LAETITIA CLARK

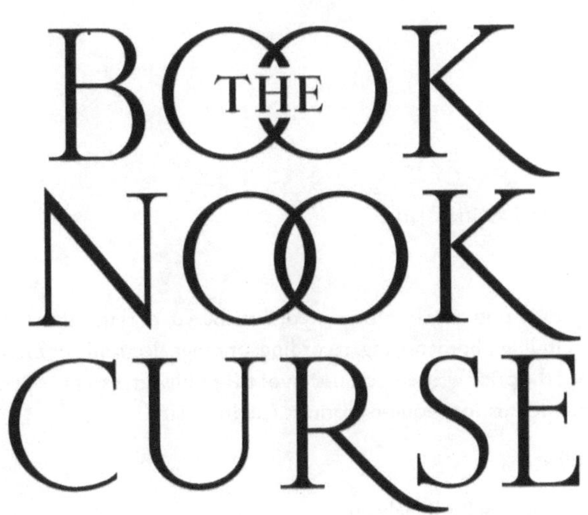

Covert art by Milbart

Developmental Editing by Karli Jackson

Formatting by Brittany Gossin

The Book Nook Curse, edition 2024

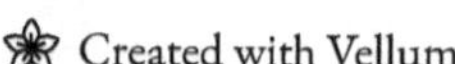 Created with Vellum

For the ones who like to play with fire...

CHAPTER ONE

"Why do you read so much, Hannah?" Brandie whines in an attempt to draw my attention back to her.

She can't stand when I ignore her—even during our daily *quiet* time together. The weight of her feet resting on my calves is suddenly more noticeable. My surroundings—including my friend—had disappeared. Somehow, the words on the pages grew tiny hands—yet again—and pulled me right inside the book.

"Did you happen to notice the kind of business I run?" I teasingly say back, barely looking over the book to meet her gaze.

Brandie is leaning against the gigantic window of my bookstore, the one that bridges the floor and the ceiling, where I piled countless pillows and blankets hoping readers would settle here and forget about the world.

I take another sip of coffee and sink deeper into a fluffy brownish pillow. Its softness braces the bare skin of my legs. The window nook is my favorite spot. I named my bookstore after it, *The Book Nook*. Crafted from rich, honey-colored wood, bearing the marks of time, it's where the sun casts its brightest and warmest light. Perfect for reading.

Brandie's gaze rakes over the countless shelves, weighted down by never-ending rows of books, all neatly organized. One book cover hugging the next one, and some random pieces of paper here and there, sticking out as if to peek at the world.

"This would be the perfect scene for an erotic scene," Brandie whispers with a malicious grin splitting her face.

I roll my eyes at her, but my skin prickles at the thought—I can't say I haven't thought about it myself before. Perfect for a gorgeous woman to get lifted by a strong, broad-shouldered man, her legs locked around his waist. Where she gets fucked against the shelves, to the sound of books falling like rain around them.

"Maybe it's time for you to go back to your flowers, huh?" I offer as a tease, without truly meaning it.

She scoffs, looking at the book I'm holding—one of my newest acquisitions.

I sell both new and used books. I wanted to build a concept slightly different from other bookstores—not that there are many of them in Willowbrook, anyway. Readers find all the new and trendy books here–the ones with the shiny covers and the overwhelming new-car-like smell.

But in the heart of the bookstore, I also gather older manuscripts. Some of them are so old, they barely hold together. The pages are crinkly, the bindings fragile. They're so damn precious to me. Each book—whether it comes from the cobblestone streets of forgotten cities or the dusty libraries of ancient churches—is a treasure in its own right, and it lies right here, in the heart of our small town, all thanks to me. I offer them as *read-only*—not to purchase. My collection is rotating, in theory at least. I like to hold on to the most precious ones a little longer. I'm quite the possessive book lover.

"When are you going to write your own?" Brandie jerks her chin towards the book in my hands.

My friend knows I've always dreamt of seeing my name in bold, embossed letters on the front cover of a book I wrote–the fruit of my imagination.

I sigh. "Some people naturally have an imagination that runs deep. Mine is a shallow grave lazily covered with a few dead leaves, at best," I remind her. "Maybe I could write about Arthur and his fluffy ass one day?" I giggle at the thought.

Brandie echoes my amusement. "Your cat deserves a million stories written about him."

"He would sell my soul for thirty seconds of scratches behind the ears," I argue. "I can literally picture him purring loudly as someone drags me by my feet once the deal is done."

Brandie laughs–sunshine in the comfortable darkness of my bookstore. A comforting dark, though. Not the spooky kind. Devouring a good book by candlelight; that's what my store feels like. I watch as my friend hops off the window nook and stretches with a gentle moan.

Her light, flowy white dress—maybe more beige than white—cascades along the riverbed of her body. It's got beautiful lace atop. It's like a spider wove a web of moonlight and stardust and decided to gift-wrap it around this dress, showing just the right amount of cleavage. Her long, thick blonde hair is wavy today. Wild, even. It suits her oh so perfectly. She looks strong and tanned. *Someone made sure to lie naked in the sun.*

I steal a glance at my reflection in the window—unconsciously comparing myself. A bunch of my fiery copper hair escaped from the bun I foolishly trusted to remain tight. I will never completely have control over my hair. It's a creature of its own. I wonder if I should feed it.

Brandie continues her stretching dance as the sun filters through the large front windows and bathes the store in a warm evening light. It's not quite yellow, not quite orange either; it's the perfect in-between. The sun's rays shine on dust floating in the air, creating ethereal beams you can effortlessly follow from one corner of the room to another.

My gaze follows the light to the back end of the store. Every little dust particle now takes part in a slow dance between the tall, oak bookshelves that stand as the guardians of all books' secrets, the sun as their guide. Brandie looks like nothing but a dancing fairy in the midst of it all.

Sure, the place is a little dusty. But dust belongs in a bookstore, anyway. It adds to the mystery and the coziness of the place. I mean, *anything* to make me feel better about the fact that I refuse to spend hours dusting and cleaning around here.

"I should get back and close the shop." Her grunts punctuate

Brandie's words as she keeps stretching her body so thin it might snap in half. "Believe it or not, I have a few orders to finish up before we go out."

Brandie is the florist next door—and my closest thing to a best friend. Well, no. She *is* my best friend. I know many people in this town. From the outside, it seems I have a lot of friends. But I wouldn't call any of them if I had a body to hide at 3 in the morning. I bet none of them even owns a shovel. *Useless.*

But Brandie, *oh Brandie.* She would run to my door in an all-black outfit, thick paint smeared across her face, asking me whether I loaded the corpse in my car's trunk or if she should get it. There's an amused smile on my face as I imagine Brandie dressed as a ninja, quietly knocking at my door at dawn. She's the definition of optimism. And waves of laughter. And kindness.

"They will be perfect, as usual." I encourage her and mean every word.

Though she doesn't need the encouragement, she's an extremely talented florist, and she knows it. She often says she could get anyone to do just about anything with a beautiful, hand-picked bouquet—I believe her. Though I think most people would bend over and backward simply for her looks; she wouldn't need any floral tricks.

I love sitting amid her flowers, pretending to be one myself. Her boutique smells like summer all year round, one flower challenging the next with its beauty and otherworldly colors.

"Where do you even find such incredible flowers?" I remember asking Brandie one day, my eyes roaming over the delicate plants like a kid in a candy store.

"I collaborate with florists spanning the globe, sourcing the most extraordinary flower species," she had said in such a cheery voice I swear she was hopping, too.

Some of her flowers resemble delicate insects, while others mimic majestic birds. Yet she always orchestrates them flawlessly. I think I adore her art because I love stories—and she can tell the most wonderful ones with her arrangements.

"My mom was an avid gardener, tending to the earth diligently at the first sign of the sun in the early days of spring," she'd clarified—her tone turned to honey. "She'd spend hours on end growing all kinds of flowers, fruits, and vegetables. I wanted to work with flowers as incredible as hers."

To this day, Brandie recalls the sun warming her skin to the point of sunburn at times. The grainy feeling of the dirt between her small fingers and the sound of her mother's laugh like it was yesterday. I never fail to see the bright light in Brandie's beautiful ocean eyes when she tells how she fell in love with flowers—and inevitably became a florist—all thanks to her mother.

Brandie's mom passed away almost a decade ago. That's when she decided to run her own flower shop. An homage of sorts. She named it *Marguerite*; her mother's name—and some foreign language's word for *daisies*. How fitting.

Her walls are tall, and pearl white, covered with various mirrors reflecting the light rushing through the gigantic windows that run the length of the building. Funny, it's quite the opposite of my bookstore. I always thought it was perfect this way. We truly complement each other.

I opted for emerald green and dark blue to paint my walls—rich, deep, vibrant colors. I too own a lot of plants, but colorful is *not* how I would describe the lot. Most are dangly houseplants that spread their long skinny arms around the store. I strategically placed golden chandeliers that give off antique, castle-like vibes. I rarely light the candles. I would knock one over eventually and set the entire building on fire. Such a catastrophe has my name written all over it.

I decided to lease the space and make it mine just a few years after Brandie started her flower business. It's been five years now. She was the first neighbor I met when I moved in.

I vividly remember the day our worlds collapsed. Considering all the furniture and boxes I had to move by myself, I wore something comfortable that day. What I thought looked comfy and practical ended up making me look somewhat desperate. Black cycling shorts and a large red hoodie with more holes in it than I care to admit. I had stolen it from an ex-boyfriend a while back and pretended that I had never seen it before when he came asking for it.

In contrast, Brandie looked like a real-life fairy queen—straight out of a fairytale. *Of course, she did.* She had sprinkled fresh flowers in her long, flowy hair. The almost see-through fabric she wore—that most people would not consider a dress—was barely covering her skin. It was a greyish-pink color, hugging her body perfectly as if crafted specifically for her. Sexy as hell, but in the most dreamy ways.

"Welcome! You're Hannah, right?" she'd say. How did she already know my name? I never figured that one out. "I heard you're opening a bookstore. I read very little myself but I can tell we will be friends," she babbled, vomiting words at me.

She came over carrying the biggest bouquet I had ever seen. I could barely see her angel-carved face behind it. The flowers were blue, purple, and pink. The most astonishing arrangement, competing with its own creator for first place on the gorgeous scale. I suspect she matched her dress to the bouquet that day—that's the kind of shit Brandie would do. I didn't have the heart to tell her that the carefully picked flowers would most likely die within the hour under my watch. Maybe she knew already.

Her sapphire eyes lit up as she handed me the bouquet. I hadn't said a word yet. I was right at home.

Surprisingly, I kept the flowers alive, perfectly placed in the center of my unorganized, half-empty space. I caught myself gazing at them a few times and realized how much I loved the bouquet. And how much I adored Brandie for it.

As I reminisce about the first time we met, looking up at the dried flowers—if anyone, I had a million books to press and preserve them—I almost forget about the little lady still roaming freely in my store. She's been humming a little song for a while now, her angelic tone filling the space, dangerously close to singing me to sleep. *I probably could use more coffee.*

"Have you read this one?" the lady inquires from behind a bookshelf, poking her gray-haired head on one side. Not quite gray, her hair shines with an incredible silver hue. It looks soft, her curls bouncing with her slow steps, as she makes her way across the store, soft as a feather.

I can see her wrinkly hand holding a fairly small book in the air. I recognize the cover pretty much immediately. I want to say that I read every book in this store. What I tell her instead—with faked enthusiasm —is, "I have!"

I gaze up and meet my customer's eyes when she finally moves into the aisle. She seems pleased with my answer, though she keeps staring at me. Another blue-eyed lady. Did she look anything like Brandie back in her days?

An uneasy silence lingers between us. I assumed that's all she wanted to know. *It appears I was wrong.* She gives me a compassionate look as she adds in a high-pitched, curious voice, "So? How is it?"

She thinks I'm an idiot. Or at the very least, a very *simple* bookstore owner. I shrug off the intrusive thought as I rise to my feet.

"It's mediocre, at best."

Wait, what?

I did *not* say that. The voice sounds deep, yet soft as silk, purring, almost. I bet Arthur reacted to this secret cat-like tone. I glance at the sleepy cat still lounging by the window in the warmth of the evening sun. *Nothing.*

The gray-haired lady's expression mirrors mine—both undoubtedly surprised. I peek over her shoulder to follow the suave, honey-like voice.

The voice of a man, *obviously*, about my age—in his thirties—maybe slightly older? It's hard to tell anything about him. He's not even looking in our general direction. He just snorted a comment without even considering looking up.

The man holds a book split open in his large hands. Talented, to say the least; he's capable of investigating said manuscript all while eaves-dropping *and* answering a question that was not aimed at him. The guy stands between two bookshelves, near the corner of the room—the read-only section. *He's not looking to purchase anything.*

It's like he purposefully stands in the shadows—belongs to the shad-ows. Despite the small distance that separates us—which suddenly feels much too big—I become very aware of his gentle breathing, of the way his fingers graze the grainy page of the book.

I didn't hear this man come in, I abruptly think to myself, startled. The little golden bell perched above the heavy door always alerts me. I must have missed it this time. It's odd. I'm always very mindful of the gentle tinkling. If only so I can properly greet my readers.

"So you don't like Zephrey Wenfrield's work, I take it?" I accuse, walking a fine line between criticism and jest.

I couldn't explain the reason, but I feel the need to be a little shit right now. Maybe it's because the man snuck into my store. Maybe it's because he answered a question meant for *my* professional opinion. I notice the edge of his mouth lift. Is that a smile? *A smirk?!*

"He writes about magic but knows nothing about it. A little research goes a long way, you know," he counters, arrogance leaking into his tone.

He still hasn't taken his eyes off his book, like we are not worth looking at. His voice seems to grow deeper by the minute. The lady still stands between us. She's glancing back and forth, standing witness to the silent battle. I can't tell whether she's extremely curious about the outcome of this upcoming debate or just a little frightened by the anger that now colors my cheeks.

"The author writes fictional stories, sir," I say firmly, crossing my arms over my chest and shifting my weight. "Can you blame him?"

Zephrey Wenfrield writes about witches and warlocks, healing potions, and wars waged on dragons' backs. Sure, research around magic can be diverse and interdisciplinary, blending elements of anthropology, psychology, folklore, and esoteric traditions. I've read plenty of texts about it myself. But it remains pseudo-science. Why wouldn't a fiction author make it spicier? Crazier? This guy is out of his mind.

First, he cuts me off to give an answer no one asked for. Then, he pretends a fiction story is mediocre—at best—all because it lacks realism. I don't even like the author that much, but when challenged, I can die on any hill. Even the witches and warlocks hill—which I don't know shit about.

The tall stranger stays silent for a few more seconds. Despite the dark corner he found a home in, I can see the edge of his eyes wrinkle as his lips upturn ever so slightly. *Jerk.* He's making fun of me.

Affronted, I continue, "What would be your suggestions, then? Maybe I can pass them along."

His silence sounds like a challenge and I'm up for it. Though that finally gets a reaction out of him. The short lady—still standing by my side—is now smiling too, clearly amused. I don't think she realized how genuinely offended I am.

Shadow man slowly closes the book he was holding this whole time —so slowly I'm wondering if every move he makes is nothing but an insult, a challenge. He takes a second to study the shelf in front of him and carefully puts the book back where he found it. I can't say I'm displeased to witness that. The read-only section can get messy really quick—considering readers pick up books and put them back on their own.

The man steps in the dim, natural light that battled to reach the back wall. The sun is setting, its light now competing with the artificial one inside the store.

"So you know the author pretty well, huh?" he barks, amused. *Prick.*

But I don't think I caught that, anyway.

His words melt together, forming a bunch of noises my brain can't decipher. When he finally has the decency to address me directly, his eyes catch the sunlight. Did someone just slap me across the face? Or is it just... his eyes? I didn't know such a color even existed. It's not quite green, and not quite yellow either. It's a pool of emerald and liquid gold, teasing and refusing to pick one color. I hope I don't need a swimsuit to enter said pools, because I don't particularly want to wear any clothes at the moment.

His eyes twinkled with a sly, almost comical charm, as if they held the world's best-kept secret, but couldn't help bursting into laughter at the absurdity of it all. *That's not helping.* Who is this man I've never seen step foot in my store before? He's quite tall, just like I thought he was. Taller than me, but not the weird kind of tall where you feel like a mere speck next to a giant mountain.

The stranger makes his way towards us, grinning. Every step he takes seems to echo with an unspoken invitation as if he'd just emerged from the pages of a romance novel. I know he wasn't just reading one, though. None of my *read-only* books are spicy romances. *I would know.*

I was expecting lighter-colored hair, but his is dark. The darkest night sky I could ever paint—if I were talented enough to paint. A handful of his supple curls are escaping, tumbling on his temples and over his ears, contrasting his caramel skin tone. He's not *beach-boy-tanned*, but he's got a delicious golden tone to him. The man's high cheekbones—underlying the beauty of his golden pools, meeting a strong, square jaw—are not helping the situation at all. Did gods carve them on their coffee break? That's just not fair.

An air of self-assurance that borders on arrogance unsurprisingly completes his perfect looks. I don't know who came up with the idea to compare this feeling to butterflies, but my stomach feels more like I need to issue a tornado warning and everyone must evacuate *quickly*. My insides twist as if a gang of monkeys used them as percussion instruments.

What is happening to me? I'm *not* the flirty kind. I've never been. No one would describe me as a great lover, either. But in this moment, I wish I could be all of that.

I want to rip my clothes off, launch myself at the tall stranger, and lick his full lips until I know nothing else but what he tastes like. I'm not wearing anything enticing, so I might as well lose all my clothes, right?

He keeps walking towards us, his bright emerald eyes fixated on me, and I'm pretty sure I'm about to lose all sense of reason. I wish he would wrap his arms around me and scoop me up—I don't even know the damn man. Instead, he turns to my elderly reader and gently taps on the book he was trash-talking just a minute ago.

"I didn't mean to spoil it for you. I apologize. You should take it home. You can only know what it's like after you read it," he says, somewhat kindly.

This damn voice of his. His smile. I never wished to be a book held by a sweet old lady more than right now. Gently pat me too, Mister Golden Eyes?

The stranger walks past us, effectively ignoring me. As he reaches for the door and opens it, the bell rings. So *it is* working. I'll be damned. He throws one last look over his shoulder, then coldly points out, "It's 7. I wouldn't want to keep you."

The man escapes through the heavy, intricately carved front door, and by the time he crosses the street, I still haven't muttered a word. I simply watch him leave. It's not that I didn't want to say something back, put him in his place—cocky asshole—but I simply couldn't. My body went on strike. I lost all control. My will escaped through the door with him.

I stand there for a moment longer, looking through the window, watching my literal dream man walk away. Was my mouth open? Was I drooling?

The summer breeze that rushes inside is warm and cozy, but I feel empty and cold. I think that's what realizing I'll never see him again feels like. A man I don't know the first thing about. A man I've never spoken to before today.

I watch a few cars drive by in silence, stunned by the absurdity of the whole interaction. Nothing about what I just experienced or the emotions that overcame me makes sense. By now, the night is chasing away the warmth of the summer sun, and the street follows suit. All is slowing down and falling quieter. Though Willowbrook doesn't have much car traffic—even during the day—this evening feels particularly silent, as if time itself slowed down.

I snap back to reality when I hear the curly-haired lady enthusiastically say, "I'll take it!"

Of course, she would. He told her to do so. I would do anything this man tells me to do, too.

CHAPTER TWO

"Oh, it *is* 7," I whisper to myself.

I lost track of time. Not just of time, I also lost my soul somewhere in this conversation. The butterflies can't seem to settle, and I can't tell if I am aroused or about to be sick.

The lady picked up a couple more books after she kept Zephrey Wenfrield's, despite the torn opinion Mister Golden Eyes offered. I check her out and wish her a wonderful evening before she exits the store.

Once the door shuts and the damn bell tinkles one more time, I let out a sigh. What just happened? I've never felt this attracted to anyone before, never felt so alive, yet disappointed that it's all a waste.

He's probably just a traveler, a tourist. This is Willowbrook after all. It is such a small mountain town—I would know him if he were a resident. I've lived in Willowbrook for some time, and I'm pretty sure I know every cow's name by now.

People treated me a little differently when I first arrived. I was the new girl from the big city—a busy city girl trying to start a new life in a quiet little town. The classic romance movie unfolded right in front of their eyes. I can't say I blame them for believing I wasn't worth their time at first. I wonder if they thought I had a dark past I was trying to run away from. Little did they know I was merely escaping a relentless sense of boredom and an enduring feeling of not belonging.

For the first few weeks, it was impossible to ignore the whispers. I caught all the side-eyes. No one knew what to think of me. I was taking over a vacant business space, piling books inside, without talking to anybody. They must have found that strange. Thankfully, I became Brandie's friend very quickly—that helped. People assumed that if *she* liked me, I was probably worth liking—maybe even worth being trusted.

Brandie would take me to all the cool bars and introduce me to every business owner. I would follow my blonde-haired friend around and let her convince me to drink all kinds of weird cocktails until the world around me spun just a little.

"Come on, you *have* to try this!" she would enticingly yell at me.

Before I knew it, I was a member of this community. In a matter of weeks, I had met almost every resident. But I have never seen *this* tall man before. My stomach would remember. My underwear too.

I must seem flustered, confused, or both, because Brandie jokingly says, "You look like you just saw a ghost," as she joyfully trots into the store again.

She pauses for a second and looks at the never-ending wooden shelves around her, worried. "Wait, the place is not haunted, is it? You know I don't mess with this shit, Hannah."

I suppose a bookstore would be the perfect place for a proper haunting. She believes that all flowers have spirits, and a story, so I'm not surprised that she believes in ghosts, too. If I were a ghost, I would want to hang around a beautiful woman like her. I wouldn't want to terrify her, though, just mess with her a little. Move some vases around or tap on some of her mirrors, just for fun.

"It's not haunted. At least not that I know of," I say, amused. "Though I suspect Arthur was an evil man in a previous life. Maybe he brought some old friends with him," I add, playfully shrugging my shoulders.

Brandie bends over to kiss Arthur's face. He loves her, and he's not ashamed to show it. The cat gently gets up and stretches his black fur before he sits and looks up at her. He's got puppy eyes—funny, for a cat.

"No, he was *not,*" Brandie laughs. "He's the best boy in the whole wide world." Her voice takes this childish tone that the cat loves. More pets for Arthur. *Spoiled little thing.*

I take a moment to study my human friend and my furry companion. They really *are* my best friends. I am lucky to have them both.

"Shall we?" my very own little fairy asks.

"We shall!" I mimic her tone. "Let me feed my evil feline first," I add, throwing my arms in the air as I rush towards the back of the store.

Brandie groans, amused. "She doesn't mean it, love." I don't.

On my way to the back room, I hit boxes and send random plastic things flying about. The back room is a tight space. Admittedly, it's also a bit of a mess. Every day, I promise myself I will clean it up. And every day, I break said promise.

I look around for Arthur's food. Though I know exactly where it is, I'm evidently still distracted, getting lost in the smallest room the world has ever seen. Lost in the thought of the sexy stranger who walked this floor a few minutes ago. I shake my head, reminding myself that this is real life—not some romantic fantasy—and that I do *indeed* have a hungry cat waiting for my return on the other side of this wall.

As I get busy filling Arthur's bowls, Brandie clarifies, "Are we still meeting them at MysticBrew?"

MysticBrew Tavern is hands down my favorite bar in town. The owners are an adorable couple—Eric and Matt—who make love look like a gods-given treasure bestowed upon the chosen ones only. The perfect pair is extremely creative, and always fun to be around. Their bar's decor is unique, and the food as well as the drinks are perfectly curated. It's got an enticing contemporary witchy vibe. Hell, Mister Golden Eyes would love it, considering he pretends to be so knowledge-able in all witchy things. But tonight is not about reminiscing about the broad shoulders of my mysterious crush. Tonight is about friends.

We meet up for after-work drinks at least once a week. I always look forward to this time. We always promise to meet for a couple of drinks and head home at a reasonable hour. It never happens. Never. We end up stumbling home, holding on to each other, all while laughing a little too loud for the standards of a small, quiet mountain town.

Brandie leans on my counter, looking down at her phone while I finish getting ready to head out. She's vigorously typing, captivated by whatever conversation is going on.

"Hot date?" I muse as I wink at her. She snorts.

"*You're* my hot date tonight," she says, abusing a fake flirting voice.

I haven't seen Brandie with anyone in a long time. It's a shame. She was made for love and happiness. She gives more than she takes—to a fault, sometimes.

She *was* dating this older guy when I first met her, but she was fairly secretive about it. It seems it was not the kind of romance you live out in the open. I had only met the man once. I'd just happened to walk in when he was leaving her store one random afternoon. We were kind of forced to meet each other awkwardly—the space of the door frame was only so big. She never said much about him. All I know is that when it ended—for whatever reason—it really affected Brandie.

I walk past the counter and around my friend before I drop my head down, spilling fiery copper hair on her tiny tanned shoulder. Her spaghetti-strap leaves plenty of bare skin for my cheek to soak up her warmth. Of course, she'd feel as velvety as a freshly baked croissant.

"I am lucky to be your date. Anyone would kill to be," I say to her. I squeeze my friend and gesture toward the door, "Okay, let's go then, hot stuff!" I slap her ass and we head towards the main street.

The MysticBrew Tavern is only a short walk away. Brandie leads the way. She's always been a fast walker. Or maybe I'm just slower in general.

The evening breeze is still warm on my bare arms. I'm not necessarily dressed for a night out with the girls; but I never am, anyway. Jean shorts and a light white blouse will do. At least I kept one extra button open to show cleavage. My hair's up in a ponytail, which I like to think makes me look like I mean business.

Willowbrook is gorgeous at this time of the year. Every street is lined with massive flower arrangements and bushes of all sorts. We walk through a symphony of colors. I always wonder if Brandie judges what the city council comes up with every year. They don't consult a professional florist for this kind of thing—maybe they should.

In contrast to the brown flower pots filled with colors and strategically scattered on the sidewalk, tall trees tower along the main road. The oaks are old and massive. Their foliage is still full and bright green, now reflecting the last rays of the sun—sign that summer's not over yet. The air fills with a mix of blooming flowers, homemade soaps from one of the stores nearby, and food from all kitchens in full swing around us.

Brandie is still glued to her phone as we eat the distance between The Book Nook and the bar. I notice the text screen opening and closing—she's talking to someone. They go back and forth quickly.

"This is the time you catch me up on your day and tell me more about yet another man hitting on you, hoping to take you out for coffee —or bolder, dinner," I joke as I look at my friend with wondering eyes as if clues will appear on her tanned skin.

Brandie chuckles—a polite dismissal.

"Are you alright?" I ask.

She takes a second to peer up from her phone and smile at me before she answers. "I am, love! Sorry. Family stuff. Let's have some fun, shall we?"

I nod in agreement, and we pick up the pace.

After the rollercoaster of emotions my handsome stranger took me on earlier, I'm ready to have a few drinks, share juicy gossip, and forget about the seriousness of the world. Though all things considered, my own little world is not that serious. Is this why I can't think of a good story to write? My life is pretty much perfect. I must be a poor choice for gossip. Nothing exciting ever happens to me.

At the exception of the co-op, of course—though most people would beg to differ. Being a member of such a concept puts me directly in the box of book nerd and cat lady.

The co-op is the very reason I created the read-only section at The Book Nook. It's also its source. What feeds it. I partner with book collectors, historians, and other scholars spanning the globe. Each member of the cooperative—me included—contributes their prized treasures, whether they be weathered scrolls from ancient civilizations, illuminated medieval manuscripts, or handwritten diaries of historical luminaries. They are the heart and soul of the cooperative.

I like to imagine that some books travel on camels back across the desert to end up at my door. Some are novels, some are religious texts, historical, rooted in magic—a little bit of everything. Most are too old to be shipped in a palish envelope and require special care.

Every week, I hope to receive another written gift. And when I'm ready to let them go, I share them with my fellow collectors. Some pieces are harder to let go than others, of course, but I remind myself that beauty exists solely to be shared with others.

Brandie and I fall into a comfortable silence as we wind through the historic downtown of Willowbrook. It's one massive block of concrete, where old houses and shops display various colors of paint. Clearly, there was no rule when it came to picking them. They're vastly different and reflect each owner's personality and creativity. Just a massive rainbow-like square.

The kaleidoscopic paints are outlined by massive wooden beams, creating a unique separation for each property. The houses, most of them built in the 1800s—from what I've read—are far enough from the road to leave space for a large sidewalk where people can easily walk, bike, and yet constantly bump into one another.

I hear the piano leading the not-so-coordinated children at the dance studio ahead. It always warms my heart. I never was much of a busy kid—the kind with a full schedule of extra-curricular activities. Maybe that's why I appreciate the radiant expression on their faces as they tiptoe around the polished hardwood floors.

We don't need to see the MysticBrew to know we're near, we just have to spot our loud group of friends standing in the front. Four women in high heels, laughing like hyenas. *Yep, that's our friends.*

They're all tall, skinny girls. I'm probably the shortest of our group. If we were a bunch of thieves, I would be the one they send inside the smallest places to retrieve the gold. "But babe, you're the only one who fits!" they'd say in unison to convince me. I know they would—cheering me up through the mud and other sticky substances of the narrow tunnel I'd have to snake through.

They're the kind of women who will turn any boring gathering into a drunken party. That's just what they do. I've learned to accept it for what it is. They don't care about much, take nothing seriously, and gossip a lot. But they also give so much love. Unconditional love and support, pouring out of their every pore. And for a sometimes lonely wanna-be-writer like me, that means the world.

The girls let out a screech that sounded more like an alarm to greet us. I wonder if people will start running away, taking the screams for a hurricane warning. Which would be even scarier—there are definitely no hurricanes reaching Willowbrook. Aside from somewhat judgy looks from passersby, no one's evacuating just yet.

We suffocate one another in a giant group hug and make our way inside the bar. It's warm, and a little humid. It now smells like women's perfume. Though I know Brandie does not wear any. She wants to be able to smell her flowers during the day. And I'm not that kind of girl.

Eric and Matt wave their arms in excitement as we enter. You'd think it's because they just love us so much. I suspect it's because we are moneybags on legs. Six women getting ready to get a *couple* of drinks every week sounds more like a bunch of dollar bills laid out on a bed to dive in. I picture Eric and Matt making money angels and I can't help but giggle to myself.

We find our usual table. We used to sit at the bar—balancing on the cool swings as opposed to the more traditional bar stools. But a bunch of women sitting in a line is hard to manage. How do you expect us to properly share gossip if we can't face one another?

Our dedicated table is in the bar's corner, granting us the right amount of darkness. The only proper light comes from a neon sign hanging on the wall above the table that reads, *good times!* It's a little corny but accurate. We always have a good time here.

As we get settled and comfortable, Amanda doesn't waste any time and starts ordering. "Okay ladies, I met someone," she then blurts out the second the coast is clear.

She darts around the table, excitement flashing in her eyes. Her hands slap the surface in front of her. I understand now why she wouldn't wait to order. She had something as spicy as her margarita to share.

"He's Italian," she says in an accent I don't recognize—not entirely sure what she was trying to accomplish.

A grin tugs at my lips. When my eyes meet Brandie's, she's already looking at me with an amused look. We love Amanda and want to see her happy, of course. But she starts a conversation with *I met someone* probably once a month.

"He's the kind of man who makes door frames feel inadequate," Amanda describes. "Tall and...*dark*."

It's impossible not to think of my encounter with my own tall and handsome stranger earlier today. Though I'd be lying if I said I *met* someone. I mean, technically, we met. But we quickly got into a pissing match and he left without even telling me his name—or asking for mine.

The memory of his distractingly perfect face makes me both really hot and a little sad. *Damn stranger.*

It's not that I don't like the idea of dating. It's just so much work. And yet, my body reacted to his commanding presence in ways I can't put into words. Every hair standing guard on my skin at the sound of his suave voice, my stomach twisting in such tiny knots like it was about to snap in half. The energy this man exuded in the bookstore seemed to shrink the room, as if unable to contain the sheer magnitude of his charisma—all while my body seemed to expend instead.

Rather than thinking of my nonexistent dating life, I force myself to focus on Amanda's newest fairy tale. I picture her Diego on a white horse. It's probably the wine. I order another drink.

Next thing I know, all six of us have tears running down our cheeks. I forget what we're talking about. We're being way too loud—but no one complains. I bet Eric and Matt just keep their eyes on the numbers that will add up on our check when the night comes to an end.

I stand up, squeezing Brandie's shoulder in the process, before I attempt the trek to the bathroom, focusing on every step. The world gently spins around me — but I keep my composure. No one could guess I had one too many.

In the bathroom's newfound quietness, I let out a deep, satisfied sigh. Happy. Serene. These ladies are the icing on the cake of my life. I feel a little dizzy, but I know the business of the bar will make me forget. I just take a second to breathe, here, alone.

When I come out, Eric and Matt are pouring shots neatly lined up on the sticky bar. I hear Amanda call me over. *Oh, no.* We're not done.

As I join the group of excited ladies, Brandie traps me in a bear hug.

"I love you, Hannah! We'll make a writer out of you yet," she screams over the music raging in the background, her voice thicker than usual, lined with the remnants of the honey-like liquid she indulged in —whiskey.

I know she means well. I know this is meant as loving encouragement and nothing else. Yet her comment feels bittersweet. It's just been a long day. I smile back and scream, "I love you more!"

CHAPTER THREE

The air of the late night lies a frosty kiss on my cheeks, like a lover would, or at least from what I remember a lover feels like. "It's so late," I whine.

We pour out of the bar. We are the last patrons, which doesn't surprise any of us. The girls all hold their high heels in their hands. Thank the gods for my white sneakers. They might not be enticing, but guess who's not walking barefoot on the nasty bar floor? I don't necessarily fancy the idea of coming anywhere close to whatever lies on that floor.

Eric and Matt give us each a hug and a kiss and send us on our way. They know we are safe to walk home by ourselves. In this town, we're probably the biggest menace.

I gaze up at the tapestry of stars painted on the cloak of darkness above our heads. It makes me dizzier, but it's not enough for me to look away from the wonderful sight. The moon is suspended high in the night, and bathes Willowbrook in its soft, silver radiance, illuminating the whole town with an ethereal glow. Wisps of clouds drift lazily across the sky, their ghostly forms casting ever-changing shadows upon the streets.

The sun is still a few hours away from starting its shift again, yet I can already see lights glowing behind several windows. *Night owls.*

Brandie and I always walk home. Our friends live in the opposite direction. We love the walk by the river that runs through town when we had a little too much to drink. The microscopic pearls of humidity filling the air near the water probably help. I hook her arm tight as we head for the river walk and send invisible kisses to our friends. Our laughter fizzles out as we walk away until it is entirely silent.

It's just her and me and the sound of the running stream below.

Brandie stops briefly—I think she's about to throw up. Which is hard to imagine from such a beautiful creature. She doesn't need any kind of makeup or any artifice, she's a true natural beauty. Her fresh flowers are her favorite accessories.

She ends up keeping it together and takes a loud deep breath as she rises again, stretching her arms high towards the sky. A spinning, giggling beauty in the moonlight. She grabs my wrist as she leads me towards the handrails guarding the water. We let a familiar and comfortable silence fill the space between us, taking this beautiful, warm summer night all in. That's what years of friendship will do.

I notice instantly when her smile fades away. Her eyebrows flatten as if in deep thought. Because I'm not clear-headed, I prefer not to ask questions. I just want her to be okay. Sometimes, all one needs is a presence—even a stumbling one—by her side, and nothing more. *That, I can do.*

"It was my dad. On the phone earlier," Brandie finally says so quietly I almost miss it.

She looks straight ahead, her dimly lit face a mask of calm, and... something else. A feeling I can't quite describe. "Well, not my dad, but it was *about* him. It was my cousin texting me. She saw him in town yesterday and got curious."

Confusion gets a hold of me and it must be obvious, because she lets out a soft chuckle and proceeds to clarify, "I haven't talked to my dad since I was eight."

"You never said much about him," I dare say, and compliment with a smile.

I'm not one to talk about my family much, which led me to believe it was somewhat normal to never hear about him, I think. There's so much love and appreciation when Brandie mentions her mother. But I've never even heard her dad's name.

"He left us when I was a little girl," her voice echoes the pain of the memory. "We've never heard from him again after we found out he had more children with a different woman."

My heart aches for my dear friend. I can't help but wonder if her incredible aura, her unyielding confidence and positivity, is a product of this deep-rooted pain. I was expecting Brandie to be ready to throw hands. Instead, she softens and tells me how she used to see the world through the lens of her father's love.

"He was my hero. My guiding light." Brandie's voice trembles. "Until he no longer was."

Brandie's mom took over beautifully, strong, and determined; a reflection of everything that Brandie is today.

"It's the kind of wound that never entirely heals. Sometimes, it pretends to close, until the next lonely night, when it comes scratching like a feral cat at the walls of your brain." Brandie's eyes fill with tears.

I want to joke about the cat comparison but now is not the time.

"It follows you around for the rest of your life...the fear of abandonment," her voice borrows a tone I've never heard from her before. And I've seen it all with Brandie.

"So, is he in Willowbrook?"

"I'm not sure," she whispers. "I have not seen him. My cousin has. Not that he would come see me, anyway. I'm nothing but a faulty memory to him, I'm sure." Her voice shakes as if her throat is sealing.

I slap her arm. "He's a monster. *He* should be the faulty memory to you. You, my dear, are a dream." I cup her pretty face into my hands and manage to steal a smile.

I know how weak my words are compared to her pain. Like attempting to take down a massive steel door with a stick. But I had to say something. Deep in my heart, I know it's not as simple as that. I can't fathom what kind of pain she had to go through as a child—and now still. She stays silent, blinking the tears away, then adds, "It's in the past, anyway."

I wonder whether she would prefer to see him again or avoid him entirely if given the chance. What does one even say to a forgotten father? Would she find forgiveness in her heart or only rage? I don't want to ask too many questions. I'm a decent friend, but I'm not good with this sentimental shit. And if I poke the bear, I have no honey to give her. We stand there for a few more minutes, leaning against the chilled metal of the handrail.

"I wanted to jump someone's bones today," my drunk self blurts out.

"Excuse me?" Brandie replies, emphasizing every syllable.

We laugh like kids sharing the story of their respective first kiss. Her laugh is a treat. She needed something stupid like that. "Wait, what did you just say to me, Hannah Scotch?" She wants to know more and I said too much already.

"There was this arrogantly handsome man at the bookstore earlier."

I tell her the whole story. How he crawled out of the shadows and how I suspect him to be a trained spy, considering he didn't trigger the bell above my door. No one walks past this damn bell without being spotted. His training must be outstanding.

I describe the way we argued; how his eyes left me devoid of any wit at all when they finally caught the setting sun and raised their honey gaze on me. How I wanted to excuse myself from my elderly customer and rip my clothes off. *And his, of course.* How the bookshelves appeared to be the perfect spot to be held against and fucked for hours. They always have, she knows it as well as I do.

Yet that's when Brandie stops me. "You are naughty, Hannah!"

"That's just the thing. I'm not," I whine out loud. "Not typically, at least."

But for Mr. Golden Eyes, I could be. I proceed to describe the fine man who stood in my store with too many details. My eyes most definitely lingered long enough on every soft line of his face, on every defined muscle of his body.

Brandie nods in agreement, her eyes still locked on the empty space in front of her.

"Well, did you get his number?" Brandie asks, hope leaking through her tone, as she turns away from the water to face the street again.

"I didn't even get his name."

Let's be honest, I might have felt all hot and bothered at the idea of this complete stranger's body on mine, but he clearly didn't show any signs of interest. None whatsoever. After he challenged me, he simply walked out the door and didn't turn around as he crossed the street. He would make a terrible main character in a romance novel. They *always* turn around—the one last look.

As I recall the memory of our encounter, it hits me. My fantasy was a one-way street. *More like a one-way highway.* He thought nothing of it. Showed no sign of any kind of fire lit under his tight black jeans. Damn jeans.

"Well, would you just look at us," Brandie says in a newfound accent, "Two poor souls desperate for love."

"I don't know about you, but I was more desperate for good sex than for love," I joke, grabbing her arm again as I start walking away.

The short walk from the bar to our stores appears much longer tonight—in the best kind of way. We keep joking about our miserable dating lives and remind ourselves that thankfully, we have insane friends who keep us on our toes, always.

I spot the big shiny gold letters glow in the silver light of the moon, against the wine-red, worn wood. *The Book Nook.*

When I leased the place, I was pleasantly surprised to learn that it came with a living space right above the store. For someone who is usually late to pretty much everything, it became very convenient to live above my place of business. Every morning, I unlock the store precisely on time—not a minute sooner. My fancy coffee maker is on the store level. I make my morning cup right before I open. I adore the smell of freshly brewed coffee unapologetically flirting with the scent of books. Most of my customers do too. The mornings are my busiest time, surprisingly.

I give Brandie one last dragged hug and reach for the wooden handle. It's been hand-carved, what looks like centuries ago. Its intricate design and overwhelming details fit perfectly on the massive door.

I drop my purse when I step inside my sanctuary, a dull sound filling the space as it hits the original hardwood floor. I know this space by heart. Every corner. Every book. And yet every time, it takes my breath away. *It's mine.* I poured my heart and soul into this place. If I can't be a writer, I'll be a damn good bookshop owner.

My gaze lands on every detail of the room. The pillows and blankets in the window nook. The tall stools with sturdy legs that taper gracefully towards the floor, put away under the large table on one side. My eyes find the rocking chair I carefully thrifted. Delicate scrolls and floral patterns adorn the armrests and backrests. The rockers are curved with precision, allowing for a gentle, rhythmic sway that soothes the soul of my readers. I prefer to call them my readers—not my customers.

I inhale the particular scent of my books, old and new. It's imprinted on my walls. It makes one with the air. I sometimes wonder if, because I spend the vast majority of my time here, I smell the same.

I lay on the floor, right here, in the entrance. I don't remember making this decision, yet here we are. Knowing I probably won't remember it in the morning, I don't think it counts as a dumb idea.

The wood floor chills my back and legs. I stretch every inch of my sleepy body as I groan. I could drift to sleep here, but I should make my way upstairs. I don't fancy the idea of greeting my readers from the floor in the morning. That's the kind of reputation that would follow me forever. The risk is too high.

"I could always turn the bookshop into a bar," I point out before I burst out laughing. I notice Arthur in the corner of my eye, bedding down by the window. His shiny black coat reflects the argent light of the moon.

The cat opens one eye, then both. He needs full power to give me the very judgmental look that flashes across his tiny eyes. If not an evil one, I suspect him to be a very grumpy old man who reincarnated as a cat. That's the only explanation I can come up with to justify his extremely lazy lifestyle and constantly condemning looks. "Come here, kitty kitty," I yell at him. But he chooses to ignore me—the wisest choice he's made to date.

As I lay here, between the published books towering to the ceiling, the dying dream of becoming a writer—and not just selling other authors' work—grips me with sharp talons. I imagine myself sitting in my store in front of a line of people who came to sign their copy of *my* book. Share their stories, and inspire my next one. It would be warm inside and the aroma of coffee would linger in the air, of course.

The local press would stand against the wall, collecting sparkling reviews and taking pictures for the newspaper edition. My copper hair would finally be tamed. I would walk in a long, emerald dress that would give me the appearance of a garden witch—*or something.* Mr. Golden Eyes would not be the mere fleeting memory of a stranger anymore. He would stand by my side, his warm hands on my shoulders, smiling with pride at the line snaking through the store.

I flop to my belly as I whine. *Stupid irrational dreams*—and wine.

I clumsily rise on my two feet again, grab my purse—which contents have spilled—and head upstairs. The stairs creak under my heavy foot-steps. It signals Arthur, who follows me, light as a feather, ready to snuggle up in bed.

I step into my living room, a delightful blend of vintage and contemporary. A leather armchair sits beside a sleek, modern sofa adorned with a colorful array of throw pillows. I wished to create a striking balance between old-world charm and modern comfort—I achieved it. The walls are adorned with framed vintage book covers and literary quotes, giving the space a sort of intellectual coziness that I like to believe fits me. Not that many people have seen it—it tends to be voiceless; sometimes lonely around here. Well, I'm not lonely, just alone, I suppose. Only Arthur's meows break the pleasant silence of the night.

Did I feed him? Without being absolutely sure I have, I drag myself to bed. I'll deal with the guilt in the morning. The room is spinning. I'll text the girls when I wake up and blame it on them, it'll make me feel better.

CHAPTER FOUR

I forgot to draw the curtains last night—to no one's surprise. The sun is using my drunken mistake to illuminate my bedroom way too early. Though its light is usually comforting and warm, this morning, it's sheer fire.

I end up waking up a little too early for my taste. I have no idea what year it is, but I *do* know that it is too early to wonder. I pull the sheet over my head, trying to recall what happened last night. It only takes me a few seconds to realize that what happened is what always happens; we met at the MysticBrew, had too much to drink, and I ended up alone in my bed. Well, not quite alone. Arthur had decided a while back that half of this king-size bed was his.

I sit up on the bed, thankful for the empty sheets after all. If I had a lover lying between Arthur and me, the poor man would have to see this. *Me.* Looking sick and smelling like a wine cave. Not my proudest moment.

The only thing that will save me this morning is a strong cup of coffee. Damn it. At what point in my life did I think having coffee in the store made more sense than in my apartment?

When I meet my reflection in the mirror, I almost let out a terrified scream. I appear... barely alive. My skin is as pale as ever, contrasting with a set of crimson eyes. Today is going to be a long day. My usually lush copper hair is all tangled up and appears to be shorter because of it. *I can fix this.* I have to open the shop shortly. I have to seem pleasant and, at the very least, awake.

As I hop in the shower—after gulping a full glass of water—I make a mental list of the things I wish to accomplish today. Many books need to be put away. Accounting is on the list as well.

But most importantly, today is the day I receive more hidden treasures from the co-op. I know this because the sender tipped me off with a brief and enigmatic email. The subject line was blank, and the body simply read, 'Get ready, for tomorrow holds something special.' That was all I needed to realize that a delivery was on its way.

The co-op system allows us to communicate without revealing our real emails, mailing addresses, or names. Most members choose to remain anonymous, which I've always found peculiar. I'm one of the few who openly shares all my contact information. Perhaps it's because I don't see myself as particularly special. It's as if these people prefer to stay hidden, which only adds to the allure of the system, I suppose.

I often let my imagination wander when it comes to envisioning my fellow co-op members. Are they men, or women? Do they have warrants out for their arrest? Are they banned from certain establishments? Are they devout religious or, on the contrary, known for their indulgence? Regardless, I'm never disappointed to see my collection of rare pieces grow.

In a few hours, I should receive yet another box containing one or several books, maybe parchments. I never know what's coming.

The thought of the precious cargo arriving at my door brightens my gloomy mood—I instantly feel better. As I drag myself toward the stairs leading down to the store, I catch a new glimpse of myself in the golden, full-body mirror strategically placed in the hallway. Still blood-chilling. I look more alert, but not any better. That will have to do.

By 8, I already had three cups of coffee and managed to have breakfast. I considered making a fresh batch of crepes but quickly realized that was too ambitious, considering the state I'm in. I settled for bland leftovers.

The sun didn't wait for me to rise high; its rays now stretched across the floor of the shop like spilled gold paint. The world outside is bustling. Leaning against the frame of my door, I gaze at all the passers-by rushing to wherever they have to be. I try to stay unnoticed, welcoming the fresh air deep into my lungs.

It's another warm summer morning. The flowers are in full bloom, attracting migrating monarchs through town. Despite the early hours, the day is already hot. I'm thankful for the carefully cooled air inside my shop—where I will hide all day like a beast in its cave.

The thick yellow cardigan I've thrown over my black T-shirt has to go. I can't afford to add sweat to my list of troubles. I'm pretty sure my shirt is already stained, but I lacked the motivation to search through my closet. The shirt hung on the metal chair, guardian of the corner of my bedroom, buried under a layer of slightly dirty clothes—too grubby to put away but too clean to wash. Perfect for a day like today.

I straighten my long skirt to fix the flower patterns before looking up at the clinging of Brandie's keys approaching. I would recognize that sound anywhere. She's wearing sunglasses. To hide the little sleep she got last night, I suspect.

"So, how are we doing this fine morning?" she cheerfully asks, leaning against the wall next to me. I will never understand where she gets that bottomless well of energy from.

"You know how we're doing. You did this to me," I say in a fake upset tone as I bump my shoulder against hers.

"It's going to be a hot day," Brandie adds, before she clarifies, "I don't think I picked the right outfit."

Her flared light blue jeans and long-sleeved black top are simple, but efficient. Though she wears it like a second skin, it does seem a little too hot for the season, indeed. I wonder if it's the amount of alcohol consumed last night or the thought of her father being in town that got her all confused this morning.

I sense a pinch in my heart again. I won't comment on her outfit—considering I picked dirty clothes off of a chair this morning, I'm in no place to give sound advice.

Brandie disappears into her boutique with a bright smile on her face. I do the same. The blinding light of the morning sun did not make my condition any better. I'm happy to be back in the soft darkness of my natural habitat.

The first few hours of the morning are flying by. I put some serious effort into welcoming my customers with warm hellos and bright smiles, though I *do* catch a few intrigued looks and side-eyes. As much as I sometimes indulge during our cherished nights out with the girls, I very rarely get to the point of feeling sick—or worse, waking hungover.

I look up at the massive, ancient clock that's steadily hung upon the north wall of the store. I needed extra—and professional—hands to hang it up. The sole idea of dropping such a masterpiece terrified me. The old clock looks more than a mere timekeeper. It's a storyteller, a witness to countless moments, and a guardian of memories. Its presence in the room adds a sense of nostalgia, a link between the past and the present, reminding me daily that time is both precious and eternal. It always gives me full-body chills.

The hour chime, when it strikes, resonates with a deep tone that seems to carry the weight of history itself. I found it by sheer luck, at an estate sale. Luck is right, considering I showed up at the very end of the sale. Everyone knows you want to arrive at dawn or else all the good pieces get snatched. But not my clock. It's as if it was patiently waiting for me. And I found it.

At 10, both the ancient clock and the golden bell above my door ring at the same time. A symphony that doesn't sit well with my migraine.

I forget all about it when I realize that it's not a reader this time, but a delivery man. He's carrying a medium-sized box that seems to be made of dark old oak—or some kind of similar wood. I spot the red dot adorned on the top of it right away. For most people, the red dot would mean some kind of sale. For me, it means sheer excitement. The hair along my arms rises in anticipation.

The anticipated delivery from the co-op.

Although this delivery was announced, there's no guarantee it will arrive. The timing and contents are always a mystery. It could happen weekly, monthly, or sometimes, months may pass without any new arrivals. The uncertainty is both part of the passion and the torment.

I let out a little screech when the young man holding the carved box says my name, "Delivery for Hannah Scotch?"

I jump from the window nook and meet him at the counter. After signing all the required paperwork and ignoring the unease on his face at the sight of me, I'm left with the heavy wooden box. There's no mention of the co-op on the package. The only recognizable sign is the red dot glued on the top. Delivery men must think that I belong to a dark cult. They have no clue how precious their cargo is. Admittedly, most people probably wouldn't care as much. It's rare to find *genuine book lovers.*

I carefully unravel the box. I breathe in the ancient, light dust that escapes from the top as I do. By the time I get rid of the top part, I'm hopping with anticipation. The worn leather-bound book lay at the bottom, its cover a patchwork of faded brown hues. This piece immediately shows it's more than just a collection of words; it's a relic of forgotten tales and bygone eras. The title on its spine, *Chronicles of Lost Journeys*, was embossed in elegant, now-fading, gold letters.

The delicate pages rustled like autumn leaves, revealing meticulously handwritten entries, sketches, and all sorts of hand-drawn maps. Each page tells a story of explorers venturing into uncharted territories, chronicling their adventures, and sketching the landscapes they encountered. The ink has aged gracefully. The margins are adorned with annotations, questions, and occasional stains. It's obvious that this book had been a companion to those in pursuit of knowledge and adventure a long, long time ago.

My eyes are watering. To think that so many hands handled this very manuscript. So many brains took part in its conception. So many hearts filled with eagerness at the idea of discovering new worlds and filing it all in this very manuscript. I close my eyes and hold the book against my chest. It's fragile, but I want to squeeze it. I promise myself to find an hour or two later today to devour its pages.

I take a deep, satisfied breath and... Wait, what is that? Salt? I taste salt?

It's as though I'm standing by the raging ocean, where the air is highly ionized. I open my eyes in disbelief. My jaw drops to the floor. A too-high-pitched squeal escapes through my clenched teeth.

Facing me, standing in silence, is Mr. Golden Eyes.

It can't be. Am I still intoxicated? I blink rapidly to make sure I'm seeing what I think I see.

"Good morning," he says, a captivating melody that resonates with an irresistible, yet icy charm.

His face shows no expression, no excitement. He's the personification of cold and placid.

Oh, no, no, no. Not now, not today. Please, not today.

Dark circles still cling stubbornly beneath my eyes, a stark contrast to my pale, sickish-looking skin. I'm pretty convinced my eyes are as red as my hair and I'm not even wearing clean clothes. I'm covered in Arthur's hair—not to mention the unidentifiable stains on my black T-shirt. If I had to choose the worst possible day to meet Prince Charming, it would be today, hands down.

As all the shamed and embarrassed thoughts rush through my head like a tornado—making my headache close to unbearable—I realize I haven't said a word yet.

"*Ugh*, Hi. Hello," I clumsily mumble, stumbling on every word.

I wonder if he notices that I'm slightly shaking. But to notice, he'd have to actually look at me, and his eyes never really fall on me. He's picking at his perfectly manicured nails, his gaze darting around the room. I avoid staring for too long and instead, place the manuscript on the counter, pretending to be busy with the most random pieces of paper I can reach. I have no idea what's on them, but he doesn't know that.

Wait a second. I didn't hear the bell yet again. How is it that when this man enters my store, my usually faithful bell decides to betray me and stay silent? If I had heard him walk in, I would have had time to get on my knees and crawl to the back room before he could get close— well, in theory, at least. And yet here I am. Stuck in the worst version of myself, standing in front of the man of my dreams.

He's dressed pretty casually, but each piece molds to him like a shadow, each garment a seamless extension of his being. The blue jeans and white shirt combination has been invented just for him—I'm now certain of it.

When did it get so hot in here?

"Can I help you?" I shakingly say to break the uncomfortable silence between us, hoping my tone doesn't betray my anxiety levels.

"I was wondering if you received a new shipment this week?" he says, his voice dipping and swaying, luring me into its seductive rhythm. *Or so I tell myself.*

Stunned, I stop whatever I'm pretending to do. My gaze shoots up to him. I'm pretty sure his eyes just devoured me whole. It's as if I'm gliding on air, not touching the ground. He's nothing but a stranger, yet all I can think about is finding the quickest way to get to the other side of the counter and pressing my lips against his. I wonder what his dark curls would be like tangled between my fingers. I don't even know the man's name.

"How do you know about the...?" I try to get out, but he interrupts me before I can finish.

"The shipments? I read about it on your website. I have a weakness for literary treasures, you see. Few bookstores offer this kind of... concept," he calmly explains, his charming smile barely reaching the corner of his face.

The website. Of course. A long time ago, I put into words my feelings about the co-op and what the concept is. Its purpose—its magic. No one ever mentioned reading those lines. I can barely remember them myself. Unless this is all an act, he genuinely *is* interested in the idea and the books from which I source.

I take a steadying breath. I need to get a hold of this conversation. But no rational words come out of my mouth. Instead, I awkwardly stare at him—with tired eyes.

"So, any new treasures to share today?" the stranger inquires, probably wondering why the crazy lady on the opposite side of the counter can't put two words in a sentence.

So, this man is not only incredibly handsome but also a bookworm. This isn't turning out the way I hoped. I can't let this teenage crush overwhelm me—it's absurd. I'm an adult. And a respectable one at that. If only he were a jerk—or illiterate. The latter would be a bit surprising, given that when I first saw him, he was holding a book. And I'm fairly certain it wasn't upside down.

"I received this manuscript today. Funny you should ask. But I haven't had the chance to prepare it for the shelves just yet," I finally manage to say without stumbling on my words, or swallowing too often. "I received a couple of new pieces, just two…"

"Two weeks ago, I know," he interrupts me again, cunningly, with obvious disappointment in his voice. I swear he rolled his eyes, too.

I can't decide whether the fact that he knows everything about everything around here is fascinating, or straight-up annoying. Last time I checked, I ran this bookshop. Yet he seems to know just as much about it as I do. He must notice that I feel puzzled by his way of interrupting me and knowing things most customers wouldn't even ask about because he comments with a gentle scoff, waving his hand between us.

"I'm sorry. I tend to get excited about rare texts. I shall patiently wait until the new one is ready to share with your readers."

Readers. Not customers. This interaction is growing weirder and more frightening by the second. How do we share the same brain?

The man puts both hands on the counter that still sadly stands between us, as to show that he'll be patient—and that he's sorry, maybe? I glance down at the smooth skin wrapping around his hands, and something shifts inside of me. As if my heart skipped a beat. As if a blurry picture flashed in front of my eyes and a familiar warmth grazed my sides. I urgently want to caress his fingers with mine. *Control yourself, Hannah.*

"You could always kill time with the newest Zephrey Wenfrield novel," I joke.

I'm not entirely sure where this newfound sense of humor came from. It was probably tired of being overshadowed by the relentless stress and anxiety that bubble up inside me whenever I face him. But I'm glad it managed to break free and jest because Mr. Golden Eyes laughs. His laughter fills the room with an infectious energy, revealing a perfect set of teeth—aligned like pearls on a delicate string. A string I wouldn't mind having around my neck. So he's capable of laughing after all, despite the icy front and all.

"I will pass," he says, still chuckling, "But Zephrey's lucky to have you in his corner to boost his sales. You know damn well his latest novel is not good," he winks. And I melt.

Before I can respond, the man spins on his heels and strides to the door, effortlessly pushing it open and disappearing once more.

I want to run after him, *movie-like*. I want to tell him he can have all the books and ancient texts he wants. He doesn't need to wait. He can have everything that's inside my shop—*including* my body. But only in rom-coms would such ideas take me anywhere.

I click my tongue. The taste of salt has vanished. Is tasting salt a side effect of being extremely horny? I should probably research it. I'm not positive that's a normal bodily function.

The consequences of indulging a little too much last night slap me in the face—back and forth. He will never forget the way I looked today. If I had a tiny chance of gaining his interest at all, it died today—along with my dignity.

CHAPTER FIVE

I madly type on my phone before hitting send. Brandie shouldn't need much more context than that. I don't remember the last time I told her about a man. She should put two and two together pretty easily.

Maybe not.

Before I get the chance to text her back, the warm breeze from the world outside rushes in, battling the cooled air of my store. Brandie pretends to run towards me, swinging her arms and taking big, exaggerated steps.

"So, did you guys do it?" she mischievously asks—too loudly.

"Brandie!" I hiss, looking at a couple of readers lingering in the aisles with an apologetic look. I add a polite smile for good measure—and slap her arm.

"Of course not. I mean, just look at me!" I vaguely gesture at my body from head to toe.

Her glance transforms as she looks me up and down. I'm prepared to welcome a sarcastic comment, but she doesn't make any.

Instead, she says, "You are beautiful, Hannah," and lays loving eyes on me as a kind smile tugs on her full lips. "Besides, it doesn't matter. You're amazing!"

"Well, that's not written all over me today, is it?" I keep whining, realizing how shallow I must sound.

Brandie smiles and pats my hands, her touch is always a magical balm for my restless soul.

"So, did he tell you where he lives?" she asks innocently.

I start laughing nervously.

"He didn't, but I assume he's local or staying around here for some time. He said he'd come back for this," I point at the ancient manuscript still lying on the counter.

Brandie never understood the value of the co-op and what we share with each other as members. But she can tell a book that was sent by the co-op from a regular book, which is a good start, I suppose.

She slaps the book a little too hard for my liking as she screams, "Well, something good is finally coming out of this co-op thing!"

I can't be mad. She could never grasp the enchantment behind the secret exchanges of time-old books. She grew up amidst fruit trees and blooming flowers—no wonder she looks like one herself. Besides the year-round harvest of fruits and vegetables cultivated by her mother, they also kept animals that freely roamed the grounds. They had eggs to pick and horses to ride. She never needed to escape real life because hers was fairytale-like as it is.

I know now there was more darkness hidden behind the beauty, but Brandie locked it up and threw away the key like the badass woman she is.

Not that my childhood wasn't beautiful—it was. I was happy and cared for. But I lived in a small, dark house with two parents who were loving, yet often absent. Dad traveled constantly—for work, I believe. Mom was too busy with our local church, devoting most of her time to coordinating charity events and quietly walking around during sermons, doing things I never fully understood. Dad wasn't religious, and I sided with him early on. I imagine my mother felt quite alone at home, as none of us truly supported her.

As a result of being alone a lot, I found my escape in books. I read for hours on end, through days and nights, in the bathroom, and at the dinner table. Hidden beneath a pitched blanket, reading forbidden texts by headlamp at night. Not that anyone ever noticed. Our house had a pervasive sense of sadness, feeling quiet—if not empty—when my parents were busy, which was more often than not.

Dad had hung a small bookshelf above my bed one day.

"So your books don't have to be on the floor," he'd said with a shy smile. I've always loved to scatter all my toys on the floor, and my books suffered the same fate.

The newly installed shelf was much too small to hold all my copies, so I would rotate them. I would pick my new favorites and strategically place them on the shelf every week or so. I always hoped that one of my parents would notice the new titles and ask about them. They never did. So I just kept reading to myself. Take notes from every book I read. When particularly inspired, I would even write stories. Sometimes, a different ending to my favorite reads. Other times, a sequel. It was never good—I was but a kid. But at least I had the ovaries to write. It has never happened since.

"So, when is he coming back?" Brandie asks, pulling me from my reverie.

"Maybe tomorrow? I have no idea. He didn't say," I say without looking at her, my eyes still fixated on the windows, hoping that the tall stranger would reappear.

"Did you guys even *talk*? Do you know *anything*?" A very obvious joking tone leaks through. Though she is not completely off base. I barely said a word to him. I throw a warning look at her. She gives me puppy eyes in return.

She's already back to looking down at her phone. Her expression suddenly turns more intense. I think she's done with the jokes for now.

"Well, shit. Have you heard about the gift store being robbed?" Brandie asks, "The owners got pretty beat up," her eyes seemingly raking over a news article.

I shrug at the words.

"What do you mean, got beat up? What happened?"

She reads the news out loud for me, genuine shock spreading across her face. My heart shatters at the thought of the owners getting hurt. Our little town knows no crime, remember? I always say us drunk girls are the biggest threat this place has ever heard of.

"It happened last night. Two men dressed in all black covered their cowardly faces before they entered the small gift store." Brandie keeps reading.

Strange. The gift store opens up to the main street. It's always busy, filled with wandering tourists. It's not a quiet, hidden place. The fact that they got targeted is very odd to me—and quite scary.

Charming Trinkets & Treasures—the gift store in question—is owned and run by an older, adorable couple. Eleanor and Walter. Eleanor is a petite woman with a gentle, grandmotherly aura. Her eyes are dark, yet delicate, and wrinkle at the edges when she smiles—which she does *a lot*. Eleanor has a wealth of knowledge about Willowbrook's history and its residents. She loves to share scandalous stories of the past, regaling us with gossip about the quirky characters who once lived here.

Walter is much taller than her and doesn't appear any younger. He wears a kind smile all day—just like his wife. Every time I walk into their store, he's busy rearranging shelves and opening boxes of newly acquired knick-knacks. The gift store has no theme whatsoever, which makes it so special, I believe. They work with local artists too. They offer upcoming creatives a place to share some of their good work—and some of their bad ones too.

"They were found cuffed to each other, sitting on the floor, quite bruised up," Brandie's voice is shaking with emotion as she relates the story.

A tight knot seals my airways. That doesn't sound right at all. That kind of story belongs in the big city, where crimes like this one are just another headline in the news. But not in *our* mountain town. Not here. It doesn't fit. Eleanor and Walter don't appear to be a logical target.

"Did they catch these assholes? I'd love to pay them a visit," I angrily spurt out, hitting my fist against my palm, picturing poor Eleanor and Walter on the floor, afraid and in pain.

"Well, that's the scariest part... they haven't."

Go figure. Our local police are most certainly not equipped to investigate such cases. The worst part of their day is probably writing parking tickets to rich visitors—on the weekends.

"Eleanor and Walter decided to reopen tomorrow. They *refuse to let fear win*, they said to the journalists," Brandie continues reading.

I love that about them. I would probably close up shop and move far, far away.

"We should go see them tomorrow. Do you know how to make cookies?" My friend brainstorms.

I laugh. Her innocence lightens the mood immediately.

"I can figure something out, I think. Who said they had to be good?"

Brandie giggles and lovingly squeezes my arm. I know it means 'stay safe'. She makes her way back to her store after promising to come check on me in a little bit. Funny that she doesn't even worry about her own safety.

The rest of the day is a blur. I desperately need rest—and water, only water.

It's hard to believe such an intense day unfolded when I was at my worst. If the Universe wanted to teach me a lesson, mission accomplished. I learned today. I'm caught between ecstasy and fear, my thoughts oscillating between the hope of seeing my dreamy stranger again soon and the terrible crime that has occurred.

I make myself another cup of coffee as I get ready to settle and explore my newly collected literary treasure. I need to get it ready to share with others—*meaning primarily with Mr. Golden Eyes*. I sit down, pull a soft, light blanket over my shoulders, and grab the book.

My *get-ready-for-the-shelf* process is simple. Before I share the co-op's books, I take pictures to remember the condition I receive them in—that's imposed by the co-op. If needed—like if the manuscript is too old—I cover it with a special protective paper. In some cases, I require readers to handle the pages with cotton gloves, to prevent oil stains and other unwelcomed bodily fluids.

I'm speeding up the process today. I won't admit it to myself, but I'm not-so-secretly hoping that Mr. Golden Eyes will make his grand entrance again this afternoon. If that's the case, I want the book to be ready. That would give me a chance to talk about something interesting—anything—instead of standing in awkward silence. I want to make an impression. So far, I'd be nothing but the memory of an uninteresting—at best—bookstore owner to him. It's time to change that.

When I realize it's too late to keep hope alive, I decide to close shop a little early. I make my rounds, checking every aisle and corner for any lingering customers. My body aches, each muscle heavy and pleading for relief. I can't recall the last time I felt this exhausted. It must be the punishment I deserve.

Arthur's already waiting by the door, gracefully posted on the last step. He tends to be hard to pull away from the window nook—even when the sun is set and gone for the night, there's something about the window that the feline can't resist. That, or he likes to secretly spew evil words, targeting the people outside. I laugh at the idea and scratch his fluffy butt as I open the door to our home. Arthur trots in and disappears to the bedroom right away—he must be pretty tired, too. I wonder what on earth could drain him?

I considered the idea of following him to bed right away, but I promised to make cookies. They won't heal the wounds, but they could heal the heart.

I want to support Eleanor and Walter; and show whoever's still out there that we are not afraid. This neighborhood stands strongly together. Maybe I'm trying to convince myself more than anything. Truth be told, the grim news really got to me today. I thought about being a possible target myself. I shake my head, dismissing the terrifying image of being beaten in my store, and head to the kitchen.

I'm not a particularly good baker, though compared to Brandie, I'm probably a Michelin-starred chef. I do know a good cookie recipe, though. A forgotten ex-boyfriend used to love them. At least I can keep a man around by pleasing his stomach. It's pretty simple and quick, and I have all the ingredients. It will do.

The summer night's glow bathes the kitchen in a tangerine-tinted light, soothing my nerves. Though small, the space serves its purpose well—it's not like I'm cooking for two. The original yellow walls–that I once despised for their tackiness and outdatedness–have become a cherished backdrop. Their faded hue evokes warm summer days near the ocean somewhere, and the hum of cicadas. I've adorned the room with a few self-grown herbs, a collection of colorful thrifted pictures, and a pair of red and white hand towels, completing the cozy atmosphere oh so perfectly.

H: Cookies are in the oven, missy.

The entire apartment smells of warm sugar and melted chocolate. I promise myself not to eat the whole batch before bed. Even Arthur comes out of his hole to join me in the kitchen—most likely motivated by the perspective of stealing a cookie or two.

B: You're the best. Should we plan to go at 9? Late opening?

I agree to the idea in a somewhat short—but kind—text, before I throw my phone on the chair close by, risking throwing it on the floor instead.

I closed early tonight and will open late tomorrow. This means I'm losing precious minutes when Mr. Golden Eyes could decide to stop by. I wonder if he heard the news, too.

CHAPTER SIX

Predictably, I headed to bed right after the cookies were done and out of the oven. I wake up to the sound of the rain tapping against my window and of the wind whipping leaves in the trees. I stretch my arms out as I peer through the windowpane. It's definitely raining. Interesting. We rarely get gloomy days in the summer around here.

I hop out of bed, slowly reaching the cracked-open window. Though it is gray and stormy, I spot patches of blue, cloud-free sky in the distance. That's what I thought. Another beautiful and sunny day on the forecast.

I check the weather app just to make sure. I need to know what I can wear. Today is the day I make sure Mr. Golden Eyes remembers who I am—and not just because I intend to dress in a manner that will make it so. I intend to bring my A-game; to sound and be interesting— reflecting the educated, mature woman that I am.

The smell of baked goods still floats in the air. The usually comforting sugary smell sadly reminds me of what happened yesterday. I can't let my mood get all dark again. Today will be a good day. I can feel it. For starters, I feel much, much better. I also look better, which is easy to imagine. I'd be hard-pressed to look worse.

Even though the sun, still hidden behind the blanket of clouds, is noticeably gaining altitude, a constellation of twinkling lights peeking through windows still stands out, like scattered stars hinting at the arrival of a new day. Willowbrook looks like a postcard at this time of the morning.

I welcome the brisk fresh morning air in. Arthur seems bothered by my decision. He's still snuggled up in the warm, tangled sheets, and the crisp air that accompanies the rain is not what the feline hoped for this morning.

'Today will be a good day' I keep mentally repeating to myself, clapping my hands together. Before I head downstairs to meet Brandie, I pack the freshly baked cookies in a glass container. I taped the note I wrote for Eleanor and Walter to it. I couldn't find the right words—*I really will never write anything good, will I?*

As I open the door to the staircase, I stop and have a look at myself. *Behold* the new and fresh Hannah. I spent some time carefully picking what I thought was the perfect outfit to face Mr. Golden Eyes. It's a captivating mix of sexy and bookish, designed to catch the eye without crossing any lines. It's a small town, after all. I don't need to spark gossip about myself. I slipped into a maroon dress that hugs the little curves I have just right, showing a bit of leg with a small slit that leaves you curious for more—*I hope.*

Over the dress, I wrapped a forest-green cardigan adorned with delicate patterns that begs to be touched. It'll be easy to take off if the day gets too hot. Or if Mr. Golden Eyes decides it should be thrown on the floor. *A girl can dream.*

Brandie's already waiting outside.

"Well, well, well, who are you and what have you done with Hannah?" she greets me.

It's true that I rarely dress up—or show any skin, really. In general, I prefer comfort over looks. Come to think of it, I never felt the need to dress up to catch anyone's eye. I never felt consumed by the fire of passion, of seduction. And without it, who am I dressing up for?

"Good morning to you, too," I playfully reply, pretending to be obnoxiously seductive. "Do you like it?" I ask, spinning on my heels so she can get the full picture.

"You look gorg!" Brandie says distractedly, as she reaches for the box of cookies.

I slap her hand before she reaches the glass, clearly hoping to pop the top off and stuff her pretty face.

"Not in your wildest dreams, missy," I bark. "Let's go before you rob me."

We both laugh at what turned out to be some dark humor shit, even for me.

The rain has stopped, though the clouds are still looming over our heads for now, covering the main street with an uncomfortably eerie light—fitting for the recent events. The street is fairly quiet this morning. Brandie and I walk mainly in silence. She seems to be captivated by her phone again. I don't ask questions about it. I know she will share if she needs to.

As we approach the gift store, I notice a few people have gathered near the entrance already. A quick glance reveals many familiar faces. The long hazelnut hair cascading down the back of the pet store owner stands out—her little white dog by her side. I've never seen this woman without that dog. Does Arthur think I'm a mediocre owner in comparison? Our local baker has brought some baked goods, too. I should have seen this one coming. I feel stupid with my cookies now.

There are a couple more heads hanging out in a tight group, discussing what happened at the gift store with kind eyes and compassionate smiles. Brandie hooks my arm as we get closer.

I stop dead in my tracks and almost drop the glass container full of cookies, which causes Brandie to be abruptly pulled back, too. She whips her head towards me, startled.

"Are you okay, Hannah?"

I'm okay. I think. I'm a little shocked—maybe excited, or both. My heart settles into a rhythm that's both familiar and fresh. Something inside me that feels both unfamiliar and oddly intimate.

Amidst the small crowd gathered for Eleanor and Walter, Mr. Golden Eyes' handsome face stands out, like a beam of light. He's smiling, looking everyone confidently in the eyes as he seems to handle multiple conversations at once, effortlessly. His charisma shines past the flesh and bones of everyone around him. A lighthouse in the storm.

"He's here! Right there! The guy in the black vest!" I shout-whisper, my eyes gleaming with what must resemble a mix of excitement and confusion.

I didn't need to describe his outfit. Brandie would have picked him out instantly.

"He's here!"

I hate the fact that I can't seem to control myself when I'm close to him. There is no rational explanation for such feelings, such behavior—it kills me. I want to scream, as much as I want to hate myself. But in reality, I quite enjoy the freeing sense of attraction—and lust.

"Someone's feeling like a teenage girl amid puberty," Brandie jokes, raising both her eyebrows with a grin, before she pulls me towards the crowd.

Eleanor and Walter stand by their door, flanked by two large window panes adorned with various stickers and fading welcoming words, framed by weathered blue wood. Despite being in deep conversation, they glance up with warm appreciation as we approach.

My heart drops—pulling away all colors from my face with it—when I finally take a closer look at the elderly couple. I don't want to joke anymore—or rip off my clothes for a mere stranger.

Their forever-smiling faces are marked with the harsh evidence of a painful encounter. Bruises of varying shades mar their aging skin, awful reminders of the violence they had endured just a couple of nights ago. Eleanor's eyes are swollen. From the tears—or other horrors. Her lips harbor a deep cut near the corner of her mouth.

Walter is wearing a tender black eye. Dry blood is still lingering under his nose. A patch of hair is missing from his scalp. Both have bandages scattered over their arms. My insides twist. I have the strong urge to embrace them both tightly as if my hug could somehow mend their broken hearts and make them whole again.

Despite the visible wounds, their determination to move forward and heal is clear. They won't take shit from anyone.

First, because they reopened today. These two didn't waste any time staying away, hiding in fear. And second, they seem to be completely open about the incident. It takes me back a bit. I'm not entirely sure I'd have the guts to share with such graphic details everything that happened with neighbors—as well-intentioned as they are. But the couple holds nothing back.

Brandie and I don't interrupt. We quietly join the group and listen, nodding with visible emotion at every word.

I glide over Mr. Golden Eyes' face for a fleeting moment. Time stopped. I think I caught a small smile—more a nod of acknowledgment than a genuine smile. But I'll take it. I would have never guessed he knew Eleanor and Walter—considering I had never seen him in town before. But by the way they both focus on him as they tell their terrible tale, I assume they must know him well—and most importantly, trust him. Weird.

"They came in around 8," Walter explains, "Just before closing time. I thought nothing of it. My back was turned. I didn't look over my shoulder. I thought they were just late customers."

"Tourists like to wander the streets in the evening. Most of them don't pay attention to closing time. So, I kept working on the shelves. But my lady over here," Walter lovingly gestures at his petite wife, "She knew something was wrong. She's always had a sense for this sort of thing," he smiles as he turns to her, eyes half closed.

Eleanor takes it from here. "They were dressed in all black, long sleeves and pants. Even a hoodie!" her tone peaks as she throws her arms in the air in disbelief. "That seemed quite odd to me. It's the middle of summer, you know?" we all nod in silence.

"Did they say anything to you?"

I don't need to glance up to know who's speaking. That smooth, velvety tone strikes a chord deep within me as if it's been playing my heartstrings for years. Mr. Golden Eyes is leading the conversation. This whole time, Eleanor and Walter were answering *his* questions.

"Not a word, dear," Eleanor answers. "They just walked towards my Walter and hit him right on the back of the head. I knew we were in trouble then."

Eleanor raises a bruised arm and gently strokes her husband's cheek. He grabs her hand and holds it there. My eyes are flooding. I squeeze Brandie's arm so tightly she might leave with bruises, too.

"I didn't see it coming," Walter admits with a breath, shaking his head. "I fell to the ground. I didn't know what was happening. They hit me a second time, and that's when I told them I didn't want any trouble. But they didn't care."

The horrifying tale continues and they don't leave any details out. They answer every question with such precision that my heart shatters at every word. Mr. Golden Eyes has *a lot* of questions. He seems pretty invested.

The couple's faces contort with horror as they recount the traumatic events of that fateful night. Their voices tremble with each word, reliving the nightmare they had been victims of.

They explain how the burglars never showed their faces—mere faceless shadows lurking. Aside from screaming orders, they said very little.

The two assholes beat Walter with unbridled savagery, raining blows upon him with relentless force. The strikes left the once formidable man crumpled and defenseless on the floor of his store. Hitting him in the face, in the ribcage—all of it was fair game to the monsters.

They dragged Eleanor by her thinning hair towards the heavy metal desk the couple had been found cuffed to. The assholes hit her head against the sturdy metal, cutting her lips open, opening the gates for her blood to pour all over the desk and floors.

I flinch, giving myself permission to look away and catch my breath. My face grimaces with a cocktail of anger, rage, disgust, and pain. My stomach sends waves of nausea every time I lay eyes on their beautiful, hurt faces.

"Were they after the money?" Mr. Golden Eyes asks.

I can only assume he's intentionally leaving out any kind of emotion —he's just seeking answers, it seems like. I can't imagine he's fishing for details just to feed a gruesome kink.

"I believe so, that's all they took anyway," Eleanor shrugs her thin shoulders. "But we don't have much in here, you know. They didn't like that."

In a trembling voice, she explains that after realizing the prize would be somewhat minimal, they took out their rage on the couple one more time, before cuffing them to one another and rushing out.

"You didn't recognize any of them, or saw anything that would stand out, did you?" The source of all my fantasies keeps inquiring.

Both Eleanor and Walter simply shake their heads in silence.

"Do you have any security footage?" This man just won't let it go.

The couple explains that they have a camera facing the entrance of the gift store and that they shared the footage with the police. With the attackers wearing all-black clothing, they couldn't make much of it. It really starts to sound like a movie.

The group falls quiet for what feels like an eternity.

I wasn't prepared for such a harrowing tale this morning. I'm trembling, my legs buckling under the weight of overwhelming sorrow. I can't decide whether I'd welcome the flood of questions or find them maddening if I were in their place. Yet, Eleanor and Walter seem unfazed —perhaps they truly trust Mr. Golden Eyes more than I realize.

The silence quickly becomes suffocating and though I'm usually not a leader, I decide to break it first—not thinking twice about the language I'm about to use.

"Well, I think these pieces of shit know they didn't break you. They know they failed. We're all so happy that you are back. Here, this is for you," I hand the pair the container full of treats.

Eleanor grabs my hands and holds them into hers for a moment. Her wrinkled skin wraps around mine; warm and grandmotherly. I make sure to mention the cookies are from both Brandie and me—it was her idea after all.

The group of neighbors naturally breaks into smaller groups, like it always happens when people gather. Hugs are shared and more tears rain on the pavement. I watch the group in silence—still pretty emotional myself.

"Hi! I'm Brandie, the florist! I own *Marguerite*, right down the street," I hear my friend's enthusiastic, high-pitched voice. My blood turns cold. I know what she's doing.

"I'm Max," he responds.

Max. So *that's* his fucking name.

I've been around this man three times already, and I still didn't catch his name. It took Brandie about five seconds to uncover it. I'm incredibly mad at myself. And maybe—*just maybe*—a little jealous. The fire of resentment builds on my cheeks. Jealousy scratches at my chest walls with lethal talons, begging to come out and strangle Brandie.

I know my gorgeous neighbor noticed his unique golden green eyes and the dark curls that frame them perfectly, supply extending on his forehead. I'm sure she didn't miss his advertisement-worthy teeth, either. I turn around slowly, my eyes wide, my lips a thin line. Her hair is flowing oh so perfectly in the morning breeze; a golden waterfall cascading down her strong, tanned back.

"So, *just* Max?" she playfully asks, setting a hand on her hip. *Traitor*.

"Just Max," he purrs, his voice as deep as ever. A gentle smile tugs on his mouth. His eyes twinkle with a kind of playfulness I hadn't had the chance to witness yet.

So that's what it's going to be. The classic *best friend falls in love with crush, and crush falls in love with best friend*. I couldn't compare, anyway. I might have a novel-worthy story to write after all. Though I'm pretty sure this plot has been written about too many times to count. I wish I still had the cookies to hold on to because I'm not sure what to do with my body. Everyone's busy talking to each other while I'm standing here, watching the man of my dreams fall in love with my perfect best friend. *Ex best-friend.*

The painful pit growing in my stomach overcomes my entire being. The butterflies are now angry little hornets. My face is burning. I wonder if it's turning red, too. I should have known that would happen. I've never met a man who could resist Brandie—she doesn't even have to try. Why would he be any different?

"Oh, and that's..." Brandie tries to say—as the wonderful friend I doubted she was just a second ago—gesturing in my direction.

"Hannah. I know," he finishes her sentence with close to no fluctuation in his voice. Like my name was old news already.

He turns his gaze to lay it on me and his smile fades away, a grave countenance written all over his face. *Well, fuck me.*

"Oh?" The sound comes out of Brandie's mouth—she seems as surprised as me. He knows my name. He's never asked. We've never *properly* introduced ourselves.

"The website," he calmly explains, as if he had just read my mind.

His now emerald eyes are fixated on my face. I think he's paused on my lips, though his face remains statuesque. There's a strange warmth that blooms within me, starting from the depths of my soul and spreading outwards to every fiber of my being. It's as if his gaze is a ray of sunlight breaking through the morning storm clouds, casting away the shadows that have lingered for far too long. I wonder if he notices the desire that lingers in my eyes when I stare at him.

The rage transforms into exhilaration—or a little bit of anxiety. His face is a painted picture I've spent hours looking at. I doubted my friend a little too quickly—she would never let me down.

Brandie gives me a daring look as a response to the obvious, one-sided sexual tension she's witnessing. What am I supposed to do? Throw myself at him, hoping he will accept me? I'm already ashamed enough that my frivolous self is coming to flourish just now, in such dark circumstances.

Max keeps staring at me in silence, his face a page that's impossible to read. Even for the avid reader that I am. There's something warm buried deep inside his eyes, efficiently concealed by his expressionless, cold visage.

He visibly snaps out of it as he says, "It's terrible, isn't it? What's happened."

Brandie's and I's expressions mirror his, as we both agree.

"I can't believe this happened to them," Brandie adds, her empty gaze looking straight ahead, "It doesn't sound like Willowbrook."

There's another silence, so thick I could grab it. There's been plenty of it this morning. A silence that speaks volumes, echoing the horrors and sorrows. The ghosts of the awful memories.

I sense Max's eyes on me again—the comforting warmth that envelops my body. I don't even need to make sure he's looking. I look up to meet his gaze but he blinks, shrugs his shoulders, and quickly says, "I have to go. I should say goodbye to the owners."

As he brushes past us to shake Walter's hand, Brandie's long fingers aim for my hand. Well, *she tries*. She tries to squeeze it real hard—and I know why—but she misses and grabs only one finger, which actually hurts.

"Ouchhh," I whisper to her. "What the...?!"

She giggles. I take it as an apology. She doesn't care.

"Thank you again for the cookies, ladies," Eleanor says with a smile.

"You better share them," Walter jokes as he kisses his wife's forehead.

"Enjoy them—both of you," I say in a soft voice to settle the cookie's custody battle.

"So, how long have you known Max? He seemed very worried about you. You guys must be close?" Brandie has never feared asking questions. She's not in the business of making people comfortable. If she wants to say something, she will. So when she wants to know something, she will ask.

I can only assume she also noticed the obvious way both of them were focusing on him, earlier. And the way he was firing one question after another.

"Who?" Eleanor asks, looking up at Walter—a silent question. Brandie's eyes fly wide open and meet my mirroring confusion.

"Oh, right, *Max*! Oh. We met him just yesterday."

Brandie stops the questioning. Some things start to make sense—like how I've never noticed Max in town before. While others just become more and more confusing. Like how he asked so many personal questions to people he didn't truly know.

Brandie and I say our goodbyes and promise to come check on the pair during the week. The morning is warming up considerably as we walk back.

"Maybe he's a psychologist?" Brandie thinks out loud on our walk back.

"What do you mean?"

"Well," she starts, "He knows how to make people comfortable. How to make them talk, you know?"

I nod. That's not a terrible guess.

"That doesn't explain why he would do it, though," I say, still struggling to comprehend this man's behavior, and quite honestly, entire existence. "What if he's just sadistic? What if he likes pain?"

"In that case, you better get some ties and ropes. You're in for a treat." Brandie laughs uncontrollably.

She can't stay serious for one second. I genuinely believe everyone needs a friend like her. Sad times always appear way lighter with her around. I blow air through my lips as an answer, rolling my eyes.

CHAPTER SEVEN

By mid-day, Max still hasn't stopped by the store. I pretend to focus on something else all morning, but the reality is, I can't stop thinking about him. His name is an oddly long-staying guest inside my chest. The anticipation is killing me.

I spend some time making sure the shelves that hold the co-op's books are absolutely spotless. If someone had been watching me all morning, they'd think I was trying to hide evidence of a murder by deep cleaning the area repeatedly, making sure no hair or fingerprint was left behind. Little would they know that I'm just trying to impress my crush. I, a 32-year-old woman. *Shame on me.*

I hear the bell above the door and turn on my heels faster than I ever thought possible. It's not Max. I let out a little sigh of disappointment —a feeling that I try really hard to hide before I greet my new readers. It seems they are on a mother-daughter date. They both hold cups from the coffee shop down the street. The pre-teen girl is still finishing her sandwich. Her mom strokes her golden hair before she disappears in the young adult section, leaving her mother standing alone in the center of my store.

The lady looks around in silence, as if unsure of what to search for

—or what to do at all. She's got a gentle aura, radiating kindness mixed with a touch of helplessness.

"She seems to know what she wants," I say, gesturing towards her now-missing daughter.

The mother giggles in response. "She does. She's most definitely a book nerd," she pauses and looks at me, horrified. "I meant that as a compliment. I'm sorry, I didn't..."

I hold my hands between us to reassure her immediately—no offense taken. She sighs in relief as her shoulders shrug.

I look at this mother with appreciating eyes as she proceeds to describe her young daughter's love for books, fantasies, and fairytales. How I wish my mother had been so supportive when I was only a kid with my nose stuck in books all day. This little one is in good hands. When I'm old, wrinkly, and retired, she could take over the shop.

I never once thought I could have someone around—let alone a pre-teen girl—to help me in the store. Someone to share my passion with, to pass it along. I can almost picture her shadowing me around the bookstore, listening to my biased opinion about certain authors, and about the co-op, of course. I'd have so much to share.

"So, what are *you* looking for?" I inquire, "Maybe I can help?"

She looks around. I notice how her face twists in confusion as if she doesn't belong here. Something tells me she's merely trying to connect with her daughter. A soft pinch finds the center of my heart. This is wonderful.

"I wouldn't know..." she whispers, embarrassed. No one is left behind in this store.

"Mhhh. Let's start with what interests you so I can guide you to the right author?" I say, while crossing my arms over my chest—fully invested now.

Though she looked confused a second ago, the woman barely lets me finish my sentence before she blurs out, "Horror! I love horror stories. I'm a sucker for scary shit," she whispers, making sure her daughter's ears don't catch the language. I softly laugh as my gaze finds my feet, a grin on my face. I like her.

After a brief moment of pondering, I lead the way toward the book I have in mind. I think she'll love it-if my instinct is right.

"I would recommend Isabella Nightshade. She's a rising star in the world of horror fiction. Her writing is filled with vivid descriptions, spine-tingling suspense, and a knack for creating unforgettable, nightmarish scenarios." I chuckle as I finish my sentence. "Here, this one should do."

I watch the woman grab the book with obvious anticipation. She thanks me and leaves to find her daughter with a promise to tell me what she thought of it. Part of me wonders if it's the first book she'll ever read from cover to cover.

"That was a great recommendation." His voice, a mere summer breeze, lifts the light hair along my arms and neck. Max is standing at the counter, obviously eavesdropping.

Fuck me. When did he get here? I ignore the drumming behind my chest walls and dismiss his nice comment to make one of my own.

"Do you always sneak up on people?" I say, walking past him.

The fumes of his cologne are sweet like honey. It's a scent I've never breathed before, yet it depicts a somewhat familiar vision; something I couldn't quite put into words. It's complex, with notes of... lavender? Interesting choice. A treat I wouldn't mind devouring.

Focus, Hannah.

"It's one of my talents," Max says back, turning around as his gaze follows me.

"You should make a list, so I can be ready next time you use one of them on me."

Our conversation is casual, comfortable, almost like we've known each other for a long time. That's a first. I shrug at the memory of our first encounter. *That* was a disaster. Today, I wanted to sound confident, educated, and witty—I'm winning. The air is warmer around him. I can't decide if it comes from the odd sense of closeness or the whispering warmth of the summer.

"So you like Nightshade's work?" I tease him, "Last time we argued about an author, we didn't see eye to eye, did we?" I embrace this freshly born confidence.

Max chuckles. The grave sound rumbles along the inside of my skin, straight to my guts.

"Nightshade doesn't pretend," he argues. "Have you heard her talk about her work? She doesn't hide the fact that she's a young author and that her writing is passionate and emotional."

I love that he knows much more about books than just the text printed on their pages. It dangerously raises my body heat. Max researches authors. He knows their style, ambitions, and motivations. *He's good.* It irritated me, at first. Not anymore.

"Are you coming for my job, *just Max*?" I joke, referring to the interaction he had with Brandie earlier.

"I just enjoy researching literature. It's something that comes in... handy." His gaze drifts away.

Hanging on his every word, I didn't notice the taste of salt in my mouth. I wonder if it's some kind of allergic reaction. I also didn't realize that I was leaning on the counter, closer to him. It happened naturally. My arms braced against the cold surface—it makes my breasts perk up. They appear fuller than they are. I catch him looking—it's working. Not that I had planned it, but it's working nonetheless. In a different life, he would ask me to close the store, so he could make me revisit every corner. Every surface. Every seat. Against every shelf... *Enough, Hannah.*

"I noticed you had time to prepare the book. I hope you didn't feel rushed," he says as his golden eyes fill with intensity. There's a trace of disappointment in his voice. Is it about the book—or me?

"Was it not what you were hoping for?"

"It's great, just not what I'm looking for."

"Did you get the chance to read it all?" I can't imagine he had. My conversation with my other reader must have lasted ten minutes, at best. And this new piece is *thick.*

"One look was enough," Max says, matter-of-factly.

I keep investigating, asking more questions about what he's looking for—hoping he will say *my body*—but he dismisses it politely.

"That's a story for another time," he whispers.

His noticeably bored tone fills the store, echoing against the walls like a death sentence. Fuck. I thought this curas going well. I can take a hint. He doesn't want my help. I will leave it be. His demeanor shifts again. He suddenly seems restless. The conversation is about to end. I don't want it to. I need to learn more about him.

"So, do you live near?" I ask, trying to get him to talk and stay a little longer.

"Sort of," he remains vague, yet again, as he looks outside through the front window. "I have a house in the big city. I prefer the one I own here."

So he owns multiple properties. I wonder what he does for a living. If he comes from money, it's not *obnoxiously* evident. His outfits have been pretty casual so far. Enhancing every dip and curve of his perfect body, wearing every piece like a second skin—madly efficient, but casual.

I can't keep asking too many questions, I'd take the risk of crossing a line. He had already dismissed my questions regarding the book. Then again, he's out and about mid-afternoon—and it's not the first time. He didn't seem too busy with work this morning, either. What if he's not busy tonight?

"Maybe you could tell me more about your book preferences over dinner...tonight?" The words roll out of my tongue too quickly for me to stop them. They bypassed the approval process of my own brain. It just happened. I just asked a complete stranger out. This is not like me. This is *not* me.

Max meets my eyes, while the corners of his own wrinkle thanks to a small smile. If he was surprised that I asked, he didn't show. Was he just waiting for this? My heart wants to jump out and kiss his face. It beats so fast that I wonder if he can hear it. I can't say I dislike this new Hannah. She's confident and doesn't wait around for things to happen to her. *You go, girl.*

"That sounds lovely, Hannah," he says.

My knees wobble. Before I can propose a place and time, Max finishes. "But I can't."

The smile that graced his face has vanished, leaving behind only a transient hint of mild satisfaction. Embarrassment uses its ugly hands to wrap my guts around my throat and choke me with it.

I'm glad I held off on the wedding preparations because that was humiliating. I summon all the rational thoughts I once had and try to play it cool. He probably *is* busy tonight. That doesn't mean he won't go out with me...*ever.*

"Oh, that's okay! Another time. There's enough days in a week," I say as I clumsily wink at him.

Max doesn't reciprocate my smile or my playfulness. If there was a light sense of familiarity and comfort between us, it's long gone.

His face has turned into an icy blanket again. "I don't think... We'll see," he mumbles. His words are daggers in my romantic heart. *Ouch*.

A half-hearted apology later, he disappears.

CHAPTER EIGHT

After such a blow, an odd sense of vigilante creeps into me. I decide to investigate a little further. I don't think Max poses a threat to our community—my heart somehow refuses to believe it—but I can't ignore how strange it is that no one *really* knows who he is.

While I wait for my water to boil for dinner, I settle at the kitchen table, despite my usual preference for the living room. Normally, I find the latter's brighter light and the expansive view from the large windows overlooking the street to be more inviting and comfortable. But I need to keep an eye on the boiling water. I've learned the hard way what neglecting it leads to—a time-consuming ordeal of scrubbing burnt salt residue from my stove, bent over in frustration with whatever sharp enough knife I can find.

Arthur comes out of his hiding spot and climbs up my leg. You'd think a cat would effortlessly jump, but not Arthur. Arthur likes to keep it spicy. And by spicy, I mean painful. His claws find my skin through the sweatpants I changed into like small needles. I fight the urge to yank my leg away and let him have his fun until he makes it to my lap, where he transforms into a ball of fur. I can't decipher his head to his tail anymore. The heat of his tiny body is not unpleasant, despite the warm air from the summer evening.

I log into the online group of Willowbrook. It was initiated as a small neighborhood group, from what I've heard. The *expensive* neighborhood. The one with the brick mansions perched high up on the mountain ridge surrounding the downtown area—the ones that look down on us.

But gradually, as more people settled in town and new businesses—like mine—arrived, the small online community grew into the go-to source for all things Willowbrook. Residents use it for various purposes, from selling odds and ends that get little attention elsewhere, to sharing freebies, finding lost pets, announcing town hall events, organizing parades, and everything in between.

I spent enough time searching said online group when I first moved here to realize that everyone in town joined it. I suspect it's more about gossiping and monitoring what the person next door is up to than anything else. But it comes in handy when you are trying to uncover the mystery of a new stranger in town.

With a quick search, I should be able to find Max. I don't know his full name, but "Max" should be enough to narrow the list of names down, peek at the profile pictures, and find his pretty face. Pretty sure it stands out. I go ahead and type the three letters. Well, that turned out to be easy; only two profiles came up. I graze over the screen. I look again, to make sure I'm not missing any third line.

Nothing.

There's a Maximus—which sounds like a nickname, hopefully for this guy—and Maxime Parriet; the man who runs the ice cream store. But no trace of enigmatic Max.

I fall against the back of my chair, crossing my arms, which pushes out a deep sigh. That doesn't mean anything, I convince myself. I'm disappointed. Almost as much as I am intrigued.

I think what I wanted out of this search was to see more pictures of his smile, of his otherworldly golden green eyes. To dive a little deeper into his secret life. I was hoping to see where I could fit. How much room I could take up. What I *really* wanted to see was more pictures of him...*alone*. That would mean I have a slight chance of filling this hole in his life. I slam my laptop shut and force myself to forget about Max, at least for tonight.

It's another beautiful summer evening and even though I seriously considered staying on the couch to watch something mindlessly boring until my eyes felt too heavy, I choose to get some fresh air after dinner instead. A chill jolts down my spine at the thought of what happened at *Charming Trinkets & Treasures* only a couple of nights ago. Eleanor and Walter mentioned the intruders came in around closing time. The darker the night, the more dangerous.

But I will go out anyway. Inspired by the memory of Walter and Eleanor standing strongly together, concealing any sort of fear and refusing to let evil win. I should do the same. In reality, I'm not half as brave as the pair. But a walk by the river can't be that serious. Though if I had a large and vicious dog, I'd probably be better off.

"Sometimes, I wish you were a big scary dog, Arthur," I sigh at the feline still lounging on my lap. He opens one eye and yawns, sticking his pink tongue out in response. Unbothered—and somewhat useless.

I let the warm air swallow me whole as I step into the darkened street. The scent of flowers in full bloom and freshly cut grass over-whelms my senses, reminding me yet again of the season. I stroll through the main street, headed towards the river that travels through Willowbrook. The river walk that is so special to Brandie and me. I wonder if she's asleep right now. I could text her, but take this moment for myself instead.

Though not bustling with crowds, a few people are wandering the main strip leisurely, their footsteps punctuating the quietude. The occasional car passes by. Sparse chatter drifts from nearby porches. It's not as busy as a typical summer night, but there are subtle signs of life. The morbid news of late must have pushed people to stay inside—and safe. *I'm not sure what I was thinking.*

I peek through the store's windows lining up on both sides of the large street. Some of them still have dim lights burning inside, contrasting with the night that's starting to seriously settle in. Some are still open. In the summer, most businesses like to stay open a little later.

The light is out longer; the air is warmer and most importantly, visitors are still out and about and ready to spend money on pretty much anything.

I naturally smile as I cross the main street, letting my eyes freely linger on each and every boutique. This is my home. This is my community. It took me a long time to find a place I could call my own; to build a life where I felt like I belonged. My heart fills with joy at the sight of every little store, nested together.

I make a left turn through a small alleyway. It's a shortcut to the riverwalk. I can hear the water running only a short distance away. The breeze is already growing colder, despite the furnace of the sun today. I throw my cardigan over my shoulders, though I don't slip in the sleeves. I just need a little something on my skin. The sound of my footsteps resonates on the narrow paved road. The steady rhythm could lull me to sleep if I wasn't actively walking. I let my mind finally relax—for the first time today.

Before a screeching noise pierces through the quiet of the night and drags me back to reality, building small bumps over my skin. I jump, terrified. My heart is pounding in my chest. It's not that the noise was scary in itself, it's just that I didn't expect it.

Once my heart rate slows back down to a normal cadence, I make a better image of my surroundings. At the very end of the dark alley, one of the stores' alarms is going off. It's loud. Too loud. Possibly waking up the whole neighborhood at this point. I half expect someone to pop their head out of one of the windows above me and start complaining—I would do that—but nothing.

"Let's go! Fuck, man, let's go!" Someone muffles a shout a few feet away.

I freeze, a terrifying feeling tugging at my senses—something is wrong. My skin tingles. My intuition tells me not to take any step forward. I don't want to run in the other direction either, for fear of being spotted.

Despite the darkness engulfing the alleyway, I discern two men rushing away from the store from which the alarm has been set off. I can't see any clear features in the thick of the night, but they seem to be fairly tall, dressed to blend with the shadows, and, most importantly, not being recognized. The lights from the river walk ahead filter through the narrow space between the walls framing us. All I can see, in contrast, is the outline of the men's silhouettes. My throat tightens as I swallow the scream that's rumbling up my windpipe.

One of them pauses for an instant—seemingly to decide which way to flee—granting me enough time to notice a gun in his hand. My stomach climbs up my throat. The comfortably warm summer breeze turns hellish-hot. I'm afraid to even breathe, should I do it too loudly. I could pee my pants out of fear, but I'm trying to be an adult—even in one of the most terrifying moments of my life.

Every instinct screams at me to run, to flee from the obvious danger. But fear holds me captive, rooted to this very spot as I grapple with the reality unfolding before my eyes. If they spot me, who knows what they will do to the only eyewitness? This is not the time to stand out. I need to disappear. Hide.

But where?

I spot two large dumpsters on my right, along one of the brick walls. There's a little space in between them. I could fit. I could make myself small enough. I don't hesitate more than a split second and jump in between the massive trash cans. The smell is unbearable, but it's better than a bullet in the head.

I drop and grab my knees—which I bring tightly to my chest. As tight as I can. My eyes burn as I squeeze them shut, releasing two silent torrents of tears. I lodge my chin between my knees and hold my breath. I want to disappear.

I am not here. I am not here.

I overhear the men arguing amongst themselves–they can't determine which way to go. They realize that time is running out. They're on edge. Nervous, and obviously angry, by the rise of their tone. I pray to the gods that they will run in the opposite direction. I could really use a miracle right now.

But I hear their rushed footsteps creep closer as they shout at each other, "This way! Come on!" Of course. *Damn you, gods.*

I make myself even smaller, holding my body tighter and tighter. I can't tell how long I've been holding my breath at this point, but I'd rather die of suffocation. I can't make a sound. They're getting closer. My heart is racing. I'm afraid they could hear it beating against my chest; a drum in the night.

Though it might as well have lasted for an eternity in hell, within a few seconds, they're gone. They ran past me in such a hurry they didn't notice the little ball of human flesh sandwiched between the dumpsters.

They're gone.

I release my fingers, one by one. Every single one hurts from the tight grip I kept on myself. My muscles attempt to relax, aching from the uncontrollable shakes that take over my body. My chest is a pit of burning fire—a result of the stress, the anger, the fear, the lack of oxygen. A little bit of everything.

I try to take a slow, deep breath, but I can't quite move just yet. I want to make sure they are *gone* before I even consider standing up. My eyes, literal waterfalls, keep my vision too blurry to see—which I wouldn't recommend in the dark.

If I stay one more minute next to the trash, the stench will inhabit my clothes and I won't ever be able to get rid of it. I stretch my legs, still sitting on the ground. The coolness of the paved road soothes my over-heated body. I welcome the temperature drop seeping through my jeans. I slowly come back to reality, to my surroundings—which I had care-fully tuned out.

The alarm is still going off at the other end of the alleyway. A piercing symphony that became mere background noise in the midst of terror. As I rise to my feet, still wobbling and shaking, I realize that a small group of people has gathered near the store. The police are with them. Lights are coming on left and right and the alleyway doesn't seem so scary anymore.

It's over.

Friendly silhouettes are popping out, bringing this nightmare to a slow end.

It *is* over.

I should go meet the crowd. I should tell the police what I saw, tell them what happened. But I physically can't. From the organized chaos at the far end of the street comes a blood-chilling scream.

"Is he alive?!" someone shouts as sheer terror noticeably overcomes the narrow alleyway.

I know instantly that someone got hurt once again. I stand in the middle, watching them from a distance, numb and confused. My body betrays me. It just wants to crawl home and get the fuck out of here. I oblige.

CHAPTER NINE

The walk home seems to stretch time. I know this route by heart and yet, but I'm a lost wanderer in a foreign land. I look around frantically and barely recognize our town. What happened woke the neighborhood up. Lights are coming on all over downtown, one by one. The news spreads fast. Everyone was already on high alert after what happened to Walter and Eleanor.

I made my way back to the main street, where some tourists whisper to each other and check their phones, concern written on their faces.

I finally lay eyes on my wooden door. It looks even more massive at night. The wood seems thicker, darker even—a fierce protector of secrets inside. I will need to repaint it soon. Maybe next spring. I've been thinking about it for a while. It's such a beautiful, intricate piece of art. I wouldn't want to ruin it. I like that it looks beat down; it adds to the charm and the mystery. Though according to Brandie, if I really wanted to fit in, I'd pick a bright color to paint over the old, tired remains of the tree that died for that door.

With trembling hands, I retrieve my keys and slip into my store. The silence envelops me, a comforting embrace, and I find solace in the tranquility. I'm home. I welcome the familiar dust particles forever dancing with the moonlight. It looks like I am being greeted by friendly ghost figures—Brandie would be mortified.

The dried tears on my cheeks tingle and stretch my skin uncomfortably. My hair is stuck in the remains of the water crashing down the sides of my face only a few minutes ago. My eyes are burning—I can only imagine how red they must be. I'm warm and cold, and everything and nothing all at once.

As I let out a grounding breath and push off the counter, my front door flies open, hitting the wall loudly. The bookshelves shake in unison, threatening to spill their content on the floor. The thick glass of the front window vibrates dangerously like it's about to shatter. A high-pitched scream escapes me. I jump around to face the intruders.

They must have followed me. I was convinced I was being discreet. I was convinced they didn't notice me, back in the alleyway. Now they're here. Ready to get rid of the eyewitness. And here I was, worrying about repainting the front door. That won't be necessary. Who will feed Arthur?

"Are. You. Hurt?"

The voice is thunder in the summer night like a powerful lightning bolt hitting the ground and shaking the premises. Every word is accentuated, punctuated with a breath.

"Hannah. Are you hurt?" Another thunder.

The storm is thickening, so is the air in the store. The voice is deep, grave. Yet, composed. I blink to beat the light of the moon streaming through the front door where the figure of a broad-shouldered man stands.

Max.

Max is standing at the door that he swung open a minute ago with more force than I could imagine any man having—not the robbers. His body betrays him, exposing the anxiety he can't contain. He sounds angry, even. I'm too stunned to speak. So he repeats the question, one more time—louder, adding more concern to his tone.

I remain silent.

I carefully watch as Max crosses the obscurity of the room, swallowing the distance between us with such soft steps he seems to hover over the floor. I can see his eyes now. His pupils are wide. Two huge black balls in the white of his eyes. A wild animal that has been hunted for hours. He places both hands on my shoulders, his grip firm yet not threatening, exuding an unsettling power as if he could shatter me with two fingers. His gaze pierces into mine, eyes glistening with an unsettling sheen. Wait... he looks alarmed.

"Hannah, talk to me," there's a plea in his whisper, begging for an answer.

I put one hand on his—he's still gripping my shoulder. The other on his chest. Max is shaking. I recognize the fast heartbeat I sense through his thin linen shirt—I just experienced it myself.

"I'm good. I'm okay," I say in an almost inaudible breath. Confused.

His tensed body finally relaxes under my fingers at the sound of my voice. His head drops between us as he breathes out loudly. His shaking slows down. I keep my hands where they are for a little longer, soaking up the warmth of his body. I caress the edges of the full muscles of his chest, ever so gently. Which seems to work—his tight features soften. The temperature within the store magically comes back to normal. We breathe as one.

I'm as confused as I'm relieved to see him. There is something very special about a man who worries about you—only this man in particular is a stranger to me.

A tornado of questions loops in my head—why is he here? And why is he so worried about me? How does he know? This doesn't make any sense. I'm nobody to him—a random woman he turned down. And yet, here he stands, right in the heart of my store, with only the smallest distance between us, clearly terrified of what could have happened to me.

I have so many questions that need answers, but I don't have the energy to ask them. All I want is to run into his arms and cry myself to sleep there. To hell with the fact that I don't know him. That he doesn't know me. There's evidently something very intense between us.

Perhaps that's what was meant for me. Maybe the peaceful surface of my life was meant to ripple with waves of confusion; to spin and fall into scenarios that make no fucking sense. Maybe I was never meant to fight it logically. Maybe I don't *want* to.

Max finally looks up as he takes his hands off me. His movements are slow, and calculated, like he's afraid to break something. Funny, considering he almost took down my front door with one swing. I will have to check the wall for impacts tomorrow.

"Max," I whisper—a silent question. A question of *why are you here? How did you know?*

He doesn't say a word. His golden eyes are raking my face as if scanning for injuries. His charming smile grows back when he sees that I'm fine—truly. It warms my throbbing heart. I taste salt again. It must be all the tears I shed earlier.

"Get some rest," he orders, back to his cold, indifferent self just a blink later. I know he's about to leave again, with no explanation whatsoever, leaving me begging for more—*for more of him.*

I grab his wrist as a plea for him to stay. To explain. To make it make sense. He brings my hand to his mouth and softly brushes my fingers against his lips. He doesn't really kiss it. All promises and no delivery. He lets his warm breath do the job. I shiver. Damn it, this move is pretty efficient.

"Lock the door," Max says, roughly joking.

CHAPTER TEN

I painfully pull myself out of bed and quickly find a pillow to hug. My migraine is beating the inside walls of my head with hammers. A million of them. My sleep was loaded with nightmares. I woke up gasping for air, thinking of what those men would have done to me had they found me hiding in the alleyway.

So I can't write a good story *for shit*, but turns out my imagination —when it comes to torture—is pretty damn savage. That's what I should write a story about.

So much had happened last night. None of it makes sense. A frightful thought runs through my body. What if Max knew, because he was part of the dangerous organization? *No. Impossible.* I shake my head to rip the thought to shreds. It can't be. He genuinely seemed concerned about me.

I consider the idea of staying in bed all day to bury my racing thoughts under the sheets and never facing the world. It's very tempting...but I can't.

In just three days, I'm flying out of the big city for the annual *Words and Letters Conference*. A literature conference. It brings together authors, publishers, and other book nerds of the country in the most beautiful venue. It's quite a big deal. The gathering lasts three days and is the perfect occasion to play dress up as a real-life princess, get one-on-one manuscript critiques—*for the real authors, that is*—and relax during mixers and happy hours.

The thought of getting away brings a smile that reaches my sore eyes. Away from the crime, away from my nonsense crush. Away from it all.

The bigger bookstores have their own booth, usually decorated in the colors of their biggest sale of the year. It seems to be a good marketing move. I know nothing about marketing strategies. The Book Nook is too small to justify a whole booth—not to mention, it would cost me an arm and a leg. I can easily picture the colors I'd pick for my booth, though. Dark emerald green. The deepest, richest, darkest blue. Golden chandeliers and half-burnt candles. *Fitting*.

The three-day-long gathering hosts various speakers going over the latest trends in the industry. And many other topics. Most of them thankfully more centered on literature and its rich history.

Words and Letters is the perfect place to meet upcoming authors and the biggest, most popular ones too. It's easy to guess which lines are always the longest. I personally prefer the shorter lines—the quick ones.

The conference is also the perfect opportunity for me to ask questions about the precious co-op. I'm convinced that some members attend it every year. I can't imagine none of them would. Each year, the conference turns into a scavenger hunt for me—where I try to uncover clues among the attendees, all in the hope of finally meeting a member in the flesh. That has never happened before. I'm undeniably one of the most invested members. That is to say, one of the least secretive about the whole thing. Which sounds counter-intuitive. You'd think the unique concept would want a chance to grow. Then again, I suppose the idea is to be pretty selective among its members.

Most of the preparations gravitate around the carefully picked outfits I'd never wear anywhere else than at the conference. My very own fairytale away from real life. Ball gowns and cocktail dresses that both trail onto the floor and are cut short enough to show the toned muscles of my thighs. Colors that belong to the rainbows, bejeweled to purposefully attract attention.

Every night ends on a festive note by means of a fancy dinner hosted at the venue usually accompanied by an elaborate show. Half-naked dancers, fire artists, and sometimes even animals. None of it you think would belong at a conference originally designed for book enthusiasts.

Brandie will keep an eye on things while I'm gone. Though I love the woman to death, I know she'll keep a *loose* eye on my business—at best. So I want everything to be in order before I go—my morning is suddenly filling up quickly. At least it will keep me from thinking about last night, desperately striving to decode Max's actions. Of the deep worry lines webbing is perfect face.

I watch Brandie enter the store and walk straight towards me. Impressive, considering she hasn't looked up from her phone to either open the door, spot my location in the room or walk in my direction without hitting a shelf—or a whole ass wall.

"Hello to you too," I joke, as she seems to have forgotten her manners this morning.

She looks up, seemingly puzzled. "What is happening in this damn town?"

So she read the news this morning. I didn't need my phone or the local newspaper to tell me what happened last night. I knew about it oh too well already.

"Did you hear?" she continues, her eyes fixated on me, wondering why I'm staying silent.

"Briefly."

"They nearly shot the owner to death. He was found unconscious in a pool of blood. Broken bones piercing the skin, and major cuts... But they think he might make it." Brandie did open her mouth, but these words are not hers.

He beat her to it.

Max's voice ripples along the walls of the shop all the way to my ears as music would. Entering without triggering the bell and eavesdropping seems to have become a habit for him. He just happens to finish sentences—or start them, in this case—and appears to always be nearby when anything significant happens around me.

He holds two cups of steaming coffee—which makes me wonder how he managed to open the heavy door without so much as signaling his presence. His face looks more at ease this morning. The deep lines on his forehead and around his eyes that I noticed last night—despite the darkness—have vanished. His features, yet sharp, are softer again. The concerns have faded, leaving the stage open for his cocky confidence. It makes me melt like butter in the sun.

He approaches us as an old friend would. No one could guess we barely know this man. Brandie's attitude certainly wouldn't hint at the fact that we both met Max only a few days ago. She flashes a smile at him before returning to her screen, frantically scanning the content to verify the validity of what Max just greeted us with.

"The register was found empty after the attack. They broke quite a few things in the store, too." he continues with the flat tone he masters.

"Do you think it's the same guys?" Brandie asks no one in particular. "Is the threat multiplying?" She whispers, worried.

Since Brandie is asking, I assume the police have not caught anyone. Nor have they shared any decent theories with the public. Which means monsters are still running free in Willowbrook. I swallow loudly as my stomach twists into multiple knots.

Max must have noticed my empty stare. He breaks the fallen silence.

"Coffee delivery. I ordered it black. It's easier to add than to take out," he winks at me as he hands me the hot paper cup.

He then turns to Brandie and apologizes for not getting her anything—she much prefers tea in the morning and seems way too preoccupied to even care about who brought her what anyway.

"I'm getting an alarm system. And a gun. Hannah, we're buying guns today." Brandie barks, speaking so fast I thought I misunderstood what she just said. I can't picture her pointing a gun. Or can I? She would look lethally hot.

"I don't think that will be necessary, love. Plus, I'm sure those robbers know we're broke," I joke, pointing toward the counter behind me, attempting to keep the mood as light as possible.

"I'm not joking!" she shouts back.

"Alarms. You and I will start with alarms. How's that?" I compromise. "I know a guy. I'll give him a shout this morning. He will quote us both, cameras and all," I wave my hand in the hair before blowing on the perfectly black coffee—exactly how I take it—brought to me by the perfectly charming man.

"Wait, are you talking about that guy you used to date? What was his name again...?"

I feel the blood rushing to my face. I can't quite explain why, but I was hoping Brandie wouldn't bring up this tiny detail of my past in front of Max. It shouldn't make any difference, but I feel embarrassed nonetheless. Another thing to add to the list of things that don't make sense anymore. Max's body straightens, barely noticeably. He hits the floor with his heel ever so gently, his gaze aiming down at his feet. Is he... nervous?

No... *Jealous?* Well, well, well, that might play out to my advantage after all.

"Chuck," I say, sounding as removed as possible. He's not necessarily someone I'm proud to mention.

"Chuck! That's it. Yeah, thank you, but no thank you. This guy was a loser. I don't want our systems to go down within an hour. *I* will make calls. You sit tight. Plus, you have your conference to prepare for!" Brandie answers with enthusiasm.

I heartily witness her smile brighten her face again. Brandie never cared for the conference, but she knows how exciting it is to me. She's always been supportive. I already know that—per her usual—she will text me every day asking if I got laid yet. And will always text me back, "What the fuck are you waiting for?" When I tell her I didn't.

The conference is nothing but a big orgy in Brandie's mind, where people engage in outlandish sex—multiple times a day. I've been attending for a few years now, and never once have I got fucked in my hotel room—or anywhere else around the conference, for that matter. I can't deny the appeal, though.

Max doesn't inquire about the conference, and about the fact that I'm leaving. As a matter of fact, he ignores it and lowers his voice to a whisper to address me—when Brandie is back to focusing on her phone.

"Feeling better?"

I have so many lingering questions about the whole incident, but with Brandie right there, it's hard to get into too many details. I decided not to tell her what had happened. What I saw last night. It's for the best. The eerie atmosphere that's suffocating our small town is already gnawing at her. I refuse to add to that. She would worry sick about me.

I believe Max quickly noticed that she knew very little about the attack—at least didn't hear anything from me—and agreed to keep it all to himself, too. Which he uses as a valid reason to avoid any further questioning and excuses himself.

Clever boy.

Before I know it, he vanishes again and my coffee has gone cold.

CHAPTER ELEVEN

The drive to the big city has always been a favorite of mine. It's barely more than an hour away—a little more to reach the airport on the outskirts of town. My flight is only tomorrow. I could have made the drive and flown out all in the same day, but I must admit, I'm a lazy traveler. I don't necessarily enjoy my days packed in action.

I made a dinner reservation for myself at a lovely restaurant—near my hotel. I love one night or two in the big city, but never more. One thing I know for sure about myself is that I'm not made for the business and the even more complicated dating games of the city. The tall buildings that obstruct the view, the spiral of concrete, and the overpriced rents. I left it behind for a reason.

It's the middle of the afternoon, another warm and bright summer day for the books. My open window allows the forceful air from the moving car—quickly eating the miles ahead of me—to mess with my fiery hair.

The air tastes like sugar—a warm breeze that feels more like a kiss on my cheeks. Flanking me on both sides are lush rolling hills, painted in various shades of green, gracefully rolling for what seems like forever, eventually meeting snowy, sharp peaks in the distance. The dark gray of the rocks contrasts with the bright sun. The mountains seem so far removed, yet I know they're only about another hour or so away.

Summer is in full swing; the grass is neon green, and the trees full and lush, just like they are in Willowbrook. Neatly delimited property lines create a patchwork of little squares of rustic split-rail fences, reaching for the mountains. Wildflowers and ivy climbed some of the fences, adding a touch of whimsical charm to the scene.

Some have animals. Lazy cows grazing and lounging on one another. There are horses, too, usually not too far from gigantic ranches scattered on the horizon. They evidently are the home to farm activities, according to the tall piles of grain, more animals, and huge tractors—not all in running condition. Classic farm stuff. Not that I know much about this life.

It reminds me that there's money around here. The mansions perched high up on the Willowbrook ridge are an everyday reminder, too. What if sheer greed encouraged this new wave of crime? As simple as that. Though it doesn't quite explain why this all *just* started. It's not like the rich discovered our mountain town on their quest for gold and all settled in last month.

I try to shake the feeling. I refuse to think of the grim events. To be reminded yet again that very little makes sense in my life at the moment. I just want to focus on the multicolored blanket of wildflowers spreading for miles around me and the smell of fresh hay in the air.

As I sit down at a table set for two, I can't dodge the small wave of sadness washing over me. I've been alone—though independent and happy—for quite some time. Is it the all-consuming feelings nipping at my body every time I see Max, the recent events harming my beloved town, or just the many couples enjoying a nice dinner in the city? I couldn't tell. But tonight feels unusually lonely.

I find myself wishing Max was sitting across from the round, white-clothed table, eyes burning with love. The word tastes bitter in my mouth. Unreasonable and illogical. *Love.*

Thankfully, the feeling is fleeting. The second my loaded plate of pasta comes floating in the hands of a very attractive server—the burden that held me down flies away. I can't quite say if it's the amount of cheesy carbs coming my way, or the dark features of the man who serves them to me, but either way, I feel better immediately.

I requested a table outside on their patio. Despite the tightness of the space, they turned it into the coziest corner on the street. Warm, yellow lights are strung up from the brick wall, criss-crossing above our heads. Climbing vines took over the gray bricks gradually over the years, creating a fairytale-like sight up to the stone roof. Their green, hanging, never-ending arms remind me of the plants inside of The Book Nook.

Across the paved street, a trio of jazz musicians fills the air with their melodies. The harmonious blend of live instruments and the vocalist's soulful voice seamlessly merge with the sultry summer atmosphere.

Though my sweaty thighs may stick to the chair, my ears are treated to a symphony of delight. Meanwhile, a burst of exquisite flavors dances upon my palate, igniting a sensory firework display within my mouth. I close my eyes as I take another sip of my red blend. The loneliness of moments ago is far, far gone. All I needed was carbs. And wine.

I'm beyond excited to leave. This trip is all about me. Did I wish to travel as the new and hot upcoming writer? *Yes, yes, I did.* But even wearing the hat of the somewhat boring bookstore owner, I can't contain my excitement.

CHAPTER TWELVE

The train of the flowy black dress I chose for the first day of the conference is following me like a faithful sidekick, a mere whisper over the marble floor and down the stairs. The click of my stilettos resonates with every step. I can't say I dislike the allure it gives me.

For the sake of balance—perched on high heels I'm not used to wearing—I attempt to fix my habitually bad posture. I pull my shoulders back and hold my chin a little higher. This once-a-year event is the only time I feel more important than I actually am in real life—it's worth the effort.

I couldn't decide whether I wanted to wear my hair down—casual yet sexy—or up in a tight ponytail; imposing and elegant. I opted for a loose bun tightened high on the top of my head. Somewhere in the middle.

For regular life, it would be too early to be dressed up and dolled up the way I am. But one quick look around the hotel lobby would prove anyone wrong. Women glide gracefully in flowing gowns adorned with shimmering sequins, or cascading silk; the colors ranging from rich jewel tones to delicate pastels. Some opted for sleek, form-fitting dresses that stress every curve, while others exude timeless glamour in vintage-inspired ensembles.

For men, impeccably tailored suits reign supreme, ranging from classic black-tie attire to daringly modern cuts. Crisp white shirts are paired with meticulously knotted ties, adding a touch of subtle refinement.

As I descend the grand staircase to the lobby, I dramatically pause in the middle. *Why would I not pretend to be the main character, after all?*

My eyes scan the lobby. The first thing that catches my attention is the dazzling crystal chandelier hanging from the ceiling. Its myriad facets catch the morning sun permeating through the glass spinning doors and are now reflecting prisms of clear light dancing across the marble floors.

Plush, velvet-upholstered armchairs and sofas are scattered around coffee tables, offering an inviting space for people to gather, chat—and most likely flirt a little, too.

The walls of the main room are adorned with large oil paintings that depict scenes from classic literature. I notice that they also added massive bookshelves, filled with leather-bound tomes, just for the occasion. It is a literary conference, after all. They had to set the scene, I suppose. The hotel is grandiose. The classiest of the area. In terms of fantasy-living; this is the place to be.

The smell of coffee and freshly baked pastries claws its way above the various colognes and perfumes filling the room. The opening ceremony is always held around brunch. What I suspect to be the real reason people gathered early this morning was set up in an adjacent room, buffet style. But a royal buffet, obviously.

Two gigantic tables on opposite sides of the room display artisan, hand-baked sweets, and other appealing piles of food; as two smaller tables in between offer fresh coffee, floral teas, and freshly squeezed juices. It's a funny sight to see so many elegant people stuff their pretty faces with breakfast food. These are my kind of people.

Toward the back of the room, plush chairs were thoughtfully arranged in close proximity, all oriented toward the spread of food and the double door that serves as the entrance. They expected attendees to load up their plates and settle into said chairs for the opening speech.

From my experience, however, most of us prefer to gather around the tall cocktail tables, standing with our coffees and sticky fingers.

I gracefully glide towards the coffee table, hoping to convey the illusion of floating more than walking in my ethereal dress. While the lower part of the garment flows effortlessly thanks to the fluid fabric, the upper portion clings to my body with exquisite precision, striking a delicate balance between elegance, and *I would totally fuck her*.

As I fill my plate with sugary delights and pour myself a cup of black coffee, I look around the room in awe and excitement. Some of these people are living my dream. Some of them published their first work recently and are presenting it for the very first time at the conference this week. They might still be nobodies this morning, but in a few hours, everyone will know about them and their story.

A *ding ding ding* breaks the chatter.

The founder of the conference just entered the room, shaking hands like a monarch would. He kind of looks just as official. As much as I love the event, I don't much care for the guy behind it. He looks spoiled by money and as fake as they come. His thinning dark hair is slicked back on his head and his teeth are too white, too straight. A man this age can't possibly have such perfect dentistry.

The man owns the biggest bookstore chain in the nation. In other words, he's the head of my main competition—this may cloud my judgment a little. But that's okay. I'm good at pretending when it's time for everyone to smile and clap for him. I enjoy the annual event he put together for us book nerds enough to play the good court subject for a few minutes.

His speech sounds longer than usual. Faker than usual. I'm dangerously close to yawning loudly but somehow remain a lady. I take another look around the room to distract myself. I recognize a couple of faces from previous years. A handful of us exchange polite smiles. My mission to try to uncover my fellow co-op members starts now. I take another bite of my buttery croissant, dropping a couple of flakes in my décolleté in the process, as I search the crowd for clues.

Nothing stands out. Nothing obvious, for now. No surprise here. It's not like members wear a red dot on their forehead—like our packages do. Maybe I should suggest we all wear funny hats next time.

The first few hours of the conference fly by. I float from one booth to another, from one speaker to another. I even sat down in one of the marketing sessions I was wholeheartedly trying to avoid. I dipped out quickly, though.

A sudden urge to check my phone tugs at me.

Brandie has sent me five messages. My stomach drops. I truly wanted to take this time. To stay away from all the horrors happening at home, but my best friend is still in Willowbrook—and could be the next target. What if something terrible happened to her while I'm playing princess here? I would never forgive myself.

Five messages. I frantically unlock my phone with shaky hands and nearly drop it.

> B: On the phone with Secure & More. We're getting secured… get it?! LOL

> B: Damn, his voice sounds hot. Do you think he's hot?

> B: I'm getting us the WHOLE package girl (not his package). Hope you're ready.

> B: They're out of their damn minds. What are we ordering, fucking gold? Did you know how expensive this shit is?

> B: I got this. I am getting us a discount. And no, I didn't sleep with the guy, before you ask. I might still if he's as hot as he sounds…

I roll my eyes as I finish reading her continuous flow of random thoughts.

One would think she could have fit it all in one text and saved me the near heart attack. But it's Brandie we're talking about. Of course, she couldn't. I know she shared every thought without filters, all while muttering the most flirty tone on the phone to ensure the best price. This damn woman. I'll text her back later.

A break, remember Hannah, this is your break.

As I walk back towards the coffee table to get my much-needed third refill of the day, I catch sight of a petite woman sitting alone at a table, almost completely concealed behind a tall, leaning pile of books. Several copies of the same book are piled onto one another. Her amber-lined eyes dart around the room. Though there is a small fire in her gaze; it's dimmed by an emotion I know too well.

Her hair is cut short, blond, and curly. Her shy smile—aimed at every person who walks by—screams *wanna stop by?* But no one does. My heart aches for her ignored invite for conversation; a stinging deep in my chest.

Oh no, not on my watch.

I make quick work of refilling my coffee and grab a second cup, just in case she's a coffee lover, too.

"Hi! I'm Hannah!" I motion to shake her hand but catch myself just in time.

I don't hold one, but two cups of coffee, and any sudden moves would be a recipe for disaster. Her eyes lit up at the sound of my voice, brighter than the sun. Either she really loves coffee or she desperately needed to talk to someone. After a small giggle, she gives me her name.

"Hi, Hannah. I'm Samantha, Samantha Lee. Is this for me?" She jerks her chin up towards the coffee.

"Yes, yes! Absolutely. It's black. I didn't know..."

"It's perfect, thanks. That's quite...kind, Hannah. Wanna sit?"

Both her hands reach for the steaming cup I'm holding dangerously close to her face as she points to the empty chair across from hers with her eyes. The seat is still cold—a sign that no one has sat there in a long time.

We awkwardly smile at each other before I ask, "So, Samantha, tell me your story."

She takes a deep breath, clutching her coffee cup.

"I never knew what I wanted to do with my life. I never fit in, so I wrote a book," she admits. "Now I'm promoting it at an empty table at one of the biggest book conferences in the country."

The weight of her situation shows on her face.

"Well, the table is not empty anymore," I say, winking. "Why do you think it was to begin with?"

Samantha explains she self-published her book out of passion but lacked industry experience. She booked a booth, hoping for the best. I check the agenda and see her name isn't listed among the signing sessions—a shame.

"What's your book about?" I ask. She tells me about her story—a cursed symphony and greedy musicians—with delightful tact.

"Listen, Samantha. I'm no big name, but I can help you sell a bit. Send me a hundred copies of your book. I'll promote it at my bookstore and share it with friends in the industry and within the co-op." I say the latter as if that was an evident source to mention.

Samantha is polite enough to keep the signs of her confusion to a minimum. She *does* inquire about it, though—that's a personal win. After I paint the most detailed picture with great enthusiasm, I write my address and phone number down, and she agrees to send copies the second she gets back home after the event.

"If you don't have a date yet, come to dinner with me tonight," I order young Samantha.

The first of a string of dinners-with-a-show. It's also a great time to network and meet some important people over drinks and *not-so-funny* jokes. Her lips curve higher as she agrees. We agree to meet around 6:30 pm. in the lobby.

With one hand holding on to my phone and the cards and fliers I collected, the other clumsily gripping the steaming hot coffee I poured yet again for myself, I run towards the elevator that I see closing already.

There were signs—obvious signs—of an upcoming disaster, but I chose to ignore them. In my rush, I didn't see the tall woman walking from my right and I inevitably collapsed into her, spilling coffee all over myself—and her beautiful vintage skirt.

I let out a mortified shriek the second I realize what I've done, my hands finding my mouth. *Fuck fuck fuck.*

"Oh no, I'm so, so sorry. Here, take that. I'm so very sorry," I blurt out, quickly grabbing a handful of napkins neatly folded on the table near us.

I'm expecting her to lose her composure, to call me names, maybe even slap me across the face. That skirt looks expensive. And this coffee is *hot*. Steaming. But instead, I look up to a flawless, dark-skinned face looking down at me with a gentle smile.

"Oh, honey, that's okay. It's nothing, please," she begs me to stand up and stop forcing napkins onto her never-ending legs. "It's all good, I promise. I was about to change anyway!" she jokes.

I finally rise to my full height to face her, my face twisted with embarrassment. I wish I could disappear into a tiny hole. I try to ignore the looks coming from all directions, raining on me like gunshots. I follow the woman's gaze as it shifts to the many pieces of paper I'm still holding—though all covered in coffee now.

She unexpectedly screams out, "Oh, you're the co-op lady! I've heard about you!" She genuinely seems excited by the news.

I close the gap between us with my upper body and whisper, "Are you a member?" One eyebrow arched.

Here it is, the laugh she was holding back. A crystal sound that gives my entire body the green light to relax after what just happened.

"I am not," she says after she's able to breathe again, "But I love the concept. I heard about the lovely lady who promotes it every year at this conference. I keep telling these people I've never had the chance to meet you."

"I bet you will remember me now." I grimace as I gesture to the catastrophe that adorns her skirt with black and brown stains—still steaming.

Another laugh. She really is not mad.

"I'm Emily, but please call me Em. Join us for dinner tonight. We will be at table five. I'll save you a seat."

"Two, please. If possible. I'm bringing a friend." Samantha could use some good connections.

Table five it is.

CHAPTER THIRTEEN

I join Samantha in the lobby at 6:30.

She looks beautiful, and somehow, even younger than she is. She's a doll. One with a possibly bright future. She opted for a flattering, flowy pink dress that lays right above her knees. Tall, elegant white boots complete the outfit. Simple, but dangerously efficient.

I, on the other hand, chose to continue to live my fantasy. I picked a cocktail dress I hope will turn heads. Brandie diligently asked two times if I got laid yet—on the first day. Maybe this year, I will finally tell her *yes, yes, I did.*

The neckline of the dress plunges gracefully into a deep vee, giving a hint of elegance, all while revealing just enough. The waist is cinched with a matching satin sash that ties at the back. Another trap for imprudent males. *Come too close and I shall tie you up with it.*

Samantha locks her arm with mine and hops towards the reception room where dinner is held. It's refreshing to have her around. It feels like we've known each other our entire lives. There is no awkward silence, no small talk. She seems comfortable around me and I feel the same around her—despite our age gap.

We politely force our way past a few groups of people blocking the entrance of the grandiose ballroom. I'm pretty sure we just stepped inside some kind of enchanted castle, or into a parallel world.

The room is adorned with intricate gold work, covering the walls, ceilings, and even the chairs. The dim light casts a muted glow over the colors, enhancing the elegance of the scene. A balanced combination of gold and deep dark red dominates the decor. It's simple, elegant, and perfect.

Long, ebony-skinned arms waving at us from the center of the room catch my attention. Em noticed me before I could find her. Table five is perfectly positioned in the middle—which means not only will we get food immediately when service begins, but we are also dead-center to watch the show. *Perfect.*

I drag Samantha towards the table—and our new group of friends.

Em is waiting with open arms, welcoming us into a warm hug.

"It's so nice to meet you, Samantha," she says to my new friend. Em squeezes my shoulder as if to say '*And nice to see you again, skirt-ruiner-coffee-monster*'. She steps aside and gestures to the table behind her, already full of people sitting and laughing.

"These are your people for the night," Em declares. A queen introducing her queendom. "Meet my book friends," she tries to say loud enough to beat the music already raging in the background.

Almost everybody looks up at Samantha and me. Their eyes light up. Hands are waved in excitement. Only a few people didn't notice us yet and kept chatting. I meet everyone's eyes with a friendly smile. Then I freeze.

Bile creeps up my throat. My whole body turns cold, then burns inside. I feel like my knees are about to give out. The music turns to a chaotic buzz in my head, overwhelming and dizzying. I click my tongue at the staggering taste of salt—it's back. Maybe it's a symptom hinting at a panic attack?

Sitting on the left side of the table, I recognize that tight jawline. I recognize those soft dark curls bouncing up and down as he laughs.

Max.

You've got to be fucking kidding me.

As if my vision just turned to slow motion, he turns his head in my direction and his golden eyes meet mine with an intensity I haven't witnessed yet. His genuinely kind smile—aimed at the woman sitting next to him—turns to a feline grin. His fist loosely closes on the table. Max casually leans back in his chair, extending one arm to the back of the seat next to him, never losing his wicked smile. He found his prey. He looks beastly.

I can't decide if I'm utterly excited or desperately offended that he's, in fact, here. So much for leaving the drama at home. How could he not tell me? *Why* did he not tell me? Brandie mentioned the conference just a couple of days ago and he didn't say a word about attending. I'm seeing red, possibly breathing fire. *But I'm also delighted.*

The heat in my lower region just turned up to a painful high. As introductions come to an end, Max whispers to the lady on his right. She suddenly gets up, grabbing the person next to her. I almost jump across the table to stop her. To tell her there's no need. But I don't *really* want to. The beast politely orders Samantha and me to join him—by tapping on the seat.

"You have some serious explaining to do," I say coldly, looking straight ahead as I sit down next to him.

Max's arm meets my shoulders. A mere featherweight against my delicate frame. He leans against me but addresses Samantha over my shoulder as if I were a mere obstacle on the road.

"She's a little grumpy at times, but don't let it fool you. She's got a heart somewhere in there," Max lightly taps the side of my collarbone with the tip of his fingers.

I can't help but chuckle. *Bastard.*

"You two know each other?" Samantha innocently asks as she carefully unfolds the large napkin onto her lap.

"Barely," I say, still forcing myself to sound upset. Though that's hardly a joke. I *barely* know Max.

His eyes meet mine for a heartbeat before they travel down to my cleavage, and then to the rest of my body. He licks his bottom lip. No one could have noticed. The man knows how to play a subtle game. But I caught it. He truly is hunting tonight.

"What are you doing here, anyway?" I inquire.

"I thought this was a public event?" Max cockily jokes, gesturing at the grand ballroom.

I throw a warning look at him. Not that it's any of my business, but I want to know.

"I research literature, remember?" Max vaguely references our conversation back at The Book Nook.

"And to what end?"

"So many questions tonight," he whispers with a grin as he braces his elbows on the table.

I notice his golden eyes are more...green. Almost... *neon green*? A slightly faded, somewhat muted version of the overwhelming hue. They look out of this world. And glossy. He's drunk. Well, that would explain his newly revealed playfulness towards me. I never imagined Max abusing anything—except for my body, of course—but then again, the conference is a known place for fun and indulgence.

The rest of the dinner is a blur. I barely focused on the show—some fire was lit, that much I recall. There were half-naked dancers, red sparkly outfits, and other things. It was hard to concentrate—let alone remember anything—when Max's hand kept getting menacingly close to my thigh. He didn't touch me. Merely laid his hand strategically close to my skin, right on the edge of my seat, the heat of his skin seeping through mine. More like a bonfire in the dead of the winter—not like a hand on the stove. The kind of heat that takes command over your body. You don't fight it.

The only vivid memory I have of our conversations is the fact that he promised Samantha he would introduce her to a renowned publisher. The guy owes Max a favor. Max pledged to use it to help Samantha promote her book and every next story she wishes to work on. That was charming—which didn't help my crush on him.

"I can't thank you enough, Hannah," Samantha said while giggling, squeezing my hand repeatedly.

The reality is, I hardly had anything to do with this. I didn't even know Max was supposed to be here.

The group casually separates by the close of the show.

I turn around to find Max but, of course, he's vanished. A mere shadow swiftly dissipating. I make my way back to the elevator as fast as I can, despite the stinging under my feet from the stupid high heels I was wearing all day and night. To hell with class. I lose the shoes and welcome the cold marble beneath me, slowing the sweat pearling down my back.

The ballroom is still crowded—and smells like it—but I manage to wait for the elevator all alone and embrace the quiet. I watch the door close after I press the button for the second floor, releasing a satisfied sigh. Before the door seals, a hand grips the heavy steel.

Damn you, Max.

His hunting grin is back, twisting the tip of his lips sensually. His eyes narrow with mischief. Max leans against the opposite side of the elevator.

"What floor, sir?" I joke.

"Second."

"Of course," I roll my eyes. The coincidences keep on coming.

We fall silent. I can sense his glossy eyes on me. Every part of my body can. He scans every inch and obvious desire ignites his features. I don't recognize the man standing only a few feet away from me. His face is familiar, sure. But his energy is...different.

"You look stunning, Hannah," his voice is suave and deep, sweet like honey.

My panties vibrated under my dress at the mere sound of it. I pretend to ignore the compliment.

"Why didn't you tell me you were coming?"

"Come where?"

"Max."

"I was quite *distracted* that day, Hannah. I didn't want to intrude, either. You seemed pretty excited about this," his hand draws a vague circle in the air.

The playful expression slowly fades away and turns to something darker. He's recalling what happened that frightful night—and the following day. All of it was so intense, so emotional—building obvious tension in the air. I feel guilty for spoiling the flirty mood. Some questions are better left unanswered—especially considering he doesn't owe me any explanation, anyway.

"Well, I shall forgive you. *If* you buy me a drink tomorrow." I attempt to bring the fun back.

"Does the all-inclusive bar count?" he grins, looking down at me.

Straight into my eyes. I chuckle, swallowed whole by his presence in the tight, confined space.

The elevator reaches our floor, and the door slowly opens. Max leans on the wall, one hand in his pocket, the other arm bent at the elbow, supporting his head. He lost the jacket he wore most of the night, revealing just enough of his full, defined muscles wrapped in tanned skin. I want him to unravel me, right here in this elevator. I look back at him, a silent invitation. He doesn't move.

"I lied. I'm on the fifth floor. I will see you tomorrow, *babygirl.*" Max winks at me.

The light of the corridor reflects in his drunken gaze. My mouth drops, and my eyebrows shoot up. Before I can say anything back, the door's closed and the elevator's gone.

That night, I touched myself and climaxed to the memory of his lips mouthing *babygirl,* over and over again. Dumb, dumb crush.

CHAPTER FOURTEEN

Safe to say that my attention shifted from the actual conference to its attendees by now. Well, *one* in particular. But even without Max being here, I met such amazing people in just one day that my cup will be filled for a while.

As I make my way to the breakfast table, familiar broad shoulders are already standing there. *Of course.*

"You're early," I say to Max, as I tap on his left shoulder.

"Black, the way you like it," he purrs as he turns around to hand me a full cup.

"I thought we agreed on a drink. Coffee doesn't count."

"Who says we can't have both?" he winks.

This day doesn't even need sunshine. His smile will suffice. He seems refreshed, as if he slept deeply and comfortably. I wonder what it feels like to sleep in his arms, on his chest. Did he touch himself to the ghost of my memory last night, like I did?

"I got us a table for tonight," he says. "But don't get too excited, it's one of the hotel's restaurants. I will see you at 7 in the lobby."

Max grabs my hand and pretends to kiss it. Once again, he doesn't touch my skin. This move is driving me insane—in the best of ways. I must have shot for the sky at this point. The butterflies in my belly are creating a full-blown hurricane, accompanied by the usual flooding of my underwear—whenever Max is around, that is.

He's swift to disappear in the crowd. This day better goes by fast. As a matter of fact, is it seven yet?

One session piqued my interest yesterday and it's happening in just ten minutes. Perfect. A glance over the schedule later, I find the room it's happening in. Paganism.

Witches and potions, let's go!

"Paganism has ancient roots, and the sessions delved into the historical evolution of pagan traditions," the speaker says, pacing around the stage.

Max was right. I suppose there's more to magic than Zephrey Wenfrield leads us to believe.

"Contemporary pagan practices draw inspiration from ancient practices while incorporating modern elements," the gentleman continues, his voice resonating a little too loud inside the small room.

His hands draw circles and waves in the air as he shares his knowledge with the attendees. "It's rich in mythology and folklore," he continues for about two hours.

That was the perfect session to keep me distracted. Plus, I can use that at dinner with Max. It's a win-win.

I sit down with lovely Samantha for a quick lunch in between sessions. She spent the morning mingling and networking. Her eyes carry the light of hope and excitement—it suits her.

As I bite into my five-star sandwich, I notice Max's figure approaching us. I can't discern the expression on his face. The heat plummets when he comes closer and puts one hand on my chair. *I wish he had put it on my body instead.*

I look up at him, ready to greet him with a joke, when I realize that there's no smile on his face. The space between his eyebrows wrinkles with worry. His severe look surveys the space around Samantha and me, never landing anywhere in particular. I think Samantha notices, too. She swallows a sizable piece of her lunch and looks straight at me, her eyes full of silent questions.

"Have you talked to Brandie?" Max's voice echoes with somber resonance.

I speed up my munching. I haven't checked my phone this morning.

Max's question feeds a sense of panic that takes my stomach hostage, tightening the bottom of my neck. I rub my hands together to get rid of the remains of food—instead of using a napkin like a normal human being—and reach for my phone.

"Is everything okay?" I ask. "Nothing from Brandie. What's happening?" My tone grows more worried.

Max gently grabs my wrist and pulls me up and in, to where his lips are almost brushing the delicate outline of my ear. He's facing me, though his eyes still refuse to look *at* me.

"There was another robbery, Hannah. The jewelry store. I just wanted to make sure Brandie was okay."

My knees wobble, threatening to give in, and this time, Max's proximity has nothing to do with it. *Another* robbery. How the hell is that even possible? Surely there must be a wave of crime plaguing the entire country. It can't just be Willowbrook, can it?

"They found a body," Max gravely adds as if reading my thoughts.

What I read in the greenish pools of Max's eyes is somewhat confusing. Does he want to pull me in? Embrace me? Here it is again, the overwhelming and uncalled-for protective instinct mixed with worry, emanating from him just like the night I hid from the robbers—and their gun.

"I will call Brandie right away. I didn't hear from her. Hopefully, that's good news." I finally mutter.

Max grabs the phone out of my hand and starts typing—without warning or permission. I simply chuckle.

"Of course, help yourself," I say, throwing my hands in the air playfully.

"My number. In case you need a superhero before dinner," he hands me my phone back and pretends to yank it away when I try to grab it. *Child.* I love it.

Max puts his hands on my shoulders and leans down to match my height. With kind eyes, he asks me not to worry too much.

"Just call Brandie. I'm sure she's okay. I will see you tonight. We'll forget about all this. Don't be late."

CHAPTER FIFTEEN

I've been sitting on the bed for the past thirty minutes, staring at the alarm clock on the side table. It's 6:30 p.m. I've been ready since 6. For someone who's usually fashionably late, this date with Max has turned me into a professional get-readier.

Brandie didn't know what had happened when I called, as Max suggested. I almost felt bad for calling at all. Her voice was noticeably growing more worried by the second. I didn't mean for her to obsess over an invisible—yet very real—threat.

It turned out to be a great opportunity for Brandie to update me on our alarm system situation and to proudly share how she scored us an incredible discount. It involved a lot of wine, dropped panties, and plenty of moaning–her words. Brandie has her own unique negotiation tactics. I decided not to think about the details too much. We're saving money, and however she achieved it is none of my business. What's undeniable is that we need some kind of security system.

For our first date, my outfit had to be a true showstopper. I didn't think I would find the right night to wear this particular dress when I originally packed it—even here—but you never know when an incredibly sexy beast of a man will brush your hand with his lips and ask you out, I suppose.

The attire is made of silky, soft, red fabric. The open-back design leaves my spine fully exposed, tracing a delicate path to the small of my back. The daring cut *demands* a lack of underwear, a choice that wasn't hard to make. The front top of the dress plays with delicate lace, showing just enough of my cleavage, covering the rest and leaving it up to the imagination. The absence of sleeves or straps leaves my shoulders temptingly bare, inviting a touch that promises to be unforgettable. I kept my hair down, slightly wavy and wild—mirroring the way I'm feeling tonight.

I find Max standing against one of the walls in the lobby, one foot up against it. One hand tucked in the pocket of his black jeans, the other holds a colorful cocktail.

He's casually looking around, punctually nodding at passersby. The movement of his head following the travels of strangers opens his blouse a little further on his chest. An invitation to touch. To taste. He's wearing a light, short-sleeved dark blue shirt, from which he kept the top two buttons strategically open. It looks like he captured the night sky and all its starlight and used it to embellish his body tonight.

Max spots me on the stairs. The way he bites his bottom lip gives it away. And though I can't hear it, I'm pretty sure he groans as he gently shakes his head. The dress is working.

I'm ready to play.

"Long time no see, Hannah," he jokes, handing me the cocktail meant for me. "Ready?" He grabs my hand and leads the way towards the restaurant.

Reflecting the whole hotel's design, the restaurant opens up to high ceilings adorned with crystal chandeliers. The walls are dark, lined with small light fixtures drawing a path to the back of the room. On each side of the central path, intimate booths are separated by thick wooden structures, supporting intricate steel designs. It's almost impossible to see each booth from where we stand. They're divinely discreet. It's ideal.

We sit on the same side, sharing the comfortable velvet booth.

We're both on our second round of cocktails when we finally decide to order food. The petite woman who's serving us can't keep her eyes off of Max. How could one ignore his full lips, tight jawline, and golden eyes? Who could possibly dismiss the veins running along the full shape of his forearms, inviting the wandering gaze to his powerful hands? There's only one way out of this—hoping said hands will tighten around your neck all while his lips crash into yours. *I get it, lady, I really do.*

Aside from the normal amount of polite and thankful looks, he doesn't seem to pay attention to her at all. Despite her silky blond hair and generous curves. His eyes are on *me*.

"So, what should I know about you?" I finally ask as I lean deeper against the back of our booth. It's one thing to be uncontrollably attracted to a physique; it's another to connect souls.

"How much do you *want* to know?"

"Everything. I want everything," I smirk. My comment is loaded, and it didn't go unnoticed.

"Of course you do," he grins. "I grew up in the big city. I've always been a bit of a loner. I can't say I ever liked to mingle with my peers. I wonder if anyone there even remembers my name." Max softly chuckles. "I like my life in the suburbs better, anyway. In Willowbrook," he takes a quick breath. "I suppose most people would consider me to be slightly obsessive over literature, as I'm sure you well know by now." He pauses to allow his lips to part and smile, staring at my décolletage. "Turns out I'm a bookstore owner lover, as well." He winks as if to punctuate the end of his sentence.

I don't know who this *conference Max* is, but I like him. Flirty, straightforward, daring. He's willing to play, and he's not shy about it. Something about him is undeniably different here.

"What does one do to own two houses in a town like Willowbrook?" I half-ass joke. I'm not certain that kind of question is acceptable on a first date, but I'm genuinely curious.

He takes another bite of the medium-rare steak he ordered, then clears his throat before he continues, a more serious expression on his face.

"My parents died when I was in my early twenties. They left behind my younger sister and myself. They also left a lot of money in the bank. It has made purchasing houses and other things a little easier. That's the only thing that got easier."

I glare at him in silence. That's one explanation I didn't expect. Way to spoil the mood—yet again.

"I'm sorry. I didn't know."

"How could you, Hannah? It was a long time ago."

I faintly nod, genuinely sorry for prying. My loose tongue is going to get me in trouble someday.

"How did you even manage? I can't fathom," I exhale.

"We tried the best a couple of young adults could do. My parents left a trail of burnt bridges in their wake. It was impossible to lean on any family or friends. I just became the man of the house—and of everything else."

"That sounds like a lot to manage," I say, and mean it.

"It was. I rapidly sold almost all of our family's properties and focused on us in one household. It made it easier in many ways. My sister now lives in our house near the city. I took over the family's mansion in Willowbrook." By the shrug that runs through him, I can tell he didn't mean to use the word mansion. Too presumptuous? It steals a small smirk from me.

"You didn't leave the *mansion* to your sister, huh?" I attempt to joke.

Max chuckles. "I don't think she's ever kept a houseplant alive. Watering a succulent once a month is too much to bear. Let alone take care of an entire house and lawn. She would suffocate in weeds. Trust me, it's better this way," he ends his sentence with a wink.

I laugh—loudly. And so does he.

"You guys are pretty close, then?" I ask between two sips.

There must be some kind of magic in the air because Max opens up to me as an old friend would. He doesn't hold anything back, painfully contrasting the cold front he harbors dutifully in Willowbrook. I eat it all up while I can.

"Extremely."

I don't have any siblings—it's a kind of connection you can only understand when you have it, I believe.

"What happened to your parents?" I dare ask, using the resurrected comfort between us.

"A car accident. The classic drunk driver story. Someone got behind the wheels intoxicated and hit them. They died instantly. I'm sure you've heard it a million times. Every superhero story starts this way."

"So, does that make you a superhero?" I smirk as I nudge an elbow into him.

There's no right word for this kind of situation. I grab his hand with cold fingers and leave them there. A blink later, he takes his hand back.

"How come I never saw you in Willowbrook before?" I suddenly come to wonder aloud.

A quick flash of something I can't quite identify materializes in Max's eyes, like a lightning bolt—gone as fast as it came.

"Like I said, I don't mingle much. I very rarely leave the house; it's on the outskirts of Willowbrook. Not the most convenient, but perfect for someone who likes to keep to themselves." Max waves his fork in my direction and winks.

Fair enough, I suppose.

"You know, most people would ask the *what's your story question*, in return," I say with mischief in my eyes.

Max playfully groans as he wipes his delicate mouth with a silky napkin. The next thing I know, his arm is around my shoulders. He leans in close. So close I can feel his warm breath on the bent of my neck. My scalp prickles as heat runs down my spine.

I sense the closeness of his lips travel from the tip of my shoulder, following along the curve of my neck, all the way below my ear. I can't see it, but I *know* that he's grinning. His lips never land on my skin. He works his breath as a torturous toy. It's working. The ache between my legs grows stronger as I attempt to keep it together for the sake of being in public.

"Well, let me guess," he whispers, remaining nested in my neck, "You left the city to start a cozy life in Willowbrook. Most people would think that you would simply start working at a local coffee shop and get a small dog. But not you, Hannah," my name is nothing more than a murmur floating on his lips. "You started your own business because you can't lift your nose off a book. But also because you're brave and resourceful. You dream of becoming an author, but you refuse to even try, though I'm convinced you are quite talented. So instead, you spend your time reading someone else's work, constantly doubting yours. And instead of a dog, I believe I saw a cat roaming at *The Book Nook.*"

My throat shamelessly displays my heavy swallowing. I can't decide whether I should be offended—again—or merely impressed at how accurate this was. Am I really this transparent? This obvious? Can people just read me like an open book—or is it just Max? He's still softly laughing in my ear, proud of what he just accomplished.

"Am I right?" Max teases.

"You're wrong about one thing." I bluntly say.

"And what is that?"

"I'm not a writer. And I'm not talented," I say, lowering my gaze to my drink, and swirling the colorful liquid perilously close to the brim.

"My point exactly," he clicks his tongue and waves his index finger toward me with a victorious smile.

He wouldn't know. He couldn't. Apart from a few lines from my website, Max had never read anything I wrote. While I appreciate the sentiment, he doesn't realize that my imagination grows drier with each passing day. There's no dormant author within me, waiting for the right moment to emerge and surprise everyone.

We linger over dinner, intentionally stretching seconds into minutes, and pouring more drinks down our throats. I learn that Max has never held a real job—since he inherited quite a fortune. Over the years, he collected hobbies to pass the time: golfing, boating, skiing. The list is endless. Though it never filled the hole his parents' death dug in his heart, it certainly granted him an interesting and adventurous life.

"Did you ever miss having an actual job?" I ask, almost immediately regretting it. Who would? Maybe I'm more asking about a purpose than a job.

"With my parents' reputation and my love for solitude, I can't say I did," Max chuckles. "Sharing my passions with someone is something I missed more." His gaze lingers on me, the remnants of a fire that seems to have once existed in them.

Hours have passed, and the perfect night must eventually end. If everything goes according to plan, it will end with our bodies intertwined.

We sip on our last drink in the brisk air of the summer night, out on the patio, under the stars. The night unfolds like a dream painted in hues of warmth and tranquility. The sky above our heads is a canvas of deep indigo, sprinkled generously with a myriad of twinkling stars, each one a glimmering beacon of enchantment.

I catch my date looking straight into my eyes in silence quite a few times. The hopes of feeling his skin gliding up and down against mine grew stronger every time I did.

We walk back inside the hotel. Max grabbed my hand and led the way. It's just us two in the small space inside the elevator now. The elevator makes a first stop on the first floor.

We're not alone anymore.

A group of college kids pour into the elevator as if a dam broke and the water was released all at once. The young men are giggly, having the time of their lives. I don't refrain from smiling back at them. The elevator fills with the smell of cheap liquor and fruity mixers. They are in good spirits—I can get behind that. Their bodies, cranked inside the small space, push Max's closer to mine. My back presses against the corner as Max's chest is only a few inches away now.

His right arm stretches over my shoulder, a feeble attempt to maintain a safe distance between our faces. The crowd behind him is large, and the space inside the elevator is quite small. I welcome the cozy fire of his breath, a ghostly caress against my lips—nothing more than an intimate promise of a kiss, but not yet. One of his perfectly defined curls escaped and landed on my forehead. He smells like cinnamon and lavender. It makes me want him even more.

The arm that's not holding Max up comes crashing onto the side of my hip. His hand lays flat on the wall behind me. His forearm makes one with my side. He swallows me whole with his golden green eyes. Two pools of liquid desire. Electricity jolts down my spine and dangerously south, aiming right between my legs. The tingling sensation takes full control over my body and mind.

Max is so close.

I would only need to tilt my head up ever so slightly, and our lips would collide. A fragile barrier, a minuscule world, separates our burning bodies now. A distance too easily consumed. I wonder what he tastes like, what he feels like. The anticipation is intoxicating, pulling me deeper into the abyss of desire.

I relax in the bubble Max creates with his body. The college kids have disappeared—at least in my mind. My vision narrows on the sculpted man standing only a breath away from me. He's grinning as he stares at my lips. I know this look. I've seen it before.

A quick breath empties my lungs when I feel his hips crash into mine. He didn't come alone. Max is hard, pressing insistently against me. By the size of the bulge I feel through the thin fabric of my dress, I can tell tonight will be particularly memorable.

The elevator rings for the second floor and the door slides open.

"That's me," I whisper through my teeth.

Max growls and creates a path through the college kids, still squeezed in tight.

My date hasn't let go of my hand as we approach my door. I swipe the card to unlock it. I can't get to the other side fast enough. As I turn around to let him in, I find Max staring at me. He leans to kiss my forehead but stops before he reaches me. One flutter of an eyelash later, the desire flees from his eyes.

Max shakes his head and wishes me good night. When he turns around one more time, halfway through the narrow hallway, I think he's about to change his mind. To come back to me. But he simply grins and blows me a kiss. Then disappears.

I'm pretty sure the floor just cracked open below my feet and hell swallowed me in one stingy bite. There was only one viable outcome to the night, to the elevator situation—and it was *not* me sleeping alone.

CHAPTER SIXTEEN

I start the day with a pleasant soreness in my favorite, delicate area. *Desire.* I'm horny. *Damn you, Max.* This isn't how I expected the last full day of the conference to start.

I replay last night's events as I slide into my clothes for the day. Every time I close my eyes, I'm transported back—feeling Max's breath flirting with my skin, his golden eyes on me, his smile. I relive the sincerity of his fingers intertwined with mine, leading us away. The playfulness in the air, the bold passion floating all around us. *Then nothing.* An empty hotel room.

I'm not mad. I *can't* be. Do my insides hurt for Max's body? Yes. But I respect and understand boundaries. If anything, I value how much of a gentleman he's been. I can appreciate the tease, and the patience forced upon me. I'm learning to enjoy the ride. No one has ever made me feel close to the way he does. Every time I think I have him all figured out, eating in my hand, he shrugs and a new version of him comes out.

I ditched the high heels this morning. The conference nears its end and the signs are clear. Most women have abandoned their extravagant dresses, opting for more comfortable yet still alluring outfits. Tuxedos have transformed into jeans and button-up shirts, somehow making the men look even sexier. More tantalizing eye candy for me to feast upon.

My phone vibrates in my hand as I reach for the breakfast hall.

> M: You are driving me insane, Hannah.

Good morning to you too, Max. I had almost forgotten that he saved his number on my phone—*in case I needed a superhero*. Now, this is undeniable evidence of the connection between us, isn't it? I mull over the unexpected text repeatedly, half expecting to awaken from a dream.

> H: Tell me something I don't know.

If Mr. Golden Eyes wants to take his sweet time with me, I'll give him extra homework.

A giggle creeps into my ear. So close, yet it sounds like a mere whisper. Instead of the text I was expecting, it's Max's soft lips I feel, sneaking up from behind. Max's touch is fleeting, brushing against my earlobe so delicately that it's essentially ghostly.

"You smell divine, Hannah," his voice hardly carries over the background noise of the room.

Maybe I'm dreaming after all. I feel the heat of his body travel from my left side, across my back, all the way to my right. I tilt my head once he arrives, offering him the full length of my neck. Max pauses. I think he's about to kiss it. My whole body shivers.

True to his manners—and the dangerous game he revels in—Max merely brushes the tips of his fingers across my lower back. It's as if he's intentionally teasing me with a tantalizing preview of his touch, offering just a hint of his caress without fully letting me feel him. Sweet, exquisite torture.

"You are playing with fire, Mister, it's a crowded room," I softly say back as I spin on my heels to face him. I dive into his eyes, our faces close enough to feel each other's breath.

"What can I say? You are hard to resist." The corner of his mouth curls into a smirk.

He knows I can barely handle the tease, and he takes great pride in it. I need to own this. If anything, as payback for last night. I can't let him win again. Without warning, I inch closer and firmly grasp Max's jeans right beside the zipper.

"I'm hard to resist, and you, mister, are just hard."

A sharp breath swiftly slips between his teeth, emptying his lungs. His eyes widen in shock, yet his smile remains, unyielding.

"This is new," he breathes as a challenge. "Who are you, *really*, Hannah?"

Max holds my gaze, refusing to look away. The room is crowded with onlookers, but I am not letting go of my hidden prize. Let them watch. Let them yearn. How many would envy me, wish to trade places, to touch what I touch? I never imagined I could be so bold, but here I am, holding on tighter, as a statement to my fiery, lustful mood.

Max *is* hard, indeed. And full. And big.

To look at his length through his pants is one thing; to feel it in my hand is entirely another. Even through the sturdy fabric of his jeans, it makes my palm look quite small. The kind of size that requires it to be handled with two hands.

For what feels like forever, neither of us has budged. Our eyes locked in a challenge, brimming with pride, satisfaction, and unmistakable desire. Is he going to take me right here on this coffee table? Max finally gives in and guides my hand away. I win this round. He chuckles, shaking his head. The hunter's grin on his face appears to be permanent now.

"Go enjoy your last day. I will catch you later, *babygirl*."

Max proceeds with this strange *grab-my-hand-but-won't-kiss-it* before he fades away into the crowd. I look around with mischief written in big bold letters all over my face, curious to see if someone did indeed notice us.

Strolling across the room, an older gentleman holds a bunch of paper in his wrinkled—obviously marked by passing time—hands. I take a moment to see him. His silver hair is neatly combed and the small smile etched on his face exudes a quiet kindness. His eyes crinkle at the corners as he looks around. He's wearing a faded but meticulously kept tweed jacket. Despite the obvious sense of wisdom exuding from him, something else entirely catches my attention.

Among the various pieces of paper trapped in his long fingers, one tiny detail stands out. A red dot. *The* red dot. *The co-op's symbol.*

I want to bolt toward him. But let's be honest, a crazy red-headed lady running full speed in your direction is never a good sign—it wouldn't make for a good first impression. I take a quick but deep breath before I trot in his direction.

"Excuse me, Henry?" I try to catch his attention.

Luckily, I'm able to read a name on one of the envelopes he holds. Only a first name—the rest was hidden behind the stack of various papers—but that's all I needed, anyway. Assuming it's his name, of course. By the way he turns to face me, obviously toying with confusion and surprise, I think it is.

"Hi! I'm Hannah, you don't... I am sorry. I..." I painfully mumble.

He raises a brow. I struggle to start a conversation—maybe I should have thought that one through before calling out a stranger's name. Might as well get straight to the point.

"I'm sorry, sir. This must be peculiar. I noticed the red dot on one of the envelopes." I point to the stack in his hand. "Now, it could be a funny coincidence, or it could be a sign that you are part of the co-op." I pause. And wait. Time stretches.

The co-op doesn't have a real name. All we know is the concept, the sharing, the sending and receiving of rare and ancient books. If he's a member, there will be no need to explain. His lips curl up and his eyes squint in response, accentuating the wrinkles in their corners.

"I think you must be the youngest member I have ever met, Miss Hannah," his voice is trembling, but not in a sick or worried kind of way. A sole sign of his fairly advanced age. "And I must be the oldest," Henry chuckles. "Well, not a member. Not anymore, at least."

Not anymore? No part of me could possibly let this go. I need to know more.

"I don't know where you were headed, sir. But I sure would love to have lunch with you?"

"Please, call me Henry. *Sir* makes me sound older than I am. If that's even possible."

We spend over two hours together. I thought Henry would grant me a few minutes, a quick lunch before he'd politely excuse himself and try to free himself from my insistent questioning. But he doesn't. It feels as though time itself has suspended its relentless march forward, gifting us a precious sanctuary of shared memories.

"Believe it or not, I've grown up with the founder," Henry explains, a genuine smile on his face. "He's one of my dearest friends, still to this day." The tip of his fingers repeatedly taps the table as he finishes his sentence.

Strangely, I joined the co-op long ago and never wondered about the founder's identity or even if he was still alive. I find it fascinating. I would have so many questions for the man if I could ever meet him.

"So, why did you join in the first place?" I ask enthusiastically. "Was it because of your friend?"

Henry chuckles. "Though it was out of love for my friend, I found the idea fascinating from day one, and wished to see it prosper," he says, his gaze scanning the room behind me, a literal sparkle circling his pupils. "I was a teacher. I aimed to kindle a love of literature in every one of my students. The co-op's treasures and uniqueness were a wonderful way to do so."

"Your students must have been thrilled," I say, envious of the young people sitting in Henry's class throughout the years. "How did you take part in the co-op with a full teaching schedule?"

"Balance, dear Hannah. If I wasn't teaching, I was traveling," his tone spikes with eagerness. "My travels brought me to the finest literary works in existence and allowed me to spread the word about my friend's idea."

Henry's passion for books and literature keeps a fire burning deep within his seemingly frail frame, and it ignites something within me. I tell him about The Book Nook and my childhood, my words spilling out as if drawn by some ancient magic he possesses. I even find myself confessing my dream of becoming an author, how desperately I want to write well—and how I can't. He disagrees, of course. Go figure. Max would love him. Henry seems to believe that anyone can write. I suppose not everyone should, though.

"What caused you to leave the co-op, Henry?" I ask, a hint of sadness in my voice. Something that echoes in Henry's eyes, too. If not sadness, regret?

"When you love something, sometimes it's best to let it go, dear Hannah," Henry answers in a whisper.

My brows furrow. That's quite vague, but I read in Henry's face the depth of the topic. Something that he might not be ready to share with a stranger.

"Are you still in contact with the members? Do you still receive packages?" I ask, trying to redirect the topic to something more concrete.

Henry shakes his head. "I am not," he says gravely. "I don't have any contact with any of the members. I'm out of the loop."

"What about with the founder?"

"My old friend and I have a strict rule; we don't talk about the co-op, its members, or its prizes," Henry clarifies.

CHAPTER SEVENTEEN

"Call if you ever need anything or just want to chat," Henry said while patting my shoulder. He then handed me the precious little square piece of cardboard with his contact information printed on it.

The mood Henry left me in pushes me to run to the gardens instead of going back to my room. The hotel is home to the most beautiful gardens, infinitely spreading just outside its back doors.

I step outside, skipping like a kid, welcoming the bright afternoon sun and taking in the burst of colors. Flowers in all shades wave hello as I stroll along the paths. Further back, there's a massive fountain made of copper-tinted stones doing a choreographed water dance. Gigantic oak trees share their shade with old wooden benches—the perfect spot for a nap. The air smells like a mix of flowers and honey that attracts a ton of birds and butterflies.

The path made of red gravel crunches underfoot as I spin on my heels, drawn deeper into the greenery of the gardens. On either side, arches of thick green leaves and pink roses open the way to more hidden side trails—ideal for a romantic stroll. *Or a full-blown fuck, away from curious eyes.*

Despite the hotel's bustling atmosphere, the gardens are eerily quiet.

Not a soul in sight. The only sound is the gentle clap of butterflies' wings. I relish the solitude; it's the perfect ending to a fascinating conversation with Henry.

I make a random right, letting the faded stepping stones lead me to the gods know where. It's not like I can get lost in a hotel garden anyway, right?

I finally pick up human voices as I travel deeper between the neatly cut bushes. The gardens are not abandoned after all. My aimless exploration brings me closer. Two men are chatting and laughing—undeniably drunk. I shoot a polite smile their way as I walk past them, looking down at my feet quickly after. They seem to have quite a fun conversation, and I'm not one to interrupt.

A few steps later, I hear one of them whistle in my direction. Disgust spreads across my face as I consider turning around to shout. Give them the finger, insult them—anything that would put them back in their place. But I don't. I just keep walking, redirecting my focus to the beautifully curated garden. After another second passes, I catch their shadows growing beside me. Before I know it, they stand in the way, blocking my path. *Idiots.*

"So, you're not gonna say hello?" one says, bumping elbows with the second.

I ignore them and turn around, deciding that the best way out was the way I came in. But before I can take another step, they both jump and block my path again, their faces inches from mine.

"What's wrong, baby? You're not gonna give us a smile?"

"Listen, I would say you're being pathetic, but you already know that, don't you? Just move out of the way," I say back, in the most confident and cold tone I can muster despite the growing pit of fear in my stomach.

These guys are quite large. Nothing my slender frame could take down on my own.

The two men exchange a daring look, seemingly offended that I talked back instead of smiling—like I was asked to do. I try to walk forward again, but the first man bumps his chest against mine, all while the second walks around to stand in my back. My heart gallops. My palms are now complete with their own waterworks. I need to get the hell out of here. It appears I can't get lost in the garden, but I can get mugged—or worse. My breathing catches, then picks up. They both notice, laughing a little louder at the apparent panic clawing at me.

"Someone's excited," the man facing me whispers as he attempts to bring his face closer to my neck. I jerk and use both my hands to hit his chest as hard as I can.

"Get out of my face, asshole," I yell, hoping to sound somewhat threatening and alert a passerby.

I can feel their eyes boring into me, stripping away my defenses, leaving me exposed and vulnerable.

The man in my back suddenly grabs my wrists and yanks me back. I yelp—he seems to enjoy that. Fear grips me like a vice, squeezing the air from my lungs and sending my heart into a frantic frenzy. I try to kick— considering both my arms are stuck under my aggressor's—but the one doing all the talking found his way standing between my legs.

He's dangerously close, leveraging his size and weight to prevent me from kicking or moving at all. His hands aim for my waist. I close my eyes, struggling to gather my thoughts. If I scream loud enough, someone will hear me, right?

I attempt to take a deep breath, but it's cut short by a sudden gust of wind swirling in my face and around my body. A wind so strong it's forcing my eyes shut. It pushes on my face, then circles my body. A second later, the current of powerful air has redirected its focus away from me. Confusion wins over the next few seconds. I let it.

When I finally open my eyes, my mind can't catch up with the scene. Both assholes are kneeled down on the floor. One is covering his eyes, moaning in pain. The other one has a bloody nose and is running out of air. *The irony.* I look around, puzzled, but I can't see anyone—or *anything.*

My heart was pounding so loudly in my ears that I must have missed the fight. I must have missed the man—if it was a man—who came to help me. But why would he run?

Fear prevents me from trying to make sense of any of this. There's no time for questions or common sense. This is my one chance. I bolt back toward the hotel. I didn't wander deep inside the gardens—though it felt far too secluded just a moment ago. The back doors come into view quickly. I clumsily rush inside, pulling on both glass doors at once.

In my hurry, I didn't notice the large body standing in the way. I come crashing into Max like a gigantic wave on sharp rocks.

My eyes burn—not with fear but with sheer anger. I refuse to accept that something so vile could happen in such a beautiful venue, at my favorite event of all time, my one escape. After all the wonderful experiences this trip has gifted me, that one sickening encounter threatens to stain the exquisite picture I have painted of the conference.

I look up at Max with teary eyes and see it then—the angry predator within, the animal enraged. His lips press together, jaw muscles tight and throbbing with fury. When they meet the sunlight, his eyes don't even narrow. If anything, the sunlight brings them to life. I swear I can see an actual fire burning in them, the usual golden flecks replaced by something far more dangerous. He's taking deep, slow breaths, giving him a truly ominous expression.

"What the f..." I breathe.

Max grips my shoulders. "Stay inside," he orders, his voice low and commanding. "I have something to finish."

He doesn't run; he doesn't explain. The gardens are still completely empty.

"Finish?" I question with a trembling voice, turning my question into a nonsensical sound.

Max ignores me.

I briefly ponder whether I should stop him, but I dismiss the idea the second I remember the last image I saw of the guys. Hurt, whining on the ground. I know Max's large, powerful hands. The silent force that fuels his muscles along his back and arms—even under his clothes. One day soon, I'll be more intimate with the valleys and hills of his body. But for now, I walk up to my room, the only refuge when sense and logic have fled my body like a cat sprayed with water.

An odd sense of satisfaction wells up in my stomach at the thought of Max handling them. That's what they deserve, a proper beating.

CHAPTER EIGHTEEN

I use the back of my hands to angrily wipe off the tears that continuously swell in my eyes, battling the need to weave coherence from chaos. Shit happens, even in the most magical settings. That's it.

Tonight is the last night of the conference. Which means the most glorious and extravagant dinner is hosted for the occasion. If the newest attendees thought the first night was grandiose, I can't wait to see their faces tonight.

I practically forced Max to accompany me. I originally wanted to bury him in questions about what happened in the gardens—but I won't. I should use all this energy to perfect my seducing act so I can finally feel Max slide inside of me before the sun rises tomorrow and this fairytale comes to an end.

Samantha and Em will join us as well—my *friendly* orders. I want tonight to be perfect. They all agree to meet one more time and end this thing with a bang.

I meet my friends in the lobby to head to dinner together.

Max's expression is back to normal. The furious predator is back in its cage. His eyes are shining this familiar bright yellow light again. His face is relaxed—though his muscles always look ready for battle, no matter the circumstances. I watch him discreetly bite the corner of his lips as his eyes travel down my body. He likes what he sees. We're off to a great start.

I opted for a flashy scarlet dress tonight. The fabric is like smooth fire, sizzling in a sultry shade of red. It's short, cutting the higher part of my thighs. I find it sassy. It makes a statement—sexy and fun. The neckline is a little more than a tease and should be enough to keep things spicy.

Upon entering the grand ballroom, I don't need to look at my friends to know we all look mesmerized.

The room displays round tables that stand in tidy arrangements beneath tall ceilings, infinitely reaching for the sky. A number of crystal chandeliers bathe the space in a soft glow, their light bouncing off the delicate diamond-shaped glass and onto the marble floors. The walls are licked with a pale golden paint that reminds me of Max's eyes. Draped red curtains cascade from the ceiling to the floor, framing large windows that open up to parts of the garden.

The sight of the gardens makes me shiver. Max must have noticed because he squeezes my forearm. On cue, my entire body eases. He waves his hand, gesturing for me to follow the jolly group and forget about the rest. I do as I'm asked, caressing his jawline with the tip of my fingers while I stride past him. Max grins in response.

We spend a good part of the night drinking and eating. The founder of the conference makes an appearance again and engages in the usual closing speech. Maybe it's the fact that Max is staring right into my eyes—his golden pebbles, immovable objects fixated on me the entire time—or maybe it's the whirlwind of recent events, but I can't hold back the tears that are building up as the man on stage thanks everyone for attending. He goes on to explain how much this conference means to him and to the community. It sure does mean a lot to me, too.

I sneakily dab away the tears threatening to ruin my meticulously applied makeup. I spent too long perfecting the black wing on my eyes to let it smear down my cheeks.

The music grows louder after the round of applause that follows the closing speech. Before I know it, Em and Samantha own the dance floor. I watch Em release her beautiful hair, locked in a tight ponytail until now. If life has taught me one thing, it's that a woman who releases her hair this way is ready to have some fun. *Same, girl.*

Max is sitting across from me, and now that dinner is nearly over, the distance between us must die. I extend my bare leg, my foot reaching for his. I trace the length of his black pants up and down, never breaking eye contact. His shoulders relax as he sinks deeper into his chair, biting the inside of his cheek. Satisfied, I bring my foot back and lean forward on the table, anticipation crackling in the air between us.

"Take me to the dance floor," I order him.

"I'm not much of a dancer."

"Oh, you are tonight."

Taking my time to stand up, I allow his gaze to feed on every inch of me from where he's sitting. I sway my hips from side to side, accentuating every move, using my hands to outline my curves. My eyes close, and I tilt my head back as I let the rhythm of the music guide the waves I draw with my thighs. I lose my fingers in my hair, grinning, giving him a taste of what he can have should he finally decide to collect it.

He remains patiently seated on his side of the table—too far away from me. Since he doesn't seem inclined to get up, I slowly walk around the table—a mischievous grin still drawn on my face. I slide behind his chair and drop my hands on his shoulder, gliding over his chest, aiming south. His shirt feels like pure silk under my palms. I almost wish I wasn't dying to rip it off him—it certainly would be a waste.

Max seizes my wandering hands, stands up, and spins me with a swift, fluid motion until I'm facing the other direction. His chest cups my back, his warmth enveloping me. I'm unsure how he managed such a trick, but it's undeniably efficient. The power and precision in his touch send heat down my spine. Max's body feels strong against my small back, reassuring—it's where he belongs. His breath heats my neck. His fingers—still intertwined with mine—dominate my hips.

"Shall we, *babygirl*?" he whispers through his teeth.

Shivers run freely all over my skin as he presses against me for a split second. An overwhelming sense of joy sweeps over me as he leads me toward Em and Samantha. This is shaping up to be the perfect night. I can't remember the last time I felt so damn happy.

I've lost track of how long we've all been dancing together. My attention is solely on Max's shirt—now open a little further down, revealing the smooth skin of his tanned chest.

Pearls of sweat glisten on his forehead, a testament to the fire we've been building up. Our bodies move in unison. He has not touched me yet—*truly* touched me. He's been teasing all night, gliding over my skin, closing the gap between our bodies until it's almost all-consuming. But never fully embraced me. I never knew someone could be so incredibly sensual, so desirable, all while keeping a safe distance from their prey. He's quite good at this gentleman's shit.

My entire being is a raging inferno of desire, yearning for his strong hands to either extinguish the flames or fuel them further—but he must choose. The sun set long ago, leaving the starry darkness to seep through the ballroom's many windows. Someone announces the last song of the night.

The last few minutes of the conference.

It's a slow dance. *Classic.* If that's not a closing song—and I'm not talking about closing the event—then I don't know what is. Max chuckles when he realizes the song has changed, along with the atmosphere. My arms loop behind his shoulders, pulling him closer as he feathers my waist. Max slows us down to the rhythm of the song.

"Look at you," he murmurs, "You gorgeous little thing."

I accept the compliment with a smile just before he grabs the curvature above my hips a little tighter and takes me spinning around the room. My gentle smile turns into laughter. His soft curls regain their original place on each side of his yellow eyes when he slows us down again. I notice the glossiness of the first night in them—he's been drinking tonight. We both have.

"I need you to be mine, Hannah," he growls, staring at me.

Though that was quite the unexpected comment, I quickly get distracted by the fact that the hunting beast is back out. I can see it in his eyeballs, feel it in his grip. He's not threatening, but he sure is possessive of his prize—*me*.

"Will you claim me?" I challenge him, arching an eyebrow, fully playing into the unexpectedness of the mood.

Max blinks, and the feral in him disappears. The gentleman takes the lead again. *Fuck.* He smiles as he caresses my cheeks, merely floating over my skin.

"It's getting late, Hannah."

"You know the way to my room." I purr.

After hugging our friends for the last time before long, we make our way back up the stairs. Max must know the elevator is a dangerous teasing zone.

The door to my room is in sight. My heart builds up to an earthquake at the thought of what I will do to Max once it closes behind us. As I step inside the room, I'm being yanked back. Max is still holding my hand but refuses to move.

Oh no, mister. Not tonight.

I awkwardly attempt to pull him inside, but he won't budge. He just looks at me, *all of me.* What's the point of all this teasing if I can't make him mine in the end?

Without thinking, I quickly move closer. And kiss him.

Max moves to the side before my lips reach his, dodging me. He cups my cheeks between his large hands. My face disappears inside his grip. I drop my arms along my sides like heavy bags with a long-drawn sigh. I'm not upset, not quite. Just genuinely confused, I suppose. He picks my hands back up and pretends to kiss them like he always does.

"I will give you what you deserve. Soon." His voice is soft and genuine. Something is obviously holding him back, and I want to believe it must be a valid reason.

I sigh again, lost in the labyrinth of uncertainty Max sketched for us.

"You better be the best fucking lay of my life," I snarl with one hand gripping Max's strong jaw before my hold eases into a caress.

"Good night, Hannah. I will see you in Willowbrook."

CHAPTER NINETEEN

It's been three days since we got back from the conference. I haven't heard a word from Max. I messaged him more times than I care to admit and may or may not have left a couple of voicemails as well.

He's been entirely silent ever since our last night at the hotel. I opened and closed my text messages multiple times, only to look at his last words to me. The ones I received right after he left me desiring him more than ever in this damn hotel room.

> M: For the record, I will be the best lay of your life. Good night, darling.

The fact that I had to scroll up quite a bit to find it is pretty embarrassing. I'm starting to wonder if I drove him away with my incessant calling and texting. Maybe I misread his energy, blinded by my own lust.

I reminisce about our memories at the conference, dissecting every word, every touch, every glance. It's hard to believe I misinterpreted things this much. Unless he intentionally led me astray. But why? He was showering me with so much attention and compliments, as if the world disappeared, leaving me the only woman alive.

Though he remained a gentleman, he openly teased me, making his desire unmistakably clear. I chuckle at the memory of Emily's and Samantha's knowing looks, arched eyebrows, and side grins as the days at the conference went by. They noticed it, too. Max had no intention of hiding his longing for me.

A pit in my stomach grows as I consider what could have happened to him. My mind runs wild and draws up all kinds of morbid scenarios —scenarios I don't like. I need to calm down. Maybe he lost his phone. He could reappear at the store today. Everything will be fine.

This would be much easier if I knew anything about this damn man other than the fact that I want to devour him whole—skin and bones and all—for a reason that I couldn't even put into words.

Brandie's bubbly voice bounces between the walls of my apartment as I put her on speaker so I can get dressed. My anxiety shrinks as soon as she says hello.

"I arranged for our alarm systems to be installed today," she informs me. "He'll be here around 10."

She describes the man she's been sleeping with for the past few days —so I don't get confused when he enters my store or something. *This damn woman.* I didn't necessarily need all the details, but that's what friends are for. At least, there's no doubt I will recognize him the second he approaches.

I didn't tell Brandie about what happened at the conference. Something inside me held me back. She's my best friend, and I wouldn't hesitate under normal circumstances. But for some reason, the words wouldn't come out. Perhaps a part of me knew this was just a fool's dream, a fleeting fantasy, and that I might never hear from Max again.

Nonsense. I will. I must. Something incomprehensible inside me refuses to move on, holding on to the hope with sharpened nails.

When the clock strikes 10, Brandie's new play toy enters my store and introduces himself. The poor man has no idea I know pretty much everything about him—down to how *much space he takes.* Of course, I show no signs of Brandie's gossip as I welcome him and show him around.

Brandie depicted a terrifying picture of our town's new wave of crimes while I was away. I purposefully stayed away from the news. I'm relieved that we're getting these things installed today, considering the violent string of attacks that has clearly escalated while I was living my own personal fairytale. Reality bites me in the ass on its way back into my life.

Despite the fear—and as much as I enjoyed myself at the conference—I'm happy to be back. The smell of books mixed with aged wood was thick in the air when I stepped inside the store. The consequence of remaining closed for a few days. Brandie was in and out to feed Arthur, but that's not enough to air the place out. Not that it needs it, anyway. The combined smell of new and old paper is melted sugar to me. Nothing compares—except maybe for the smell of cinnamon that clings to Max so sexily.

As anticipated, I spent the day like a ghost to my readers—absent-mindedly staring out the windows, hoping to see the familiar silhouette I long for walk by—or better yet, walk in. But nothing. *What's wrong with me?*

After checking my phone about a million times and resisting the urge to send one more message, I decided to close the shop and get some dinner. I should ask Brandie to come out and take my mind off things, but the conference has me all partied out. What I need is to get sushi and walk back home to sit on the couch with my black furry companion by my side—begging for a piece of salmon.

Now that the alarm is installed, locking up the store takes on a new routine. Brandie's man-friend diligently showed me how to set it and disarm it when I walk in to avoid any mishaps. Even though he did a wonderful job, I know I will trigger it by mistake someday.

When I step outside, the sun is about to do its nightly disappearing act, bathing the city in a warm, golden glow—the same hue I see in Max's eyes. The air is kissed with a gentle breeze, getting ready to cool off the summer night.

The main street is saturated with tourists tonight despite the current atmosphere. So many faces all around me, and yet, none I want to see. I glare at every man passing by. Not for attention, of course, but hoping my eyes will finally meet my favorite golden circles. *Watch me build a reputation for myself, studying everybody like a lunatic.*

The sweet smell of flowers is rolling in and triggering my nose to sneeze. I walk unhurriedly on the pavement of the main street toward the sushi restaurant. I stop along the way, drawing inspiration from various shop windows.

I smell warm chocolate in front of the candy store. They went all in this summer—and it's working. The line pours out of the store onto the curb. Large, swirling lollipops in every shade imaginable stand tall, catching the eye of both small and big children. The window is alive with movement. A chocolate fountain cascades down in a mesmerizing display, and a conveyor belt carries gummy candies in a perpetual dance. I should probably get dessert on my way home.

I reach the Italian restaurant I also considered for dinner, though I was craving something lighter. They make the best lasagna I've ever tasted and probably own the prettiest building on the main strip.

Large red bricks hold on to small drop-shaped lights permanently dangling across the front, mingling with green leaves above the stained glass entrance. This place is always insanely busy, and a quick look inside the restaurant confirms it. Every table is taken—most of them couples. Servers are running like chickens without heads.

I look at the orchestrated dance happening inside—then almost collapse.

My heart drops to my gut, and my gut goes straight to my heels. I try to shake the hollow sensation digging its talons inside of me. My legs are about to give in. I can almost picture how the pavement would bust my head open if I were to fall now. *That wouldn't be a good look.*

I can't take another step. I can't turn my head either. I'm fixated on one table inside the Italian joint. The sweet summer air is suddenly burning my lungs and the inside of my mouth. I'm unable to take a full breath.

Through the windows and amidst the business of the restaurant, one figure stands out. Well, *two*.

He's sitting across from a beautiful young woman. Her skin is porcelain, and her eyes the color of frost. Her thin, whitish-blond hair hangs past the back of her chair; I can't see the end of it. She belongs in a cartoon as some kind of ice queen—*as gorgeous as she is lethal*. I've never seen her in town before, either. I would remember her elegant form and her perfect features. Her beauty strikes the center of my chest.

Max reaches across the table, caressing her hand—I'm about to throw up.

None of this *almost-touch-but-not-really* bullshit. She gets the special treatment. Their hands make one on the white and red tablecloth. There's no keeping a chaste distance between them. He brings her fingers to him and presses them on his lips, holding them here for a second as he closes his eyes. His lips move, but slowly—most likely whispering.

He looks...apologetic.

Wait.

Her rosy cheeks can't be blamed on the warmth of the night. She's crying, and Max is trying to console her. The rise and fall of her chest is quick and shallow, distressed. Did she find out about the conference—and about us? Is he trying to undermine everything that's happened between us? *Bastard.*

I thought we had something special. All these indescribable feelings. I thought... no. I can't even think right now.

I'm still frozen in front of the glass that separates us when Max whips his head around as if he sensed my presence.

His eyes—two vibrant jades—collapse with mine. His face drops, its colors draining away completely, mirroring the pale skin of his date. If one thing, he didn't expect to see me here, watching him and his woman.

It's not guilt that's written all over his face when he spots me—it's something much, much deeper. He jumps out of his seat and straight up as the blond woman looks up and lays her icy blue eyes on me. I can't hold her murderous gaze for more than a millisecond—at best. Her eyes pierce right through my soul. They carry the greatest depth of the ocean. The fatal freeze of the highest glaciers. Her lips split open, swallowing tears that were still falling down her cheeks. She knows.

I need to get out of here. *Now.* I shake my head as if to shake a bad dream off and rush away. Sushi will have to wait.

Tears—fueled by sheer anger—well up in my eyes, turning my vision into a blurry mess my brain can't even process. I feel the flames of fury dancing across my cheeks, igniting an inferno on my face. Pain, jealousy, and humiliation build, swell, and crush me from the inside.

I hasten across the darkened streets, letting my cardigan trail behind me and dragging across the pavement. The usually pleasant explosion of smells from different restaurants makes me nauseous. I walk as fast as my legs allow it—the speed just before running.

I find myself lost in a cloud of memories from the conference, now realizing how much I've been played. Every word Max uttered, every smile, every tender touch—as light as they may have been—was just a cruel game. I can't make sense of how genuinely concerned he appeared when danger loomed, how he seemed to truly care for me. This entire story feels like a riddle spoken in a foreign language, resisting my effort to crack it.

Many times, he had the opportunity to tell me about her. At any point, he could have—no, *should have*—stopped me. Instead, he fed my obsession.

A deep exhale escapes through my faintly open mouth when I finally lay eyes on my front door. The downtown buildings have been flying on my sides. I didn't realize how much distance I had conquered already. Only a few steps separate me from my bed and from the crazy world I now live in.

"Hannah! Stop!"

I have no idea how he managed to catch up with me so fast. I'm fairly confident I didn't spot him tailing me through the streets despite the night already draping its dark wings over us.

I choose to ignore his suave voice—shouting yet still resonating like a soft melody in my ears. He won't win this one. I pick up the pace to reach my door faster.

"Hannah! Please," he's moving closer.

"Hannah!" Max's voice sounds like a roaring tempest.

He seizes my arm, halting me from taking another step towards my door. I quickly gaze at his reflection in The Book Nook's window. He's standing behind me, his grip tight and tough on my arm.

"Hannah," my name emerges as a plea from his lips.

"Let me go!" I yell, breaking free from his grip. "Let me go, please," I beg in a broken voice, silently sobbing.

Raw anguish is all I can voice right now. I realize how all the screaming and crying might come across and dart around the street—only to find it eerily empty. The area was crowded just a few seconds ago. Now, it's just Max and me.

CHAPTER TWENTY

I turn on my heels, aiming for my door again when my breath is abruptly cut short—a light but noticeable pressure on my chest. I'm stopped dead in my tracks. Only this time, I don't feel Max's hands or any warmth anchoring me back. I glance down at my body —nothing.

It's as if invisible chains came out of the ground and ensnared me, ensuring I remain right where I stand. There's a gentle resistance against my arms and waist, but I still don't see what holds me back.

I attempt to take another step. I can't move. I groan as I try again— to no avail.

This is impossible. The taste of salt in my mouth is so strong I'm about to give out the dinner I didn't even have yet. Did a heartbreak just turn me insane?

I can blink; I can breathe just fine. But I can't move. I attempt to wiggle my toes and fingers, but my body ignores my commands. I lost all control over my very own flesh and bones. I'm stuck. Yet, somehow, it doesn't feel threatening.

As slow as a predator readying for the kill, Max shifts from behind me and slides to my right. When he finally faces me, he's looking down at his feet, both hands held up in my direction.

"Hannah, please. I am begging you," his voice is deeper than the core of the earth.

I must look incredibly panicked because Max doesn't wait to add, "I'm going to release you. But please, don't run. Let me explain." he implores.

He's not on his knees, but he might as well be.

Release me?

"How could you possibly release me from the games my mind is playing on me?"

I'm tripping, hallucinating. I must have eaten something rotten. That would explain the insufferable taste of salt waltzing on my tongue and the mirages.

Max stares at me with eyes covered with a shiny layer of glass. Tears line up beneath his eyelids, poised for a grand entrance on the flawless canvas of his face. His skin seems to glow in the moonlight. If I weren't mysteriously paralyzed right now, I might lose myself in the dark sea of his soft curls. *I assume I have more pressing matters at hand.*

He lowers his hands with a long exhale, shyly looking up at me. On cue, the pressure around my body dissipates. I look around, allowing my arms to fall down freely. I can move again. The ground has swallowed the invisible restraints that held me in place just a second ago.

"What the actual fu..." I murmur, leaving my thoughts unfinished.

As I look at Max, I can see his expression more clearly now. He seems devastated—as much as I am. If not more. The tears flooding his strange eyes reflect the street lights in a magical dance. His body is noticeably tense as he looks at me with the intensity I've only seen in him when I find myself in danger.

"What just happened?" I calmly ask.

Part of me urges me to flee, yet the other part feels oddly safe. The salt in my mouth is unbearable, digging into my tongue and cheeks. Sensing my distress, Max gestures for me to take a deep breath and calm down. When does that ever work?

"Hannah. My name is not *just* Max. I'm Maximilian Linus Forstthorn. I come from a long line of magical blood. From an ancient line of warlocks."

Silence falls like a boulder between us. There is no pressure left around my body, and yet I can't find the strength to move a muscle. I was pretty convinced I knew a lot of things for certain until a second ago. I would confidently say that I know what isn't real and what is. Magic most definitely didn't fall into the latter category.

Magic isn't real.

There must be another explanation. My breathing picks up again as I quickly realize I don't have much of a logical one. I look at Max, tracing his full height, still shaking.

What is one supposed to say after hearing such...*lies*? The only thing I can do is laugh. It just escapes me unintentionally. I laugh uncontrollably.

"Do I look *this* stupid to you? Is that the best you can come up with? Please run back to her. I have nothing left to say to you." my voice breaks under the heavy weight of sorrow, rage, and confusion.

"It's all true, Hannah." Max's lips don't move. The sound doesn't come out of his mouth.

The voice is crystalline, light as fog in the night. A female's voice. The air turned cold in my back as if winter had made its grand entrance in the middle of summer. The humidity in the air seemed to have turned to small, tiny pearls of...ice?

I turn around, anticipating the next chapter of this insane story, and meet those frosty blue eyes yet again. The silver-blond-crowned young woman stands behind me.

"Hello, Hannah. It's nice to see you again," her thin lips draw a slight upward curve.

"Again?" is all I can bark back.

She can't possibly be referring to the awkward disaster that happened at the restaurant a few minutes ago.

She chuckles softly, placing her hands on her stomach and arching a well-defined brow at me. She looks so elegant. Every move she makes is soft and calculated. With one look, I can tell she's not the kind of woman who will shout or lose her composure. *I could learn a thing or two from the girl.*

"You two have a lot to talk about," she says, gesturing at the space separating Max and me. "I'm not your enemy, sweet Hannah. I will see you soon."

One last smile at me, and the woman evaporates into thin air—not figuratively. Her body fades away in the night, right in front of my eyes, cell by cell, leaving nothing but a white smoke looming behind.

What in the actual fuck!

I don't simply jerk. I jump back a few feet, letting out a shriek. Instinctively, I grab Max's arms—comfort and protection. I jolt my hand back when I realize where it landed. Max clicks his tongue while whispering a name I've never heard before.

"Alice...She can be quite the dramatic witch. Normalcy is not my sister's strong suit."

His sister.

Alice. The young woman he looked after and protected after his parents died.

There's no doubt. Either I'm clinically insane and need to check myself in, or magic is real, and I just witnessed it firsthand. I have no desire to admit that I'm going crazy, but the alternative is just as challenging to accept.

Why didn't I fall for the damn postman instead?

"Hannah, please let me come up with you. I need to explain. I need to talk to you."

My stomach hasn't stopped its twisty dance since I saw Max and Alice sitting together. My breath is still catching in my throat. My body aches from the anxiety it stubbornly clings to.

"I... I can't. I don't..." I breathe out.

Thoughts come and go, a tsunami of confusion. I can't finish a damn sentence. My entire world just turned upside down. Everything I've ever believed in is a lie. This world is not what I always knew it to be.

"I understand. I do." Max pauses. "Give me a chance. Just meet me at my house when you are ready. I will text you the address."

After a deep breath, he adds, "I will wait for you, Hannah."

CHAPTER TWENTY-ONE

My phone rings before I can make it up the stairs and inside my apartment. Max texted me his address the second I left him behind, dazed and confused.

I will wait for you, Hannah.

His words resonate in my head. In my heart. I drag myself to the couch and fall flat on it, face first, hugging the pillow with both arms. My head is spinning, making it difficult to try and summarize my night.

I just encountered an insanely gorgeous witch and discovered that my biggest crush ever is a freaking warlock. I watched the woman literally disappear as a cloud dissipates after a rainstorm. He held me back with nothing but imaginary force. I pinch myself, both arms still under the pillow, just to make sure. Ouch. I'm not dreaming. It was worth a shot, though.

Reality just pulled a disappearing act on me. I live in a world where magic exists. A world where it isn't confined to children's tales—it's a tangible reality, and I'm surrounded by damn witches.

Arthur comes climbing on my back, meowing in protest, knowing his dinner is late yet again.

"Are you magical too? Will you start talking to me now?" I say to him, my voice muffled by the pillow pressed over my face.

When I turn my head to look back at the cat, he's just staring at me, obviously questioning my sanity. Turns out I might go insane after tonight.

I will wait for you, Hannah.

Damn it, Max. Why do I have to be so obsessed with this man? Why can't I simply be mad at him, ignore the fact that he's not entirely human, and move on with my life? It was pretty perfect before I met him. I could go back to that.

Something is pulling on my heartstrings. I ache. I long for his presence. I crave his feather touch, his gaze over my body. My logical thoughts demand that I let rage consume me and forget Max ever existed. My heart sings an entirely different song.

I sit back up, letting go of all the air stuck in my lungs. The harsh reality is that I can't seem to ignore what happened tonight and pretend Max never existed altogether. The soft marks he left on my body and heart will never fade away. I can't explain why; I just know it.

He didn't exactly fool me. There was no other woman in his life—only full-blown magical powers.

After checking the map on my phone, I realize that his house—while on the outskirts of Willowbrook—is not far enough to discourage me. I must talk to him. I owe him that much. Plus, I can't possibly trust that I can step into the dawn of a normal life after witnessing very real acts of magic. It's not exactly a topic I can casually bring up during girls' night without sounding mentally ill or causing mass panic.

I made my decision.

The drive to Max's house takes me through a long, winding road. The moon shines its comforting light over me, piercing through the veil of darkness. It gives me a bit of reassurance, considering the forest on both sides thickens with every passing mile. It's giving murderous vibes around here—am I making a mistake?

I bring Max's beautiful golden eyes to mind. How he bites his lips when he looks at me—that alone dissolves any fear I have.

There's no house to be seen for miles and no light either—the warlock definitely was going for privacy. I remember him mentioning his family's mansion. If that story was true, that's where I'm headed right now.

After a few more minutes of driving in the middle of nowhere, a small light catches my attention in the distance.

I'm greeted by a tall, black steel gate—as large as three cars—guarded on either side by brick walls, wrapping around the property. No one is entering without an invitation.

As I drive the car closer to the gate, it opens for me, breaking the silence with a loud creaking sound. A shiver runs down my back as it does. A massive, old willow tree stands sentinel behind the gate. It seems to bend on its trunk as if to say hello, its gnarled branches hanging low, wisps of silver-gray moss cascading like ghostly tendrils. That's fitting—not creepy at all. I chuckle nervously, gripping the wheels a little tighter.

Beyond the towering tree, an expansive property unfolds before my eyes. It's lit like a Christmas tree and looks absolutely magnificent in the night. Every inch is bathed in the soft glow of artificial night lights, accentuating not only the grand driveway but also meticulously illuminating the neatly trimmed grass of the front lawn.

A few steps lead to a double wooden door. Tall white columns support an intricately designed roof—though I can't see every detail in the darkness. The mansion boasts a facade of expertly laid bricks. Among them, intricately carved scenes unfold, capturing moments of human life—the irony—with remarkable detail and artistry. The property stretches across three levels, each adorned with large windows, spanning the entirety of the front facade.

That's quite the bachelor pad—even for a warlock bachelor.

I park right in front—unsure of the etiquette—and shyly approach the front door. Just like the gate, the front door opens on its own for me.

Max stands in the hall, wearing a loose black blouse folded to his elbows. His face, a canvas of chiseled perfection, betrays a subtle tension, his furrowed brow and tightened jawline adding depth to his flawless features. The remains of his worry and anxiety are evident in the furrowed lines etched around his eyes and the restless energy that flickered behind his gaze.

As he lays his eyes on me, I watch the tension dissolve. His face softens. His eyes shift from a golden hue to neon green, back and again. I can't believe I never noticed the magic in them before. It's obvious to me now. My anxiety flies away through the open front door the second our gazes collide.

Max was waiting for me, standing there in silence.

I want to run up to him and throw my arms around his neck, but I restrain myself. I suppose a more remarkable woman would be angry at him right now. But I'm not. Not really.

Clinging to his silence, Max welcomes me into the grand entrance. The walls are licked with a light rust paint. Multiple painted portraits hang around the circular room. I automatically assume they are family portraits. I'll have a look later. Thick, velvet emerald curtains torrent down the sides of the front windows, adding to the elegance of the mansion.

I take a few steps deeper inside the hall, which seems to have triggered the large chandelier hanging from the round, textured ceiling. It starts swinging on its own, threatening to break the chains that bolt it into the ceiling. I jump.

"Ghosts," Max chuckles.

What did he just say to me?

"Oh, don't worry. They're friendly. Well, except for that one," Max casually remarks, pointing towards the grand staircase that leads to the first floor from the middle of the hall.

Sensing my noticeable lack of amusement, Max takes my hand and reassures me, "I'm teasing Hannah. I mean, they're real, and they're here," he shrugs his shoulders, "But no harm will come to you. I promise."

My throat bobs, trying my best to ignore that, though I can't see them, ghostly figures crowd the space around us. I remain silent as Max leads me to one of the adjacent rooms.

Despite the season, a raging fire cracks in the hearth. Oddly enough, it doesn't produce an insufferable heat—rather, a welcoming warmth—not too hot, just the perfect temperature.

In contrast to the entrance's painted walls, the living room is all wood-paneled. The authentic beams crisscrossing the ceiling give it a log-cabin look that wouldn't work as well without the large brown leather sofas arranged in a U-shape around the fireplace.

In one corner, a wet bar is filled with all sorts of wines—and stronger liquors. This particular room—and what I've seen of the house so far—unapologetically attests to the fortune Max mentioned at the conference. But nothing screams magical powers.

There's no cauldron steaming in a corner, no broom hovering mid-air, or any other kind of shelf filled with spell components. Well, except there are ghosts. I don't know what I was expecting. Probably something more book-worthy. I suppose having spent most of my life lost in pages doesn't help me set realistic expectations.

Max gestures to one of the couches. I oblige.

"Wine?" he offers.

I discern his anxiety in the trembling of his voice. It's a new feeling I haven't seen him openly expose yet. Under normal circumstances, I would run to him and tell him everything would be okay, but I must keep the act up. I need answers.

"I'm feeling more like tea. Is that okay?"

"Anything, Hannah."

I was expecting him to leave the room and boil the water—you know, the usual steps one would take to make tea. But not Max. He wiggles his fingers mid-air, and a hot cup of tea appears floating in front of his chest.

He moves his controlling hand towards me, and the hot tea lands on the coffee table before me. The floral smell fills the air quickly, mixing with the scent of burned wood. He picked the perfect herbal tea for me. If it wasn't for the clear skies and hotness of the night outside, one would assume we were in the midst of the winter, lost somewhere deeper in the mountains.

"So, aside from making tea from thin air...what do you do with your magic?" I can't stop the playful smile that tugs at my lips as I grab the cup.

His shoulders relax a little at the sound of my joke. He sits across from me, crossing his fingers on his knees.

"It helps stop beautiful women from running away, too," he jokes back, raising an eyebrow along with a wide grin, which twists one side of his face. Damn you, gorgeous warlock.

I laugh, and so does he. The air between us is not as heavy anymore.

It becomes easier to breathe again. I look straight at him as I take a sip of the tea—too delicious.

Max takes a deep breath and whispers, "Ready?"

Oh boy am I ready.

CHAPTER TWENTY-TWO

I sense the room's atmosphere shifting as if the house recognizes the significance of this moment. It feels more still and quiet. Even with the table lights on, only the magical glow of the fire is taking its job seriously. The orange hue it casts creates an intimate atmosphere, and if I didn't know better, I would swear the couches moved closer to one another. The house is up to something.

"Welcome to the Forstthorn Mansion, Hannah," Max shily starts, uncomfortably chuckling. "It comes with lots of lawn to mow, some-what friendly ghosts, and a silly warlock," his voice trails off with the last few words.

"But that's not why you're here. I owe you an explanation. I will tell you everything. I will not stop you if you wish to run and never hear from me again after you hear it all." Max pauses, his eyes fixated on mine, only confirming how profound his last statement is.

I nod—a silent permission to continue.

"We descend from a long, powerful line of magical folks. Magic runs in my blood and in Alice's. It ran in my parents' too." Max's voice quivers at the mention of his late parents.

"As I mentioned before, said parents set a lot of bridges on fire in their quest for power and wealth, leaving a path of ashes and painful wounds to mend around them. Which cost them their lives." Max pauses, scanning my face for a reaction.

"So, the car accident...?" I ask, leaving my thoughts unfinished.

"Just a story that fits the mortal world better," Max admits. "Remains of magical burns scarred the room their bodies were found in. They were murdered using magic."

I swallow loudly and tighten my grip on the teacup. "I'm sorry," I whisper.

"They made a lot of enemies. I can't say I'm surprised." Max's voice is cold. "When they passed, I took over this," he gestures to the ceiling. "And most importantly, I took care of Alice. She was only nineteen. Not quite a kid anymore, but not quite an adult, either."

"I managed to remain a stable figure in her life. Our relationship grew stronger and stronger over the years, especially after what we've been through. We're basically best friends," he chuckles.

I release a small, genuine smile. I love that about them.

"She's a powerful witch and a force to be reckoned with, and despite her cold front, she's nothing but sweetness and love—deep, deep inside," Max chuckles as he realizes that his sister's kindness might not be the first thing people notice about her.

"You used to know that about her, Hannah."

My eyebrows meet in confusion. "Max, I've only just met Alice."

"I will get to it," Max counters gently.

"A few years ago, Alice fell sick. Right after her 25th birthday." Max takes a deep, grounding breath, visibility fighting away the shaking in his voice.

"The disease took over her body in the most painful way. Her organs were failing one by one. Alice was fading away," Max's voice disappears in nothing but a whisper.

My focus shifts from his full lips to the tears pooling into his golden pebbles.

"She was dying, Hannah. Painfully," he swallows the knot in his throat. "No doctor in the mortal realm could figure it out despite the extensive testing they did. I visited many of the most prestigious covens, too. Our most powerful mages couldn't stop the disease. It took over, creeping over Alice's body and claiming it as its own."

I remain silent, my lips trembling as I scan the face of this man I've been craving without knowing the horrors haunting him. His eyes, wide and glassy, seem to look beyond the present, seeing horrors invisible to me. His brow furrows deeply, creasing his forehead into lines of anguish and dread.

"That's when I turned to The Collector of Souls," Max announces.

The name makes me tick. The mansion seems to jolt too—strange little thing.

"The what now?" I let out without entirely controlling my tone.

"The Collector of Souls," Max repeats. "I'm sure you've heard of good and bad magic in your stories," he chuckles. "It's not as simple as that, of course. But it *is* real in our world."

"Dark magic is real. Extremely dangerous and highly frowned upon. The dark arts took quite a few lives within our family. Most witches who attend to control it end up miserable, lonely, and suffering unfathomable ends." Another much-deserved breath as Max's voice trembles again.

"Is the Collector...the Devil?" I innocently ask.

Max smiles. "Not quite, no. But he's the closest to it as far as dark entities go."

The cozy living room becomes quieter as if this creature just walked in—though I suppose such a terrifying being would make a grander entrance. The fire stops spitting embers, and the dancing of the flames slows down. The mansion is setting the scene for Max's tale.

Max continues, "The Collector is a dark, ancient creature, fueled by anger, lust, and fear. Just like the fairytales speak of pacts with the devil —or selling your soul to it—you can make a pact with The Collector," he pauses. "But it's never free."

Yet another heavy silence falls.

"The Collector wields the most ancient magic in existence. The most powerful, too. He sets the price. He sets the rules. You are free to deny or accept a pact, assuming you are willing to pay the price." Max takes a deep breath, his gaze getting lost in the space behind me as if his vision filled with memories too dark and terrifying to talk about.

"I thought the price he set in exchange for saving Alice's life was fair at first. A small price to pay to save my young sister's life. Eradicate her pain."

Max's eyes scan me carefully, carrying the weight of his last statement.

"What did you do, Max?" I ask.

Something inside me tells me that this very pact is intricately intertwined with my life in ways I might never fully comprehend. Are those the answers I was seeking tonight without knowing it?

"The Collector would save Alice from her illness, but in exchange, I shall never touch a woman I fall in love with. If love ever were to grow in my heart, it would be but poison." Max pauses, and I replay his last words, attempting to make it make sense.

Max continues, "It's clever, in a sense. The Collector didn't take love away from my heart. Love, he would let me feel it. Fully," he pauses. "But I shall never touch the woman who owns my heart. Should I ever meet this woman's lips, take her to bed, embrace her with the wrong intentions, or leave my hands on her skin for a little too long..." Max takes a full breath, "Both Alice and my lover would die instantaneously. Their souls both collected for the monster to do with them as he pleases."

I shiver. A suffocating silence envelops Max and me, the gravity of his words hanging in the air like a dark cloud. The space between us grows colder, each second stretching into an eternity.

Max breaks the silence. "The Collector made sure love could find its way into my heart, all while ensuring I should never know what my lover feels like in my arms. What she tastes like. I should never show her how much she means to me. It's a different kind of torture. An ingenuous one. A horrible one."

My heart free-falls inside my chest. I never once imagined the pain love could bring if you could never embrace your lover, never be with them despite the desire. It's like being trapped in a beautiful, tantalizing dream that turns into a nightmare when you reach out to grasp it.

"How long have you lived with this curse on your shoulders, Max?" My voice carries the emotions I can't quite contain.

"I made the pact about two years ago."

"Is that why you don't leave the mansion much?" I ask, remembering that Max referred to him as a bit of a loner.

"It surely didn't entice me to go and meet people," Max admits.

"Could you be with someone you're not in love with?"

If the rules of the curse are very focused on *true* love, maybe I have a chance after all, I jokingly think to myself, forcing myself to alleviate the seriousness of the moment.

Max chuckles. "I wouldn't take the risk of finding out."

Fair enough. Max's eyes follow my every move as I shift on the couch, pulling my feet up to sit in a bit of pretzel shape. The sofa becomes softer, molding my body and offering a soft place to land and lean in. Caring little thing.

I exhale loudly before I address the elephant in the room. "What does this have to do with me, Max?"

Max sighs. "Well, it gets lonely around here," he vaguely gestures to the walls. "Alice came to visit about six months ago with some earth-shattering news. She heard of a possible way to undo the pact I made with the creature and break the curse looming over our heads."

My eyes widen in both surprise and something that feels awfully close to excitement. Hope, maybe?

"I grew curious," he explains. "Not that I had anyone in my life worth the risk. But if I had but one chance, *well*, I'm just a man after all." Max shrugs his shoulders, seemingly apologizing for very normal needs.

"Is it a spell?" My mortal-ass asks. Magic equals spells. Makes sense, doesn't it? "Were you looking for a spell?"

Max smiles as he tilts his head. "Yes," he answers. "But more specifically, a spell book. An ancient text said to offer a way out of any deal made with the Collector through intricate spells. It's said to be hidden somewhere in the human world. That's all Alice and I knew. That wasn't much to go off on." Max shrugs his shoulders.

"I'm still struggling to see why I'm here, Max."

"Well, I spent a lot of time and energy trying to locate said manuscript using my own research methods—magic—but to no avail." he pauses. "That's when I found just what I was looking for in the human world—you." Max's gaze locks with mine with fervor. A familiar warmth runs down my spine.

"Well, not you. Not at first," his voice is a low murmur. "The co-op is so beautifully described on your website; I instantly knew it could be the perfect way to support my efforts and access rare scriptures. I never expected to find you in the process." Max halts again and looks up at me for any reaction.

"That's why you were in the read-only section the first time I met you." My brows furrow as I start to connect the dots.

"That wasn't the first time we met, Hannah."

CHAPTER TWENTY-THREE

ax's expression shifts to one of strong determination. His eyes are dark and piercing, as if daring anyone to challenge his revelation. His jaw tightens, and a heavy silence blankets the room.

"What do you mean?" I breathe, a pressure inside my chest preventing me from taking a full breath. My knuckles turn white from gripping the cup so tightly it might break.

"I started visiting The Book Nook *a lot*. Every day. I incessantly questioned you about the co-op. Which you loved, of course," he chuckles. "I needed to learn more about the origin of the deliveries and how it worked. I could feel in my magical heart that this could be the way to reach my goal."

"That's impossible." I interrupt, but Max ignores me and keeps going.

"For weeks, we spent nearly every day together, Hannah. I think I came to forget what I was even searching for in the first place. I was so captivated by you. I *am* captivated by you," another whispered chuckle.

"You told me everything you could think of about yourself over coffee dates that slowly turned into dinner dates. You shared stories about your parents and your childhood, your love for books, and the dream of opening your own bookstore." A genuine smile splits his beautiful face, his eyes sparkling with the sweetness of the memories that make zero sense to me.

"You confided in me about the stories you think you'll never write because you believe you can't. But I still know that's nonsense." Max shrugs, then falls silent.

"Do I even have to say it?" His mysterious, fiery pupils drown out all details in our periphery. I feel the beating of my heart pick up behind my chest, a slow drum morphing into a full band.

"I fell in love with you, Hannah. So incredibly in love."

His voice barely carries all the way to me—hesitating and shy. And yet, I hear his words as if Max just shouted in my ears. My heart travels to my throat, where the taste of salt still lingers. It's been for weeks now. My breath hitch, caught in the whirlwind of disbelief and euphoria, as if every nerve in my body danced to the rhythm of Max's words. Tremors of excitement reverberate through my limbs, leaving me momentarily paralyzed.

Well, fuck. That story took a whole different turn.

In the shadowy corners of my mind, someone partially lifted a curtain off my memories. The pieces vaguely fall into place. The picture is not entirely clear, but something inside of me clicks. Cracks open. Pools out of my heart. A familiar comfort, yet completely new and unknown. It all starts to make sense—somewhat. The looks, the smiles, the texts, the caresses. They would come from a man who's in love. Someone I thought until now was a mere stranger.

Love. Every letter of the word frantically dances in my mind.

"I don't..." I mumble. "I don't understand."

"It's because I erased your memory, Hannah."

His words jolt me into a physical response. My body recoils instinctively, sinking deeper into the plush cushions of the couch, hands pressed flat against the smooth leather.

He did what now?

"I had to," Max rushes to explain, his tone laced with what sounds like an apology. "I couldn't risk it. Every day, the temptation grew stronger and our connection more intense. The more hours we spent together at the bookstore, the more hours we spent together here," he shakes his head. "The stronger our love grew. With every shared story, with every joke, with every dinner."

Our love?

"If I had slipped, if I had given in my true desires," his voice fades, haunted by the horror of what could have been. I watch as his face, bathed in the soft glow of the flickering fire, crumples into his hands, the pain of his confession etched into every line of his face.

I suppose any good love story needs its share of heart-wrenching twists and turns.

"Why would you do that if you loved me?" My voice is breaking, demanding an explanation. And a good one.

Max clears his throat, his eyes flushing away the ever-living spark inside them.

"That's the issue," he says gravely. "This fondness I feel for you prevents me from touching you. Our time together only brought us closer by the minute—bringing us a step closer to the worst possible outcome. One misguided hand and... Hannah," Max lets out a deep, trembling sigh. "If I were to kiss you, to hold you close. Just the way I yearn to... I couldn't risk it."

Max's gaze drifts upward, his fingers fidgeting nervously, his knee bouncing with restless energy. I struggle to make out his features through the curtain of tears clouding my vision. The collision of true love and the stark reality of mortality feels almost unbearable. We lapse into a heavy silence, yet again, the weight of unspoken words hanging in the air.

"Every second of every day, you consume my every thought, Hannah Scotch. And you have for quite some time. My heart is burning for you in a way I will never be able to describe in words."

My body goes numb. A silent whisper begs me to make the distance that separates us disappear. To find the delicate skin of his neck. Graze his chest with my tongue. Something that, until now, I couldn't quite explain. Maybe I can now.

After a deep breath, Max announces, "Not so long ago, Hannah, you loved me, too. You don't remember it now, but you did."

My arms naturally release the weight of my body and cross over my chest. There are a million things I could say, a million questions that need to be asked, but I can't make a sound. Not one. It's all too much and not enough.

Love. We were in love?

The air of the room fills with a sweet smell. Honey, maybe? The fire's gleaming turns to something more intimate, imbued with hues of pink. Is the house trying to be romantic right now? Because I would have a thing or two to say about this.

"Why are you telling me this now, Maximilian?" My tone is flat, defeated, and confused. "Why didn't you tell me the whole truth back then?"

"I panicked," Max says simply. As simply as a mere human soul would. "I've never felt this kind of love before. Let alone feeling loved and appreciated the way you loved and appreciated me." More tears swell up his beautiful, sparkling eyes. "I thought I could break the curse before I could find you again. Before we could start over, safely. I thought I could save you. And save Alice. And save myself. I didn't think I would hurt you the way I am hurting you now."

"You let me fall in love with you just to vanish? Guess The Collector is not the only one doing the torturing." My eyes throw fire. I bite my lips in regret immediately after lashing out. Not that the situation is fair, but I do not need to be cruel.

Max laughs, which takes me aback. "Hannah, no one alive can *let* you do anything. You decide what you can and can't do, babygirl," he grins like the devil—fitting. "I panicked when you admitted your love for me. I was smitten with you the second I laid eyes on you, but I never suspected you would fall for me, too. The night you revealed the reality of your feelings for me, I realized there was no way to stop you. Stopping you from claiming me. I had to keep you safe," Max explains, with a sense of both pride and endearment.

"Why did you come back to The Book Nook, then?" I challenge. "If you attempted to break the curse on your own?"

His plans have quite a few holes in them.

"Turns out I can't stay away from the beautiful bookshop owner. I needed my fix," Max attempts to joke. "You forgot all about our love, but I didn't. I had to live with it."

"I tried to stay away," Max says when he realizes his joke didn't land.

"To stay away from the co-op for good until I could meet you again. But my magic isn't cutting it. I can't locate that damn spell book," Max grumbles, frustration seeping into his voice. "The co-op is my only viable option. You are my only chance, Hannah."

His eyes look straight into my soul, reaching for my heart.

"Did I know back then? That you were a warlock?"

Max shakes his head from side to side. "I wanted to protect you and keep you away from the curse as long as it wasn't lifted."

"Does Brandie know about us?"

"Brandie knew. The whole town knew about us, Hannah." There's an intensity in Max's voice, and I know it is preparing me for what's next. "I erased your memory, but everyone's in town, too."

My emotions are being dragged onto a wild ride that feels like there is no stopping—only a deep-end jump at the end. The kind of roller-coaster that gains speed and spits you out into the void.

"That's why the residents of Willowbrook answered all my questions, even though they believed I was a stranger. I saw the confusion in Brandie's eyes that day; it was clear it didn't make sense to you," he murmures, his voice a haunting whisper. "But deep within, their souls recognized mine. And they trusted me, against all reason."

"You lied to me. And to everyone else."

"I protected you. And Alice," he responds matter-of-factly.

"You took control of me, of my free will, Max."

His silence is the only answer I get.

It's not just the memories themselves that I suddenly mourn; it's the sense of control and agency that has been callously ripped from me. I feel exposed, violated, and vulnerable, as if the very fabric of my identity has been unraveled before my eyes.

If he loved me, the decision should have been mine. *Ours.* Not his.

There's a lot of different ways tonight could have gone. I certainly didn't expect this one in particular. I feel like a brick wall has been carefully placed over my skull throughout his monologue, brick by brick. Now crushing me, turning me into a pool of upset human goo. What a way that would be to ruin the leather couch.

"What if I didn't see you and Alice at the restaurant? Was your plan to disappear on me again?"

"I didn't have any plans, Hannah. Our time at the conference was proof of how much I wanted this. How much I want you. I let myself get close to you. Dangerously close. Too close," his lips tremble, mirroring the fast movement of his pupils. "Alice felt sick again. A grim reminder of the pact I've made, of the consequences I accepted."

I look down at my feet. I couldn't live with myself if Alice got hurt because of me. If *anyone* got hurt because of me.

"I'm glad you saw us, Hannah. You deserve the truth. I should have given it to you sooner." Max admits, and it sounds a lot like a closing statement.

Oddly, Max's eyes remind me of my father's. The two men have nothing in common, only the way they look at me. Maybe it's the love lingering in their gaze. My dad has dark features—thick brown hair and eyes that flirt with ink-black. I most definitely inherited my mother's physical traits—her green eyes and red hair.

Astray in Max's eyes, walking the line between confusion and madness, I'm brought back to one particular afternoon.

My father was pretty absent growing up, always drowned in the next work project. But when he was around, he truly was. That one cold afternoon, Mom and Dad had a terrible fight. They didn't fight much, so it's easier to recall the days they did.

A winter storm was raging outside. I recall the snow whipping against the windows, swirling with the strong winds.

Mom was furious, stomping in the next room. Though I couldn't see her face, I could picture it clearly. Mom has always been very expressive. The deep wrinkles that map her face now are proof of the emotions she felt and showed throughout her life.

I remember her high-pitched voice throwing insults that sounded like sharp knives. They might as well have been. Dad's face was creased with anger, too. He was sighing repeatedly, sitting across from me on the floor, trying to tune out the screams on the other side of the wall.

My toys were scattered between us, and I was busy reorganizing them in a well-thought-through manner. Dad hadn't noticed my new arrangement of books, proudly standing on the shelf he built—but that's okay. I didn't expect him to, anyway.

"Are you and mom going to get a divorce?" my child self had innocently asked, without looking at Dad. "Wait, does that mean I'm getting two birthday parties?" I lit up, thinking this would be my chance to double down on gifts.

Not only did I inherit my mom's temper, but also her pragmatism and a touch of wit. Come to think of it, that's what sparked my relationship with Max on the first day we argued at The Book Nook.

Dad only chuckled and brushed my hair away from my forehead. "That's not how love works, sweet girl," he'd answered.

The rest of our conversation faded into a foggy haze in my memory, but Dad made sure I understood a critical notion that day; love can conquer all.

"Sometimes, people make mistakes, Hannah," Dad had told me, "But you know what binds them together? Love. Good people can make mistakes, too. What matters is what you feel for them and what they feel for you. One day, I hope you will feel it in your heart. I hope you'll experience the kind of love and respect that not only deserves but also has the power to broaden your perspective. People can be angry yet still madly in love. Love doesn't stop at anger. Love soothes anger and fixes cracks. I've learned that from your mother, and I want you to know that, too."

Mom and Dad weren't perfect, but they were in love. True love.

I'm beginning to wonder if this is why I've never fully immersed myself in any relationship. Perhaps I've been subconsciously seeking the stable, enduring love that my parents share. I convinced myself that I wasn't a romantic at heart. That a committed relationship wasn't for me. What if I've always been too much of a romantic, searching for a kind of love that never materialized for me?

CHAPTER TWENTY-FOUR

"I need to call my dad," I say absentmindedly.

I rise from the couch, feeling numb, clumsily gathering my things. I do everything in my power to avoid meeting the two golden fires that are Max's eyes. I can't handle what's written in them. Two invisible hands reaching for me, begging me to stay.

He remains silent. True to his promise. He said he'd let me go if I wanted to run—so he does.

As I rush through the entrance hall, the chandelier starts its swinging performance once more, and for a second, I almost expect the front door to slam in my face. This is a magical house, after all. Who said the warlock and his ghosts would allow me a happy ending?

By the time I get inside my car, the lights scattered throughout the large front yard shine brighter, clearly illuminating the path away from the house, away from Max—my Max.

"What does it feel like?" I urgently inquire. I couldn't wait until I got home to talk to Dad. He picks up on the first ring. I realize it's late, but if anyone has a good chance to answer my call now, it's him.

"Hello, sweetheart. I've missed you," Dad greets me, the weight of years passed echoing in his voice through my car's speakers.

He overlooks the fact that I didn't say hello, didn't ask him how he was doing—or pose any question a normal person would to start a random phone call, for that matter. The moment I heard the click of the conversation starting, I blurted out, *what does it feel like, Dad?*

I sound panicked—because I'm freaking the fuck out. Dad most likely picks up on it, but he remains calm. That truly is his strong suit—nothing can shake the man.

"What does *what* feel like, sweetheart?" he asks.

"Love, Dad. The real deal."

He chuckles softly, breaking up a little over the speakers. "You will know, dear girl. Trust yourself."

Without warning, he hangs up the phone. Or maybe I lost him; I'm not sure. I'm driving through the thick of the woods again. My service could be bad right now. Either way, I know how he operates. Dad wouldn't have said much more than that. He always loved to keep things somewhat mysterious—particularly *important* things.

We exchanged two-word sentences and talked for maybe fifteen seconds. Yet, I felt profound relief—a guttural sense of reassurance. He mumbled a few words that meant nothing—it was exactly what I needed to hear.

You will know.

I spend what's left of the night tossing and turning, to much of Arthur's dismay, trying to process everything that fell on me like a gigantic boulder tonight—it seems impossible. I fell in love with a damn warlock in a past life I can't even remember, all because said warlock played with the gods—or the devil—and wiped my memory clean.

Though perhaps he had a damn good reason to do so.

This is why Willowbrook trusts him so much. This is why he knew so much about my store, the co-op, and our little mountain town. That explains his insufferable way of finishing my sentences, almost reading my mind every time we talked.

He *knew* me. Truly knew me.

It explains the way my body feels when I'm around him and how it feels when I'm not. I get it now. I understand why he stormed into The Book Nook the night he thought I was in danger after the robbery. It explains the bloody nose and black eye gifted to the two assholes at the conference—seemingly caused by a random gust of wind. I understand the live fire I swore I could see in his eyes back then. It all makes sense now.

Despite the fact that I couldn't remember the love we shared, we found each other again. My body knew the way, racing towards him every chance it got. My hands knew what they wanted all along—which was to rip his damn clothes off and travel along the edges of his full muscles.

Focus, Hannah.

What am I supposed to do with this twisted tale, anyway? The past couple of days alone have shown me it would prove very, very difficult to stay away from Max. If not impossible. Doing so would mean robbing him of the only chance he's got to save himself and Alice. I could ask him to erase my memories again, though that feels like opening the door to your house for someone to rob you a second time. I'm not particularly eager to let that happen—not if I have a say in the matter this time around.

So what are my options?

I don't have any magical powers to find a damn book I know nothing about. I've read enough fairytales to know that someone with no ability—like myself—rarely ends up being the hero of the story. The fact that magic is real alone is still incredibly hard to wrap my head around, let alone hope that I have some of that magic in me. My parents have great qualities, but superpowers are not one of them.

I'm just Hannah. Simple, boring Hannah.

All I have are my books, my cat, my shop, and the co-op.

Wait a second.

I *do* have the co-op. I have the damn co-op.

The co-op might be the very reason this whole mess started, but it could also very well be the answer. The only chance that Max has to get his freedom back. A blessing and a curse of sorts.

I jump out of bed and bolt towards my desk, where stacks of papers and notes are starting to dangerously lean, threatening to spill on the floor. The room is still bathed in the darkness of the night, and aside from shadows stretching on the walls and blurry outlines of the furniture, I can't see much.

The ceiling light blinds me. I hear Arthur's meow coming from the corner of the bed. The cat is upset he won't be able to get his beauty rest tonight. I frantically search the shelves and the various stacks on my desk. Drawers fly open, and pieces of paper go waltzing around the room. I empty every folder I own and keep digging for more.

By the end of my frantic search, I'm on my knees on the bedroom floor, head bent down. My eyes quickly scan every page, every note, and every picture thrown around me, my index finger posted on my bottom lip.

To most people, these scraps would be meaningless—but to someone deeply invested in the co-op, someone who's been tracking down its members, their contacts, and their origins for a long time, every single piece of paper here is gold.

Now, that is my superpower.

CHAPTER TWENTY-FIVE

As I unskillfully park right in front of the mansion, the front doors open for me once more. Max is nowhere to be seen this time. I rush up the front stairs and into the grand hall. The chandelier is swinging, of course. The giant double-paned front door slams shut behind me in a loud, deafening sound.

"Not now, ghosts!" I scream, infuriated.

Maybe they are mad at me, too. Mad for leaving their warlock companion without a word just a few hours earlier.

Something tells me I will find Max in the room where we had *quite* the conversation not so long ago. I wonder if he even moved after I ran away. My eyes are burning from the lack of sleep, though I know I couldn't fall asleep even if I tried. I'm not sure what time it is. The thickness of the night outside tells me it must be 2 or 3a.m.

I put my hair in a messy bun and didn't bother changing or cleaning up. I still wear my comfy leggings and a loose shirt over them. A weird mix of elegance and coziness. *A hot mess is what it really is.*

The mansion smells of cinnamon and roses, the latter of which is new and seems to emanate directly from the walls.

I enter the living room and find it the way I left it. My magical man is sitting on the couch. Only the glass of thick amber liquid he's holding is different. *Whiskey.*

The fire is still lit in the fireplace, though it looks tame, almost melancholic. The flames are not as tall anymore; their dancing has slowed down. It looks sad.

I stand in the doorway, my eyes meeting Max's—two shining pebbles that could easily shoot fire. As our gazes lock, I feel an explosion inside my chest. It burns—beautifully. The feeling breaks my heart open and mends it all at once. I feel weak in the knees, yet stronger than ever. As if invisible wings were lifting me toward the skies. The butterflies return, turning my guts into a giant rave.

Here it is, the very feeling I've been craving without knowing it. Dad was right. I *would* know.

Eager to be near again, I reclaim the seat I left earlier. I dramatically drop the large folder I've been holding on to like my life depended on it —quite literally—on the low-lying coffee table.

"This is everything I know about the co-op, its members, and collections. Everything I've tracked over the years."

Max's eyes are wet, never leaving mine.

"Hannah," he whispers.

I don't like the tone of his voice. I was expecting excitement, maybe even gratitude. Instead, Max greets me with a voice that sounds like an apology, like he's given up on us—*on me.*

I can only imagine what went through his mind after I left. At any moment, he could snap his fingers and erase my memories again. At any second, he could disappear from my life again, maybe for good this time. I can't let this happen.

"I love you, silly warlock." I blurt out, clearly not thinking anything through. It rolls off my tongue like a prisoner who's been banging on their cell door, begging to break free. My body has known it this whole time, forced to remain silent. Not anymore.

"You think I wouldn't remember, but in a way, I do. Every fiber of my being does. If you think I consume your every thought, just wait until I describe what the thought of you does to me." I chuckle, shaking my head.

I must be honest. I can't lose him again. This is all or nothing. I'm all in.

I might not remember the path that brought me here, the first few moments we shared, the increase of my heartbeat when I initially realized I was falling for this dark-haired, golden-eyed man. But I know now there's a reason I couldn't recognize myself around Max from the very second I met him.

There's a reason my body has been screaming his name ever since. It remembered it all. My love for him might have been forced to hide its flowers, but its roots are deeply anchored inside me. They are weaved through my heart and my very flesh, and no rational thoughts can't combat this.

"I hate that you took that away from me," I continue. "I hate that I can't remember. I hate that it's senseless. But in reality, it never left me. Though my mind couldn't remember, my heart did all along. Clear as day. Maximilian, I want you. I want to love you. Magical powers, intimidating sister, angry ghosts and all," I laugh softly. "So, we are doing this together. This isn't a question. I know the co-op better than anyone. We don't have much to start, but we have *something*."

I don't know if we can break this curse, but I know we can try. I'm his only chance. I might not be magical, but I sure as hell am not useless.

My breath catches as Max remains silent. I suppose I'm due a taste of my own medicine by now. The seconds that pass in stillness feel like hours. Just like earlier, it feels like the mansion is holding its breath, too. Even the fire went still, leaving nothing but the sound of cracking ambers.

"Max," I find myself begging, my voice trembling.

I despise what I did earlier. Despise the fact that I ran; my judgment clouded by selfishness and anger. Why couldn't I talk to Max when he opened up to me? Why did I have to leave without a word? Damn pride. I feel like an idiot. I made this whole thing about me when everything he did was to save us all.

The silence stretches. My mouth runs dry.

"I would kiss you... if I could," Max finally says with a grin on his face, his joking tone floating in the air.

The walls breathe again; the fire is back to swaying. My warlock is back. Relief pulls my lungs up so I can take a full breath.

"Kiss me? Listen, I have an idea what you are hiding underneath those jeans, Mister. If you think we should stop at *kissing*, maybe I should leave after all," I laugh, pointing at the door.

Max growls. We are right back where we started. My heart is full. His eyes are burning again—literally. This feels like home—a familiar sense of belonging that feels so new all at once.

"So, where do we start?" I say enthusiastically, moving to the other couch to sit by Max.

His arm finds its way around my shoulders as he brushes the loose strands of hair away from my neck. He leans in, his lips dangerously close to my skin. I know now he will not kiss it; oddly enough, it arouses me even more. The fire is not just raging in the fireplace anymore—it moved to my underwear, deliciously burning my inner thighs.

"We start by getting you some sleep," Max whispers in my ears.

Sleep is the last thing I want, but he's not wrong. We have a lot of work to do, and I can't be helpful if I can't think straight—which is hard enough to do around Max, even with many restful hours of sleep.

"I don't want to leave you," I admit.

"I wasn't going to let you leave. There are enough bedrooms here," he gestures to the ceiling, which I know means one of the top floors of this gigantic mansion.

I gently trace the tips of my fingers through his black curls. He can't truly touch me, but I can safely tease him. Our time at the conference proved it. I learned the rules without even knowing them. Or so I think?

"I need to know the ground rules," I say, brushing a featherlight touch over Max's cheek.

"The ground rules?" he mimics, clearly laughing at my choice of words.

"Of the curse," I counter, my tone more serious.

Max scoffs.

"What's that for?" I nudge his ribcage with my elbow.

"I don't know if they are rules as much as safety measures," Max says, shaking his head.

"Oh, we're playing with semantics now, are we?" I tease. "Look, at the conference, we were physically close. We never crossed a line, considering I'm still here to tell the tale," I chuckle. "But Alice also felt sicker. So I need to know where the balance lies."

Max's face turns grave, the weight of the curse suddenly pressing down on him again. "A warning from The Collector," he sighs.

"Let's not give him any leverage, then," I say.

Max turns to face me; his gaze is tender as a caress. "Most of the burden falls on me," he explains. "My intentions are what trigger the curse. What I want to do to you. How I feel about you. But there's an obvious physical component, sure."

"So, *I* can touch you?" I ask, hopeful.

"Yes and no."

"Okay. Lips?" I go down the checklist.

"We can't kiss, obviously," Max starts. "I can't kiss your lips, your breasts, between your legs. Nor taste you with my tongue," he growls.

I shift in my seat, attempting to shake off the soreness between my legs at the mention of his lips and tongue on me.

"You can't fully kiss me either," Max clarifies.

"Okay." I think for a second. "Hands?"

"Like I said, there's no absolute rule," Max says. "But as long as my hands and fingers remain in chaste enough areas of your body, we are safe."

I nod, pensive. "You caressed my neck before," I think out loud. The thought steals a smile from me.

"You'll notice I always only dare graze your warm skin, Hannah, as a true gentleman would," he whispers with a grin, aiming to lean into the bend of my neck.

I push him off, giggling.

"That's fair," I admit, thinking the whole situation through.

"Clothes help, too," Max offers. "Your hands tend to wander, my dear," he teases, "But with my intentions as much in check as possible and clothes separating our skins, we can play. It's a dangerous playground, I should add. But not necessarily deadly."

"So you can touch me, as long as it isn't in a desirable part of my body?" I ask.

"One would argue every single part of your body is desirable, Hannah," he snarls. "Now, can we get you some sleep?"

Max shows me to my room, where the focal point is an imposing king-sized bed dressed in crisp white linens with a plethora of plump pillows. Too bad the two of us can't make a mess of this inviting bed set.

My now bare feet kiss a plush, warm carpet as I enter the room. I'm walking on a cloud. A more contemporary chandelier, resplendent with cascading crystals, hangs overhead. If I'm lucky, this one won't swing in the middle of the night.

The larger wall consists entirely of ceiling-to-floor windows, providing an open door for the moonlight to light up the whole room. A door merges seamlessly with the glass among the windows, revealing a spacious stone balcony enchantingly illuminated by delicate string lights draped overhead.

With a quick look through the windows, I can see that the room overlooks the backyard. It's so vast I can't even see the end. I discern various large trees and more night lights.

"I hope this will do?" Max's voice reaches my ears from behind.

Leaning against the doorframe with his legs crossed at the ankle and arms folded on his chest, he remains shrouded in dim light. But his eyes never seem to meet the darkness.

I notice he has laid out a large T-shirt and shorts on the bed. I wish my own clothes were scattered on the floor instead, but that's a story for a future day—if all goes according to plan and we don't die.

"Is this where you tell me you can't fuck me because you would hurt me?" I joke, bringing all the vampire stories I've ever read to mind. "It always hurts the dumb mortal, you know," I wink.

"Good thing you are everything but a dumb mortal, then," he whispers with a smirk, creeping closer until the heat of his body engulfs mine. It takes everything in me to not devour those lips of his—and some. "Good night, my love," he mouths, caressing my cheeks so gently I can barely feel his fingers.

He makes it sound so natural—to call me this. Like he's been doing it for a long time. I suppose it will take some time to readjust to this newfound yet deep-rooted love, at least for me.

It appears we won't be sharing the same bed tonight. It's for the best. Every one of my nerves has been tingling all night, the sensation intensifying whenever I find myself closer to Max. This forgotten love is no joke and comes with *many* beastly desires I never knew I was capable of feeling.

I whisper a shy *good night* back as Max slips behind the closing door.

CHAPTER TWENTY-SIX

The aroma of freshly brewed coffee tickles my nose as I groggily awaken. I slept like the dead. This is hands down the best sleep I've ever had in my entire life. This bed must be magic, too.

As my senses slowly come to life, I sit straight up in bed, clutching the sheets tight against my chest. I dart around the room, a momentary panic setting in. I take a deep breath of relief. I'm still at the mansion. I'm still in one of Max's beds. This was not a dream. As twisted as our story is, it's very much real.

I let myself fall back into the plush pillow and stretch my body, savoring the divine silkiness of the sheets. I want to stay here forever, but the smell of coffee and the muffled voice of Maximilian downstairs are calling me like a carrot would attract a donkey.

I spring out of bed, draped in the oversized t-shirt that smells like my favorite man. In the dimness of the night, I didn't notice the incredible number of books stacked on a massive built-in wooden shelf. Is this why he picked this room for me?

I walk around the bedroom, trailing one hand behind me, exploring every texture and piece of furniture. One book has been left on the nightstand beside the bed. *"The Side Effects of Magic"*. Well, well, well, let's see.

I'll be damned. The number one side effect listed is none other than the taste of salt in the mouth. You've got to be kidding me. *Damn warlock.* I chuckle, carefully closing the book before setting it back down on the nightstand.

I rush over to the glass door and step outside. The sun is already high in the sky—I must have slept in. The cold stone balcony beneath my feet perfectly counters the heat outside.

After adjusting to the bright light, my eyes roam over the sprawling yard before me. My jaw drops. Stretching for what seems like miles, lush green grass unfurls, creating a green ocean in the breeze. Countless trees stand tall, all fruit-bearing. Brandie would be in heaven.

A neat gravel path separates the trees from raised growing beds. I spot a large wicker hat floating among the growing leaves and stems. The hat rises, revealing the face of an older, tanned gentleman. Clad in a white t-shirt and gardening gloves, he diligently tends to the soil and prunes the vegetables. *Of course, Max has staff.*

Even though I don't know the mansion's layout, I quickly find the way to the kitchen, as if on my way to meet an old friend.

I took a moment to refresh myself in the attached bathroom—which could be a room on its own. I'm pretty sure it's bigger than my apartment. In the center lies a grand clawfoot bathtub, its gleaming surface beckoning invitingly. Every surface is adorned with gilded accents and intricate mosaics, each detail meticulously crafted to evoke a sense of timeless beauty and refinement. A vanity table gleams with polished silver and crystal perfume bottles. Plush towels and robes hang tight, their softness a promise of *otherworldly* comfort—quite literally.

I'm wearing nothing but Max's t-shirt when I walk downstairs, greeting the ghosts for good measure. Might as well keep the invisible figures on my side.

The man fueling all my fantasies is sitting at the kitchen table, facing away. An expansive assortment of breakfast food stretches before him. Steaming, melting, filling the air with scents I didn't know existed. When he notices me, Max happily trots in my direction.

"There she is," he says with a kiddish hint.

Before I know it, I'm spinning in his arms. I suppose a morning hug is chaste enough, even for the curse. When my warlock releases me, I shyly look down, feeling the heat of my cheeks turning them pink. Another thing I will need to get accustomed to, I suppose.

A petite woman stands on one side of the kitchen, flipping pancakes. *Oops.* Instinctively, I pull down on my shirt, attempting to cover as much of my body as possible. I didn't expect the company. Max chuckles at my embarrassment, pulling me closer to the petite lady.

"This is Annie," he says proudly, gesturing to the gray-haired lady focused on the griddle before her.

"It's good to see you again, Miss Hannah. You look well-rested." Her voice is as sweet as the pancakes she's making.

The wrinkles on her face deepen into a grandmotherly smile as she turns around to greet me—a grandmotherly smile I unexpectedly realize I've never had the chance to enjoy in my life. I never knew my grandparents on either side.

'It's good to see you again,' she said. Of course. I had met her before. I wonder how many times. I can't remember, but I can feel it. A slight pinch flutters in my chest as if my heart is saying, *'Hello, it's good to see you, too.'*

This woman, this kitchen, this man—it all feels too familiar, yet it feels like the very first time I stand here. Sure, my mind has forgotten, but some feeling deep inside screams, *hey, dumbass, I remember.*

"Black coffee, Miss Hannah?" Annie asks, transferring the golden tower of fluffy pancakes she's been working on onto a plate.

"Just Hannah, please. And yes, that would be amazing. Thank you, Annie."

My plate fills up with fresh fruit, pancakes, fruit cakes, and other delicious things all on its own. Magic is cool. I'm starving. The clock strikes noon. *Damn, I did sleep in.*

Max sits with me at the kitchen table, holding the folder I left in the living room last night. He sure had time to review it while I was nearly unconscious in bed from such a deep sleep.

"Hannah, this is amazing," he says with genuine gratitude. "Incredible, even. You're incredible, my love."

I chuckle, nearly choking on the strawberry I've stuffed in my mouth. I don't know if I'll ever get used to these cute little pet names.

My love. Did I ever, previously, I mean? I gently shake off the butterflies that rush through my body and brush Max's hand with mine.

"I'll start sending emails today," I finally say after emptying the food pit that serves as my mouth, "And letters. Some members are very old-school and use PO boxes instead of anonymous emails. We have to start somewhere. Ask questions, look around," I say in between bites. "If someone has seen such a manuscript, we'll know. Maybe you can describe it to me?"

Max's golden eyes sparkle, a literal glimmer. He stares at me in silence, a broad smile on his face. We don't need to say much more. We silently agree on a vague strategy, exchanging loving looks like college kids falling in love for the first time. I look down and away a few times. This feeling is all too new and scary to look at too closely. Just yesterday, I thought the only man who'd ever truly caught my eyes had disappeared on me.

Max notices. He grabs my chin with a feather touch, and his golden-ringed eyes send a silent, comforting message. My body settles when he does, guided by the ghost of our profound love.

"This is delicious, by the way," I enthusiastically say to Annie. "I must say, it would be even better without the salt." I slowly turn back to Max, tilting my head with a grin. He laughs as I wink.

"It'll get better soon, now that the main spell on you is lifted."

By the main spell, he means the obliteration of my memories. But let's not get back to that. Telling me the whole truth was Max's way of lifting the spell cast on me, but there was no counter-spell strong enough to bring my memories back. I might not recover the entirety of my memories, but at least I'll recover my taste. I'd say that's a win.

We lounge around the breakfast table for a little longer, exchanging stories that Max has heard before. But he owes me that much. The more I learn, the more the dormant feeling lodged deep inside my heart starts blooming again. I forget what day or time it is. All I know is that I should be at The Book Nook. I could get used to slow mornings in his company, lounging in this gigantic kitchen.

The real hardwood floor reflects the sunlight, refracting through an array of small glass squares joined together to form one substantial yet slightly imperfect window. The charm of the floors extends to the robust wooden cabinets encircling the room, gracefully embracing the walls. Crafted from dark, rustic wood, they look freshly polished. Annie's doing, I'm sure.

Long green arms—dangling house plants, not much different from the ones at the bookstore—creep all around the kitchen, hugging the top of the cabinets and the door frames, giving an ancient apothecary feel to the room.

I almost expected to see a bunch of jars and other glass containers filled with frog legs and crow feathers preserved for potions and spells. *Magic must be different these days*, I jokingly think to myself.

The food Annie made is delicious, and the coffee is the boldest in flavor I've ever had. It's pretty unfair to think that everything is nearly perfect in this house. And by nearly perfect, I mean absolutely fucking perfect. From the bed—though a little empty—and the sleep to the coffee and the host's flawless face screwed on his sculpted-by-the-gods body.

Unfair, indeed.

As I stretch my legs further down under the table and grab a magically refilled, steaming cup of coffee, one of the doors leading to the kitchen slams shut. I don't know how I manage to keep the cup in my hands, but by some miracle, I do. I jerk back up.

"They have been out of control, Maximilian," Annie says without losing her composure. If anything, she seems used to it. She's demanding action, though. That much is obvious.

"It will get better. I'll talk to them," Max responds kindly, taking another buttery bite of homemade bread.

"The ghosts, Miss Hannah." Annie reacts to my confused expression. "They've been angry...and acting up," she waves a bent finger at seemingly nothing. A warning.

"They're just brats," Max jokes. "I'll talk to them, I promise."

After Annie leaves the room, not entirely convinced by Max's promise, I learn a couple more things.

Firstly, Annie, though accustomed to the ghostly inhabitants of the house, can't see them either. Oddly enough, that makes me feel better. It felt like I was missing out. Like I was unworthy. Max explains that the spell he cast on me—and Willowbrook—in addition to the incessant magical work he's been doing to locate the grimoire, has been agitating the ghosts.

Most of them are ancestors, angry at Max for humoring the Collector of Souls' pact in the first place. A few of them are not quite human but *entities*, he calls them. They're not necessarily dangerous, just not exactly loving creatures. I'll ignore them, and they'll ignore me in return. Easy enough. I can follow a simple rule.

The entities came to the Forstthorn family, attracted by their undeniable power. *Greedy little things.* The ancestors just piled up in the mansion as the family grew older and new generations came to live. Some came and went, some stayed.

"Did I used to come here a lot?" I absentmindedly ask Max, my gaze drifting, floating over the room.

"Though it was quite tortuous for me, yes. You did." Max chuckles.

"Sleepover?" I ask with an arched brow.

Max grins. "That too. Most times, you'd fall asleep on the couch. After dinner, movie nights, game nights…" A warmth envelopes Max's voice as if the memories, though complicated, softened every edge of his.

"Game night?" I shout with a chuckle. When was I ever a game night person?

Max laughs in response. "You are pretty good at it, too."

I can't recall the last time I lingered over breakfast for more than an hour, but then again, I can't remember ever feeling anything close to what I feel for Max.

Though I wish this morning never ended, I must return to my business. I lightly kiss Max's forehead as I head toward the living room to find my phone and purse—I abandoned both last night.

> B: Have you heard? Call me when you get up. I need to know you're safe.
>
> B: I can't believe this is happening. So sad.
>
> B: Where the hell are you, Hannah?
>
> B: This dick better be good, girlfriend…

CHAPTER TWENTY-SEVEN

Along with the long trail of texts, six missed calls from Brandie were waiting for me. That's beginning to look all too familiar —I hate it. I did let the morning just fly by. I wasn't ready to deal with reality again just yet.

Max's footsteps trail behind me.

"Something is off. I need to call Brandie," I absentmindedly say, looking down at my screen to read the myriad of texts one more time in case I missed an important clue.

"You should go see your friend. I will meet you in town shortly."

My warlock sounds worried and a little too serious again. It would be too easy to forget that our world is not just about magic—some serious shit happens. The light mood that carried us through the morning has already faded.

"There was another burglary, Hannah. I just learned about it." Max's tone is grave.

Willowbrook must be breaking records of criminality. A chill runs down my spine. Not the sexy kind. Fear grips me from head to toe.

"I took the liberty of flying some of your clothes over. Take a moment before you go back. Don't worry, Brandie is fine. And everything else will be too. I'll see you later." He purrs in my ears.

He's trying to conceal the seriousness I heard in his tone just a second ago. Max is all about balance—and protection. He doesn't want me to worry. He delicately caresses my skin where the fabric of my shirt ends, right below my butt cheeks. The world could be on fire right now. I wouldn't care.

~

BRANDIE IS PACING between her counter and front door, poking her head periodically to check on my side of the wall. I don't see any cops, which means she hasn't *entirely* lost it just yet.

I catch a reflection of myself in the windows as I walk closer. Max did well. He picked a flowy jumpsuit in warm red fabric adorned with yellow flowers. He even thought of a white hairpin with matching flowers. I look perfectly recharged, which, considering the current circumstances, might seem out of place.

Still fairly oblivious to what happened, I catch my friend's attention. The smile I crafted just for her crumbles when I see her tense face.

"You better have the best fucking excuse..." Brandie yells at me in a motherly tone, pretending to be mad, as she hugs me—tightly.

"It's a long story. For another time. Are you okay?" I inquire, attempting to breathe through her grip.

I reconnect with reality when I realize how genuinely worried Brandie is. It's not every day I don't make it home from a one-night stand. Funny, considering I did not get laid last night.

I lead Brandie inside The Book Nook and get some tea going for her and coffee for me. The opposite fragrances collapse and float around the shop. Arthur promptly finds one of his favorite spots—Brandie's lap. It seems they both need it today.

I'm about to join my friend in the nook when I feel a strong breeze caressing my neck. Max is standing inside the store, already greeting Brandie. No bell to be heard above the door. *Damn wizard.*

Brandie, unfazed by the man's sudden entrance, proceeds to share what she knows so far. Max's expression is unmistakable—he didn't hear the whole story from her *first.*

"Which store got targeted?" I anxiously question Brandie.

"It was someone's home this time." She corrects me.

"That's quite the escalation…"

Now, both homeowners are in critical condition. The woman had been savagely stabbed—the blade entering below her rib cage, perforating the lung. Her thorax had been slashed open in multiple places. There was no telling if she could survive this.

According to the press, her husband had been shot in the leg. Though bruised up and undeniably traumatized, he had a better chance of making it. Not sure he'd want it if his wife didn't.

I sit down next to Brandie, laying my hand on her lap—the one that's cat-free. The sorrow and grief are palpable. I chose Willowbrook in part because of its safe streets. Crime rates were nearly zero—and remained pretty much nonexistent until now.

"I checked our security system but didn't see anything. I was hoping our cameras would have recorded something useful for the investigation." Brandie explains matter-of-factly.

She's not one to be kicked down easily, but the late malfeasance seems to get to her in a way I've never witnessed before.

"That was a great idea." I squeeze her hand.

Brandie's resilient. More than I will ever be. She's always been. I will never forget the night she learned about her brother's death. Nico. She doesn't speak much of it, but I happened to sit across from her at a sticky bar table when her cell phone rang that night.

Like his sister, Nico was known to love nature. So much so that he made it a focal point in his life. He lived on a farm, recluse somewhere. You couldn't hand the guy enough money to come close to any city— even small mountain ones like Willowbrook.

Brandie would visit him once a year or so. She'd pack light and spend a few days on the homestead—particularly when she needed a break from our mundane lives. Tragically, it's his love for nature that killed Nico. A freak accident during a camping trip, where he fell off a cliff at night.

I sometimes wonder if the most heartbreaking stories I've read are based on true stories like this one. I would never, but I imagined writing my first novel about Brandie and Nico. I never met him in person, but I knew him just the same. Brandie was very fond of her brother and drew quite the picture for me. Their relationship was beautiful.

I remember this terrible night mainly because of my friend's reaction. She was devastated, as one would expect. But she didn't let the feelings linger. She used her love for Nico as fuel to get to work. Someone had to manage his estate and get his stuff in order. Nico didn't have a care in the world—he left a messy trail for his sister to sort out as a result. Brandie got it all figured out without shedding a tear.

That's when I got confirmation of how strong this woman is. She might look as delicate as the flowers she tends to, but *man, oh man,* is she not.

Max isn't worried—he's angry. He's beating the floor, pacing around The Book Nook. Before I know it, he softly brushes my cheeks and is out the door.

"Wait a damn minute, are you guys a thing now? That's where you disappeared last night, isn't it?" Brandie lights up at the idea of Max and me tearing each other's clothes off.

I still haven't told her anything—not about our time at the conference, the incident at the restaurant, or Alice, and especially not a word about some magical powers or minds being erased, including *hers.*

I chuckle, trying to find the best possible story to dodge her incoming questions.

"It's... complicated," I mumble, hoping she'll leave it at that for now, "And right now, it doesn't even matter. Are you feeling alright? Do you need to spend the night tonight? The both of us can beat down some pussy robbers easily."

"Who are you kidding?" She jokes, slapping my arm. "I'm alright, babe. I'm actually staying with security-system-guy. He lives out of town. I like that idea better. No offense." Her voice holds mischief when she mentions him.

I hope the poor guy doesn't get his hopes up. He's probably just her favorite playtoy at the moment. But if that means she gets someone to look after her, I'm all for sexy hobbies and safe leg spreading.

"Does the security system guy have a name and a phone number? Maybe even an address?" I ask as I stand up to finally start my business day.

"Joffrey," she says, scratching Arthur's butt a little faster. "I'll send you his info. I'm already sharing my location with you anyway." Brandie grabs her phone to double-check the latter.

"So, you and Max..." she waves her free hand in a circle in front of her mouth, meaning *get to talking, girl.*

"Later, missy. Now get out of here. Expect me to check on you every hour until we close." I shoo her out of questioning range.

This conversation was gearing up to be an important one and I don't even know where to start. I don't know if I could mention our *relationship.*

Is it even a relationship?

CHAPTER TWENTY-EIGHT

The recent events are heavy on my mind, but we have work to do. Progress to make. I start by sending emails to all members. Though addresses are anonymous, the co-op system ensures it reaches all members. I don't need real names; I need the goddamn spellbook.

Max had never seen it, leaving me with few details to share. Short emails it is. I'm not entirely sure what to ask for. I basically beg for anyone to share any knowledge of a book containing what would look like spells and incantations.

It's not uncommon to find such literature within the co-op. We frequently come across all kinds of texts. Fiction, historical, treasure maps, texts rooted in magic and folklore, and more. Though it isn't out of the ordinary, with no solid description—or any detail—it is a shot in the dark. One I'm willing to take.

My afternoon of email writing is punctually interrupted by a few readers. I find comfort in smiling faces and everyday human interactions.

Brandie continues to check in throughout the early afternoon. Pretending that she wants me safe, she insists that I should stay close to

Max, throwing wink after wink in my direction. "Maybe even spend the night again," she adds.

She and I end the afternoon together, sitting in the nook. I'm not mad at the idea. We haven't had some real time together in a while—ever since before the conference. I missed my friend. I make more hot drinks despite the heat of the summer day.

I've sent all the emails by the end of the day. Next, I will have to write letters, which Max decided to enchant to give them a better chance to hit the mark.

After helping my last readers, I spot the broad frame of my magical man sitting next to Brandie again. *Classic sneaking-in move.*

I watch them with loving eyes, chatting and laughing. Arthur found Brandie's lap again—*traitor.* I suspect he loves her more than anything in this world, and clearly, more than he loves me. Though that's easy to do, she's pretty damn lovable.

As I join them, an article in the corner of the newspaper Brandie is holding catches my eye.

Wait, a minute.

I recognize this pretty smile and short blond hair—it's Samantha. Samantha Lee. The lovely doll I met at the conference. I snatch the paper from Brandie's hands—who lets out a small screech.

Samantha is being recognized as a best-seller and author of the month. The article goes on to discuss her undeniable talent and bright future as a young and upcoming author and how incredibly fast her first novel sold worldwide. I gaze up at Max, already grinning.

"I said I knew a guy. I didn't say who the guy was or what he could do to help her," Max shrugs his shoulders and winks.

He followed through.

He promised to connect her with the right people and, well, he sort of did. I couldn't tell what kind of voodoo he used to get her book on the front page, but I read it. It's fantastic. Samantha is talented. She deserves the recognition, *magical push or not.*

I would kiss Max—if I could.

CHAPTER TWENTY-NINE

The emails I sent out bring the co-op to life. All members love a good scavenger hunt—I know that for a fact—and this one is quite the wild goose chase. According to the first responses we receive, no one has seen the book or knows where to find it. But everyone who engages promises to look and ask around. That's all the help we can hope for.

The enchanted letters will arrive in the next couple of days. The co-op's newly lit fire brings us hope. Everyone seems invested. We're doing the right thing and receiving the right kind of help in return. Max continues his magical work in parallel, casting location spell after location spell. We double down on our efforts, using it as a reason to spend a *lot* of time together.

Tonight, I'm working late at the shop. Arthur is roaming freely between the bookshelves, chasing dust balls. The sun has set, leaving the stage free for the night to take over, but not before having bathed the whole place in a breathtaking alpenglow.

The store is quiet, still warm from the hot sun punishing the windows throughout the day. I gather my stuff and half-ass organize the mess on my desk, preparing to go upstairs. I grab the empty cups of the day and mouth a clicking noise for Arthur to follow me. The cat doesn't move—go figure.

A piercing sound fires as a response. Gunshot. *Boom*. Gunshots.

Sadly, it's not the first time I've heard them in Willowbrook. I recognize the loud bang immediately. I jump and drop the mugs. The thick clay shatters when hitting the ground, scattering by my feet. That's going to leave a mark on the hardwood. I'll have to pick it up before Arthur gets hurt—once my heart stops thundering, that is. It's currently digging through my throat, one beat at a time. This heart-pounding bullshit has become a constant in my life.

The gunshots were close. Maybe a couple of blocks away, at best. This is getting out of control. I don't understand. I gather my thoughts and rush to the front door, tiptoeing around the sharp clay to lock the door.

The main street is already filling. People pool out of the buildings and into the dimly lit streets. This constant menace has made Willowbrook bitter—residents seem to not be afraid of gunshots anymore.

When I peek outside, loud screams and cries leak inside the store. Heads move fast, and hands are thrown in the air. There are more screams. Quicker than anticipated, emergency lights flash in the distance.

I was right; the gunshots were only a couple of blocks away. I look up above *Marguerite*, no lights. Brandie is with security-system-guy—I mean Joffrey—thank the horny gods.

I wedge the door with my body and keep it cracked open, poking my head out to survey the scene. I can't make much of what's happening with all these people in the way.

I squint as I work to figure out what I'm looking at. A literal tornado passes through the soft glow of the streetlamp across the street. My brows furrow, following the strong winds kicking dust and dirt in a cone shape.

The tornado reaches me, throws me out of the way, and enters the shop. It doesn't disturb anything inside. You'd think books and pieces of paper would be a perfect candidate for a windstorm. The gust of winds morphs into a humanesque shape. The statuesque back of Max comes into being in its place. Damn, that's quite the magic trick.

His eyes are two black pits—no fire to be seen. His jawline pulses with tension, highlighting the prominent vein that snakes across his forehead. In opposition, my whole body relaxes the second I sense his presence.

"You're staying at the mansion. Grab what you need for the night. We'll pack the rest of your stuff tomorrow." Max is not asking; he's ordering.

His voice is throaty. I instantly notice his hands—closed in tight fists. He's darting around the room and through the windows.

"I'll cast a protection spell for Brandie. Let's go, Hannah." Another command.

"She's not here, she's... she's staying... away. She'll be okay. I think. What happened out there?" I stumble over my words, confused.

More screams come creeping through the open door. I know gunshots have been fired dangerously close, but that's about it. I quickly realize that if Max appeared out of thin air at this hour, ordering me to leave my apartment, something terrible must have happened.

"Hey, are you okay?" I reach for his arms, but he keeps pacing and dodges me.

"Pack your stuff. Now."

～

BACK AT THE MANSION, I throw my overnight bag in a corner. Arthur carefully enters the grand hall, overthinking every step as if the floor was on fire. He's never left the apartment or the bookstore. The feline gazes up at the chandelier that starts to swing on cue. Arthur tilts its head. *Can he see the freaking ghosts?*

"Cats *can* see ghosts." My warlock brushes my back. His voice is honey again.

"Do wizards read minds?" I chuckle.

"Some do. But I don't. Though I don't need to read your mind to know what you are thinking, *babygirl*," his voice trails off into a whisper —it seems impossible to keep this desire at bay, even during the darkest hours of our lives.

Standing behind me, Max's hands are now hugging my hips—never *truly* touching me, of course. His face is lost in my hair. I hear him breathe me in. A long, deep, satisfied breath. I let my head fall backward, melting in the column of his neck.

"Oh? What am I thinking right now?"

My hand travels to his lower abdomen, above his silky shirt, and past his waistline. I learned at the conference that this was a safe enough move. I push my body closer to his. Only my hand stands guard between our bodies.

My fingers fiddle with his zipper and slowly pull it down. Max growls. He knows I won't cross the line, but he can take a good tease just fine. My fingers find their way past the zipper. I caress the thin fabric that separates my hand from my prize. It's warm in here, and rock-hard. Throbbing, even.

"You're evil, woman," he moans, biting my ear ever so gently. I can't truly feel his teeth sink into the delicate skin, but I can't miss the gentle heat traveling down my shoulder.

I turn around, more in an effort to ease the sexual tension that could get me killed than to simply face my lover. His eyes found their natural golden color again. The wells of infinite darkness are gone.

"Thank you," I whisper to him, floating back down to the real world around us.

Max always puts my safety first. If the burglaries are escalating, I'm the safest right here, by his side.

"It appears the cowards only hit at night. I'd feel better if you and Brandie closed shop earlier. You can't stay at your apartment alone, Hannah. That's non-negotiable. There's plenty of room here. Make this place yours. Please." He smiles down at me—a kind, genuine smile.

My independent nature would usually resist this, but honestly, I'm terrified. Letting stubborness win is tempting, but being practical is necessary. Closing early and staying here is hardly an inconvenience until things quiet down in town.

"How can I help around here, then?" I ask, wanting my lover to know I don't attempt to freeload.

His lips twist into this familiar, beasty grin. The lion is on the hunt again, his prey at his fingertips.

"Oh, you know how to do that."

CHAPTER THIRTY

"Who got targeted last night?" I dare ask, bracing myself for Max's answer as I butter up some fresh bread.

I watch as the thick dairy delight melts on the warm slice. Despite last night's events, I slept like the dead—yet again—and woke up like a flower in the spring.

"The art gallery. They had an intern working the floor to prepare for an upcoming exposition. The young man didn't stand a chance. He was shot in the head." There's sorrow in Max's voice as he shares what happened with me. His eyes darken, and so does his face.

Yesterday's news finally hit me like a bag of bricks. I don't think even the mouthwatering loaf can fix it.

Downtown, the main street is buzzing. I'm fighting the crowd to get to my door. It appears the residents organized a march in honor of the young man who died last night—and in the memory of all other victims of this incomprehensible wave of terror.

There's a mix of heavy hearts and exasperation in the air. The people of Willowbrook are grieving and demand action. It's been weeks now since the first attack. Things are not getting any better; they're getting out of control.

Willowbrook's Mayor has appeared on the news several times since, his greasy face glinting under the lights, offering us a concerned smile that barely masked the depth of his anxiety.

"Authorities are working tirelessly to apprehend those responsible for these atrocities," he declared, concluding his address with a note of cautious optimism, acknowledging the fact that though they had no leads, they had hope.

There are reporters and officials near the scene today. This day should be an interesting one.

Because of the enchantment cast on the hand-written letters we've sent, Max knows they arrived. A magical notification of sorts. We now play the waiting game while Max casts more location spells to support our search.

He devotes much of his energy to his magical work—but his strength doesn't seem to deplete easily. He spends a lot of time behind this enormous steel door at the mansion. It's thicker than the walls and looks like a vault. Three large round bolts protrude from the frame and serve as a lock, resonating so heavily when it closes that the entire house shakes.

This room is where he channels important spells and keeps his components, too. Sometimes, the smell of damp moss wafts through. Other times, straight decaying *something*. Once it closes, trapping Max inside, there is no opening until my warlock decides to come out.

I spent most of the morning roaming around an empty shop. Readers were not too keen to come out, and Brandie decided to stay away for a couple of days. As for Max, he simply said he had some business to take care of this morning, and that was that.

After a few hours, my broad-shouldered warlock enters the store like an ordinary man. No windstorm, no slamming the door against the wall —threatening to demolish it. Just a handsome man walking in—using the doorknob and all. He's carrying a small gray box that I recognize instantly; he bought treats from the bakery down the street.

"You're trying to get laid." I grab one of the sugary buns out of the box.

"Am I being too obvious? I haven't done this in a while."

"Tell me about it!" I let out, half screaming. We both laugh.

The happy sound is interrupted by the ring of the bell above my door. I wipe my mouth clean of the crumbs and remains of sugar. I stop dead in my tracks when I realize that two officers just walked into the bookstore. Chances are these guys won't buy the latest trendy read. And I don't sell donuts.

"Maximilian Forstthorn?" One officer shouts, rudely ignoring my presence—the one that looks like he *would* buy donuts if I had some. "You will have to come with us. We'd like to ask you a few questions."

My eyes widen as I look at the officers, then Max, then back at the officers.

"This must be a mistake," I nervously chuckle.

Why would the police need to talk to Max? With the chaos of late, my mind is swiftly drawing up scenarios. Scenarios I don't like. There's no way in hell Max is linked to any of this. It can't be.

"It's okay, Hannah," Max says softly.

"I'm coming with you," I shout, throwing my body in front of Max, my chest puffed—like I would ever impress anyone with my build.

"Hannah," Max's hand lands on my shoulder. I feel his thumb stroking me gently. "Go back to the mansion. I will meet you there shortly, okay?"

Not okay.

"No! This is ridiculous!" I turn to the two men in uniform. "What the hell is happening?"

"I'm sorry, are you Miss Forstthorn?" The larger cop inquires.

"Not yet," Max answers in a whisper, too close to my ear, before I can say anything.

Every bit of my body quivers at his words. His tone is sweet as caramel. My panties suddenly feel tighter. The heat rises around them.

Not yet.

"Then we can't share anything with you, miss. Mister Forstthorn, you will have to follow us. *Alone.*" The officer insists, his eyes narrowing on me.

I don't budge. Max grabs the side of my head with one hand and gently pulls it so I face him. He's looking down at me, locking his now-greenish eyes with mine. There's no panic in his fiery pupils. Whatever is happening, Max can't possibly be guilty of anything.

Aside from being incredibly hot when he hints at giving me his last name.

"Go home, my love. I will meet you there. Annie will be there if you need anything." He lets go of his gentle grip with a caress.

I watch the man I love framed by two officers—whom he could disintegrate with a snap of his fingers—walk out the door.

CHAPTER THIRTY-ONE

I find Annie cleaning the countertops in the kitchen. The sun is filtering through the glass wall, each ray breaking into the colors of the rainbow. The real world feels so far removed when I'm at the mansion.

Annie's calm spirit brings a kind of quiet peace to any room I've never truly felt before. Would it be too selfish to lock the damn doors and forget about the world? Max and I couldn't fuck, *sure*, but we could be with each other, grow vegetables, and never leave this house.

I suppose we could adopt Brandie and keep her safe. We'd only need to accept the line of men parading in and out of her room. That'd be too easy.

Annie is preparing fresh coffee that I assume is meant for me.

"How's your morning been, Annie?" I sigh.

"Quiet, Miss Hannah," she smiles at me.

I sit down at the kitchen table.

"You've heard, haven't you?" I ask her.

"Yes dear, I heard."

She doesn't seem worried that her employer just got escorted to the police station. Her trust in him runs deeper than I thought. What if they found out about his magic? What if he's somehow involved with the recent madness? Did I fall for a fucking criminal?

Annie's coffee must be magic, too, because it kicks my anxiety away after just one sip. I blink my eyes closed, and the mansion falls quiet around me. I embrace the sun, kissing my back. The chair feels more comfortable. When I reopened them, I found Annie glaring at me, her grandmotherly smile on. I swear she's glowing. A literal glow.

"Will you have coffee with me, please?" I beg, craving for her angelic company.

"I would love to miss Hannah."

"Just Hannah."

Annie recalls the first time she met me—*the actual first time*. She tells me how ecstatic Max was to introduce me, how I'm the first woman he ever brought here, the first woman who stayed with them. *The man sure kept that precious piece of information for himself.*

Annie was originally employed by Max's parents. She obviously stayed when they passed and took the role of, if not a mother, a grandmother.

It's everything my fairy tales have taught me. She's witnessed Max and Alice grow up, applauding at their every milestone. She tended to them from day one. There's no denying the love she feels for them both. I can tell she didn't care much for Max's parents, though. He *did* mention they were complicated people who didn't mind setting a few bridges on fire. But I don't know much more. Which leads me to believe Alice and Max were lucky to keep Annie in their lives.

I can't tell if Annie has magic in her, too. Her aura still appears to be glowing, but I didn't notice any tricks. She hasn't pulled any coins from behind my ear yet.

Annie knows a lot about the Forstthorn family and confirms my suspicions: Max's parents were rarely around, too busy chasing fame, money, and power. I can relate to that, to some degree, though my parents never did it maliciously.

I've seen a handful of other faces passing through and helping around the house. No one compares to Annie's role, though. She lives here, at the mansion, even though she can be so discreet you'd never guess.

"Have you written something yet?" Annie asks after a kind laugh triggered by a different topic.

"What do you mean?" My head tilts.

"Well, I know you want to write. Have you started?" Her voice is filled with genuine hope. Like she *believes* in me. My chest tightens. I'm surrounded by people who think I can—and should—write.

I smile down at my cup, trying to find the words Annie would like to hear when the front door opens. *Saved by the bell.* Annie nods with a small smile as if to say, 'Go get him.' I jump out of my chair and rush to the grand hall.

Max doesn't have a chance to say a word before I lock my arms behind his neck, the weight of my body fully hanging from it. I feel my eyes flooding, though no tear escapes. I guess I was more worried than I thought. Max chuckles, lazily grazing my back. One day, he'll squeeze me so hard I might break—but not today. Not with the curse still hovering over our heads.

"It's good to see you too, my love," he whispers through his teeth.

He grabs my face when I finally release him. "I guess I owe you an explanation, don't I?"

You think?

We sit in the living room, on the same side of the coffee table. This room has a way of holding quite the conversations. I brace myself. I think Max notices.

"You can relax. I didn't kill anyone," he jokes, trying to alleviate seriousness.

His fingers find the higher part of my thigh. "They found two suspects this morning, tightly roped together in an empty warehouse—bound and gagged." There's a mischievous spark in the fire of his eyes—pride, maybe?

"Let me guess," I interrupt, "One sexy wizard just happened to find the assholes."

Max laughs and nods, looking down at my body in the process.

"Well, did you give them a good beating at least?" I ask enthusiastically.

More chuckles.

"I might have," he winks. "But I didn't want anyone to know I found them. It appears the building across the warehouse had cameras. I didn't cast any concealing spells. I wanted to do this, you know, *old school.*" He says jokingly as he grabs the collar of his loose blouse and pulls on it gently. "The police wanted to know why I left an empty building, leaving two criminals behind."

"How in the world did you explain that?"

Max looks up at me, grinning like the devil. The dreamy kind. The kind of devil who means no *actual* harm.

"Of course. You snapped your fingers." I tap my forehead with the palm of my hand egregiously, obviously joking.

"It's actually a little more complex than snapping your fingers, you know," he purrs, leaning against me.

Max's lips naturally find the proximity of the arch of my neck again. I moan at the idea of his tongue finally gliding over my skin. To think I begged this man for a first date—that he kept dodging—not so long ago. Now, he's just a lick away from crawling inside my skin.

Max clears his throat while I lose myself in the dream of his body against mine and puts a little more distance between us. He grabs both my hands.

"There's more."

CHAPTER THIRTY-TWO

"Magic is more or less the mere control of energy. Magical folks manipulate the energy around you, around me, the one that lies between us. In all things," Max proceeds to put into simple words. "I suppose it doesn't describe its full glory, put this way, but it's not any less true." He pauses, a sense of pride flashing across his face. "When one casts a spell—in other words, moves energy around—one leaves... a mark, of sorts," he gestures at seemingly nothing.

"An energetic signature." I confidently say. *I read a lot.*

"Yes, exactly." His eyes narrow as he smirks; he's not surprised. "Well, you can picture that signature as a big *blob* of energy," he waves his hands, forming a round shape with his fingers, "It's strong, stagnant, magical energy. Nothing more than that. The problem is, the bigger the signature, the more it attracts *additional* energy around itself."

"I don't think I follow you," I admit.

Max's lips press together as he visibly thinks of a better way to paint the picture for me.

"The strongest energies are evil energies. The reason is that a lot goes into vice or into acting on it. When you are driven by anger, greed, or wickedness, your actions require much willpower. As you know, I've been using my magic quite a bit lately," Max chuckles. "Between the memory spell not only on you but the *whole* town as well, the location spells, and other incantations—like the enchanted letters—my magical signature is strong." He pauses. "Too strong."

His face turns grave. "Like I said, a powerful magical signature feeds on more energy. It's like they attract each other, keep one another alive, if you will. Power attracts power."

He doesn't need to finish. I can do that on my own.

"So your magical work attracted all these crimes to Willowbrook? Your energy pulled their evil in as a buffet would attract starving criminals?" I ask with a trembling voice.

"Yes, Hannah. What's happened is all my fault." He lets go of me and clasps his hands to his face.

Max's silence speaks volumes, a portrait of remorse etched into every line of his face. His shoulders slump with the weight of his guilt, the heaviness of his actions bearing down on him like a burden too heavy to bear.

I slap his arm. "It's not!" I take a grounding breath. "Maximilian, it's not. Plus, you caught the guys. It's done. You did the right thing. It's over now."

"People died because of me, Hannah." There's a rawness to his expression, a vulnerability laid bare.

"People died because there is evil in humans' hearts. You didn't do that."

I grab his wrists and pull them away from his face. The fire is blazing in the chimney. I can't tell whether it's been going this whole time or if it's just started. I think the fiery pit is trying to comfort its master.

I grab Max's sculpted chin to pull his head up. I want to see the golden spark in his eyes—all I see is more remorse and sorrow. He lets out a drawn-out breath.

"It's not over, Hannah. The guys I caught are not the only murderers. They *did* strike in Willowbrook, and I'm glad they're away. But there's more of them out there. The more I use my magic to fix this mess, the more evil I attract. I won't be able to stop this without creating more problems."

Defeat is something I haven't heard in Max's voice until now. After everything he's gone through ever since he was a boy, this is what takes him down?

My mind is a screaming cyclone, and guilt is the loudest voice. Its weight presses down on me like a leaden cloak, suffocating me with every breath. We've obviously made mistakes, and the consequences weigh heavily on my conscience.

I fidget nervously, my fingers tracing patterns on the fabric of my dress. There must be a way out of this. A win-win situation. We can't keep putting people at risk; that's out of the question. But we can't give up either. Not now. Not after everything.

"We need to reduce your energetic signature," I say, brainstorming.

"That would help," Max admits, though he doesn't sound convinced. "But that won't benefit us. Though I'm not sure what the priority is anymore."

I ignore the end of his sentence. Max has a good heart. He'd never want to hurt a damn fly.

"There must be a way," I whisper to nobody in particular as I stand up.

Pacing around the room might not help me organize my thoughts, but it does add a dramatic effect to the situation.

"What's leaving the biggest mark right now?" I ask, still pacing.

I know he's doing a lot behind that damn steel door. Something must be prevalent.

"It's hard to say for sure... but I would guess the memory spell I put on the whole town."

I look up and meet his eyes—already on me. There's a grin beautifully stretching across his face. He's pretty proud of that one.

I grab a throw pillow I didn't notice until now and do what the name says—*throw it at him*. I'm pretty sure the house has snuck the fluffy object within my reach on purpose. Smart.

Max doesn't dodge it. He simply extends an arm—showcasing bulging veins along his steel-strong forearm—without breaking eye contact and snatches the pillow mid-air, still grinning. His eyebrow hops when he effortlessly catches the pillow.

Gods, I want him.

"Well, let's lift it then, *smartass.*" That sounds like an obvious thing to do in order to get his energetic signature under control.

I already know the whole truth. Willowbrook can know, too. Max's smile reaches the side of his face, perking one of his eyebrows up. Let me guess, he thought of that one, too, didn't he?

"Okay... why not?" I continue, slightly frustrated. His amused expression told me he was about to throw my idea in the trash.

"Well, I can't just *lift* the spell. We would need to break it. The only way to do that is to tell the whole town the *entire* truth. Not just that you're madly in love with me," he teases me, playful mischief written all over his face, "But that I'm a warlock as well. Which...could create bigger problems."

He runs a hand in the dark field of his locks and leans back, sinking deeper into the couch. That would be complicated, indeed. I can do without the pitchforks and fires outside the mansion. Who knows who would want to burn us at the stake just for good measure?

I let out a big sigh. I'm running out of ideas. Max picks up on my frustration, but suddenly, his face lights up.

"We can't *break* the spell, but we can make it *lighter,*" he says with renewed excitement. Something tells me he hasn't thought of this detail until now.

"Continue..."

"The closer the person is to you, the stronger the spell has to be. We can't tell the whole town, but we could tell someone dear to you. Someone that you trust."

"Brandie!" I shout.

Of course.

"Bingo," Max beams.

CHAPTER THIRTY-THREE

When we decided to tell Brandie the truth, I thought *that* would be the most difficult part. Turns out the real challenge is to get hold of this damn woman. I know she's decided to disappear into Joffrey's sheets, but I thought she would catch a break to pick up her phone. Or some water. Or food.

Max and I thought we would invite her to the mansion for dinner. Annie offered to cook for us—we couldn't refuse. Anything I'd make wouldn't do justice to the story we had in store for Brandie. Talk about blowing her socks off. We couldn't possibly serve burnt chicken and over-salted beans for the occasion.

Flipping Brandie's world upside down was only the first step of the plan. We needed more to reduce Max's magical imprint and stop evil from swarming Willowbrook. Even if it slows down our research, we can't keep ignoring the grim consequences.

After a long conversation and some convincing—I might have used my low neckline for the latter—I told Max that the search would have to remain human only, starting now. No more location spells, no more enchanted letters. We can't take the risk of another murder or anyone getting hurt on our behalf. I will do the legwork using mainly the co-op. Max would assist as he sees fit.

"Is that going to get us anywhere?" he anxiously asked.

"Well, have you located anything yet?" I teased, playfully poking at his ego. "I don't think it can be worse than your spells. Are you even a real warlock?" I brushed my lips against his shoulder after I pulled his shirt down as an apology.

I wanted to sink my teeth in his warm skin, lick the red bite marks I'd leave, and coat his neck with the tip of my tongue. But I stopped at the soft barrier of his skin, leaving just enough space for the tiniest beam of light to shine through—if you looked closely enough, that is. Just enough space to keep the curse from ripping Alice and me apart.

I have a lot to accomplish, so I leave the mansion early. *Marguerite* is still closed. Brandie left a lovely hand-written note that she taped on her door. She framed her words with hand-drawn hearts and flowers. *Fitting.*

It's vague enough that people will know she's out but won't expect her to return too soon—it sounds exactly like her. Max and I don't know yet if our strategy will work or if the threats will die out, so it's best she stays away.

I drown in my inbox when I open it. I have a habit of subscribing to anything and everything I stumble upon online, resulting in an overwhelming influx of messages every day. I trained my eyes to swiftly scan every line and hone in on the important shit. A different name, a direct response—anything that looks official as opposed to marketing bullshit.

My learned skill strikes again. I notice an email sent from what seems to be a pseudonym. So far, I have received a handful of emails about the grimoire. Still, nothing promising—only excited members pledging to help as much as possible. This message is different.

"Call this number. Tell them what you are looking for." As suspected, the signature doesn't display a real name. My pulse speeds up, and the blood in my veins increases its speed of travel. A lead. We got a lead.

I snatch my phone to call Max first. As I unlock the device and search for Max's contact, a large hand lands on mine. Despite its velvety touch, I leap out of my seat and up, knocking my knee against the sturdy desk and stumbling over my own feet.

As I prepare for impact—the ground waiting to receive me—said hand grabs my arm. I instantly recognize the tight, slightly possessive grip—it says *you are mine*. His chest molds against the curve of my back. Max catches me before I go down. Usually, I'd be furious with anyone else. But it's *my* warlock.

Max materialized behind me so quietly that I never would have guessed.

"I'd say you almost gave me a heart attack, but let's face it, you were closer to gifting me a broken ankle." I don't free myself from his embrace, as dangerous as it may be.

"I would never let you fall, my love." His raspy voice is nothing but a breeze through his lips, a whisper from another world.

The words fall on me like a rain shower in the early spring. Somewhat unexpected yet entirely welcomed. *My love.*

"I suppose I don't need to explain what's happening?"

"I think I got it." He grins.

The sound of the phone call going through echoes across the bookshop as we settle down in the window nook. Max caresses my free hand as we wait–well, barely. After a few rings, a female voice answers.

I clear my throat and clumsily introduce myself. I'm evidently nervous. This is a big deal for us. Max shifts his fingers from my hand to my cheek, likely sensing the constant drumming of my heart.

I proceed to convey our situation to this literal stranger. Someone we're putting our full trust in. I skip the part about cohabitating with a magical—incredibly sexy—man.

Instead, I mention the co-op, the email from an unknown sender, and the unusual nature of the manuscript we're seeking. Jessie—we learned her name the second she picked up—*mhhs* a lot. She doesn't sound surprised by my random attempt to connect, though I can't tell whether she expected my call.

"One of my dear friends is a member of the co-op. He told me all about it. I think it's brilliant!" Her voice sounds genuinely enthusiastic. "I'm a professor at the University By The Sea. I studied folklore and esotericism my whole life. I teach about it now."

Max's eyes light up with a blend of excitement and approval.

Because her field of study examines hidden knowledge, including magical practices, divination, alchemy, and other kinds of mysticism,

Jessie sometimes comes across quite interesting texts—without knowing said texts might save a life.

"I have two different books in mind," her voice has a contemplative cadence. "I think they could be what you're looking for. I have copies in my office. Can I send you pictures when I get there?"

Max traps my hand in his. A warm, silky cage. His gaze, locked on me, reveals both hope and a sense of pride. Proud of *me*. It's the closest he's ever gotten to an answer.

"Would a picture do?" I whisper to him, covering the lower part of my phone.

Do magical waves travel through screens and stuff? I wouldn't know. Max nods.

"That would mean the world, Jessie!" I end the call swiftly, anxiously anticipating the pictures to come.

With too much ease, Max pulls me up, and his hands land on my buttcheeks as lightly as possible. My arms and legs find their natural place—locked around his neck and waist.

"I would take you right against this window if I could, Hannah Scotch." He snarls before lowering me back down, realizing the looming danger of this position. "Or maybe against this wall," he whispers, a grin slowly spreading across his mouth.

Max corners me against the wall between the entrance and the nook's gigantic window. I sense the cold, unyielding surface hit my back, offsetting the burning fire between my legs.

His left arm extends above my head, holding himself up against the wall. Bending down towards my face, he delicately slides the back of his fingers from the corner of my mouth down to my hips, his touch barely grazing my skin.

He makes a pit stop above my breasts, diligently following the shape of my v-neck shirt. I arch my back, eating the small distance between us. My breathing picks up. I wouldn't say no to a good fuck right here, right now.

"Am I interrupting something?" Brandie's jolly, amused voice sounds the end of the dangerous game my warlock and I are playing. "You could at least close the damn door," my fairy-like friend jokes as she walks past us—without a look in our direction—and through the store.

CHAPTER THIRTY-FOUR

"Where the hell have you been?" I throw in Brandie's direction, trying to divert the attention away from us.

"Oh, you know the answer to *that* question," she teases, pointing her index finger at me. "My phone died, though," she quickly clarifies as she sits at my desk.

"So this dude installs cameras and shit but doesn't have a phone charger?"

"You got me there. I didn't check my phone until we were done f... I mean...until I left. I was... *busy,* you see." Brandie's blue eyes now host a sinful spark.

"I believe this is my cue, ladies," Max chuckles, clapping his hands together. He feathers a soft kiss on my cheek and disappears.

"So, was *I* interrupting something?" Brandie looks up from her phone—that she's indeed charging using the cord taped to my desk.

I suppose I still haven't said a word to her about the all-consuming desire Max and I have for each other. With the speed at which each event has unfolded lately, I didn't think the desire for Max to be inside of me was a top topic to discuss. Though to Brandie, it would be.

"I was worried about you, idiot." I hiss.

"Oh, I can see that." She counters, her playful look on.

I join my friend across the shop. "Are you okay, though?" I whisper, genuinely inquiring, as I wrap my arms around her shoulders, squeezing her from behind.

She's been hiding in some bachelor's pad but must have heard about what happened. She reciprocates my hug, and we stay locked with one another for a while before she assures me she's doing just fine.

Oddly enough, she barely mentions the latest attacks—and by attacks, I mean murders—and we keep our conversation light, mainly focused on what Joffrey's bed would have to say if the damn thing could talk. It's precisely what we both needed.

"Speaking of having fun, I'd love for you to come have dinner with Max and me." I try to sound as detached as possible. I don't want her to hear the anticipation in my voice.

"Are we going to ignore the fact that you still haven't told me you guys are officially together?"

Shit.

Saving me from coming up with lame excuses, she quickly adds, "That sounds lovely, though. I'd love for Joffrey to tag along if that's okay?" Brandie side-eyes me.

Well, well, well. It appears the plaything isn't merely a plaything now, is he? I must have been wrong about Brandie's hierarchy. He must fall right under french fries.

In all honesty, it warms my heart. It must be the best news I've heard in a long time—after the phone call we just had with Jessie, of course.

"If you promise you two will behave," I slip in the middle of a laugh.

"You're one to talk," she raises her eyebrow in disbelief, throwing a pen she found on top of my desk, aiming dangerously well.

I spend the rest of the afternoon cleaning before I drive back to the mansion. Our efforts to keep Max's magic on the low have just started. We don't know how long it'll take for the attacks to stop—if at all—so I am still staying at the mansion. *For safety purposes, of course.* Regardless, Max never acted like I was to move back to my apartment—and I sure as hell won't be the one to bring it up.

I take my time between the tall stands, trailing a rag across the shelves and on every cover of every book. "It suits you, *honey bee*," Mom had said on the phone the day I signed the lease.

I had left the big city just a few weeks earlier and had yet to tell anyone what I was planning. I didn't want anyone to dissuade me from investing my lifetime savings into a project that seemed small-city-minded.

I was spending most of my money on meaningless late-night drinks anyway. I wonder when the next night out with the girls will be. Lately, no one has the guts to go out past sunset. Plus, it appears that both Brandie and I have been...well, *busy.*

I had been collecting used books for years when I opened The Book Nook. Most of the stack I started my dream business with was accumulating dust in my attic. Not because I didn't care, the gods know I did, but because I was living a very different life then. Immersed in the chaos of urban existence. Stuck in the mundane life of the bigger city.

I fucking hated it.

Back at the mansion, I'm greeted by a swinging chandelier and a happy cat trotting down the grand staircase. Arthur has been living his best life, embracing his inner diva. He took quite the liking over Annie —of course he did. I'm pretty sure he forgot who I even am.

The smell of dinner lingers in the air. I'm guessing roasted chicken. I hear the *cling* of dishes being moved around in the kitchen. Annie must be hard at work yet again. Max is already home. I pick out his voice amidst the kitchen noises.

As I make my way into the kitchen, I can't see Max's face—though I soon find out that a broad grin splits his face in two. He's hidden behind a relatively large box, wrapped in bright blue paper—I'm not sure I would have chosen this specific color. A big red bow neatly holds the wrapping in place.

"Did I miss the memo? Are we buying each other gifts now?" I play around.

"I saw you wander around the library the other night. I thought we could add a little something just for you in there."

The second floor—where my bedroom is—is home to most of the vacant bedrooms, but most importantly, the family's library. The treasure chest for literature spans from one corner of the mansion to the other. It's bigger than The Book Nook. Had I not poured an insane amount of love into my bookshop, I could have been slightly jealous.

Its walls are lined with a velvety, dark red tapestry. If it wasn't for the built-in shelves filled floor to ceiling with books of all sizes, I could have sworn the room was designed to be a sex room. On each side, sliding ladders are proof that someone, at some point, cared about this space.

Everything is now covered with a thick layer of dust, abandoned to the silence of passing time. Intricately carved wood moldings frame the windows. The polished hardwood floor reflects the gleam of small reading lights scattered around the room—though if it wasn't for me, they'd be permanently turned off.

"Oh, so you're spying on me after you abandon me in a lonely bedroom? You're an evil man." A grin tugs on my lips as I sit on Max's lap.

Annie cleared the room before I came in.

"From what I heard, your bed might not be empty much longer. I don't know if you are ready." Max purrs. His eyes narrow on my cleavage.

"Is *that* supposed to help me, then?" I point at the wrapped box as I allow my back to land on Max's chest. He chuckles and gently taps on my thighs.

"No. But hopefully, it will help you outside of the bedroom."

"Okay, now I'm too curious." I jump on my feet, clear of Max's feather embrace.

I tug at one of the trailing ends of the oversized, attention-grabbing bow, causing it to unravel and create space for my fingers to play with the wrapping paper. I hastily tear off one side and complete my messy task, leaving a scattered pool of torn wrapping pieces in its wake. I lift the box up and lay eyes on my gift.

"You are dating yourself with that one," I chuckle. "We covered that. In theory, you are as young as you look." I say to Max, attempting to conceal my emotion with sarcasm.

He slaps my ass in response. *Damn, I might need to be an asshole more often.*

The box uncovered a metallic black typewriter. It's quite large. Its keys bear no trace of any usage whatsoever, glowing. The metallic type-bars, poised to strike the paper with precision, hint at a mechanical dance that unfolds with every press.

It's perfect. Absolutely perfect. It unashamedly plays with my heartstrings. My chest aches a bit, knowing that such a masterpiece is wasted on someone like me, who's incapable of writing anything of worth.

"Why?" I turn back to my lover with wet eyes, encasing his face with my hands.

"Well, considering you won't use modern ways of writing, I thought this might inspire you."

"Is it enchanted?" I joke, "Did you make sure it writes *for* me? I don't write, Max."

"And yet, you should."

I sigh, smiling. I wish I could see what he sees in me.

CHAPTER THIRTY-FIVE

After dinner, I find myself sitting in front of the typewriter, just like Max intended all along. *Sneaky warlock*. I never thought watching a man carrying an ancient writer up the stairs would awaken such desire. Highly recommend it.

Max's bare arms tensed under the machine's weight as he ate the stairs one by one effortlessly, putting every vein in his arm on display. He then snapped his fingers—the only goal being to make fun of me—and all the dust in the library lifted at once, meeting in a dancing swirl that floated out the window.

The room is now spotless. The definition of perfection. Max presses on my shoulders for an instant before he whispers in my neck, "I'll leave you to it."

"Max, I won't..." He vanishes before I can finish.

The lights flicker in his wake, then return to their warm, stable hue after Max orders the ghosts to leave the room with him.

I'm all alone now.

I trail my fingers along the metallic keys. They feel soft under my touch. I start typing my name, hoping that Max enchanted the damn thing after all. I know we agreed—no more heavy magical work—but maybe he'd help me out here. Nothing more than what I type appears on the grainy paper. The click of the keys is comforting, but I wouldn't say it's inspiring. I'm a lost cause.

I stay still for a moment, looking around the book-filled room, keeping my fingers in position in case some lighting of inspiration strikes me right in the head. *Nothing.*

The soft vibration of my phone deep in my pocket startles me. Jessie's name appears on the screen, with a mention of several attachments. My heart drops. Breathing becomes difficult as my lungs feel like they're being squished by apprehension. The uninspired writing will have to wait. We received the pictures.

Max poured himself some whiskey, and the smell found me up the stairs. By the time I enter the living room, he's standing by the fireplace, looking into the flames, one arm up by on the mantle.

He knows. Damn magical intuition.

When he turns to face me, his eyes are filled with that neon green shade—the celestial hue I first saw at the conference. I can barely see the separation of his pupils within that pool of emeralds.

"Should we call Alice?" I ask, holding my phone up in front of my face. "She would want to be here to uncover this, don't you think?"

It suddenly hits me. I haven't seen Alice ever since the restaurant incident. Max barely mentioned her name since we started this twisted adventure. I assumed it was to keep her safe and as far as possible from the curse. Now, I'm not entirely sure anymore.

"I think we can proceed without her," he sounds vague, avoidant. That shit won't work with me. Not anymore.

"Where *is* Alice anyway?" I ask, defiant.

Max chuckles at my recently acquired attitude. I may or may not make a bigger deal than necessary out of this.

"She's staying in the big city," he offers as an answer.

"And?"

"She's staying with the Unearthly Witches."

My brows shoot up at the news. "That doesn't sound...*reassuring*," I attempt to joke.

"They're among the most feared covens in existence. They practice white magic, but together, and focused, their powers have more impact than mine. Thankfully, I have them on my good side." He chuckles.

It irritates the hell out of me.

"They're focused on Alice's protection at the moment," Max explains.

"What about their magical signature?"

"Covens work differently. Because they are separate sorcerers working together, their imprint is kept to a minimum. It won't save Alice from the curse but will delay it, making it less... *sensitive.*"

A gentle smile tugs at my lips. I'm genuinely relieved that Alice has found a safer place to stay for now. I'll never be able to erase the memory of how devastated she looked that night at the restaurant, her frosty eyes bloodshot from all the tears cascading in a continuous stream down her high cheekbones.

I can only imagine how terrifying it must have been to feel the danger of the curse slowly pouring over her again. Like a thick, sticky liquid you can't quite clean off. The creeping dread, the helplessness, the inescapable grip of dark magic.

"So you've got the witches on your good side, huh?" Pretending to be playful won't save me. Fires of jealousy chaw on my cheeks and spread to my forehead.

If witches look *anything* like Alice, I have something to worry about.

I walk across the room and stand only a few inches from Max's face. I try to conceal my bitterness. His eyes darken and lock with mine, his lips turning upward, slightly exposing his teeth. A deep growl escapes his throat. He *loves* it when I'm jealous. I feel his grip land on my lower back before he pulls me in and sighs—an order for his warm breath to brush my neck.

"I do," he says in his deep, raspy tone. "They owe me." He keeps whispering inside the shell of my ear.

I both love and hate this feeling. My guts twist and sink. I can't decide whether it's desire or the wish to *burn a witch or two.*

I intentionally break free from his light grip as I walk towards the door. Max yanks me back, spinning me so I face him. We're close again, right where we belong.

"Don't you walk away from me," he snarls with a playful grin, underlying dark golden eyes.

"Don't you have witches to entertain?" I snap back, half playing, half offended.

Max laughs as he brushes away a couple of strands of hair from my eyes, still holding my arm behind my back. "Hannah, no one. And I mean, *no one*, compares to you," he purrs, locking his gaze with mine, determined not to break it.

That'd be a good time to kiss. Or fuck. Or both. Which reminds me of the reason why I ran to him in the first place. *The pictures.*

We sit down on the leather couch and switch to my laptop.

"Okay, here we go," I say, emptying my lungs.

I'm slightly shaking. Max's knees bounce up and down frantically. I suppose even powerful warlocks get nervous.

"No matter what happens..." I try to say so low that my voice barely carries any sound at all.

"No matter what happens," Max confidently echoes as he feathers yet another wanna-be kiss on my hand.

The screen lights up, and Jessie's email pops up. The pictures are only a click away. I hover over them for a brief moment, not pressing down on the mouse just yet.

After a few more audible deep breaths, the images spread across the screen.

The seconds feel like hours. The house is doing this strange hold-its-breath-by-pulling-the-walls-up-even-straighter thing. The fire has stopped in the fireplace, vanishing entirely like a scared cat. Speaking of cats, Arthur is sitting by the door, looking at us with no particular expression, his tail waving in an S-shaped dance behind him. He's no help.

At first glance, both books are made of weathered, thick, dark leather. One shows intricate embossments, almost like arcane symbols, subtly imprinted on the cover in fine gold paper. Jessie took as many pictures as possible—one for each key aspect of the manuscripts—the drawings, the cover, and a few full pages. Both books are clearly hand-written, a rhythmic interplay of curves and angles that capture the essence of each word.

That must be a good sign, right?

My eyes hop from one picture to the other, both fast and lingering, to take it all in but miss no details. There are many hand-drawn symbols, intricate maps, and what appear to be sketches of herbs—perhaps ingredients?

This looks good. This looks *really* good.

Though I'm not entirely sure what we're searching for, that looks like a grimoire steeped in dark magic—precisely the kind that might help us fill the gap between my thighs, if ever there was such a thing.

Max remains silent. The screen's light reflects in his eyes. They're moving quickly, shifting from the color of the most frightful of nights to the brightest emeralds—that I wish to mine one day. I don't know what it means. He's motionless.

"So?" I shyly ask.

Do I even want to know?

My lover gets up without a word, releasing the hand he was still painfully squashing—but I wasn't going to say anything.

He glides towards the bar and pours himself a glass of the dark amber liquid he cherishes. With a wiggle of his fingers, a tiny swirling fog appears in his glass and turns into two perfectly cut, square ice cubes. His arm reaches to the right—putting his full muscles on display. He grabs another empty glass—a wine glass. I hear the bottle pop open, followed by the melody of the velvet elixir coating the glass.

We're celebrating. *Fuck*, we *are* celebrating!

CHAPTER THIRTY-SIX

I watch him finish up by the wet bar while I get my phone ready to call Jessie. We will have to arrange shipping as soon as possible. Unless Max wants to get the book himself. I would understand that. The University By The Sea would only be a short flight away.

Max walks back towards me, both glasses in hand. The smile on my face is about to make my cheeks cramp. I happily grab the wine.

"Well, my love," Max sings as he sits beside me. "It's *not* it."

The colors drain from my face. I feel my lunch creeping up my throat. That mise-en-scene is quite risky of Max, considering I'm holding a glass of the darkest liquid this world has seen.

The gods know how fucking hard it is to clean wine off furniture. So does my own couch. You can still see the faded yet slightly purple stain on the middle cushion from when the girls thought it would be a brilliant idea to pregame at my apartment like twenty-something-year-olds.

Max prepares to cheer, raising his glass in the air closer to mine.

"No!" I shout. "What do you mean, it's not it? It must be!"

"Hannah." He's calm. Composed. The complete opposite of me.

I clumsily snatch the laptop with one hand, balancing the full glass of wine with the other, ready to shove the pictures in Max's face again.

"Hannah, my love," he chuckles, gently pushing my laptop-loaded hand back down. "It's okay. It's not what we are looking for. That doesn't mean we won't find it. We're closer than we've ever been." He smiles at me, full of hope, while I'm battling disappointment tooth and nail.

I inhale deeply and let myself fall back on the couch, defeated.

"Fuck. Me." I say in one unapologetic breath. My voice is trembling, fueled by both rage and disappointment.

Max's grin grows larger at my words. His fingers lightly brush the tip of my chin—a breeze floating in the orbit of my face. I look up at the smirking hunter. His eyes changed colors; orange flames now in place of his pupils. His grin carries all the sins of the underworld. I feel the familiar tingling sensation expand between my thighs.

The lion is hunting, *again*. I'm his prey, *again*.

"That, I could do," he finally lets out in a low guttural growl.

Max stands up and walks towards the door. I follow suit. He turns around, and his tongue hits the roof of his mouth. "Tssk. Sit down."

"What the hell? Where are you going?"

"Sit, Hannah." He commands, pointing downward with his index finger.

The invisible chains that anchored me to the ground the night he ran after me come back out to play—much more demanding this time around. I notice the push against my chest and on top of my shoulders. Confused, I comply.

"Good girl," he purrs. "Now, get undressed," he adds after scanning my body with hungry eyes as he bites his bottom lip.

"What do you mean?"

Am I hearing this right?

"You heard me. When I come back, I want to find you in nothing but your underwear." He orders.

I feel the enthralling heat rise from the tiny spot between my legs up to my lower stomach, clinging to my skin like warm talons, climbing my body inch by inch.

"Max, I'm not wearing anything...You know." I tilt my head to the side with an embarrassed smile.

The taste of salt overwhelms my mouth. Strange, that hasn't happened in a while.

"Wait a second... What did you do?" I ask, busy clicking my tongue to fight the tangy taste off.

"Just think of what you'd want to wear first. Then get rid of these damn clothes. *Now Hannah.*"

I nod. I gave up on logic and senses a long time ago. Nothing makes sense anymore, and that's okay. I obey my warlock.

"Good girl." He repeats before disappearing through the hallway.

Think of what you would want to wear.

Well, *shit*. I haven't thought about what to wear in case anyone would rip my clothes off for a long, long time. Certainly not for someone who makes me feel the way Max does. Plus, we weren't supposed to be able to touch one another. I'm a hot mess; confused, excited, and a little scared too. This is so unexpected.

Would I want provocative, spiky black leather or delicate lace? What would Max want? I can't think. I need to make a decision fast.

I close my eyes and picture my body decorated with what I want to wear, as instructed. I opted for delicate red lace intricately knitted in the shape of small flowers barely covering my nipples. Keeping my eyes closed, I shift my focus to my bottom. I picture a red thong that connects two sheer triangles with nothing but a small cord-wide piece of fabric. That should do. The fresh blood color would compliment my skin tone. As for the pieces of fabric, they're large enough to cover just what's needed and leave the rest to Max's imagination.

I wonder if I should write it down or if I'll have to describe it to him. No time to ponder. Though I don't know what's happening, I know I should do as he says.

I start shedding layers, darting around the room to find a corner where I will be able to hide the comfy–but-not-sexy-at-all black bra and assorted panties—*very Hannah-like*. Max doesn't need a first-time peek at me like this.

My jaw drops as I pull my shirt up and above my shoulders. To my surprise, the exact replica of the set I envisioned seconds ago clings to me like a second skin. It's breathtaking, flawlessly mirroring every detail I had in mind. *I look damn hot.*

So *that* was what the salt was all about.

I throw my clothes in a ball and out of the way before eagerly finding my seat again. I lie down on the couch, holding my upper body up with one of the pillows that always seem to conveniently appear when I need them most. Placing it snugly under my arm, I draw one leg in, bending it over the other.

I run a quick hand through my fiery mane, hoping to add some volume to my hair—now gathered on one side of my face, overflowing along my shoulder and down my barely covered breasts.

Max's footsteps announce him before he appears in the doorframe, a black container cradled in his right hand. He's ditched the shirt but clings to those snug jeans. The faint glow inside the room hits him at the perfect angle, creating shadows along his powerful chest and arms that look like dark, deep valleys I am eager to get lost in. His eyes morph to a dark red glow when he lays them on my body.

Max moans and tilts his head backward as his gaze rakes every inch of me. His free hand clenches into a fist, drawn to his mouth, where he bites down.

"By the gods, Hannah, you're a sight."

He crosses his arms over his torso, clinging to the container. His shoulders perk up, looking even fuller this way. Leaning against the doorframe, he maintains his unwavering gaze, his eyes darkening as he traces his bottom lip with a slow, deliberate lick.

His perfectly defined curls spill on his forehead, framing his eyes. I want to lose myself in their thick field.

Max strolls towards the fireplace, where the fire decides to stay hidden. He gracefully leans down, supporting himself with one arm. Seizing the moment, I allow my gaze to wander over him. My eyes traverse his arms, down to his sturdy back—a sun-kissed landscape of sculpted definition. I never knew jeans could fit a man's ass so perfectly. But then again, Max is not just any man now, is he?

He murmurs something into the fire. I can't hear it clearly; some kind of gibberish. From the couch, I watch the fire return to life on his master's orders. Max reaches into the flame and grabs the glowing embers from the center with his bare hand. I let out a squeak. He chuckles in response.

"Are you worried yet, babygirl?" A grin lifts the corner of his mouth as he turns around after delicately placing glowing coal in the container. It's too easy to forget that this particular fire is magical and that the man who controls it has magical blood filling his veins.

If Max noticed my confusion, he completely ignored it.

"You look divine, Hannah. Did you like the spell?" he purrs, his gaze slowly exploring my body, lingering over the delicate lingerie covering the most precious parts of my body.

"It could come in handy," I shrug, teasing, as I gracefully stretch my top leg up, resting it on the backrest of the couch.

He's got full access to the inside of my thighs now, and he's reveling in the scenic tour. A guttural growl escapes him. I shoot back a cheeky grin—guess who's wearing the devil's crown now?

Max descends to the floor and on his knees, conveniently placed before me. I watch him wiggle his hands in my direction.

The familiar, invisible push takes over and manipulates my body like a rag doll. I chuckle at the possessive caress rearranging my legs and arms like a puzzle that needs solving. I surrender entirely and find myself sitting up, one leg on each side of Max's face, still kneeling before me.

The heat spreads across my body, leaving a tingling sensation in its wake. Max turns around and grabs a piece of the red ember from inside the bowl that magically keeps them all burning and active. *Damn warlock.*

As he surveys me with ferocity, Max carefully places the coal in his mouth, steadily holding it between his pearl-white teeth. I can't help but yelp again.

The ember pulses, its reddish shade preparing for battle. I gaze in confusion but am unable to contain a genuine laugh.

"I'm pretty sure that's straight from a movie," I joke, most likely laughing at the wrong moment. It almost feels like giggling at a funeral.

Unable to contain himself, Max spits out the dormant fire, joining in the laughter. That's why I love him.

"They use ice cubes, don't they?" I keep poking. I want to kiss his pretty face to apologize.

"Oh, it will burn just the same," he whispers with narrowed eyes and an evil sneer. One of his eyebrows arched up. "Are you done now? I have plans for you."

I take a deep breath. This is both exciting and terrifying. Nodding, my gaze shifts down to my enigmatic warlock.

Max pushes himself up above me, his extended arms framing my face. His profound gaze locks onto mine, embers skillfully stuck between his jaws. He consumes me with the entirety of his presence. He brings his face down to meet mine. We hover an inch apart, at best, before he touches my skin with the small piece of magical coal between his lips.

The piercing fire bites my mouth, forcing me to empty my lungs in one sharp exhale. The burn quickly turns to an enticing warmth, like a lick after a bite. My body tenses as I arch toward his chest, sensing the radiating warmth from his skin through my every pore.

"Is this going to hurt?" I ask.

"Do you trust me?" Max asks in return.

I nod.

"Good girl," he murmurs. I shut my eyes.

We're playing a dangerous game. This might just cost me my life. Alice is protected by the witches, but I'm just a defenseless dinner for the starved predator that's suspended above me. I fucking love it.

Max's breathing speeds up. I can feel its warm wind brushing my face. As if to complement it, the fire drops to my mouth again. I inhale deeply. Max now has complete control over me. My life is quite literally in his hands.

He leads the incandescent spark of warmth from one corner of my mouth to the other, synchronized with the rhythm of his deep growls. My whole body burns with desire—if that was ice instead, it would pool all over me before long.

The fiery sensation travels to my neck, tracing my collarbone to meet the summit of my shoulder and back. A deep moan bolts out of my body and through my mouth the second the ember meets my nipple. Max chuckles, satisfied. He swirls it around, slowly making its way to the other side.

"This will be my tongue before you know it. Can you feel me?"

I can't speak. I only mutter a guttural moan in response. *Fuck yes, I can feel him.* I've never wanted anyone more than I want him.

Another whirl around my nipples. My head sinks deeper into the leather couch as my chest collapses from evicting all the air it contains. I feel Max's soft curls caressing my skin, teaming up with the fire to work my body. The scent of cinnamon and lavender emanating from my warlock fills me. I breathe him all in with my next inhale.

Max continues his travels. My body is a playground to him, an unknown land he needs to explore—better yet, *own*. He's marking his territory without even *truly* touching me. Fear jolts down my spine, forming a strange alliance with beasty desire. One slip, one wrong move, and I'm a goner. This is the closest I've been to death—and to cum, all at once.

After a quick stop to befriend my belly button—which turns out to be quite erogenous—Max follows the border of my small but well-defined obliques, recreating the vee shape with his burning kiss.

He follows the vee south, aiming for my inner thighs. My lover halts for a second, snarling something inaudible. *I don't care*; there's no way I can focus. The burning feeling the coal leaves in its wake is the most incredible sensation I've ever experienced. I might have made fun of his idea, but it was genius. *Dire, but genius.*

When I come back to my senses, I finally hear what Max has been ordering me.

"Take this out of the way. *Now.*" He barks.

He wants me to pull the delicate red lace aside. Until now, he glided over the thin lingerie, which made me feel a little safer. As if my bra would create a tiny barrier of extra protection.

He's got different plans for my inner thighs.

"*Now*, Hannah," he repeats. I oblige.

Another moan escapes him as he glances at what my tiny thong is covering. I look down at Max. His eyes host the biggest fire I've seen in them yet. Hotter than the actual fire still between his teeth. He shakes his head a couple times, content.

"Good. Fucking. Girl."

Fuck me.

My breath catches in my throat when the top of his head moves closer to my body, bracing for the ember to gently bite my delicate skin. He doesn't head straight down; he takes the long way round. Swaving on top of my thigh, teasing me. He's toying with the prey he's about to devour like a cat would a mouse.

He ultimately finds his way to the small space between my legs. He brings the ember dangerously close to the bundle of nerves on the edge of my lower lips. After a prolonged growl, he gives in.

The smoldering spark of warmth bites my clit. Max swirls the glowing coal around without ever leaving the delicate spot. My hands grip the couch below me, my fingers digging deep into the leather as my head tilts all the way back.

I howl and push my hips up. My toes painfully curl on the polished wood of the coffee table—where I've been finding my balance. The fire doesn't burn. It's as soft as I imagine Max's tongue to be. I thrust my hips as he speeds up his mouth-play. I can't tell which is actually on fire, the ember or my feminine parts.

Time momentarily loses its grip as my body becomes a vessel of ecstasy, ready to reach climax. It feels like an ethereal dance between vulnerability and liberation. Max keeps pressing the ember against the tender spot, swirling and swaying it frantically.

I trap his beautiful face between my thighs, holding it there. All that separates his lips from my body is that tiny piece of coal. We're quite literally playing with fire.

A wave of warmth starts from my tiny core and radiates outward, my nerves stinging with a pleasurable current.

"Burn for me," my warlock demands of me in a whispery-ish scream.

My body turns to stone as it's reaching the edge. It's a cosmic release, a breathtaking plunge into a universe of bliss. Shakes take over my whole being. I scream—loudly, bent backward on the couch, legs pushing the table away. The room around me doesn't appear to be real anymore.

Fireworks of purple, and blue, and red sparkle around me. My vision gets blurry. The walls transform into a dark, starry canvas. I cum under Max's mastery. My pearl of pleasure is one gigantic blaze. My legs dissolve into a melty surrender.

I'm all his. There's nothing I can do about it. Nothing I would want to do about it.

When I finally find my bearings, I have flooded the couch. My legs build a prison of flesh around Max, unanimated. My arms feel entirely detached from my core. They're not strong enough to hold me back up just yet. I attempt to fill my lungs with renewed air, but they're not responding.

Max is sitting on the floor, his back resting against the coffee table. One of his legs extended in front of him, the other bent up so that his knee touches his chest. Shiny pearls cover his torso and forehead. No glowing coal in sight. His powerfully built arms are stretched along the edge of the small table. He's grinning up, his emerald eyes fixated on my face.

"What. The. Actual. Fuck." I manage to whisper—barely audibly.

"You're welcome, *babygirl*."

CHAPTER THIRTY-SEVEN

"That's an awful amount of work just to get laid, babe." Brandie jokes in a loud exhale as her eyebrows rise closer to her hairline.

Her blonde mane cascades freely down her shoulders and back. She didn't style it much today. It looks wild and free, just like her. If I wasn't walking the lush yards of the mansion with Brandie right now, I could have sworn she was a runaway bride about to elope to her secret lover on a beach somewhere. All thanks to that white dress she's wearing, held over her shoulder by a tiny cord. The flowy kind that hugs her body perfectly yet gives room for the summer breeze to run below the fabric and along her skin.

I dragged her outside through the expansive cobblestone terrace after the *nuclear bomb* we dropped on her and Joffrey at dinner just a few moments ago. Max and Joffrey stayed inside. We all agreed that Joffrey's memories needed to be erased. He can't know about Max just yet. Arrangements that are most likely happening right now.

Max assured me it'd be a small enough spell. His energetic signature shouldn't be affected much. Max was pouring two glasses of his finest, most cherished whiskey when I led Brandie through the glass doors. I assume it'd be his way of apologizing for messing with the man's brain.

I bump my shoulder into hers and gently push her to the side. "Tell me about it."

Our steps naturally follow the faded red stepping stones that lead us past the growing beds and through the fruit-bearing trees. Brandie looks around in awe. For a florist and true nature lover, Max's *kingdom* is the closest thing to heaven.

The yards extend beyond what our eyes can see. The line that delimits the large piece of land is not yet meeting the horizon. I'm yet to walk the entire length of the property.

As always, Annie delivered and cooked us the most wonderful food for the occasion. She delighted us with an appetizer composed of home-grown heirloom tomatoes, fresh mozzarella, and basil drizzled with balsamic reduction, each bite a burst of vibrant flavors. The main course featured perfectly grilled salmon and a medley of roasted vegetables that I know the wicker-hatted man I spotted the first day grew from seed.

Annie disappeared before I could adequately thank her. Her talent for staying discreet—if not literally invisible—is unmatched.

"Did you guys go right back to normal? When Max told you every-thing, I mean. Did you pick up where you left off?" Brandie's voice breaks the peaceful silence and carries a million questions as if trying to draw a picture with colors she didn't know the name of. Colors she'd never seen before.

"We kind of did. I don't know where we left off." I admit. "But it's like the walls around my heart crumbled simultaneously. Something shifted inside of me, and it all made sense. As if my body remembered all along and welcomed the flow of life back in." I pause, my gaze floating over our surroundings. "Does that make sense?"

Brandie chuckles, "It does. Our bodies remember more than we could ever know," she ends her sentence in a whisper. Something close to a realization flashes in her ocean eyes.

"I thought you were about to announce that you were pregnant," she says in her usual light and amused tone. And here I was, wondering if she could survive the news or if she would go insane.

"Where does your mind go?" I chuckle as I respond.

"So, what are you going to do now?" She finally asks more seriously, looking up at the full trees.

She stops and reaches for a perfectly ripe apple, its red and orange coat glossy in the sunlight. She takes a full, juicy bite. After wiping her mouth, she looks up at me, waiting for an answer.

"Well," I start. "We're searching. That's all we can do for now. We decided it was safer for Willowbrook to limit Max's magical work. Any heavy spell is out of the question. I'm using the co-op as much as I can. I spend my days making phone calls, leading nowhere. My emails didn't see much success either. Everyone is eager to help, but no one knows where to start." I sigh, looking at my feet.

"And try researching dark magic online... aside from thirst traps and hot cosplayers... you don't find much, let me tell you," I chuckle. "I just sound like the crazy lady who believes in dragons and unicorns."

The past few days have been eerily quiet, and I haven't found any new leads since Jessie. Keeping my promise to Max, I've scoured the depths of the internet, delving into questionable forums and various group chats. Despite how deranged it felt, I received a few pictures, but none Max could identify as the spellbook we're desperately searching for. I would have lost hope by now if it wasn't for him.

Max is keeping both of our spirits up. You'd never guess he's trying to free his sister and his lover from a lethal curse he put on them, all while trying to resist my advances. Sure, it'd be nice to have Max fill the gap between my legs. But what I truly need is to feel his arms around me. To embrace him *fully*. I don't want brushed air kisses on my hands. I want his tongue dancing with mine.

We have to make progress. Something inside of me is screaming. Screaming that the answer lies within the co-op, somewhere. That it *will* be the way to break the curse. And yet, here we are. With zero leads. Still very much cursed.

Maybe the answer doesn't lie within the co-op, after all. Maybe it's out there.

"What's next?" Brandie inquires about my search, forcing me to brainstorm a little harder.

I think for a second. "A list of the oldest libraries across the country and any accessible archives." I think out loud. "That sounds like a good place to keep the search going."

"How can I help?" Brandie's voice pulls me out of my thoughts and worries. "I mean, I would want it too. I get it. He's *damn* fine," she innocently laughs.

I can't stop the fire of jealousy burning my cheeks. I sometimes wonder why someone simple and common like me. Why not someone like Perfect Brandie? *No one compares to you.* Max's words revisit me and warm my heart, fighting the jealousy away.

"I'm not sure," I admit. "I just know I need to keep looking. And you barely even read." I joke, bumping my elbow against her ribs.

She squeaks and slaps my arm in return. We stay silent as we keep strolling around the greenery. I don't know if it is the magic in the air or the sheer beauty of the gardens, but I swear the birds don't just chirp here. They sing full songs. The trees are full of miniature talons gripping every branch.

The sun is descending past the horizon line, the evening air reaching the perfect temperature.

"I like that for you. You know that, right?" Brandie stops and pulls on my arm. Her eyes meet mine, genuine and loving. "He's good for you. You seem happy, babe. *Horny,* sure, but happy," she jokes, pretending to roll her eyes with a side grin. "I know it's your true heart that's guiding you. Not what's between your legs." Another chuckle.

My best friend has never seen me truly happy with a man, and I don't think anyone has. *I* haven't even seen myself happy with a man before. Her support feels like a staircase opened up, leading me straight to the clouds.

I smile back at her. She really is the greatest friend I've ever had and close to the greatest love I have ever known. Though I can't deny that Max has stolen first place on this one.

"So, tell me about Joffrey. I like him," I gently say as I force her to continue walking with me.

Brandie chuckles, and I notice her full cheeks turning pink. Joffrey strikes me as a simple man. Which is most needed for my extravagant friend. They seem to have found the perfect balance together. She likes crazy; he likes slow Sunday mornings—I'm just guessing. Joffrey was kind and patient at the bookshop when he installed my cameras.

"Well, I don't know," she shrugs her shoulders. "I like him. I didn't expect it. I wasn't looking, you know," she explains, waving a hand in front of her. "It was supposed to be a new...*hobby*." She jokes. "But I think it could go somewhere. He's a great man. I want to give it a shot." She ends in a whisper, more at the trees guarding the path around us than at me.

"That's when it seems to happen. When you least expect it," I say absentmindedly.

Our eyes meet in a side gaze, and we burst into laughter. Just look at us, two former night creatures who never truly believed in love, getting our asses handed to us. I was pretty set on growing old with Arthur on my lap, watching Brandie gracefully float from one relationship to another until one of us crazy ladies died.

"I like this version of us," I say and mean it.

"I need more of this delicious wine Max keeps pouring. Come on." Brandie drags me back to the mansion through the vast gardens.

CHAPTER THIRTY-EIGHT

We reach the side glass doors through which the last few sun rays creep in, bathing the dining room in a warm evening light. Both men are sitting at the table, empty dishes and multiple glasses spread in front of them. Max and I make eye contact. He nods. *It's done.* I squeeze Brandie's hand. She winks at me. We're all on the same page.

As Brandie and I join our respective lovers, the chandelier above our heads starts swinging. Their signature move. It's not as large and impressive as the one hanging from the grand hall's ceiling, but it's big enough to catch Brandie and Joffrey's attention.

Next thing we know, the doors leading to the living room slam shut and slowly reopen. So does every single one of the cabinet doors around us. A glass slides off the table and crashes on the floor.

I don't think the ghosts approved of the little trick Max played on Joffrey's mind—and they want it known.

"What now?" Brandie shouts, seemingly more annoyed than suspicious—or scared.

Max and I lock eyes, and I can't hold back my laughter.

"Ghosts," I say, shrugging my shoulders with my forearms bent, palms facing up.

I've grown so used to them and their little tricks that they no longer faze me.

"You've got to be kidding me," Brandie sighs, leaning back into her chair and throwing her hands in the air.

Joffrey remains silent, darting around the room, scanning every single one of us with killer focus. He's searching for either a reaction or an explanation. We can't give him any of those.

"Can you...?" I wiggle my fingers at Max with a smile.

"Sure can, my love."

A few wiggles later, Joffrey's gaze seems devoid of any thought—any life, for that matter—staring ahead. His mouth splits open before he shakes his head and blinks a few times as if he just woke up from a bad dream.

"My poor man," Brandie half-jokes.

We spend most of the evening eating and drinking together before we move to the terrace, safe from the ghosts' nightly show. The summer night is warm, the sky a perfectly transparent canvas for us to delight in the stars. The entire universe seems to be dancing above our heads.

Aside from our laughter and critters in the tall grass, the property falls completely quiet. The noises and horrors of Willowbrook can't reach us here. The lawn stretches in front of us and fades into the darkness. All the in-ground lights are on, making it look like a million candles have been lit just for us. It's grandiose.

I look around the table—where carcasses of empty glasses piled up —at my lover and at my friends. For a moment, I believe we can do this. Maybe we don't need to break the curse. Maybe we don't need to beat the Collector of Souls. We can stay just like that forever. We can live a simple life with the people we love. We can keep Alice and myself alive.

The thought of Alice makes my head tilt. I don't hear much about her. I know she must stay close to the witches at the coven to stay protected. But I thought she'd be more of the defiant type.

The hopeful feeling that grew in my chest a moment ago soon turns to an icy ache when I watch Brandie leave her chair and find Joffrey's lap. Her arm curves around his neck. She strikes his trimmed beard with her other hand.

Their eyes narrow on each other, and it's clear we have faded away from their reality. They look at each other with a hungry smile. Before long, their lips make one, and from the way Brandie's jaw is dancing, I know her tongue is *not* in her own mouth anymore.

Her fingers pet the side of Joffrey's face softly as the obvious passion slows down. She presses a soft kiss on his lips before releasing him from her sensual grip.

I'm reminded that I will never share such special moments with Max unless we break the damn curse. Dark magic can go fuck itself. We need to get this over with.

I find Max's gaze—already locked on me. A kind smile wrinkles the edge of his emerald eyes. We're both craving the same thing—each other. He reaches his arms in my direction, squeezing my hand. He might as well have squeezed my heart. His hand softly caresses mine as we gaze into each other's eyes for a moment longer.

Dear Collector, Hannah Scotch is coming for your twisted, cruel ass.

I've lost track of time. The night reaches its darkest point, telling me it's later than anticipated. Our laughs keep growing louder. No one noticed that after a while, Max no longer bothered to walk to the wine cave in the basement to retrieve the bottles; he'd just been waving his hand around to refill the already open bottle. But I got my eyes on you, desirable warlock.

Max regales us with the tales of his numerous trips around the world. My chest softens every time I notice he hasn't mentioned a woman other than Alice yet. *You were the first woman he'd ever brought here.* Annie's words resonate in my chest.

Something tells me young Max traveled a lot to stay clear from his parents' deadly wake—anything to protect Alice and build a different path for himself—one that follows the light.

Tonight, Brandie and Joffrey stay at the mansion. We couldn't possibly let them leave after the insane amount of alcohol that was consumed. A wide smile spread across my face when we all agree—it feels like a giant sleepover.

The only difference being the banging of the bed frame against the wall for at least an hour, punctuated by Brandie's moans and screams. You'd think the mansion was big enough to avoid this kind of... *sharing.*

Max prepares to leave my room as always—before we cross too

dangerous of a line—after he promises that my own screams will fill the mansion before long.

"You think you're *that* good, huh?" I tease, brushing his lips with my fingers.

"I *know* I'm that good," he snarls before the hallway eats his body up.

I don't even bother changing into my night clothes or cleaning up. I fall asleep in my clothes, above the covers.

CHAPTER THIRTY-NINE

The plane is crowded. The air is thick and humid, clinging to my skin like a wet blanket, making every breath feel like a struggle. It stinks like we mortals do when we get stuck in the same confined space for too long.

Miraculously, cinnamon and lavender always follow Max around as if trapped in a bubble. I lean in to inhale the pleasant smells as we fasten our seatbelts.

Max is close to being too tall to sit comfortably on this plane. His bent legs come up high—at an abnormal angle—as his knees press against the seat in front of him. I laugh as I gaze at my magnificent man; he looks like canned tuna.

Max begged me to allow him to open a portal for us instead of mingling with the sweaty crowd and wasting some precious hours. Though he strategically skimmed a craving hand along my body in the hopes I would agree, I stood my ground. No unnecessary spells until this mess is all over.

The past few days, I've strained away from the co-op focus, force-fully ignoring the feeling that's been tugging at my gut with sharp claws, telling me there was something to be found right in front of my nose. Instead, I spent more time researching different avenues online.

I again came across the *folklore and legends* field of study—very close to the one Jessie teaches at the University by the Sea. Considering meeting Jessie has been the closest we've been to finding the spellbook, I thought it'd be a good idea to keep looking in that direction.

Since I cut Max out from all magical work, he's been taking more of a backseat in the search. Though I must admit, I come up with ideas, and he helps with the legwork. He's seen as many late nights as I have.

Folklore and legends rang a familiar bell. It wasn't just because of Jessie or because of the many books I read in my spare time. It brought back memories of one of the sessions I attended at the *Words and Letters Conference*—the one about paganism. To think that I sat in a room where the speaker talked about witches when I was *quite literally* messing with a real one—unbeknownst to me. The irony.

I barely remember what the speaker looked like. From where I was sitting, I could only see his dark, slicked-back hair and the web of deep lines carving his forehead. What I do remember are his words about exploring magical practices within paganism, including spell work. I had no idea how valuable this would have been to me then.

Max and I ended up chatting with another professor—a big fan of legends and fairytales. Throughout our late-night conversations—mainly over emails—Professor Blackwell seemed to believe that the archives of the school he was teaching at might hold what we were looking for within its walls.

It seemed straight-up impossible that such a book was casually held within a school's library for anyone to see and use. But before I gave up on the idea, Professor Blackwell clarified that said archives had a forbidden section. A handful of texts and manuscripts were kept in a restricted area, where no student or unauthorized staff were allowed—only highly decorated teachers or researchers, whatever that means. Now, that made more sense to me.

Thankfully, the University was only a short flight away. Professor Blackwell excused himself and told us he wouldn't be able to meet us in person. But after hearing our story—the shareable version—he decided we were worthy of entering the restricted archives. He assured us that he left a note with the person in charge and that we could enter and look around.

This new discovery earned me another *glowing coal treatment* that night—the couch surely remembers as well as I do. I could have sworn I saw the fire in the chimney turn around and look away as Max worked my delighted, melting body with another piece of charcoal.

"So, how does it feel? When you know. You'll lay eyes on the spell-book and just...*know*. Right?" I casually ask Max as the flight attendant hands us our drinks, holding her cart with one hand while the plane navigates through turbulence.

"It's hard to explain, I'm afraid," he readjusts his legs to bring the tray table down. "It's like when you first saw me. *You just knew*." He smirks, side-eying me with mischievous pride all over his golden eyes.

"I thought you were a complete asshole when I first saw you, mister," I point out—which is hardly a lie.

Max chuckles, shaking his head in agreement.

"How does magic work, anyway? Could I learn?"

I guess I've never thought of this possibility before. Still, now that I've been around magic quite a bit and despite my occasional questions about it, curiosity is suddenly clawing at me.

"Our magic can't be taught." *Bummer.* "I could teach you to *feel* it, to recognize when a spell is cast or if a magical being is around. But without magical blood, you couldn't wield it." He says calmly, stuffing his pretty face with the over-salted peanuts we got handed. "Our magic is primarily elemental. Common witches—like Alice and me—wield all elements to some degree. Other creatures are more specialized." He continues, explaining between two bites.

So there are more *creatures?*

"Alice and I can practice the same kind of magic, for instance. Cast the same kind of spells. But each of our true strengths comes from different elements. My strongest magic lies in..."

"Fire." I interrupt him as a smirk carries the left corner of my mouth up.

That was an easy one. I watched Max's strange relationship with his fireplace unfold—no man cares more about his chimney than this guy. It's not healthy, I joke to myself.

"Let me guess," I mutter after a loud gulp, chugging my water down, "Alice's element is ice?"

Max chuckles. "Technically, it's water. But I'll accept ice because I love you." He purrs in my ears, and heat radiates throughout my body and down my spine.

Fuck. I wish there was a fire to use on this plane right now.

I bump his shoulder with mine. I suppose I could have thought my answer through. Ice came out so naturally. It's hard not to picture the ice queen when you dive into Alice's frosty blue, almost white eyes. Her hair so blonde it looks white. Ice was an honest mistake.

"I've never seen your true fire magic," I note. "Or how strong it is, for that matter." I tease, poking at his ego like I always do.

"There are a lot of *strong* things you haven't seen about me...yet."

The man can play. My body reacts more than I anticipated at the idea of how *strong* he is.

I can't shake off the nagging question of just how powerful the Forstthorns truly are. Alice exudes this undeniable aura; her mere presence commands fear, enough to send even the bravest souls quaking in their boots. I've felt it myself–it only took speaking to her for a minute. Her icy gaze alone could freeze the bravest creatures with just one glance. She exudes strength and emanates it from every pore.

But then there's Maximilian. *My Max.* With his fiery powers and his gentle heart. His hotness rivals the very flames he commands, yet there's a softness in his emerald-golden eyes, a tenderness in his smile that belies his formidable powers.

If his magic is as powerful as it sounds, he could fool anyone into thinking he's nothing more than a magician who performs at kids' birthday parties. Until he loses his shirt, that is. I swallow at the thought of his bare skin, illuminated by the flames he controls.

Fuck. We need to break this fucking curse.

CHAPTER FORTY

Max and I sit down on the cold steel chairs. The long bench-like row of chairs is bolted along the gray wall of the waiting area. It's not a room; it's more of a long, skinny hallway—the kind of underlit, uncomfortable one where you anticipate receiving some terrible news. We face countless windows, which would have been absolutely lovely were it not for the fact that said windows open up to the next building—a blend, faded brown wall clearly weathered by this town's constant rain and wind.

I look around, both underwhelmed and remarkably stressed. Max's hand finds my bouncing knee, and the gentle pressure stops the uncontrollable hopping. He smiles at me; my muscles ease into place. We endure the wait in complete silence—the place doesn't encourage giggles and fun.

Finally, a petite woman approaches us, fixated on the paper held delicately between her pale, slender fingers. Her hair, thin as paper, rushes down her back in a straight line, almost touching the back of her knees.

I half-expect her to trip on it at any moment. She doesn't. She glides toward us with soft steps so subtly that, had we not been focused on the black double door at the end of the corridor, we might not have noticed her presence at all.

Max and I stay seated until we are convinced she's here to get us. Her head doesn't move away from her piece of paper; only her eyes move up to meet mine behind the thin frame of her red glasses. She's yet another *blond-hair-blue-eyes* creature. I stand out with my fiery copper hair. Her eyes narrow on me, raking every inch. Until they slide to my right to meet Max's, where they soften immediately. *Of. Fucking. Course.*

"Professor Barlow..." I attempt to explain—she makes me nervous.

"I know." She eats the end of my sentence coldly. "He explained. This is unusual. We don't let just anybody in there." She whips her head towards the black door that's somehow less intimidating and more pleasant than this tiny piece of a woman.

"Oh, but we are not just anybody," Max purrs in her direction as he stands up.

Her eyes travel the distance between the ground and the top of his head as she takes in his full height. She's so tiny compared to him. Jealousy shows its ugly, furry hands and uses them to tighten my guts in multiple knots that will most likely remain here for the day. *Great.*

Without any more words, her eyes still locked on Max's perfect face, she turns to lead the way. I watch them walk side by side for a moment while I adjust my purse on my shoulder. I wish I could throw it right at the back of her head.

Max pushes the rubbery door open and holds it there for the little woman to walk past him. I might as well be on fire right now. If I could, I would burn this whole building to the ground, restricted archives included, and run away to start a new life in the jungle. Arthur might be upset, but he'll come around.

Past the double door, a new world opens up to us.

The difference between this room and the waiting hallway showcases a startling contrast. It makes me wonder if the coldness of the waiting area—which fits Blondie's attitude over here—is meant to deter people from entering this side of the school unless their lives depend on it. A little test of will, I suppose.

The walls are all wood—warm, coated wood adorned with a brilliant mix of mirrors and oil paintings. Small light fixtures in the shape of candles make the gloomy weather that peaks through the stained glass feel cozy and comfortable. I've always been more of a sunlight person, but this works—it works really well.

"You can review the manuscripts while in the restricted section, but nothing comes out. You can't borrow anything. Don't use outside light..." Blondie drones on about the rules of the restricted section, but I tuned her out a long time ago.

Her voice becomes background noise; it strikes all the wrong chords. Meanwhile, Max eats up her every word with a twisted smile, leaning casually against the wall by her side. The burning sensation humming under my skin intensifies.

What kind of game is he playing? I hear her giggle at something he said as I meander around the room.

My gaze turns upward, captivated by the intricate beauty painted across the ceiling. A stunning night sky unfolds, hand-painted in its entirety. In the center, a full moon peeks from behind a cloud, so realistic it could be mistaken for the real thing. I notice some contrast in texture scattered across the ceiling, adding to the realism of the scene. Genius.

"Questions?" Blondie throws in my direction, her voice as cold as ice.

I suppose she noticed that I didn't give a shit about what she had to say. I bet Max remembers every word, anyway. I shake my head, lifting my eyebrows. She scoffs in response. *Bitch.*

"Let me know if you need anything while you're in there," her tone turns to nectar as she faces Max again.

I should just leave right now.

The door closes heavily behind us, resonating in the small space that stretches before us. Upon entering, the air changes—it is denser and weighted with the scent of aged paper. Dim reading lights cast a warm glow, revealing rows of tall, sturdy bookshelves lining the walls.

A quick glance is enough to make out fifty manuscripts, at best. It's most likely a good sign—they keep only the rarest of rare things around here.

The worn but well-maintained wooden floor creaks softly underfoot as I navigate the narrow space. Dust particles dance in the air, caught in the occasional slant of sunlight that filters through the room's only window, high on the back wall. Below the window, a small reading table leans, serving as a crutch for the antique lamp that tries its best to cast a decent glow for rare visitors.

Max walks to my right, passing me with a brush of his fingers.

I hate him.

"So, do you plan on taking her out for dinner first or... what's the plan?" My tone cuts through the dense air like a knife.

My arms cross on my chest. Max doesn't pick up on the seriousness of my tone and chuckles softly as he turns to face me.

He clicks his tongue on the roof of his mouth as if he was tasting something new. "What's that in the air?" he whispers. "Jealousy?"

"Is this just a game to you? Am I just a way to free you so you can get laid?" I slap my sides with shaking hands, the smacking sound mirroring my trembling voice.

The rage building up in my guts fills my whole body to the brim and is now pooling out. Max slowly eats the short distance between us, the outlines of his imposing body blending with the shadows of the room.

"Oh, my love," his voice drips with sweetness.

His grin expands until he finally notices the real anger growing in my eyes. His head tilts to the side as he cups my face ever so gently. His playful smirk turns to a more genuine smile.

"We need her on our good side. I could never..." he shakes his head, guilt flashing in his eyes. "It *is* a game, Hannah," he pauses. "Towards *her*. She's nothing but a figurine to move around the board game. Hannah, if I hurt you, I apologize."

"I'm sorry, my love." Max mouths silently, his thumbs grazing my cheekbones as gently as he can. His soft touch slows down the drumming of my heart. My tensed body gives in as his words reach my ears. There's love in his eyes, and truth, and genuineness.

My hands find his, still bridging the void between my cheeks and neck. I run the top of my fingers on his forearms. A sigh of release escapes me, freeing the intensity I bottled up since we met Blondie. Fucking Blondie.

"Is that what you did to the witches, too?" I tease him now that I feel confident again.

He growls. "Wouldn't you like to know?" The words barely escape through his clenched teeth.

He looks deliciously menacing.

His body moves closer to mine. The freezing steel of the door bites into my back as Max pins me against it. His fingers wrap around my forearm—a cold, chaste enough move—to pull my arms up and hold them hostage against the hard surface. He leans in, the smell of cinnamon and lavender overwhelming me. I feel his velvety curls kiss my forehead. His breath intensifies.

Max is lodged between my hips, leveraging the small barrier that our clothes procure. The perfect position for me to feel the desirable bulge grow stronger below his jeans. I push my hips up, teasing, as I feel his length extend—more and more. And more.

His face suddenly lights up, shadows dancing along his features, sharpening the definition of his jaw and cheekbones. I look to my side to find the source of the new light, gasping. Max's hands—still holding mine in place—are on fire. *Actual* fire. It burns along his skin, following the edge of his fingers. The metal door reflects the brightness of the inferno kissing my skin through his. It doesn't burn. I'm enveloped by a soft warmth, barely stinging.

"What the..." I manage to mutter.

"You wanted to see fire magic, if I recall," he sensually whispers, his lips brushing my earlobe, "You're in for a treat, *babygirl*."

His head moves back up, and again, his eyes lock with mine with this familiar intensity that's both terrifying and exhilarating. Without moving, he whispers a few words that I don't comprehend, and I feel the bold, invisible force lift my skirt up to pull my underwear down to my knees, leaving me bare.

Max shuffles his body between my legs and forces me to spread them a little further.

"Good girl."

I don't need to look to know that the fire that's been contained in his hands is now traveling down my arms. The heat makes one with my skin, turning it into melted sugar. It finds its way over my shoulders and to my chest. My body shows no resistance. All doors are wide open for Max's fire to flood my whole being.

The flames sink under my clothes, and their teeth bite into my nipples. My throat rumbles with a deep moan. I sink my teeth deep inside my lips when the erogenous area sends waves of burning pleasure across the ocean of my body. I would have collapsed in delight if it had not been for Max's hands pinning my own against the door.

His jeans are rock hard, threatening to rip from the size of what they're trying to keep contained. *Unleash the beast already, by the gods.*

When I reopen my eyes, Max is grinning with satisfaction. If it didn't kill me, I would lean in for a kiss as the fire keeps working my breasts. The flames descend by my side, a soft caress along my thighs. It offers me a soft place to land as I still process the hedonism built on my nipples, like catching my breath after an intense run. Only I don't run. Ever.

"We don't have much time," he snarls. "You *will* burn for me."

There's no room for questioning in his voice. It's an order. No words come out of my mouth. I pant, biting my bottom lip, holding his glare as best I can.

The fire burns hotter against my sides, causing me to twitch. There's no room for me to move. There's no escape. I'm trapped under Max's muscular body, and I must take whatever he sends my way. He doesn't even blink. He stares right into my soul with a mix of uncontrollable desire and pleasure.

I'm all his.

The flames move faster. I feel them circling and swaving across my lower abdomen, playing with my belly button like a cat with wool. *He remembers.* He remembers this area is quite sensitive and easy to please. I scoff, swallowing the scream that's building up in my throat. We wouldn't want to alert Blondie now, would we?

"Burn." Max barks.

"Make me." A defiant smile grows as I slowly lick my upper lip.

Max growls. He likes a good challenge—though we both know this one is an easy win for him. There's nothing my body can resist. The fire digs deeper under my skin.

I can't keep my voice down any longer. Max notices. The familiar force that manipulates my body as if the latter had no secrets left to hide presses against my mouth, sealing my lips.

The burning light in Max's eyes contrasts with the darkness of the room, shielding us from the world. His body is nothing but a shadow hovering over me, controlling me.

His features—deliciously underlined by the light of the fire that's dangerously close to my inner thighs now—appear clearer than ever. I attempt to open my mouth, but I'm not yet free of the invisible grip. *For a good reason.*

Before I can protest, the piercing warmth eats the last inches between my legs and reaches its final destination. It caresses the edges at first. I suck in air, my eyes flying wide open when I realize it feels like Max's fingers penetrated me—only it's not.

The fire is delving in. A couple inches inside of me. Incredibly soft, yet fierce. The inferno slides up and down, teasing the sensitive area; then it's inside me again. I have no time to process or question the very reality of what is happening. Before I know it, the flames split to conquer. Some are dancing on the delicate bundle of nerves, some are inside me, claiming inches after inches. Back and forth. In and out.

The burning sensation increases as the fire speeds up, tapping, biting, slapping. I feel the pleasant aching build up deep in my core, ready to explode. I lose all connections to my muscles as the fire sends me over the edge.

I free my arms from Max's hold and grab the back of his head—his curls being the perfect support for my shaking body. His silk-encased springs slide between my fingers as I grip them tight and pull back.

My face finds the bent of his neck. I rush my tongue against his skin with all possible urgency, barely grazing the edge, before I pull away again, hitting the steel. *I know the rules of the curse.* The tangy taste of his sweat settles on my taste buds in a delicious, unexpected way. I need more. But I refrain from pushing my luck.

I hear his breath deepen, rippling against my shoulder blade. His body comes crashing against mine in a blink, pinning me against the unyielding door.

I'm all fucking his.

The fire keeps jumping on the erogenous center of my body until fireworks of euphoria paint the canvas of my senses, each burst leaving me breathless, caught in the dazzling spectacle of bliss. I'm in the midst of a cosmic collision of pleasure particles, creating a supernova that temporarily eclipses reality around me.

All I can feel or see is Max. I bite down on his shoulder, just long enough to get a glimpse of his taste, incapable of filling my lungs fully. My hands are closed in a fist, still full of his hair.

I sense the wetness built up between my legs drip along my legs as my breath slows down, coming back to what could almost be considered to be normal breaths.

Nothing compares to the orgasms Max has gifted me since we started playing this dangerous game. No man alive could come close— or has, for that matter—even while using their actual body. And that's just it.

As delightful as they are dire, our games always leave me craving more. I want to feel Max *entirely*. On me. Inside of me. All of him. It's like slapping an itch when you want to scratch it until your skin breaks. It helps...but temporarily.

The love we share is complicated. It demands more.

Max's chuckles pull me back into the dark room. My body slowly wakes from the cosmic dream he sent it on. I feel the warmth of my warlock grazing my skin, perfectly balancing the cold of the steel against my back. Another dance of Max's fingers later, my underwear magically found their rightful place. Though *rightful place* is debatable at this point.

"I love fire magic," I say in the wind of a breath. Chuckling.

"I know," he purrs, smiling so hard his mouth might rip.

He pushes off the door to build a safer distance between us. Slowly turning away to inspect the room, he runs his hand through his undisturbed hair—damn magic—and stops mid-motion. His arm flexes, each muscle accentuated by the dim light. I tear my gaze from the perfect man who just led me to climax with magical fire in a room where flames are very much proscribed. Bet even Blondie wouldn't look at him the same way after that.

"Should we look for what we came for?" My voice carries the hope and enthusiasm I've been trying to keep alive.

I slam my hands together, darting around the room. I have a good feeling about this place. I believe we've been led here, somehow—and not just to have some magical fire fuck my brains out.

"Oh. It's not here." Max turns around to face me—smiling, of all things.

CHAPTER FORTY-ONE

So much for keeping hope alive.

I open my mouth but shut it just as fast. Twice. I want to protest, but I already know it's a lost cause. Max would have felt the magic upon entering the archives or something like that. Asking him to double-check wouldn't lead us anywhere.

I release a heavy sigh. My vision blurs as my eyes well up with the waters of deception. I'm submerged in the suffocating tide of feeling utterly powerless.

Why did I think I could make a difference?

Max came to me. To *me*. I was supposed to lead the way, to crack the damn code. The plan was for me to find the damn pages.

The air suddenly feels even thicker, filling with the scent of shattered dreams. I witness the hope I diligently nurtured each day crumble with every misdirection, every false alarm. Another profound sigh escapes me.

Max cups my cheeks, his hand still warm from the fire he yielded just a minute ago. How does he keep smiling like that?

"We came all this way for nothing..." I whisper, my voice trembling.

There's a broken dream somewhere in those words, dancing with the idea of giving up. I might not be the answer after all.

"Well, I wouldn't say for *nothing*," Max's hunting grin reappears on his perfect lips as his golden eyes turn emerald green again.

I snort, slapping his shoulder. The grin transforms into a kind smile. I blink, swallowing the tears threatening to escape. Max's image becomes clear in my vision again. *He's the cure, always. The anchor.*

"I love you, Hannah Scotch," he whispers.

As if even possible, the silence in the archives grows stronger. His voice echoes against the rows of books standing sentinel against the walls.

"I love you, silly, *cursed* warlock."

"Let's get out of here."

It takes a few seconds for my eyes to adjust to the normal daylight shining beyond the archives door—where Max flooded my legs with the juice of my own pleasure.

Though defeated and disappointed, I'm overjoyed to leave this place. If only we didn't need to report to Blondie one more time. I could do without her wandering eyes and flirty tone.

Max and I stand in the heart of the room, waiting for the woman who pushes all the wrong buttons to come check on us—and release us. My eyes travel around the lovely wooden room one more time.

Something unusual catches my attention. *Blondie's feet.* Only her worn soles are straight up, facing me. Well, shit, that's not a good sign.

"Max," I whisper-shout as I grip his hand.

I turn to look at him. Concern flashes in his eyes. He's staring straight in front of him. His eyebrow furrowed, assessing the room.

"What is it, Max?"

Max's expression mirrors that of a wild animal sensing danger is near. If he had a cute little snout, it would sniff the air frantically. He grabs my hand and leads me towards Blondie, whose inert body lies on the wooden floor.

With a quick glance, I notice there's no blood, no sign of attack. The room isn't disturbed. Did she just pass out? I guess she couldn't take the heat of Mr. Golden Eyes over here after all.

Max leans down to his knees and brushes away her hair, tangled over her face. I gasp at the sight he uncovers, both confused and mortified.

There's no wound or sign of a struggle. Instead, a black mark shines on her forehead.

I get down to Max's level to have a closer look. It looks like someone used coal to trace the symbol on her forehead—except it's much shinier. At this angle, the material is glowing like a dark night sky full of stars. It's not just black, it's *center-of-the-universe* black. The darkest ink shade, yet seemingly alive. Glowing with the light of a million celestial bodies.

The mark, etched upon the skin, manifests as an ominous spiral, its contours blurred as if veiled by an eerie mist. From its sinuous twists emerge three dots, like droplets of viscous black liquid—or blood—each punctuating the design with a sense of foreboding. Beneath the spiral, a bold line extends, reminiscent of a path leading into the depths of hell itself.

Now, I despise the woman, but that doesn't mean I want her dead.

I reach, oddly attracted to the eery symbol, which seems to pulse with an otherworldly force. It's as if the very essence of malevolence had been seared into the flesh, leaving behind an indelible imprint of wickedness. Max stops me before I brush Blondie's forehead. Dread twists his pretty face.

"We need to go. Now." He barks. There's no room for questioning —is there ever?

"What's happening?" I ask anyway, hoping he can defuse the tension as his own panic finds its way to my guts.

Sometimes, I wish I wasn't so closely connected to Max, where his emotions become mine. An unspoken bond that opens up an emotional stream between us. He can't hide what he's feeling from me, and I from him.

Something is wrong. Really wrong. I can sense it.

Max doesn't bother answering. The lines on his face are harder than ever. He waves his arm in a wide circle motion, and what resembles a small tornado appears. Only the circular top faces us, its edges dancing with hues of iridescent blues and purples. It sparkles and glints and shines. It looks like a rippling pool of liquid light suspended in mid-air, its contained winds moving clockwise.

A portal.

We step through—well, Max roughly pulls me through as I feel my stomach climbing up my throat. One step later, we're back at the mansion. Nausea grips me. I stop to catch my breath before I cover the floor with what I had for lunch—which thankfully wasn't much. Max still grips my hand so tightly it might leave a mark.

He hastily leads me towards the stairs but changes course when he hears giggles from the kitchen. I can't see his eyes as he drags me along, but I can tell they're two black pits now. Their color reflects his feelings.

Annie is standing in the corner, busy with the coffeemaker, looking as lovely as always. The worries of the world never seem to reach her— her face always marked by the softness of peace and calm. The elderly lady spins on her heels with a broad smile as she pours coffee for—

"Alice!" Max shouts in horror. "What the hell are you doing here?"

"Nice to see you too, brother," she casually throws in his general direction, her voice like honey, unbothered.

Alice turns on her chair. She lifts one of her legs to cross it on top of the other. Her frosty eyes meet mine. My body freezes, but not out of fear—this time. I feel an odd sense of familiarity around her. My body remembers. My heart remembers. It's *just* Alice.

"Hello, Hannah, honey," her smile does all the talking. She's not that scary after all.

"You can't be here!" Max snarls, already pacing around the kitchen table, losing his fingers in the dark field crowning his head. "I can't protect you both. You have to go back. Now!" Anger drips from his voice. The plea in his tone isn't so much begging as it is commanding.

Alice scoffs, and her eyes find mine again as if to say, *don't worry about him.*

"He's..." Max attempts to explain, still marching around the kitchen.

"After us. I know. Do you think I didn't notice?" Alice finishes with one eyebrow arched.

Max's eyes fly wide open, and his mouth drops. The lines of his forehead grow deeper on his sun-kissed skin. He's noticeably thinking as fast as he can, drawing all kinds of scenarios in the storms of his mind as he walks in never-ending circles.

"What happened, Alice?" He asks.

"He knocked one of the witches out. I found his mark. The witches are pissed, by the way," Alice points her index finger at her brother as she tilts her head to the side, then takes a loud sip of her steaming coffee.

Whatever is happening seems to mess with Max's internal world, leaving Alice fairly indifferent. Or at the very least, unafraid.

"I pay them for a reason." Max scoffs, annoyed.

"Wait a second, you pay them?" I throw in the middle of the fight unfolding in front of me. A fight I don't quite understand. "I thought they *owed* you?" I half tease, half inquire, a side grin drawn on my lips.

Alice bursts out laughing, "*Owe* him? The witches are not keen to hand out favors, darling. I should know."

Valid point. She's a witch, after all.

"It doesn't matter how handsome my brother is," her still-pointed index finger now flies up and down, drawing her brother's height from a distance.

Max ignores her comment completely.

"You have to go back to the coven," he orders his sister as he finally stops pacing and sits at the table with us.

Annie comes around with more coffee for us both, still oddly quiet.

"I don't have the strength to protect you both," Max adds.

"I'm fine, Maximilian," Alice grabs his hands from across the table and squeezes. An incredible amount of respect and love shines through her icy gaze, directly aimed at her brother. "I just wanted to make sure you two were okay."

A timid smile lifts the corner of my warlock's mouth, and he breathes slowly and deeply.

"We found a librarian with the mark," he explains.

Alice's eyebrows raise in question.

"Long story..." Max continues, failing to stop the grin stretching his mouth upward at what I assume is the memory of what happened against the archives door.

They both say they found *the* mark. The spiral shape on Blondie's forehead? Does that mean one of the witches at the coven ended up with one, too? Confusion bubbles up in my stomach. I'm being left out of a critical conversation, and I have the feeling I might be one of the main puzzle pieces.

"Would one of you pretend to care enough to explain?" Unexpected frustration drips from my voice.

Both heads whip my way, seemingly forgetting I even existed. Annie faces away to make more coffee and gracefully dodges the explaining portion of the heated conversation. Still, her eyes shine in a way that tells me she knows what's going on.

So I *am* the only one who's left in the dark.

"I don't know if..." Max mumbles, hesitating.

"Ugh, for the Gods' sake, Maximilian!" Alice practically barks. "It's the Collector, Hannah," she blurts out matter-of-factly.

Max slaps her hand.

"What?" she shouts at her brother, emphasizing the last letter of the word. "Hannah deserves to know. She'll find out soon enough. And last time I checked, *you* got her into this mess, brother. Lying to her isn't going to get us out of it."

Ouch.

Her tone is as cold as her eyes—two ice picks going for the kill. I'm not sure whether that kind of comment was warranted, but then again, knowing Max's ways, who knows if he ever asked for her opinion when he made the pact? Chances are she never wanted it. She never wanted to be a central part of this. If it was to preserve her brother, I know Alice would have picked death.

I don't remember ever meeting someone as *straight to the point* as Alice. There's care somewhere in that tone, but it's buried under deep layers of facts. Facts that she knows I deserve to know if we want to stand a chance.

Grief settles in Max's face as he swallows his sister's words. He *technically* dragged me into this mess, though he had no idea he would when he made the pact. Or when he met me. Max just wanted to save Alice—which she now seems to remember as she extends her arm again and caresses Max's hand. I follow suit.

"The Collector of Souls?" I shyly ask, trying to divert our focus.

These two might nickname him *the Collector,* but I don't know the guy—the beast, the creature, whatever he is.

"Yes," Max gives in and gets to talking. "The mark left on the librarian is his. And it looks like one of the witches got marked too." he loosely waves his hand toward Alice.

If it wasn't for the fire magic I experienced back at the restricted archives, bitterness might have spoiled the moment, seeing that Max seems to care more about a stranger's fate than the fate of the witches protecting his sister.

"Are they...?" I whisper.

"Dead? No!" Alice rushes her words. I feel them strike the center of my chest with sweet relief.

We already have more weighing on our consciences than I can bear. I refuse to add another name to the death toll on our behalf.

"It's his way of toying with us," Max's tone is dry, his irises now glowing bright red. "He must have learned that we are seeking the spellbook. He must know that I'm trying to break the curse, to undo the pact that we've made." His clenched fist hits the table, rattling our coffee cups and silver spoons.

Anger suits him. It's hard to deny how hot he looks right now—despite the dire situation we find ourselves in. His features turn darker. I want to make them sweet again—with my tongue. *Focus, Hannah.*

Annie comes around the table and pours more steaming coffee for all three of us. She's remained incredibly silent throughout the whole argument. I watch her wrinkly, age-stained hand land on Max's.

"It will be alright, Maximilian," Annie whispers, patting him gently.

Her love noticeably envelops Max's body. I watch his shoulders sag as he leans in his chair with a newfound smile.

The old lady then turns to Alice.

"He is right, you know. You should make your way back to the coven, dear. You know how dangerous it is to have you both here." Her voice is as soft as a cloud but carries the determination of thunder. "Maximilian can't protect you both, dear." She's suggesting, yet demanding, that Alice return to the witches who protect her.

"Protect us *both*?" My pitch rises with the end of the question I've been asking myself since Max mentioned having to protect us both. "What do you mean?"

I meet Max's eyes, which suddenly shine with slight panic. They said too much. True to herself, Alice takes the lead.

"Well, magical protection works like a bodyguard gig," she chuckles. "You *can* do it yourself, but it will never be as efficient as having someone dedicated to it. Now, if you have a whole team working on your protection, well... *That's* the real deal." She winks at me. "Maximilian is obviously focused on your protection, which makes my presence here...a burden. The witches are powerful—and love my brother's fat checks—but they can't do much if I'm away."

Alice casually looks down at her coffee and stirs it. Without touching the hot liquid—only whipping her bony finger in a circle above the mug. Very *witchy* of her.

A massive boulder made of unspoken truths falls between us. I watch the strange, familiar phenomenon happen again—the walls stretch taller and flatter. My eyes narrow and I turn back to Max, carefully scanning every inch in between, as I lose myself in a cyclone of thoughts, processing the explanation Alice innocently offered.

Max sighs and grabs his face in his hands, his arms braced on the kitchen table. Alice's confusion proliferates across her porcelain face and reaches her icy eyeballs.

"You almost got me killed," I say in a short breath, barely carried over as a whisper.

"You almost got me killed, Maximilian!" I scream, connecting the dots in my head.

CHAPTER FORTY-TWO

"What?" Alice shouts back, her tone hesitating to make a true statement.

"Hannah..." Max reaches for my arm, but I dodge him.

"What do you mean?" Alice continues.

I take a grounding breath, trying to process what I just heard. *He's doing this for you, he's doing this for you,* I repeat in my head in a never-ending song, attempting to shove away the anger growing in my stomach.

"We agreed, Max. No more heavy magical work." I snarl through my teeth. "We agreed to slow down the attacks. You promised. You lied to me."

"I couldn't possibly leave you without any protection, Hannah. You can't ask me to do that." Max barks. His tone is defiant, mirroring the expression on his damn perfect face.

"And it almost cost me my life." I snap back. Two can play this game, and I'm good at it too.

"I would burn this whole city down and some before anything happens to you. Everyone in this damn town can die for all I care before I leave you defenseless, Hannah." My lover's voice is stern. He's not joking.

He's speaking in ragged breaths. His jaw ticks, and I notice an angry vein traverse his forehead. Damn, isn't he a sight for sore eyes.

No, I can't be distracted.

His secrets almost killed me. It could have been anyone in Willowbrook, too. We can't keep fucking hurting people.

"We agreed." I coldly repeat, looking away from my favorite golden emeralds.

All I want is to keep this city safe while we attempt to break the curse and save ourselves. No one deserves to get hurt—or to die—because we can't stay away from one another. That's just not fair.

"How impactful is the spell?" I inquire, still looking away.

"I'm channeling through other warlocks," Max says, getting straight to the point. No excuses in his tone. "Alice has an entire coven of witches working on her protection to make the curse...*bearable*. So you and I can even stand close to each other. None of this would even be possible without some kind of counter-spell or shield, Hannah. I needed the same for you. As Alice mentioned, I needed a team. Trustworthy warlocks are channeling their own magic through me."

"You are borrowing someone else's power?" Damn, that's a turn-on.

I mean, I want to be furious—for the lies, for deceiving me. But this display of protectiveness is quite attractive.

"Quite a few of them, yes. They're good men. I would do the same for them. I would do anything to protect you, and staying away from you is *not* an option. I'm doing this with you by my side or not doing it at all." Max keeps throwing facts at me while burying any kind of regrets deep, deep inside.

"But you lied to me." I snarl, reliving that one horrible night in my head.

"You need protection, Hannah. We could never be that close without it. I won't have it any other way." My warlock won't cave. There's still no remorse in his voice. If I wanted an apology, it's not happening tonight. "I will give everything I have to keep you away from the curse. I will risk everything if it means keeping you safe and close to me." He keeps murmuring in a settled tone. Repeating the same exact words over and over. Protection. No matter the cost. Protection. He doesn't blink, his gaze unmovable, seemingly oblivious to the fact that his own sister is sitting across from him.

"Okay, what the fuck are you two talking about?" said sister finally yells at us.

With closed eyes, I take a grounding breath as I recall what happened only a couple nights ago at The Book Nook...

Since we decided to stop any heavy magical work, hoping to reduce Max's magical imprint, Willowbrook's attacks had somewhat slowed down. Still, it wasn't where we wanted it to be just yet.

I was unaware of any protection spells or any other heavy spells that Max was still casting that would keep feeding his magical signature. I expected evil to leave Willowbrook alone soon. We were supposed to do the right thing.

That night, I was sending yet another wave of emails about our quest to co-op members. The warm summer night breeze that filtered through the open front door triggered the bell. I remember the dim light of the store bathing the place in a comforting glow. It felt so peaceful and safe, like it always does.

I had no idea what was about to happen.

I remember looking up at my giant clock when I realized it was getting quite late. I knew Max wouldn't be back at the mansion any time soon—he had some business to attempt somewhere. He was pretty secretive at times, but I never doubted him.

I got up and walked towards the front door, ready to lock it and exit through the back. As I attempted to shut the large door, I recall feeling resistance, and I watched fingers gripping the wood from the outside in. I was hoping for a co-op delivery, and my heart jumped out of my chest in excitement. This could have been it—the grimoire.

I reopened the door swiftly with a bright, excited smile, which quickly faltered away when I found myself facing the incredibly large frame of a man I couldn't recognize—even if I tried—considering his face was concealed with a black mask, resembling a ski mask.

I can still see the way his eyes reflected the light of the store in my memory, sending back a terrifyingly angry glare at me. I knew instantly. This was not a co-op delivery unless the delivery guys wore new, terrifying outfits.

I slammed the door in his face as hard as I could, but he held it in place with one hand. A knot in my throat grew so tight I could barely breathe. Thinking quickly, I attempted to run towards the back door—to hell with the bit of money I had made that day. He could have it all. I remember reaching the desk, briefly thinking of the books I would want to save if I could. Funny what truly matters to us in the end.

As I rushed towards the back door I knew was unlocked, I felt it. The weight of his massive hand slamming down on my shoulder, covering most of the space between my neck and my shoulder, like a steel hammer on my small frame.

A sharp breath escaped me. It was too late in the evening to even hope to alarm anyone. I instantly tried to wiggle my way out of his grip, but he was too strong. My breath cut short. I felt like I was suffocating in my very own haven.

My hands desperately grabbed the edge of the desk, pulling voraciously to escape, but there was nothing I could do. His hand moved, and I felt his arm snake across my neck, placing me in a headlock.

I threw my legs backward, kicking, hoping to hit a sensitive enough spot to loosen his grip on me, all while scratching his forearm.

I remember the way his skin felt when breaking under my nails. I drew blood, but nothing seemed to faze the monster behind me. I felt his large frame against my back; fear took hold of my guts, twisting and crushing. His body didn't seem muscular as much as it was massive— tall and large. He was way stronger than me; that much was clear.

"Stop it, you fucking cunt!" The guy barked at me as I had been fighting with everything I had to break free.

His sweaty hand found my mouth to keep me quiet. That's when I realized he was holding a large knife—large enough to eviscerate me in one cut. My eyes were burning, blurring my vision. I knew this place like the back of my hand, but I couldn't see anything familiar. I wanted to yell, to wake up the whole neighborhood, but his hand acted as a dam holding off the stream of my screams.

"I will fucking cut you!" he shouted. Anger guided his every move.

I harken back to the terrified feeling that prevented me from thinking logically. I just kept kicking and scratching. If I was going to die, I was going down swinging.

He hit my body against the desk in front of me in an attempt to stop me—to no avail.

Noticing that his last blow didn't land how he had hoped, he grabbed the back of my hair tightly and hit the desk again—with my face this time. The hard surface came crashing into my skull, and I heard a light cracking sound—was it my head or the wooden desk? My vision darkened at the edges when he pulled me back up by my hair.

"Are you fucking done now?"

I can still taste the blood I spat as a response—which didn't please him. He held me against his chest, still using his fist full of my hair as a lever. I felt the rise and fall of his ribcage fasten. He was furious. Tears streamed down my cheeks. The heat of the room was setting my skin aflame—and not the right kind.

I remember thinking how I was about to die in my very own bookish paradise.

My attacker's arm shifted, and the frigid blade pressed against my neck, its sharp point grazing my skin and contorting it almost to the breaking point. I held my breath. My body trembled in terror. My legs were giving in—from fear, from the blow against the desk, from rage. One wrong move and the blade would perforate my skin straight through my throat.

The monster chuckled in my ear, a disgusting, greedy laugh. His headlock closed tighter around my windpipe, preventing any air from coming in or out, as he kept pushing the knife against the thin layer of skin covering my throat. I felt the sting like a nuclear explosion. The blade cut me.

I felt the thick, slow descent of my own blood along my neck, down my chest. I recall the sound of his laugh as it grew louder—along with the sickness in it. He was about to murder me for no other reason than the evil in his heart. I was just at the wrong place at the wrong time.

That's when I heard it.

The front door slammed against the wall, followed by the sound of pieces of concrete crashing onto the hardwood. The door smashed against the wall so hard it put a hole in it. For a moment, I thought the large man expected some extra hands. But the scent of cinnamon and lavender filled the place quickly, laying a soft kiss on my nose.

I started crying so hard that I howled.

Max had arrived.

My attacker lifted my body a few inches above the ground, still holding me by the throat, and spun to face the entrance. My blurry vision had cleared just enough to meet Max's eyes. Two ink-dark pits where a gigantic, menacing fire was not burning... it was *raging*.

I attempted to let out a deep sigh, but the man's arm was still sealing my airways shut—until he saw the scene unfolding in front of us and let go of me.

I collapsed onto the floor, my body in a slumber, filling my lungs as quickly as they could take it. I could breathe again. My windpipe burnt, blood streamed down the front of my neck, but I could breathe again.

I looked up at my warlock. Max's body turned to a dark shadow hovering above the ground. Though dark as night, his muscular arms displayed strong, veiny muscles. They were extended down by his sides, his fists clenched tight. His jaw, though I couldn't find the defined lines of his face, was noticeably tight. His lips pressed against each other in a menacing line. Max's eyes never met mine. The blazing fires were locked on my aggressor—standing behind me.

A trail of fire followed Max's steps. Dancing flames of purple and red followed their master inside the store. I vividly remember how quickly the fire had spread around us. The flames crawled along the floor towards us and climbed up the walls, circling us until there was nowhere else to go but to face Max's fury. The heat was unbearable, yet I was able to breathe just fine now that my warlock was here.

Max's body extended into an inky cloud of shadows, stretching along the walls and enveloping the entire store. None of us could see past the veil Max had cast over us. The clouds were menacing, sheltering the most terrifying of storms. Sinister shadows were twisting and dancing amidst thunder and lightning. The air quickly felt denser, charged with an eerie energy I had never witnessed before.

It was all too loud and all too quiet.

Before Max locked us in the dark gloom, a quick glance through the front window confirmed what I assumed already; the fire he had wielded wasn't contained in the bookstore. It had spread across the street and to the surrounding stores. His anger was such that even he couldn't control his fire.

"What the fuck is that?!" the monster shouted, his voice trying to conceal the sheer fear gripping him by the balls. His tiny, miserable balls.

I chuckled. He kicked me in the chest in response. *What a mistake.*

Thunder cracked across the clouds and hit the ground in front of us. The robber jumped. Max's eyes turned glowing red. No fire to be seen anymore—only a glowing energy that screamed *I will destroy you.* Max took one step closer to us, then another. Calculated movements. Locked on his target.

"That? That's my man," I whispered, spitting more blood on the floor as I finally gathered enough force to pull myself up and run to Max.

I crashed into his chest—a black canvas fading into the clouds around us—and encircled his shoulders with my arms. My chest lifted with the fullest breath I had taken yet, crying and shaking. His arms never met my back. He kept them menacingly extended along his sides. I heard his breath deepen as he felt my skin meet his.

"Are you hurt?" Max asked, his voice matching a peal of thunder above us.

"Only a little," I attempted to joke, still clung to my warlock, ignoring the fact that the massive man who'd hit my face against the wooden desk and nearly cut my throat open was still shaking behind me.

I finally pulled away from Max and cupped his face—or where his face was supposed to be. His skin had turned as dark as the storm he created. He looked down and noticed the blood dripping from my throat. The stinging had started to fade already; I wasn't worried about it. But Max was.

His eyes scanned the area where the cut was, and I saw an actual explosion in his eyeballs. He growled. A deep, guttural, terrifying growl. He pushed me to the side. I didn't fight it.

Max started eating the distance between him and my aggressor. Flames raged higher around us, the fire turned redder, and the heat rose at a dangerous rate. Pearls of sweat from either the heat or the fear—or both—shone on the fat guy's forehead, dripping on my beloved floor.

Max raised his arm towards the robber and a flash of fire shot out of his palm, aiming for the large man—who squealed. The fiery rope tightened around his fat neck before the robber could process what was happening.

The knot closed tighter as the robber gripped the ablaze rope with both hands, trying to free himself. There was no escape. He begged for air, taking short, loud breaths, coughing. His eyes turned red, but not from any fire inside them—*no.* From a very mortal reaction—blood. *Death.*

His bloodshot eyes met mine. I saw despair spread across his face as I watched him painfully die. Max was killing him.

Wait.

Max was *killing* him.

That's when I snapped back to reality. I truly saw the blood filling the man's eyes. I saw the fire around his neck, turning his skin to coal. His charred hands begged for relief as they displayed more and more burnt flesh.

This guy was a monster, and he deserved every second of the torture Max was serving him—but we were not. *We're not monsters.*

Panicked, I grabbed Max's shoulder. "You have to stop this," I begged him. "You have to let him go."

"He hurt you." Max's eyes never left his target. His arm was still stretched towards the man as his fingers ordered the rope to close tighter.

"He's a monster. You're not." I said in a mere breath, clinging to Max's arm. My gaze locked in, fixed on the dying man.

"Please." I implored.

"I will destroy anyone who hurts you, Hannah." Max's voice carried the heaviness of grief. There was no stopping him.

"Then do it for me, Maximilian. I'm begging you."

"This happened because there's evil in their heart, remember?" Max used my own words against me.

Evil was a weed that needed to be burnt down to its roots so it couldn't spread any longer. Max was the weedkiller. He had *one* mission.

"But not in yours," I breathed, reaching for his chest. The palm of my hand found his beating machine. I left it there for a moment, stroking his blazing skin with my thumb. "Not. In. Yours."

The robber was still choking behind us, wet gurgling sounds escaping through his clenched teeth, walking the edge of death. Max had pulled him above the floor. I watched as his legs kicked aimlessly in the air. Maybe he deserved to die; perhaps he couldn't be saved. But I wouldn't be the one to sentence him.

"I love you," I whispered. "I love your heart the way it is now. It will never be the same if you kill him." I continued, stroking Max's chest.

Max finally blinked at my words, his eyes flooding with thick tears. I was getting through to him. His darkened face softened. His fingers followed suit, not letting go of the fire rope completely, but enough for the asshole to take a deep breath. The fat coward mustered a few swears we couldn't understand. It wasn't about him, anyway.

Max's arm finally let go completely. He grabbed my face and tilted my head up. The inferno in his eyes had settled. He softly caressed my cheeks, following the edge of my jaw to my chin.

"I love you, Hannah," the words tiptoed from his lips to mine. "I will burn alive any man who ever touches you and watch his flesh turn to char, patiently. Do you understand me?"

"I definitely do now," I joked, gesturing at the chaos only he could control around us.

My lover chuckled, looking down at his feet. He seemed to get back to his senses, inspiring large amounts of hot air. Slowly, the veil of clouds and thunder lifted. The fire around us sighed its final breath. The temperature crept back to normal.

The robber had pissed his pants. This guy truly was a fucking loser.

"What do you wish to do with him?" Max asked, as if secretly hoping I would want to stab the man myself.

I didn't. We roped him up—well, Max did. I wasn't going near this literal piece of trash—and we called the cops.

When the police arrived, the man shouted all kinds of outlandish accusations at us—at least none that made any sense in the eyes of mere mortals, oblivious that one of the most powerful warlocks in existence was standing in the room with them.

The piss-smelling man sounded insane. Exactly the way we were hoping he would.

Max and I simply told the authorities that we found him in The Book Nook, attempting to steal money, but completely delusional—and left the rest up to them. A wiggle of Max's fingers later, the cops nodded as if this was a normal situation.

What they did with him is a mystery.

"Oh, honey." Alice's tone is wet, bringing me back into the kitchen and the present moment. I blink and lay eyes on her. She swallows the tears building up in her icy-blue eyes. I see her throat bulge. I didn't think she could be sentimental, yet here we are.

Another heavy silence invades the room. I'm torn between anger and gratitude, both tugging at my arms in opposite directions, threatening to dislodge them.

Max *did* save my life that night. His magic attracted the asshole in the first place, sure. But then again, his magic was to protect me from the curse. To allow us to be near.

We all look down at our hands, carefully placed on the kitchen table. No one knows what to say. *Talk about a vibe killer.*

"You have more important matters to attend to, children. Hannah is safe; that's all that matters." Annie breaks the ice after clearing her throat.

She's right. Max did everything he could to protect us both, Alice and me.

I nod, grazing Max's hand as I firmly grip Alice's with my other hand. "So, what do we do now?" I ask.

CHAPTER FORTY-THREE

"Absolutely not, Maximilian!" Alice shouts, shaking her head rapidly from left to right. You can't do it without me, and *me* says no." Her words are grave, final. She won't budge.

"He's taken souls, Alice," Max barks back, mirroring his sister's tone.

Max is referring to Blondie and the witch. I side with Alice on that one; to hell with the flirty blond. Alice scoffs and shrugs her shoulders. She couldn't care less—which steals a barely hidden smirk from me.

"He'll bring them back once he's done playing. Leave. It. Be." She emphasizes every syllable, and I swear I see actual ice spread over her pupils.

After a lingering, warm stare that I believe was a promise of an upcoming, true apology to me—for the robber, for the lies, for everything—Max had made up his mind. He now wants to confront The Collector in person.

"You're the only one who can open the gate, Alice," Max pleads.

The foul creature lives in its own realm, which needs an opening to be accessed. A rip in the fabric between our universes, like a door of sorts.

"It's a mere game to him, Maximilian. Let him have his fun," Alice advises, throwing her hand above her shoulder.

Though her face is nothing but a mask of calm, the frozen glare she casts over her sibling says it all. She won't open the gate to The Collector's realm, even if she is his only option. A fact that suddenly hits me.

"Wait, why can't you open the gate to his realm?" I ask Max, gesturing in his direction.

"Only the ones who were willingly invited to his realm can now open a gateway," Alice answers in place of her brother. There's undeniable pride in her tone. "There's only a handful of us still alive. If you can picture a hand that has lost a couple of fingers, that is," she winks.

"So, you were *invited*?" I say to her with a smirk, my eyebrows jumping up and down, unsure if my playfulness suits the situation.

Alice waves me off, her expression the complete opposite of mine. "It's a long story," she whispers.

"For another time," Max interrupts in a bark. "Alice, listen to me. I can convince him to let us go." Max slams his open palms on the table.

Coffee spills and pools around our cups, threatening to stream off the table and onto the floor.

Max's tone lacks his usual confidence. He wants to believe there's a true chance the monster will free us. I see it in the way his jaw ticks and his lips are pressed thin, focused. But his green eyes betray my warlock. There's no emotion he can hide from me. There's a small amount of doubt in there—maybe even fear.

"Is this The Collector's way of summoning us? Maybe he's expecting us, Alice?" I offer as an attempt to support Max's demand.

Alice scoffs yet again.

"The Collector doesn't waste time summoning people, honey. If he wished to see us, we'd be pulled into his realm with a snap of his fingers," Alice explains.

"I'm telling you, he's worried, Alice. He's trying to scare us away from our goal. Two can play this game," Max insists.

Alice only arched an amused brow as she side-eyes her brother. Sounds like the monster is not easily scared. Even if The Collector feels we are getting closer to breaking the curse. Even if he found out what we were seeking.

"Plus, you seem to forget one little detail, brother," Alice mutters, taking another sip of her coffee, which surely has gone cold by now.

Max rolls his eyes at his sister and leans back into his chair, crossing his strong arms on his chest—noticeably annoyed by her know-it-all attitude. "Oh please, enlighten me, dear sister."

"He controls the game. He doesn't just play it. I will tell you one more time, Maximilian. Leave it alone."

CHAPTER FORTY-FOUR

The air feels denser here, thicker, even though the land unfolding in front of us is one of a dream. The sunlight streams down to the full trees, over the green rolling hills, and over our shoulders, scorching our skins. The sky is a perfectly blue, cloudless canvas. Strangely, there's no sun. Where the beautiful golden light that mimics the celestial body comes from, I couldn't tell.

Alice's portals look very different from her brother's. The colors dancing at the edge of the phenomenon snow-white and icy blue. It all makes sense, of course.

I wasn't privy to what Max whispered in his sister's ear to convince her to open the door to The Collector's world. All I saw was her frosty eyes filled with tears they couldn't contain long. Her face dropped, soothing the anger anchoring to her porcelain skin.

She sighed deeply and rose from her chair, ordering us to get ready.

Despite Max's insistent plea for me to stay at the mansion, away from danger and more potent magic, I followed them. He couldn't come up with a good enough reason for me to stay behind. Danger isn't good enough. I'm already knee-deep in this mess.

I don't feel nauseous this time around. I can't tell if it's because this is my second time traveling via a portal, or because Alice cast it. Who knows, the ice queen might be gentle, after all.

I don't know what to expect other than a foul monster lurking somewhere in this mysterious realm—the very monster preventing me from loving the man walking beside me with every fiber of my being, with everything my heart and body have to offer.

"Don't trust any words coming out of his mouth," Max had shared with me before we departed the mansion.

And that's not much to go on.

I know evil resides in this very land, yet it doesn't feel threatening. The beauty of the scenery around us is overwhelming. The various shades of green and purple perfectly marry the light gray and pink of mossy boulders. If I had to write about an enchanted forest on this type-writer of mine, this would be it.

Though richly green and red, the leaves are adorned with a delicate, golden iridescence, casting a warm, magical glow over the entire forest. The fake sunlight—or whatever the hell it is—draws patterns of shim-mering gold on the forest floor that remind me of my lover's golden eyes.

Amidst the rugged landscape reaching the horizon, hidden deep within the heart of an untouched wilderness, ancient towering rocks stand as guardians, their surfaces covered with mosses and lichens.

Cascading from a cleft between these mammoth rocks, a waterfall of literal liquid gold dances in the ethereal glow of phantom sunlight filtering through the dense canopy that stretches its green finger all the way to our feet. Each droplet sparkles like a piece of treasure, leaving me wondering what gold would taste like. If only I could coat my tongue with it, run it below the glowing steam, and bathe my naked body in the shiny water. It seems as though the very earth has opened its veins, releasing a precious elixir that paints the air with a radiant shimmer.

The air is alive with the heavy scent of exotic blooms, their fragrance a tantalizing blend of sweetness and spice that hangs heavy on the breeze. Each inhalation fills my lungs with exhilaration as if I'm breathing in the very essence of magic itself.

To our left, a meandering river winds its way through the landscape, its waters sparkling as they cascade over multicolor rocks. Along its banks, clusters of willow trees dip their branches into the water, their leaves trailing in the current like delicate fingers.

It's an odd feeling... to feel so at peace in such a terrible place. *Talk about a trick.*

The very ground beneath our feet seems to pulse with life. More than life, a powerful energy.

As we silently follow the winding path, a majestic sight finally emerges on the horizon—a castle. It's crafted from a harmonious blend of old white stone and pure gold. The rocks, expertly hewn, form a sturdy foundation, while veins of glistening gold snake through the structure, catching the light and radiating a soft, ethereal glow.

Four towers adorned with golden spires reach for the sky as if aspiring to touch the magic that infused the air. A beacon of wonder that seems to bridge the natural world and the realm of magic. *Dark magic,* from what I understand. Evil. Foul.

Max grabs my hand and squeezes gently. His gaze floats over my shoulder and to my side, meeting Alice's. Her face is unreadable. I can't tell if the woman is nervous or simply determined. Maybe a little bit of both. She takes a deep breath and picks up the pace, leading us towards the castle—Max and I fall behind her.

We cross the gigantic gate that leads inside the castle, and I feel my breath cut short. I grab my throat in panic. My eyes fly wide open.

"Breathe," Max whispers to me, calm and composed. *Like that's an easy thing to do right now.* "You're okay," he adds. "It's the magic. It works differently here. I'm pretty sure you're the first mortal to ever enter his realm."

"I'm honored," I tease, choking on my words as oxygen finally finds its way back into my chest. It feels like I'm inhaling fire with every breath, but at least I'm still alive.

If the air inside the castle is already unbearable, I can only imagine what kind of awful creature is breathing it. My heart turns to beating drums as I realize that I'm about to meet what comes closest to the devil —*Max's words.*

When I look up, I notice that Alice is way ahead of us, now standing ahead in the grand hall. Majestic pillars, crafted from veined marble and adorned with golden filigree, support a vaulted ceiling that seemed to touch the heavens—were we not in hell, that is.

Soft, ambient light emanates from strategically placed golden sconces, casting a warm and inviting glow. The castle, the stones, the gold... It is nothing but a trick, covering the true ugliness of the monster who roams this land.

Or so I thought.

On the spiraling staircase that oversees the entirety of the entrance stands the most beautiful man I've ever seen. My eyes are on Max, of course, *but goddamn*, this man is quite the snack. He stands far away, above us, looking down, yet I see him as if he was standing only an inch away. Despite the distance, every line of his angel-carved face and sculpted body appear to me as clear as day.

His short, chestnut-brown hair frames his dark eyes—a mesmerizing blend of deep hazel—holding a captivating allure that spoke of untold depths. Beneath a strong brow, they sparkle with malice. He's wearing tight, shiny leather—which would be a questionable choice for anyone else. But on him... The snug fit kisses every curve of his body perfectly, making him a masterpiece of strength and proportion. His muscular contours seamlessly flow along the leather top and pants in a harmonious balance. Each sinewy curve, from the broad shoulders down to the powerful chest and sculpted abdomen—that somehow peeks through the shiny material—conveys a sense of power and... grace?

I know there's a monster hiding underneath, somewhere, but at first glance, it's nowhere to be seen.

His chiseled jawline confidently underlines his perfectly shaped lips, holding a subtle charm that hints at both warmth and sensuality. Where was the foul creature? The monster who cursed the love of my life?

Max's body tense up beside mine, and I catch his side eye. I must be drooling or something because he snarls. I snap back, blinking and shaking my head to meet reality again.

"That can't be..." I mutter.

"Oh, yes. That's *him*." Max sneers.

"Collector!" Alice shouts from the middle of the grand hall. Her voice might be light, but the sarcasm it carries is heavy. She throws her arms wide open, pretending to hold the space between her shoulders just for him.

His lovely hazel eyes survey us one by one. Alice first, for what seems like an eternity. They narrow as they lay on Max, until they meet mine, where they linger. He's scanning me in silence. His full lips curl up ever so slightly, drawing fine wrinkles in the corner of his chocolate eyes.

"Forstthorns. Long time no see."

The hair on the back of my neck stands in formation at the sound of his polished voice, a sound that mirrors that of a fresh stream cascading down a mossy mountainside in the comfortable heat of a summer afternoon. The air fills with a sweet taste that tingles my tastebuds—I'm more used to the taste of salt when it comes to magic, but not around here.

"I suppose that means you received my gifts," he sings, slowly walking down the stairs and towards us, amused.

His steps are so soft that he appears to be floating above the marble floors. Not a sound is heard in his wake. Every step accentuates the strength of his leather-covered legs, his muscles pulsing with power.

"I want to negotiate the terms of our pact," Max blurts out, getting straight to the point—stern and confident.

He's lightly grazing my hand with his own, nothing more than dust landing on the pond of my skin as if he was feeding off of my energy.

"For her," The Collector notices and whispers with a twisted smile. Not a question—a statement.

His gaze lands on me again. All I see is warmth in those beautiful brown pebbles. There's malice—yes—but that of a small child, at best.

But Max said... Max mentioned the devil.

CHAPTER FORTY-FIVE

I jerk my chin up as if to say *yes, for me. For love.*

"You had your fun, Collector. Let us go now," Alice casually answers, waving her hand in the air and rolling her frosty eyes.

Max remains silent, his hunter's eyes locked on the moving enemy. The Collector stops when Alice's voice fills the gigantic room; he looks down at his feet. Eyes closed, he chuckles, softly shaking his beautiful head.

"What makes you think you can negotiate with me?" The Collector asks Max, ignoring Alice.

"You know what we are seeking. You know we are close, or you wouldn't interfere. Save yourself the humiliation of being beaten, and free us from the curse." Max demands.

A low growl rumbles through the Collector's magnificent chest. Ice prickles my scalp at the magnetic pull of his otherworldly beauty. I don't want him, I really don't—but I can't seem to fight the invisible haul. He chuckles, and I melt.

He finally reaches the last steps and stands by us. He looks so much taller now that we're all leveled. I rake his entire body with a discreet glance and still can't find any sign of a monster. If a foul creature exists —and I know it does—it's buried deep within this perfect body.

The Collector circles us with slow and steady steps—not much different from a dangerous predator. His arms are tight behind his muscular, sculpted back, accentuating their definition. His gaze travels around the room, lingering on every stone column and intricate gold design as if stretching time was a way of torture he's very much accustomed to playing with and relishing.

Max's body stiffens, never letting the menacing man out of his sight.

"It's a funny thing, love. Isn't it?" The Collector's suave voice covers us—*or me*—in honey. "You seek the spellbook for love. To save the love of your life. When it's my own who wrote it," a heavy chuckle escapes his perfect lips.

"Why?" The question escapes me as if something forced me to voice it.

"To destroy me." The Collector pauses, a muscle twitches in his jawline, betraying simmering rage. "If anyone can beat my magic, break the pacts that are made, I'm pretty much out of business, ain't I?"

He brushes his shoulder with a loose hand before adding, "What a cruel thing love brought to me." Ironic, being as he's quite literally considered the most *cruel* being of the magical realm.

"So the rumors are true," Alice breaks her silence with a tone that could kill—and probably wants to. A single of her brows arched, "You deceived her. Your lover."

She bites the inside of her cheeks, creating a small dimple on the right side of her face. Her hands are clenched into fists, arms tensed along her sides. Her eyes turned neon blue—the color of the thickest, deepest ice. She looks pretty terrifying.

In a blink, The Collector floats closer to her—only a couple inches away.

"She couldn't see past the...appearances." The Collector sneers through his perfectly aligned teeth and slowly gestures to his body, running its length. "She was young. Inexperienced. And quite foolish."

There's a silent battle raging in the small space that separates them. It's killing and spilling blood. Every muscle in the man's body stiffens, still facing Alice in utter silence. He finally dismisses her with a scoff and turns back to face Max and me.

The overwhelming gold features of the room reflect in his eyes and over his face. I feel a warm breeze rushing from the massive door we left open behind us. This would have been pleasant in other circumstances, but the summer breeze here is strangely chilling. Fear jolts down my spine the second I notice that The Collector's expression shifts drastically.

"You shouldn't have come here." His voice is not honey anymore; it's charred flesh.

"Break the curse, and you'll never see us again. No one will find the spellbook, and your business remains safe," Max negotiates.

Here is it again, the lingering hope in his voice—though still lacking confidence. My heart aches.

"I'll give you seven days," the creature says.

Alice and Max exchange confused looks but find nothing to say.

The Collector walks closer to me. I hold my breath. He smells like melted sugar and rose gardens, but his gaze is dark on me. I see it now—the evil. He grabs my chin firmly and scans my face. Max growls and angles his body by my side, ready for the kill. My warlock's breathing stops, and I notice the familiar tick of his jaw.

"If you can't beat me within seven days, that one is mine." The Collector whispers, tilting my head with his firm grip. "And that one too." He points a finger in Alice's direction without releasing my face or breaking eye contact.

"You can't..." I mumble, panic choking me, and it has nothing to do with the brown-eyed man's grip or the lack of oxygen in the room. "Those are not the terms of the pact."

"Oh, darling. But I can," he purrs, letting go of my chin with a soft caress that, oddly enough, builds little bumps all over my skin. Quite the *killer* touch. "Who will stop me? *You?*"

Alice bolts towards The Collector, her face twisted with rage. I don't recognize her. Her eyes would be on fire; was she the one wielding it. Her hair trails behind her skinny body as she races towards the beast. Her snow-white arm lifts in the air with an open palm, her fingers clenched together as one.

I wince as I brace for what happens next. But The Collector lifts one hand of his own, and Alice freezes into place, incapable of moving.

"I wouldn't do that if I were you, *witch*," he barks, defiant.

A few seconds pass as they stare at each other. I can taste the fury of Alice and the grief of Max it's so thick. I feel like the pristine marble floor cracked open and swallowed me whole. This is the hell Max and Alice were talking about. The room is bright and open, yet the walls are caving in, crushing me as they close on us.

Max shatters the heavy silence, spitting his words at the beast.

"Take me. Let them both go." His golden eyes are locked on The Collector, and his arm waves in Alice's and my direction.

"No!" The scream flees through my mouth without warning, echoing against the golden features inside the room.

A genuine plea. I grab Max's arm, my nails digging inside my lover's skin. Alice doesn't react, her icy gaze scratching The Collector's face—if it could.

This is it. The embodiment of Max's doubt. The one that was evident in the tone of his voice all along, faintly leaking through his eyes. Max must have held doubts in his heart about The Collector's agreement from the start. I now realize how uncertain he's been about our chances against the monster.

Was this stupid idea his plan all along? A mix of anger and despair washes over me. I can't lose him. I can't let him sacrifice himself.

But The Collector only chuckles and clicks his tongue. "Now, now, Maximilian. We wouldn't want to be cheaters, would we? You know offering *you* a deal prevents me from taking *your* soul," he gestures at Max. "Unless the pact is complete."

"Or beat." Alice's tone is a challenge in itself. "Or beat," she repeats.

Her jaw tightens. She's determined, confident. A true ice queen.

CHAPTER FORTY-SIX

"I told you to leave it alone..." Alice cries out once we're back at the mansion, numb and muddled. No coffee, as delicious as it is, can help us now.

There's no time to throw blame around. It was Max's idea, *sure*—but we all agreed to carry through with it. Alice's face is devastated, her mascara smudged under her beautiful blue eyes, gliding down to her pale lips. Her hair is spiking up from running her hands through it too many times.

I can't seem to feel the pain, the worry. My mind is racing but remains logical, looking in every corner for a solution, an idea—that's all we need, *one* promising idea.

"The rumors. What are they?" I ask bluntly, reliving the memory of the scene that brought us here.

Alice looks up, a silent wonder written over her face.

"You told him that the rumors were true. What did you mean?"

Alice groans, shaking her head as if she can't remember but is trying to rattle her memories into place.

"Something about his lover," I offer as a reminder.

"He wasn't always the way he is now. That's what the rumors are." Alice's lips are not moving. Max's voice took over.

"That's not nearly good enough," I snarl. "Tell me about the rumors."

Alice takes a deep, grounding breath before she tells me what she knows. What they both know. Why do they feel the need to hold it from me? Maybe to protect me. But we're all in this together now. *Knee-deep in this shit.*

"The Collector of Souls was made in a different realm. A different magic runs through his blood. Something that wields all elements and none at the same time. Much more complex and powerful than ours." Alice explains without fluctuating her tone once, looking out through the glass wall.

"For millennia, our kind has been seeking him for help. He's always made pacts with witches, warlocks, and other beings across all magical realms. They started out to be good-willed. He genuinely wanted to help people." She pauses for a moment.

"Legends say that one day, he fell in love. *Deeply* in love. With a powerful but common witch. One of us," she gestures at the space between her brother and herself, her gaze still looking at nothing in particular.

"But he deceived her. Fooled her. Something must have been evil in him all along. The fury he unleashed within her sought to end him. She truly loved him. So she wanted to hurt him back. But her magic was not nearly strong enough to hurt him directly."

"So she wrote up the spellbook. The grimoire we are seeking. She'd been around him long enough to know the secrets to all pacts made, to understand the deep nature of the magic that lay beneath every one of them. As her lover, The Collector allowed her in places he maybe shouldn't have."

"She laid on paper every spell that would destroy his very reason for existing. Spells that would defy his magic as her revenge. After she left him, he became the evil being you saw today. Or some version of it, I suppose," her lips held faintly apart.

"Something in him broke. He carried on with his business but only bargained with desperate souls, feeding on magical folks' despair and pain, like the vile creature he is. He feeds on people's suffering and makes incredibly cruel pacts. Forcing the ones who seek him to sacrifice everything. Knitting his pacts in the most terrible ways." Her voice trembles, but she continues.

"Our death is not the darkest part of our curse, Hannah. It's the way he will kill us and, most importantly, treat our souls after death. Both our souls are his, should Maximilian fail." Her frosty eyes snap back in my direction, an icy layer clinging to her pupils.

My throat bobs as I process her every word.

"I thought...I imagined our death to be quick and painless," I whisper, realizing that I never inquired about it. I was convinced it would be like being struck by lightning.

"Then you were a fool," Alice says.

Of course, The Collector would torture us for eternity. If love made him what he is, love is what he'll punish the most, in the most cruel ways. At least, in a sadistic sense, it all adds up.

"How did he do it? Deceive her, I mean?" I ask.

Max scoffs. I whip my head toward my gorgeous warlock. Back in The Collector's realm, all I could see was the leather-wearing man. His every contour. He was glowing, consuming my attention bit by bit. I tried to look away many times, but the magical pull was stronger. I couldn't help but devour every inch of his tall body, wondering what it'd look like if I shredded the leather to pieces. A dessert waiting for me on a golden platter. His traits were gods made to me. I couldn't resist.

Max was good enough to ignore it. But here, in our reality, all I can see is Maximilian. His perfectly carved features, the softness of his dark curls, the gold shining in his emerald eyes, his perfect teeth—covered by the most beautifully designed lips. *My* warlock. *My* lover.

"What you saw today is not The Collector. It is, but it isn't. He uses this body as a cover. Not only is his heart rotten—and his very soul—his appearance is too," Alice's lips grow nearly invisible as she finishes her sentence. "He seduced her using a fake body. Another's face. She fell in love with a mirage. Until she glimpsed at the real creature hiding beneath, one random day, as he changed in his chambers."

So he deceived his lover by covering his true appearance—which, from the sounds of it, was quite honestly terrifying. Alice proceeds to describe what the *real* Collector looks like. It could—and might—feed my nightmares for decades to come. I fall silent again, weighing every word, every sentence.

"But if his heart was good...?" I finally question, more to myself than anything.

Alice jolts, her eyes throw daggers at me.

"Are you trying to defend the beast?" She hisses.

I pause and embrace the silence for a moment. We've been screaming, swearing, arguing, and crying for a while now.

"Isn't that what love is all about?" I finally blurt out, looking straight at my warlock with absent eyes, lost in thoughts.

Would I love him just the same if his appearance was repulsive? Would I love his heart just the same?

I picture the indescribable traits that tales and rumors had tried to put into words about The Collector's actual physique. I try to picture two milk-white hollow voids in place of his golden-green irises, my favorite of his features. I imagine his sun-kissed skin turning an ominous, wrinkly gray. His full lips disappearing into nothingness, barely covering a row of jagged, twisted and sharp teeth that neared the color of piss. The hands I want on my body so ferociously, nothing but long skinny fingers ending in pointy, sharp, yellow nails. The velvety, full field crowning his head now empty, filled with bulgy purple veins.

My heart gently scratches at the walls of my chest at the thought. I would. I can feel it. If he could hide it as well as The Collector has, that is.

There would be no reason not to love the man he was inside. If fairytales had taught me anything, it's that I surely should. *It leads to fantastic sex.* I giggle inside, but my expression doesn't give it away. I let the silence embrace us once more. Alice had nothing to bark back this time.

"When did that happen?"

I need to get to the bottom of the story. Maybe there's something we can use, a missing piece to the crooked puzzle we're forced to put together.

"Millennia ago and a few years ago," Max says calmly.

"That doesn't make any sense," I whisper, shaking my head.

"Time works differently across realms. It's not linear. Think of it as a straight line on a piece of paper. If you fold the paper onto itself, two points in time will meet, though separated and distinctively different. That's pretty much what happened. His maiden wrote the book only a few years ago, turning him into the cold-hearted monster he is now long ago, in a complicated game of time."

The concept might give me a headache, but I think I get it—to some degree. Enough to work with it, at least. The Collector's lover affected two different points in time across realms and universes, one being very close to our current timeline.

Which means... which means... My gears are turning...fast.

"Which means she's alive. Right?" My face lights up, "His woman—lover—whatever. She's alive. She lives in our time, doesn't she?" I'm so close to screaming that it's a struggle to tone it down. Did I just find the missing piece?

"She is," Max says calmly, surveying me with silent questions in his eyes.

None of them is nearly as excited as I am, which tells me they don't get the point I'm trying to make. For powerful witches, they seem a little slow right now.

"Then we find her." I fling my hands skyward. "If we find her, we find the book. If she wrote it, there's no way in hell she won't help us break the curse. It's the *very* reason why she created it!" I exclaim, practically beaming.

Alice and Max exchange a tender look. I see a smile that doesn't reach their eyes on both their faces. It's faint, like tiny embers desperately trying to catch fire in the thick of winter—with wet wood. There's something I'm missing.

"She doesn't know where the book is," Alice says softly—almost sadly.

Her body's here, but her mind has wandered a great deal. Far, far away from the mansion's kitchen. My brows jump to my hairline.

"How is that possible? She's the one who..." I grumble, finishing my sentence by waving my hand in circles.

"She erased her memory to ensure she could never find the spells. She erased the location out of her mind, as well as any knowledge about the spells. What they were, how to perform them," Max explains. "Once she realized what she had done, she was too angry to destroy the spell-book but too fond of him to help anyone destroy *him*. So she hid it away and forgot all about it. Left it up to fate."

"So she could never be used against him," I whisper, realizing how much that absolutely sucks for us.

Max echoes my exact words in a soft tone to confirm. *Fuck*, I adore tragic love stories—though that one in particular is a giant pain in my ass.

"Do you witches do anything aside from erasing memories?" I tease. I can't fight the grin stretching across my face. The irony of the situation.

CHAPTER FORTY-SEVEN

I look at Alice, who's remained pretty silent for a long time now. Her messy hair tumbles down her shoulders and along her waist. Her face is a black and red painting on a white canvas, a mix of wasted makeup and blood-shot eyes from the tears on her porcelain skin.

I keep seeing ice frost over her eyeballs and melt instantly, streaming down her rosy cheeks. Snow is falling in the blue of her eyes—a blood-chilling winter sky. She knows there's a massive chance we are both dying in unfathomable pain.

Why am I not feeling as distressed? Why is there still determination —for lack of true hope—in my heart? I must be a fool. I've read of slow and painful deaths in many stories, of ways to torture a soul for eternity, but it doesn't hit me. Not yet.

Our very own ice queen snorts and wipes her tears clean with the back of her hands. After filling her lungs fully and releasing it all, creating small puffs of visible breath vapor—in the heat of summer, mind you—she turns to me and grabs my hand.

She's frigid. Quite literally frozen.

"I believe Maximilian was brought to you for a reason, Hannah. I believe your love is worth more than you could ever imagine. You *are* the key. I can feel it in my bones. My work here is done, but you can't give up. You will be successful. You will save us." She pauses, her voice quivering so much that her words vanish—swallowed empty noises.

More tears fall down on the kitchen table. "You must save us."

Oh, sure, no pressure at all.

She embraces Max for long, precious minutes, promising that she won't see him in a few days from now before she turns to me one more time.

Alice strikes my hair with a proud smile on her face. It feels like it's the first time I've really *seen* her—for who she is and all the big emotions she carries around, like too much luggage nobody needs for just a weekend trip. And yet, a fragment of me *remembers* the Alice standing before me.

She seems to hesitate at first, but she eventually pulls me into a tight embrace. Her tiny—but oddly strong—arms fall around my neck. I feel the rapid rise and fall of her chest as she sobs on my shoulder, leaving a stream of icy tears down my arm.

My eyes fly up to Max, who already turned the opposite way, looking outside. I can't tell whether it's to give his sister some privacy in all her vulnerability or if seeing her like this is too much to bear, even for my strong warlock.

"So, I *won't* see you soon," I muse, half choking on my words, just before she releases me.

If we are bound to meet our faith in a few days, all I will remember of Alice is that one last genuine laugh she freely let out before disappearing into her portal, her hair catching the shy sun rays and reflecting the celestial light before the phantom wind of her portal swallowed her.

I saw great despair in her eyes tonight, dancing amongst the falling snow and blue ice. More than a marriage of panic and worry, I saw desperation. I saw terror. On such a pretty face, it's quite a shame. There's a whole world living within Alice that I know nothing about. I'm not sure anyone does. I don't think even her velvety-haired brother even does.

CHAPTER FORTY-EIGHT

"Do we have to?" I fake a pouty face as Max braces his arms against the kitchen table and chuckles.

We've spent a great deal of time lounging around this table. Max reserves the great dining room for guests, and I'm not considered a guest anymore.

The walls of the large kitchen hold the memory of every breakfast we shared, every dinner, every comment referring to his body on mine, and every allusion to how hard he is just thinking about the tiny red lacy set I wore for him the first time he made love to me with glowing charcoal.

They've seen it all—the tender moments of connection, the fiery exchanges of passion, and the quiet, stolen glances that speak volumes.

The witch marked by The Collector will be kept safe and cared for within the coven. On the mortal side of things, *someone* has to pick up Blondie's body and keep it safe while we attend to our breaking-curse-and-stuff business.

Max's got a point; we can't just leave an unconscious woman's body on the floor without raising any alarm bells. It's already been an hour or so, so we must hurry. Plus, her body will need special tending until The Collector's game is beat and her soul is being released. If it wasn't for

Max's gentle heart, I would have buried her in the backyard. Oh well. I can't win them all now, can I?

He *did* agree to keep her in one of the forgotten bedrooms at the very end of the last floor of the mansion. In other words, as far away as possible. Though I was originally making that request as a complete joke, I couldn't deny the relief that crossed my chest when he agreed in a blink—not even questioning my sanity.

Annie will be kind enough to tend to our sleepy guest while she's stuck in her magical coma. There's nothing I would see Annie say no to —if Max asked, anyway.

"Annie knows what to do," Max had briefly explained and left it at that.

We portal back to the archives quickly enough to retrieve Blondie and be gone. We find out that Maggie is her name thanks to the name tag on her white blouse. Max pretended to notice it for the first time when he picked her up, though with all the fake flirting he shamelessly participated in, I'm sure he'd noticed before.

Maggie *almost* looks pleasant when she's sound asleep. Maybe it's because she looks so innocent; so fragile and vulnerable with that dark mark on her forehead. I could almost feel for her. *Almost.*

When we reach the top of the staircase, Annie is already standing in the bedroom Max picked out with a wet steaming towel neatly folded over her forearm. The room had been dusted, cleaned, and the brisk air of the night rushed inside from the window she carefully opened. I didn't realize the night had spread so fast.

It's a simple room, as opposed to the opulence of the first and second floor, as opposed to *my* bedroom—but it's perfect.

Thick, velvety green curtains frame a large two-pain window that's peeking over the gardens. All you can see now is the lights scattered at equal distances on the grounds, looking like a million stars fell to the earth and kept burning. Blondie can't see it, of course, but I hope it somehow brings her comfort, anyway.

Four intricately carved wooden pillars join above the bed. A light green couch that matches the color dancing within my warlock's eyes leans against one wall. It left marks on the white-grayish thick carpet. A sizeable wooden dresser eats most of the space between the door and the next wall. Aside from a red and gold round rug strategically placed under half of the bed, covering the vast majority of the room's floor, nothing else is in here. A simple, efficient guest bedroom.

"Did someone ever use this room?" I ask, groaning from lifting the heavy duvet on the bed and placing Blondie's legs underneath.

Max shakes his head. "Just one of the many guest rooms that never got used regularly. Aside from playing hide and seek with Alice." I see childish mischief in his eyes as he reminisces about the precious memory.

Annie left the room after placing the hot towel on Maggie's forehead, ensuring the pillow was folded at the perfect height for our sleepy guest.

"Where's her soul now?" I quietly ask when we are alone, my gaze absentmindedly grazing over Maggie's inert body.

I'm standing here, utterly unsure of what to feel. My emotions are a tangled mess, and I can't seem to make sense of any of them.

"Somewhere with The Collector, I suppose. Held hostage in his realm. Like a spiritual prison, if you will." Max's voice is quiet and grave, filling the small bedroom with worries and sorrows.

Shadows now cover the light brown walls. I think the house shares its master's pain.

"You *suppose*?" I joke, diffusing the heaviness around as best I can, putting my best grin to use.

"No one ever came back to tell the tale."

The joke didn't land; I see.

A heavy breath escapes me as I sit on the bed next to Maggie. Regardless of what happened at the archives, I don't like the idea of anyone's soul being trapped in a frightening realm no one knows much about. I wouldn't wish that upon any of my enemies, and she barely is one. She just happened to be caught in the crossfire between our two worlds. Maggie and the witch were targeted only to make a statement. For The Collector to catch our attention.

"What happens if we don't beat him?" I ask. "To them," I clarify.

I already know what will happen to Alice and me. I don't need to hear more details about how our death will be slow and painful, how our essence as living beings will be trapped in the Collector's playroom to torture as he sees fit, subject to his sadistic whims. *Bastard.*

Max remains silent for a moment. Not that he didn't hear my question. His golden emeralds are coated with a glossy layer of sadness.

"He'll keep them on a shelf, toying with them when he gets bored. He could also release them once he gets us all. Who knows what his twisted mind will decide?"

My throat bobs at the thought, but something Max said catches my attention.

"Get *us all*?"

Max understands my question right away. I can tell by the perturbed expression that sneaks its way across his pretty face, lingering over his eyes and digging deep lines into his forehead. I feel a painful cracking behind my chest at Max's next words.

"Anyone who makes a deal with The Collector pays a price greater than the *actual* terms he sets. Your soul is bound to him the second you accept the tradeoff," he explains. "If you accept the deal, you accept to pay the price, but you also willingly give your soul to The Collector. No matter what happens in the end. It's his."

This whole time, ever since he shook hands with the beast, Max knew he would never be free again, not in life, not in death. He accepted the threat of losing both his sister and his lover at once—should he dare succumb to the forbidden dance of love—knowing that his soul was no longer his, anyway, regardless of failure or success.

Ever since he signed his name, Max knew that when death naturally came for him too, he'd never be at peace, never find rest. For his soul was sentenced to travel back to this evil place. Eternal puppet to The Collector's will. Just another shiny toy to torment for the fucking asshole, forever at his mercy.

"All this time..." I murmur, despair clinging to my heart. I don't have to finish my thought. Max merely looks at me.

A genuine smile pulls his lips up. "It's worth it. Alice's life is worth it," he says as he softly chuckles, his eyes throwing an invisible rope at mine. "You are worth it, Hannah. I would die a million times over just to be with you. Just to love you the way you deserve to be loved. I would live and die just to find you in every single lifetime and do it all over again."

I might die in just seven days, but to even have known this man has been all worth it. The pain, the terror and all. In Max's presence, I have found a kind of peace—a sense of belonging that I have long searched for. In loving him, I have discovered a part of myself that I never knew existed—a part that is stronger, braver, and more resilient than I ever thought possible.

"I'm so lucky to have you, Maximilian."

Max's laugh is light as he realizes I rarely use his full name.

CHAPTER FORTY-NINE

The weight of my emotions almost dissolves the reality around us. My eyes narrow on my lover. The guest room we stand in, Blondie's inert body—everything around us disappears. The edges of my vision blur everything but the one person who truly matters to me.

I blink, then Max stands next to me, in between my body and the bed behind him. He turned his body to wind and silence and sheer speed, all to materialize back in front of me. The warmth of his skin is kissing mine. His lips so close to my own I can almost taste him. The heavy protection spell is worth it, after all.

"You realize there's a half-dead body right here, right?" I muse as I gesture towards the female's body, which is separated from her soul, getting just an inch closer to Max in doing so.

I hear the familiar whooshing of magical winds in my back, explosions of colors crowning my head. Max gently pushes me, and I let my body fall backward into the portal, trusting him entirely. A heartbeat later, I'm free-falling, my back facing the floor of my bedroom.

A bed of fire catches me before I can feel the unyielding surface crash against my bones. Nipping at my skin, back, scalp, arms, and legs.

A comforting tingling sensation that feels like a warm blanket more than a fire.

I look at my sides. I'm floating just an inch above the floor, held up by a dancing inferno. Max catches himself with his open palms, both arms fully extended, framing me. His feet dig into the carpet of my bedroom. His flexed muscles are proof of the strength he uses to hold himself up above me—though he makes it look effortless.

I'm trapped between an actual fire and the sensual heat that radiates from my warlock. I can't tell which one is hotter. Our bodies struggle to not eat the small distance between us and make one for good. The fire that serves me as a safety net dies, and I feel the velvety touch of the carpet as I land on the floor.

Max bends his arms and comes closer. *So close.*

His warm breath finds the bent of my neck, a delicate wind made of softness. Small bumps take over my entire body. The smell of lavender fills the room. His dark, springy curls hang loosely against my face—my fingers know the way. I grip his hair and arch my back up towards him, moaning his name. He growls in response.

We keep that safe distance between us, just enough for a small beam of light to travel between our bodies. He pushes himself up, meeting my gaze with raging fire inside his eyes.

Max presses his hips against mine for a fleeting moment. I sense the rock-hard length of him against my clothes. I want to rip his restraining, stupid pants off. I want to feel him at my entrance, pushing his way inside of me.

Max wiggles his fingers. My clothes disappear. My bare skin embraces the softness of the plush carpet below me. Laying down, stripped, and wide open in front of my kneeling king, I run both hands in my hair, swaying my hips, using the floor as leverage.

"I want you," I say in a breath. "Right. Now."

Max grins down at me. If I didn't know better, I'd say *he* is the evil beast of the story.

He summons fire at his fingertips; blue, red, and orange flames extend the natural length of his fingers. He doesn't say a word as he prepares to make love to me with his magical fire right there on my bedroom floor. All I hear coming out of him are growls and moans.

To the rhythm of his breath, Max's fire cups my breasts and bites my nipples before it travels dangerously south. I feel the flame flick and nip the bundle of nerves between my thighs, over and over, until my moaning turns to screams.

That's when he stops. I beg him to continue, my eyes closed, focused on the remains of the fiery sensation on my skin.

Max tells me how good I am. He likes it when I implore him to continue.

Just before my body turns cold from the torturous wait he imposes on me, fire flicks and bites again, and before long, the flames are inside of me. Carefully eating inches inside of me. In and out, a tidal wave of pleasure. Until he pushes me over the edge.

As my body arches and trembles in the throes of ecstasy, I'm swept away on a tsunami of sensations—a whirlwind of pleasure that consumes me entirely.

It's as if every nerve ending in my body is ablaze, sending sparks of delight racing through my veins. Tiny orbs of sweat cling to Max's forehead like shimmering diamonds as he gives me a smile filled with wicked satisfaction.

"You're all mine," he mouths as the fire he commands caresses my lips, my breasts, and the plane of my stomach.

"We need to kill the bastard." I breathe out, slowly returning to my senses, wanting Max more than ever.

Max carries my naked, shaking body thanks to a blanket made of fire, and gently lays me down on my bed.

"I'm serious, Maximilian," I say with a groan as I brace myself on my elbows.

I grab the comforter and cover my naked body, tucking it in under my arms. Max found his way to the rocking chair, guarding the corner of the room by the side of the bed. He flicks his index finger, and the covers go flying, landing at my feet and uncovering my bare body. He grins. I reach for a large throw pillow to cover myself as I insult him —*jokingly*.

"I've read the stories. Your library is full of them. Stories about your family, Max. I read your history. Your battles. The Forstthorn bloodline is among the most powerful of your kind. You can kill him. Get rid of the poison."

"Been busy, have we?" Max muses with a smirk.

"Well, it gets lonely at night," I tease. "And I can only get myself off so many times."

"You should spend your time writing, not reading," he playfully suggests, still laughing at my last comment.

I throw the pillow at him, redirecting his smartass wit towards my bare body. I have barely touched the typewriter he got me as a present. I sat in front of it a few times, grazing its metal keys in search of inspiration. *Just one idea,* I had whispered to myself. One *inspired* sentence. But nothing ever comes.

Max never shared much about his family or his bloodline. The few words he'd ever said were always burdened by pain and evident frustration with his parents. Their history seems dark, a rotten flower in his beautiful heart. But it was all here, written in the countless books inside the family library. Infinite rows of stories, both fictional and real. And among them, his family's history.

The Forstthorns were common witches—as Alice called them—but powerful. Their magic is ancient, rooted in the elements of the eternal universe, from before the sun warmed the earth on the first morning, the very first drop of rain, the very first fallen rock, the very first spark.

I found many stories about the Forstthorns' early generations' victorious battles against evil. Why would fighting The Collector be any different? I've learned the names of the many clans who pledged service to Max's family long before he was born—long before his parents were born—swearing to fight by their sides.

I don't understand it all, of course. The many intertwined universes and magical races seemed to be a complicated web to untangle for a mere mortal like myself. But one thing I know for sure: Max and Alice are powerful. And their family was once respected among witches.

I throw a wondering look in Max's direction, a silent question that begs for answers. "Why not kill him?"

"The Collector is much more powerful. It's as simple as that. We'd need allies, and even then..."

"Allies?" Slight confusion lingering in my tone at the choice of words, my arched brow as its witness.

"Our fate is one of many, Hannah. The Collector is a powerful entity. An important one, too. His magic is intricate and complex. A gift knitted from the fabric of a multitude of universes. A beacon of power crafted by all existing realms' very essence. But he's been using it to hold many people hostage—not just in our world. To spread suffering. Many would rather see him dead."

"Why wouldn't others want to rally to help us and help themselves, then?"

"Our allies grew smaller and smaller as my parents pushed their quest for power over the years."

I grab the light sheet, still neatly tucked, and cover my body with it —no objection this time. A low sigh escapes me.

"One day, we'll have grown old and gray and wrinkly, and you will have to tell me your family's story. All of it." I whisper, letting the overwhelming lack of sleep wash over my body like waves on the beach. I'm exhausted.

"I love the sound of that. I'll tell you...*everything*," he says as a caress, oddly insisting on the last word. There's heaviness in his tone. I don't want to pry.

I lay tired eyes on my beautiful lover. A powerful monarch on the small throne of my borrowed bedroom. His head tilts in a gentle smile as he meets my gaze before I bid the night farewell.

When I wake, I suppose he will be gone. Tonight, I will dare dream that one day, I will fall asleep in the hearth of his embrace and wake up there, too.

CHAPTER FIFTY

We haven't heard from Alice since our visit to The Collector four days ago.

The magical sibling connection Max and her share is intact, though. He describes it as an underground tunnel between their two hearts, minus the oppressive humidity and eeriness.

While clear words can't traverse this bond, nor can they share actual thoughts, Max can reach out and sense a steady heartbeat. Emotions, too—to some extent.

Max has been reaching down—he can feel her. It means she's safe and taken care of. Alice never shielded her mind. I suppose that's what unconditional trust looks like.

Maggie's body still lies on the top floor. I watch Annie tend to her diligently, ensuring she can still feel the warm flow of her breath. I sometimes stand by the bedroom, leaning on the door frame, just to make sure Annie doesn't need an extra pair of hands—always hoping she declines the offer. She always does.

Alice convinced me that I was the key before she left. Something in her eyes, in her quivering voice, told me it was real. That she *genuinely* believed it. If I'm the key, the answer lies within the co-op. That's my only superpower.

Brandie has been in and out of her shop—spending all her free time with Joffrey—just enough to entertain tourists with her extraordinary creations and keep her flowers alive. The onslaught of attacks has diminished, but they're still very much real in Willowbrook. I suppose people can use the magic of her exotic flowers to remedy the grim times our town is going through. *The magic of her smile and her perfect peach ass is more like it.*

I didn't find the right words to tell Brandie what our situation had evolved to. How can I possibly tell her that her friend might vanish in a few days? The reality is, I'll miss her more than she'll miss me. The mere thought of losing her makes me choke.

My warlock is on high alert, attempting to sense the evil before it strikes Willowbrook. I call it damage control. It's the least we can do, considering we are the very reason the robberies and attacks even happen.

I have spent every waking hour either devouring every inch of Max with my eyes—considering my time might be limited—or researching. Incessantly questioning the co-op.

I've contacted Samantha and Em, the wonderful ladies I met at the conference. Though I heard some...*confusion* in both their voices—probably wondering if they had met a fucking lunatic, after all—I explained that my research was needed for a scholar's project at our local university. It was a weak excuse, something I came up with on the spot, but it was good enough. They ate it up and promised to look around and send me anything useful. The more, the merrier.

We received a couple of packages adorned with the precious red dot—packages sent in a hurry, responding to the urgency in my emails. Every time, Max would materialize in the shop before I got the chance to call him. Every time, he would hold my hand as tears of rage streamed down my face. The co-op was active—helpful even—but it was never *it*.

Max makes a point of making our lives as normal and full as possible. His face conceals his fear very well, but I know my man. I sense his every feeling.

In four days, we have tried every restaurant in Willowbrook, devouring their most expensive dishes, savoring their most delicate desserts, topping it off with their most exquisite wine. I suspect Max has made my life a party to hide the fact that our hearts grew darker and more wary.

Willowbrook only has so many restaurants and bars to get grossly full at—and Max isn't done. Yesterday, he asked me to imagine a perfect dress to wear. I closed my eyes, picturing every detail of the dress, every inch of fabric either covering or strategically revealing my skin. I watched it materialize on my bed with a gaping mouth. Does a mortal woman *ever* get used to magic?

Crafted from a luxurious satin fabric, the dress boasted a deep, midnight blue hue that seemed to absorb and reflect the ambient light in a dance of shadows and lights. I couldn't believe how perfect it was. The sweetheart neckline traced a gentle curve across my décolletage, gifting Max a subtle glimpse of collarbones and hinting at the sensuality beneath.

Delicate spaghetti straps adorned the shoulders, providing a delicate frame for my neck and shoulders. The bodice—tailored by expert faeries, or the gods, maybe—featured subtle ruching that created an intricate play of texture.

As the dress descended, it clung to my torso before cascading into a flowing skirt that gracefully brushed the floor. The deep slit on my right side revealed a glimpse of my full leg with every step, enhancing the dress's call for fun.

My warlock had opted for a black suit. Simple, but oh so damn efficient. The vest accentuated his broad shoulders with elegance and fell right at his waist, where it met his leather belt. He had folded the sleeves up to his elbow.

The button-up shirt he wore underneath—a different shade of black—revealed just enough of his muscular, tanned chest to drive me insane. The pants were fluid yet contoured his ass perfectly, showcasing the muscles of his perky backside every time he moved. I was ready to follow him all night just to never stop watching it.

He portaled us to a different city. It took my vision a second to adjust after traversing the portal, thanks to the fireworks of bright colors inside it. I wasn't getting nauseous anymore—which was a perk considering we were about to have dinner.

Once the overwhelming brightness of the portal dissipated, my eyes landed on the most magnificent restaurant room I'd ever seen. The floor-to-ceiling windows that composed the back wall opened up to moonlit, raging waves, dominating the vastness of the ocean in front of us. With one look, I could tell the restaurant was balanced on top of a cliff. There was only one way past the giant windows—the way down.

The full moon, lodged high in the sky, dropped scattered pieces of shattered-crystal-like lights over the waters. I was walking in a dream, though the floor beneath my feet was very much real, as was the magnificent king standing by my side.

I stopped at the entrance for a brief second, only to throw a bewitched look at Max before we continued toward the dining room. The centerpiece of the room, nestled beneath a canopy of hanging lanterns, was a small, crystal-clear pool, its surface gently rippling with the softest touch of light. The water shimmered like liquid moonlight, casting delicate reflections onto the ornate ceiling above. Lush, emerald ferns fringed the pool, and floating lotus blossoms drifted serenely, their petals glowing faintly in the dim, romantic glow.

The colors of the walls—dark blues and creams—mirrored the angry ocean's hues, creating a seamless connection between the interior and the natural beauty outside. The hum of contented conversations, the clinking of glasses, the laughter, and the mellow notes of jazz music built a harmonious symphony that gently echoed around us.

"What is this place?" I asked quietly as my eyes traveled around the room, hypnotized.

"Annie used to take us here, Alice and me, before or after a walk on the beach. When my parents fought. It was a way to escape the grown-up world when the tension became unbearable at home. We've always loved the ocean." His eyes reflected the twilight.

Max nodded to a server in a neat uniform who was clearly waiting for my warlock's commands. The man vanished, only to reappear a few feet away, beside a small round table covered in perfectly ironed white tablecloths conveniently situated by one of the towering windows. The server extended his arm towards the table as he bowed down. We took our seats.

The food kept coming; the wine kept flowing—getting to my head.

I stopped noticing when Max would order more. The explosion of flavors on my tongue mirrored the elegant smells of the room. I didn't know such creations even existed. It wasn't just good food. It was a whole experience; a choreographed dance of tiny plates, innovative drinks, and professionally trained humans, barely as noticeable as shadows gliding around us.

I saw the lingering eyes on Max, of course, but I didn't care. Not tonight. I would as much as look outside, grazing over the crashing waves in the moonlight, to give them the space to explore his perfect features. His powerful arms and chest.

"Looks like quite the place to distract children," I mused, imagining what this view would look like by day.

Max chuckled in agreement. "It did the job."

"Did you come often?" A loaded question.

It wasn't about how many times Annie delighted Alice and Max with the exquisite experience; but about how many times his parents unleashed all hell at the mansion.

"Let's say that we didn't need to see a menu to order," Max tilted his head, eventually turning his gaze entirely to the ocean.

I felt the heaviness in his glare. My heart ached for my lover. I knew something dark lingered in his past. One day, when he was ready, he would tell me.

"I'm sorry," I breathed, reaching for his hand around the table. My fingers briefly intertwined with his, and my thumb swiftly stroked his cashmere skin. "When we survive this, you will tell me everything about your parents, and we will hate their memory together, as one."

His emerald eyes met mine and got lost there for never-ending minutes. I knew he felt like home in my eyes, exactly like I felt like home in his.

"You never talk about what would happen if we fail." I had already hurt the mood anyway.

Max's face told me nothing was ruined.

"Because we won't," he said that so confidently I had a hard time not believing it myself. "I have faith in you."

Again, *no pressure.*

"I want dessert," Max then announced, shaking his head as if he had just remembered. A wide smile grew on his face.

"We tried everything on the menu." I gently slapped my abdomen.

"Oh, that one is not on the menu."

That's when I realized we had been the last patrons in the restaurant. Rocked by the sound of the waves crashing against the cliff below, I hadn't noticed that the chatters had died out a long time ago. All the tables were already cleaned up, ready to serve the next wave of customers in the morning. The world had disappeared. I realized it was because Max was *my* whole world.

He nodded at the waiters standing as straight as statues against the walls, ready to jump on the chance to refill our glasses or bring more plates. They all bowed politely at once, then disappeared.

"You can't just dismiss the staff," I laughed, high on the red wine I'd been sipping all night long.

"I can. Considering I own the place."

All doors slammed shut, coinciding with the last syllable he pronounced. My eyes flew wide open, and I laughed harder. Sneaky, rich-ass warlock.

CHAPTER FIFTY-ONE

Before I could throw yet another smart-ass joke in his direction, my body went flying. Literally flying—and this had nothing to do with the wine.

I recognized the firm yet soft invisible force that sent me hovering above my chair, then above the table. I didn't protest when it laid me flat on the round surface, my legs facing my handsome warlock—who leaned back into his chair to survey the scene, to take it all in.

My knees went up, and my legs were bent, as my back was pushed flatter on the table when I tried to look up at Max.

I saw the silk of his curl spring as he ran a strong hand through it, biting his bottom lip and growling. A low, throaty growl.

"Now, that's my kind of dessert," he sneered through his teeth as he braced his arms on the small table by my feet.

A wiggle of his fingers later, the floaty skirt portion of my dress was tugged higher on my stomach, granting him full access to his favorite playground. His territory. His kingdom. He ruled over my body; no one would ever be insane enough to challenge him. This was his hunting ground. He owned me.

"Good girl."

I barely heard the words as I felt the magical fire bite my thighs.

I moaned, melting under his indirect touch. I swayed my hips, pushing them up. My toes curled and gripped the white tablecloth as the flames climbed on my sides to find my breasts.

The stinging warmth caressed the round, full bit of my underbreast. Slow, delicate strokes. A second later, the fire was biting and flicking on both my nipples, nearly pushing me over the edge. I imagined my body free-falling from the cliff we were dining on, entering the ocean like a million rocks on a lake.

"Not yet." Max played, clicking his tongue.

The magical inferno lingered over me completely, from my fingertips to my toes, licking every inch with precision and intention.

It caressed my hair, my cheeks, my shoulders. It jumped and slid all over my body, up and down. I begged for more. And more. I was melting, abandoning my body right there on the small dinner table. *I suppose the Collector couldn't get my soul if it left my body.*

Max thought it would be amusing to turn on *high* every single one of my sensations. He reached for an ice cube in the bucket where a bottle of champagne once laid.

As the heat of the fire worked my body—a path my warlock's fingers were deciding—the ice cube, lodged between his teeth, followed. Cooling down the trail of gentle burn with a different kind of stinging.

The ice—dangerously melting in contact with my skin—flooded my body and the table below. Fire and ice. Enemies to lovers. I moaned. Again and again. It was delightful torture. A building of anticipation I could barely take.

And then I felt it—the final straw. The heat of the fire. The perfect alter ego to the wetness that was patiently waiting for Max's mastery between my legs.

The flames grew brighter and higher when they finally came crashing down on the delicate and sensitive spot, flicking, swaying, and biting until my hands ripped the tablecloth from underneath me.

Screaming his name so loud it rippled over the ocean. Every single nerve inside my body was set on fire. My back arched, my eyes shut tight as I let the wave of pleasure overwhelm me completely, abandoning any common sense. Any sense of reality. Any sense of the world around us.

CHAPTER FIFTY-TWO

Our deadline has descended upon us stealthily, like a predator stalking its prey through the dense undergrowth of a dark forest. We sensed its presence lurking in the shadows, waiting to pounce from the darkness. But we couldn't see it just yet.

It's almost here now. If I reached, I could touch its sharp, deadly edges.

The sun filtering through the windows of my bedroom finds my eyelids. The gentle burn shakes me awake. I take in the intense soreness of my body. Sleep has become a precious commodity, scarce and fleeting in the face of our challenge.

Max never leaves my side anymore. Even though we can't share the same bed, he has taken it upon himself to stand watch over my sleep. He settles into the rocking chair in the corner—it's hardly comfortable, but he doesn't seem to mind. I love the sight of him in the morning.

As our end approaches, the fear in his eyes becomes more pronounced, etching lines of worry into his face. It's only in those first few moments of the morning, before the weight of the day settles upon him, that he shines an air of serene peace. When his long lashes brush against the skin beneath his eyes, and his lips soften from their daily tension, his features regain their natural softness. I find solace in the steady rhythm of his breathing. The slow rise and fall of his chest grounds me. *My sleeping king.*

We have two days left. And I will cherish every second I get to spend watching him.

My mind feels like a blank page, dotted with the tiny, damp traces of the tears I've shed. I have no idea left. No stone left to turn or corner to search. I keep pestering the co-op members. For updates, for ideas. They must think I'm straight-up crazy at this point. My browser history might alert the authorities.

I keep repeating Alice's words in my mind.

I'm the key. We've been brought together for a reason.

The vibration of my phone against the wooden side table makes me jump out of my skin. If I wasn't completely awake yet, I am now. Max's eyes widen, and his fists clench the armrests.

Joffrey is calling.

Max and I exchange confused looks before I pick up the phone. Joffrey and Brandie have been spending a lot of time with us recently. I've loved seeing my best friend fall in love. Fall in love with happiness, fall in love with life. It will be one of the precious memories that will anchor me when The Collector takes my soul as a new addition to his collection.

Joffrey calling me directly is a little surprising, though.

By the time our conversation was over and I put down my phone, my heart rate had sped up considerably. Joffrey hasn't heard from Brandie since last night—when she was supposed to meet him. He hoped to get ahold of her this morning, thinking she might have spent the night with me instead. *Nothing.*

I immediately try her cell and face the same result: *voicemail.* Max doesn't need to say much; the deep furrow between his eyebrows reveals his worry as clearly as words ever could.

We portal inside The Book Nook, and I immediately rush to the door. Max falls behind me. I see no sign of breaking in at Marguerite. Brandie's door is locked, the glass is intact. Her windows still stand. I peek through and see nothing disturbed inside the store. Her flowers are neatly organized. The humidifiers are running. Everything seems normal. Max would have known if any attacks had happened last night. He's been tracking evil every night.

I step away from the building and gaze up, hoping to see some sign of life through her apartment windows. I see no lights, no open windows.

"We need to get inside," I distractedly tell Max.

He waves his fingers by the lock. I hear the click, then the door slides open.

The flower shop is filled with exotic scents, as always. Was she not missing, I would remind Brandie how much it means to me. What it does to my soul. I walk amidst the colorful flowers and potted trees, snaking through the aisles, scanning the room. I rake every inch of her boutique, looking for clues—or a sign that she's alive and well.

Max paces around the room with narrowed eyes and furrowed brows. His perfect curls bounce with every step he takes. I sense his pulse accelerating through that strange bond we share.

The flower shop reveals nothing of use. Everything seems perfectly fine—aside from the missing owner. Like mine, her shop connects to her apartment by a narrow set of stairs. Max and I rush upstairs and promptly unlock her apartment door.

At first glance, everything seems normal here as well. I run to her bedroom first. Her bed is neatly made, her clothes are folded and put away, and the curtains are open and neatly pinned against the wall. Nothing stands out.

"Hannah..."

His voice is dark. Deep. *Too deep.* I follow Max's call and find him kneeling in the living room.

Brandie is lying next to him.

Panic throws blades at my guts and climbs up my chest with burning talons. Max looks up at me with wet gold as he shifts his body to the side so I can see Brandie's face. I knew what I would find there before I even looked.

The Collector's mark.

My heart pounds in my chest like a wild animal, a cacophony of fear and dread echoing through my veins as I rush to my best friend's side. The world around me blurs into a frenzied haze, every breath coming in short, ragged gasps as I scramble to make sense of the scene before me. My friend is pale and unmoving, her once vibrant eyes closed to the world, her body limp.

A scream rises in my throat, a primal howl of anguish and despair that threatens to consume me whole. I reach out to touch her, to shake her awake from this nightmare. My hands tremble with a mixture of panic and rage. I want to lash out, to scream and shout and tear the world apart with my bare hands. But beneath the rage lies a deep well of pain, a raw ache that cuts to the very core of my soul.

Max is still kneeling by my side, one hand laid on Brandie's arm as if to make sure this is not a mirage. The creature took my best friend's soul. Brandie is trapped, caught in the crossfire.

Max extends his arms and attempts to wrap them around me in a desperate embrace but stops himself just in time. He'd want to hold me so tight my heart couldn't shatter, and he knows the rules.

Instead, he summons a blanket of gentle fire and lays it over my shoulders and across my waist. His way of hugging me, supporting me, trying to offer whatever comfort he can in the face of such overwhelming pain. But even his indirect touch, warm and reassuring as it is, can't quell the storm of emotions raging inside me.

My mind races. I imagine what Brandie must be going through right now. How confused she must be. How much pain she must be in. The more I picture it, the more I howl.

The fiery blanket tightens around my shoulders as tears cascade down my cheeks. A seething rage courses through my veins like molten lava. Every fiber of my being screams for vengeance, for retribution—to make The Collector pay.

I will find the damn book, and I will destroy the beast. I will suck the magical life out of his pathetic body and turn it to ashes myself.

CHAPTER FIFTY-THREE

Annie is waiting at the grand entrance, sadness deepening the wrinkles on her face. Somehow, she already knew. She always knows. She holds a couple of steaming towels and what appears to be a long-sleeved, plush white nightgown. All carefully picked and intended for my friend. Annie blinks with sorrow as she watches Max carry Brandie's inert body inside the mansion. We pick the room directly next to mine. I want to be near in case she wakes up.

I change Brandie into the night dress while Annie softly sponges her face. For a fleeting moment, I dared to hope that this would obliterate the horrifying mark on her forehead. But it persists, clinging to my friend's smooth skin like a parasite.

Annie and I remain silent as we busy ourselves around Brandie, making sure she stays comfortable. I brush her golden hair and carefully tight it in a French braid, weeping. Annie helps me elevate her legs. We adjust her head pillow and cover her with a light, feather comforter that should hold the perfect temperature.

Brandie seems to be peacefully sleeping, waking at any moment. But in my heart, I know she won't. I know her beautiful ocean eyes will remain shut until we beat the fucker. Rage finds me again. I sob, holding my best friend's cold hand.

For the next couple of hours, I sit silently by her side. Annie pops in and out. Max's rage was as predictable as mine. After he laid Brandie in her new home, he let out an enraged scream, hitting the wall with a bloody fist before he disappeared behind the steel door. The magic room. I didn't stop him. To hell with the rules. Willowbrook can burn to the ground for all I care—my best friend is in danger.

If I knew my lover, he would be busy for the rest of the day. That vault-like door will not reopen until he's done processing what happened today. Until he's done casting what he needs to cast. I won't stop him.

I have an idea of my own.

I finally descend the stairs, numb and confused. A mere shell of myself hovering down, step by step. My eyes swollen from my incessant crying. Lunch is already waiting for me on the table. Sweet, thoughtful Annie.

"I need to talk to Alice."

"That's complicated, dear," Annie's voice is soft. "The coven cuts off any communication, especially now that they protect Alice from such unspeakable evil."

"Complicated, but not impossible. You know how to reach her. I know you do."

Annie's lips twist in a regretful smile. I can't decide whether she can't help me or refuses to. "I know what you are thinking of, Miss Hannah."

"Then make my life easier and help me." I've never spoken to her in that way.

I would have never dared use such a tone with my favorite elderly lady if it was not for my best friend's soul. Annie reads the plea in my gaze. She sees my raw, vulnerable heart beat through my eyes, ripped open and bleeding, a fusion of fury and desperation. She lets out a deep sigh.

"If Maximilian hears..." Annie whispers.

Before I can protest or serve her a million excuses, Annie closes her eyes and brings her hands together, both palms flat, facing each other, as if she were about to pray. I recognize this veil of calm covering her face, this hand position—from my mother, from her hours of prayers, sitting in silence.

But Annie's not praying. She's...*summoning*. So she *does* have magic in her, after all.

Alice appears at the kitchen door. She nods at Annie, who then smiles at me. The magical winds of her portal mess with Alice's beautiful silver hair. It reminds me of Brandie's a bit. Both are gorgeous creatures, but only one is free right now.

"Maximilian will never let this go," Alice sighs before my lips can open to let out any kind of demand. "What's your plan, Hannah?"

"I don't have any," I admit sternly.

Alice sighs loudly, rolling her eyes as she analyzes my face, then sighs again.

"Get him to talk, Hannah. Get him to talk and see if you can hear anything of use, anything at all," Alice says, her tone urgent. "He might slip and reveal something we haven't considered."

I nod in silence. A skeleton of a plan is better than no plan at all, I suppose.

Alice hands me a delicate golden pocket clock suspended from a stunning chain adorned with twinkling diamonds. The timepiece closes like a locket.

"When you are done, open it and shake it three times. It will signal me. I will reopen the way for you." Alice explains.

"Can't you just leave it open?"

"Who knows what creatures could use it and reach our realm. We can't take the risk." Her voice is hoarse, and her blank gaze is enough to explain. Surprising, considering I didn't see another soul the first time we visited the realm—no pun intended.

CHAPTER FIFTY-FOUR

"Are you out of your fucking mind?" Max's shout mirrors an earthquake in the mansion.

His hands are severely shaking when they land on my shoulders. His grip, though painful this time around, isn't menacing. I meet his greenish circles and see overwhelming terror and worry. A wave of conflicting emotions washes over him. At first, there seems to be relief —relief that I'm safe, that I've returned *somewhat* unharmed.

But beneath that relief lies a simmering sense of frustration and anger, a deep-seated disapproval of the risks I've taken. He struggles to contain the whirlwind of emotions swirling within him as he looks at me again.

"What were you thinking, Hannah..."

Alice is standing next to him, patting his shoulder. She understands why I had to try. For Brandie. For us. He shoots her a warning look, probably thinking she's fully responsible.

"You could have been hurt. Or worse, locked away..." My warlock's voice resembles the water rippling after a massive rock crashes in.

I read in his face that he wants to be furious. Maybe lock me in my room himself—so I never take such risks ever again. But a part of him—the part that loves me fiercely and unconditionally—knows that I'm my own person, with my own brain and my own convictions.

"It's not *my* soul he wants," that much I learned after Alice agreed to open the passage for me just a few moments ago. "This was all a waste of time and energy," I admit, rage dripping from my voice. "I got nothing out of him," I add, looking at Alice.

As I entered The Collector's magical realm, fear, anger, and determination collided within me, each fighting for dominance as I navigated the now familiar terrain.

I forced myself to ignore the scent of sugar and honey filling the air. I tuned out the multicolored blanket of wildflowers stretching on both sides of the path that led to his palace. The magic overwhelming the air commanded me otherwise—*lose all your clothes and roll your bare body in the fresh grass and soft flowers, let The Collector fuck you.*

I shook the intrusive thoughts out of my head. They were never mine to begin with. It was all part of the malicious game.

The bird seemed to sing a beautiful song crafted just for me. It found my ears as a potent drug would overcome my blood. I paid them no mind, my focus fixed solely on my goal: confronting the foul creature and rescuing my best friend's soul from his clutches.

With a fierce determination burning in my chest, I broke into a sprint, rushing towards the towering spires of his palace looming in the distance. I bursted through the doors, swinging them open with the force of hurricane winds, my breathing erratic and shallow.

I found him near the bottom of the stairs, clearly expecting me in all his sinister glory. He turned around from the window he was looking through when he heard the doors hit his wall.

His beauty was as striking as ever—a beauty tainted by darkness, by the cruelty and malice that lived in him. My eyes lingered on his soft facial features, losing myself in the chocolate basin of his eyes. My gaze traveled down the mighty, statuesque chest, down the valleys of his arms...wondering what such strong yet delicate hands would do to my body.

Yet again, not my thoughts.

I bared my teeth. The magic in this place was as rotten as his heart.

"That appears to be a wasteful way to spend your *limited* time, darling," his words flowed like melted caramel, rich and smooth, enveloping me in their disgusting warmth. "Did Alice send you, or is she the butler?"

I bolted towards the monster, fighting the urge to embrace him —*taste him, feel him*. The magical lies slowly getting the best of me. I needed to hurry. I stroked his torso with all my might. Only I didn't reach it. I hit an unyielding, invisible surface—like thick, impenetrable air. A shield. An invisible armor surrounded him. I suppose I wasn't the first one wanting to rip his heart out.

"Let her go!" I shouted, tears of rage fleeing my eyelids. "You have no use for her. She's not a part of this."

He smirked, but I refused to be cowed by his presence, by the power he wields over this realm. I was driven by a love stronger than any magic, a love that would stop at nothing.

"Let. Her. Go." I slowly repeated, meeting his gaze with unbending resolve.

He didn't so much as acknowledge my demand. The Collector looked bored as if I was wasting his time. What could he possibly do in this empty ass realm, anyway?

Get him to talk. Alice's words resonate in my mind.

"Why do you care so much if one little pact is undone?" I sneer through my teeth.

He smirked. "You have so much to learn, little Hannah."

"What did the Forstthorns do to you, anyway?"

"Maximilian and I made a pact."

"Brandie plays no part in this. Why don't you stay focused?" I challenged the monster.

"Now, where would be the fun in that?" He chuckled, redirecting his gaze away from me.

From the very moment the somewhat irrational, highly emotional idea to come here birthed in my mind, I felt like it was a lost cause. But I knew for sure the second I noticed his cocky grin. He had no intention of negotiating with me. No intention to release Brandie's soul. Not for free.

"Fine! Fucking monster," I sobbed. "Take my soul. Right here, right now. Take it and do with it as you please. Torture me for eternity, for all

I care. But release them all. Let Alice and Maximilian and Brandie go for good. I'm not the one who made a pact with you. You can easily take my soul without breaking the rules. You said so yourself."

His eyes traveled the length of my body, and for a brief moment, I thought he could actually consider my offer.

He let out a scoff. "I admire it, you know. Your courage. It's pure folly, but I admire it."

"You'll never know what that kind of love can do."

Another smirk on this perfect face of his.

"That's where you are wrong, darling. I know what that kind of love feels like. And I know what it did to me."

His expression was severe. The handsome man turned into a statue of ice. Anguish flashed in his eyes, but I couldn't fall for it.

"So? Are you taking my offer?" I jerked my chin up.

Another soft chuckle escaped his full lips. A mockery.

"A thousand human souls are not worth *one* Forstthorn, little Hannah."

Dread fell from the fake sky above and gripped me, pulling my insides to the center of the earth—or this evil realm. That's what he wanted all along. *Max's soul.* He would never accept any bargain or enter any kind of negotiation. This mission was doomed from the start.

"I will let your friend know you came all this way hoping to leave with her precious soul. She will be moved, I'm sure. I will take it easy on her. She's been a good girl," he sneered.

Sheer rage surged through me, animating my lips and giving voice to my words.

"Listen to me carefully, Collector. I've traversed realms to tell you this. We will retrieve the spellbook, and every day, we'll thank your former lover for writing it in the first place."

His eyes darkened at my words. "And then, I'll fuck the man I love over and over again. I hope you will watch closely and hear every moan. For each thrust of his hips will echo your pathetic failure, your broken pact with the Forstthorns. It will be a testament to the love you'll never experience."

A flicker of tension betrayed his stoic facade, his chest tensing beneath the surface.

"When I'm done orgasming at the thought of your defeat, I will come for you. I will find a way to destroy you. This is my promise to you. I will come back here, and I will end you myself. I will make you beg for mercy and will serve you an eternity of hell instead. I will then serve your head to Brandie on a golden platter that I will craft from the gold of your very own castle."

His typically composed features contorted into a mask of primal fury. His jaw clenched so tight it looked as though it might shatter under the pressure, while his hazel eyes now blazed with an intensity that seemed to sear through everything in its path.

I then realized the true depth of his anger, the ferocity of his wrath. I tore a deep hole in his heart when I mentioned love—*true love*—the kind that betrayed him, the kind of love he now had to witness from the sidelines.

The Collector's hand shot out, palm flat, a guttural howl escaping his lips. In an instant, darkness enveloped me, suffocating and consuming. Agonizing pain ripped through my chest and stomach as if a thousand needles pierced my flesh.

It was a relentless wave of dark energy, unstoppable and merciless. I lost my footing; the force sent me flying through the air like a rag doll. With a sickening thud, I crashed through the front door, the impact sending shockwaves of pain reverberating through my body. My head pounded, my lungs begged for air. I felt powerless—a mere mortal in the devil's realm.

Yet, despite the searing agony coursing through me, a grin spread across my lips. By the fury he unleashed upon me, I could tell that my last words crept under his skin with poisoned teeth and ate at his flesh.

As I laid battered and bruised on the ground of his realm, I knew that my defiance had left its mark on the Collector; a wound that would fester and torment him long after I was gone. Despite the searing pain growing with every move, I grabbed the pocket clock Alice gave me.

One, two, three.

Her portal opened almost instantly, granting me just enough time to drag myself up and on my feet.

"My beautiful, lionhearted woman." Max's shaking voice whispers, his eyes filled with tears. He cups my face and gently strokes my cheeks with feather thumbs. "I'm so fucking proud of you. But never again. Please."

I chuckle. Alice disappears back to the coven before Max can corner her and unleash his anger upon her. She doesn't deserve it, anyway.

When silence finds its way back into the mansion, I make my way up the stairs. Every step I take ignites a raging fire within my muscles. *The bastard got me good.*

When I reach the grandiose bathroom attached to my room, Max is leaning against the doorframe. A see-through curtain of steam dances behind his back. He ran a warm bath just for me. Whether the house magically provided the food and coffee patiently waiting next to the tub or whether Max asked Annie to whip it together, I don't know. Either way, it's perfect.

I lazily run a hand across the plane of his stomach as I walk past him and inside the bathroom.

"Did you lose the shirt just for me?" I tease.

Max smiles but remains silent. His eyes survey every inch of my body as I undress—accentuating every curve—most likely searching for hidden injuries. I stand before my lover, my form laid bare, draped only in the essence of my own vulnerability.

I make the distance between us almost completely disappear, keeping just enough to keep me safe.

"I love you, Maximilian. No matter what happens next." I breathe out.

Max doesn't break his silence. He smiles and summons a couple of ropes of fire directly attached to his hands. The fiery cords caress my cheeks and lightly push me towards the tub, where they pick up my naked body and lay me down in the steaming water.

Max comes to sit by the bathtub, where my head rests. With his actual fingers, he strokes my hair. A whisper of a touch.

"I love you too, Hannah."

CHAPTER FIFTY-FIVE

A gust of brisk autumn air rushes in from the open window. The mansion's gardens are dreamy in this season. The leaves are turning, abandoning their bright green coats for now, proof that time is a thief, passing by us fast—too *fast*.

The enormous rose bushes scattered throughout the property still hold strong despite the soft wrinkles overtaking the bright pink flowers. The sky wears a darker palette, with grayish clouds looming ominously, threatening to bring an end to summer.

The days fall shorter—just like our remaining time.

I will miss that. The human world. The lush grass, the colorful flowers, the change of colors as seasons pass. The Collector's realm proudly competes with—if not beats—the beauty of the mortal world, but who knows where he keeps his stolen souls? Most likely not in a blooming garden.

I stop by Joffrey's borrowed bedroom and watch him silently. He twisted his tall, slender body into a little human mountain. Lying on his side facing the window, his knees are drawn up to his chest, his long arms wrapped tightly around them as if seeking solace from within.

His pale skin reflects the muted light of the day. It's raining outside. Raindrops patter against the glass. I can't tell whether Joffrey found peace in it or if it has darkened his already somber mood. I'm not entirely sure if he fully grasps the finality of our situation or if he truly understands the depths of the magic coursing through Max and Alice's veins.

What I *do* know is that he's committed to helping us in any way he can. One thing he understands for sure now is that his queen is in danger if we don't break the curse, and he won't let that happen.

After we told him the whole truth, Joffrey stopped working and moved to the mansion with us. He spends countless hours brainstorming with me, deciphering my hastily scribbled notes, and sifting through my emails for clues.

Max offered him one of the biggest rooms of the house—one complete with its own balcony with a view of the gardens, a bathroom, and a kitchenette. We thought he would appreciate the space, the intimacy. But Joffrey barely leaves Brandie's room. On the first night, we found him asleep on the floor beside her bed. Max conjured an extra bed for him the following morning.

Despite his determination to help us, Joffrey is noticeably brought down by a suffocating cloak of despair that drapes over him. I know the feeling. The feeling of helplessness, of being utterly powerless to protect the one he holds dear from the looming threat that hangs over her.

We have forty-eight hours left.

It's as if the sun will never pierce through the heavy, dark clouds looming over our heads ever again. My chest tightens with every passing moment, realizing that Alice was wrong.

I will not be the key, after all. I was never the answer, always the problem.

I haven't returned to The Book Nook since Brandie was taken. I transferred everything of use, every piece of research—to the mansion. We use one of the vacant rooms to spread everything on the floor. To brainstorm, to investigate, to find a way—until our eyes burn from fatigue and the night is as dark as the center of the universe.

Forty-eight hours.

I can almost hear the cocky laugh of The Collector ricochet in the heavy silence that has taken over the mansion. The bastard is winning. We have no lead. The realization of impending defeat washes over me like a chilling tide, sending shivers down my spine and leaving my senses reeling.

Desperation claws at the edges of my mind, urging me to fight, to defy fate, and to cling to the slimmest glimmer of hope. But deep down, I know the odds are stacked against us.

Max is absent, locked up in his magical room during the day, running the streets of Willowbrook at night—*damage control*. He barely looks at me. And when our gazes *do* meet, I see nothing but a black pit of terror inside the golden pools of his eyes. Dread is eating him alive. The bond we share feels like I'm carrying a heavy quilt made of the sturdiest steel. His feelings are unbearable. And his feelings are mine.

Annie spends most of her days walking from room to room. To tend to Maggie and Brandie. Max ensured that Maggie would not be missed. Using a strand of her hair—so very magical of him—he cast a spell that would force anyone who knew her to think she was on a beach somewhere, enjoying a much-needed vacation. When she wakes up—*if she wakes up*—she will believe the same.

I hear Joffrey's voice mix with Annie's sometimes. Short, heavy conversations primarily focused on Brandie's needs and comfort. And loads of *thank you*.

Forty-eight fucking hours.

"Will you see her? When you pass to...the other side?" Joffrey's voice is ice cold.

"I don't know. He could release her," I dare dream.

Joffrey only scoffs in response. He's not convinced The Collector would do such a thing, considering the beast has been nothing but wicked.

My eyes explore the room where we scattered many notes, printed emails, notebooks, and cards. Everything that I own, everything that we've researched. We kept the desk and a couple of chairs in the room—though Joffrey and I make the most use of the floor, sitting among the scraps of paper.

He's leaning against the desk, sitting on the floor with his arms braced on his knees. He's wearing the same faded blue jeans he's been wearing for days. His soft face looks harder by the day. His short black hair has grown a little. So has his beard. Brandie would like it.

"I never told her I loved her."

Guilt gnaws at the edges of his face. His brow furrow with the weight of unspoken words. There's more than sadness in his eyes.

"I never had the balls to tell her how I felt about her."

Brandie can be pretty intimidating. Most people stumble over their words, their confidence crumbling in the face of her perfection. There's a magnetic quality to her allure, a captivating charm that draws people in like moths to a flame. And just like moths, men easily get burnt by her flame.

But I saw the way my best friend looked at Joffrey. I recognize her smile; the way her face softens when he pulls her in. I've never seen that in her before.

Grief flickers through Joffrey's eyes. Regret, too.

"If she comes back, I will propose to her." His throat bobs.

I scan his face for a fragment of a joke or uncertainty; there's none. He's very much serious.

"I know what you think, Hannah," he says, avoiding eye contact. "But this is all very new to me, and I can't contain it. I know you understand. I see the way you look at Maximilian. I see the twinkling stars in your eyes when he's near." Joffrey smiles at me.

I didn't think him much of a poet.

"I've been alone my entire life, Hannah. I've buried myself in work because what else did I have? Funny to think that my work brought me to the woman of my dreams. I knew the second I laid eyes on her. She was the most beautiful flower in her shop." his smile grows larger when he thinks of her.

I stay silent, bringing Brandie's beautiful face to mind. Who couldn't love her? I can't speak for her heart—and I won't—but I believe she'd say yes.

"Will you tell her? That I love her? When you see her?" Tears now cascade down his cheeks, forming glistening pools on the edge of his collarbones.

Joffrey's lips quiver with emotion, with guilt, with regret, and sorrow. And as he sits there, grappling with the magnitude of his feelings for her, I see his very essence. He realizes he has found the one he wants to spend the rest of his days with.

I purposefully redirect my gaze to his fidgeting hands when I realize that emotions have drowned me and my vision has turned blurry again. Joffrey picked up a card from the floor to distract himself. There's enough crap all around us. He simply needed to extend one finger to grab anything.

But he didn't grab just *anything*.

I stare at his hands as I swallow the tears and blink the water curtain away. I recognize this card. How in the world did I not think of this earlier?

What the fuck, Hannah?

I jump to my feet and bolt toward Joffrey.

"You will tell Brandie you love her yourself." I excitedly bark at him as I snatch Henry's business card out of Joffrey's hand—ignoring the fact that his jaw just hit the floor.

CHAPTER FIFTY-SIX

We all gather around the coffee table in the living room. The fire is grandiose, raging with anticipation. Now that the temperature has dropped outside, it finally diffuses real heat —just enough to stay comfortable when the autumn nights fall upon us.

The weather is still gloomy outside—as if it's been mirroring our moods—but there's now sunshine in my heart. Despite the rain tapping against the windows, a rainbow is floating over my head.

Max invited Alice to join us, but she refused. I think she doesn't want to get her hopes up. She's been riding the same emotional roller-coaster as us, but I can tell every turn has been hitting her a little harder. Right in her perfectly flat stomach.

"Do you think he has the spellbook?" Joffrey asks about Henry, his arms braced on his lap.

"No." Confusion spreads across the room at my answer. "He's not even an active member anymore."

"Is that why you haven't thought of him until now?" Joffrey continues.

I nod. "He hasn't received any of our emails or letters. From what I understand, he's disconnected from the co-op altogether. Which is why he slipped my mind." I regretfully admit. That was one *massive* mistake on my end.

"Wait a second, so if he's no longer a member and doesn't have the grimoire, why are we talking to the man?" Joffrey worries.

"I think he might know who has it."

Henry mentioned a key detail during our lunch at the conference—he knows the founder. They've been friends since their early childhood. Something in my heart flipped when I noticed his card in Joffrey's hand. The one answer that has been in front of my nose this whole time, hiding behind fear and rush and a million different thoughts.

There's a shit ton of hope attached to this phone call to Henry. I couldn't lay out exactly what we were seeking without taking the risk he'd doubt my sanity. But he insisted that I should call him should I need anything.

Well, I need something now.

Every sentence I mutter gets punctuated by guttural yet friendly growls. Henry chuckles, then mhhs again. I can sense his hesitation. Something forced him to leave the co-op behind, and I have no clue what it is.

All eyes in the room are on me as I carefully unfold a somewhat made-up story for Henry. Max's hand lands on my knee, low enough to remain chaste.

I stay as vague as possible, focusing on my eagerness to meet the one person I think might have the grimoire. The mighty founder. I remind Henry how much the co-op means to me, what my livelihood is all about, how much it would mean to have the chance to meet the man behind my *obsession*. I get a laugh out of this one—not just on the other end of the line.

The conversation stretches as Henry takes the opportunity to check in and talk about his life, too. I painfully play along and avoid rushing to our goal. It's not that I dislike chatting with Henry; on the contrary. But we only have a handful of hours left before I can never chat with anyone again.

"So, will you introduce us?" I shakily ask.

I remember the rule; the two friends don't even talk about the co-op.

CHAPTER FIFTY-SEVEN

ary Gray is the name embossed on a golden plaque above the doorbell.

Max and I portal into an alley near Gary's house. Each house on the quiet street is separated by white picket fences bordering neatly cut green grass. Towering oak trees flank the road, their foliage showing signs of autumn.

The tiny house is entirely made of red bricks. The white window frames and green blinds contrast with the fiery hues of the square stones. The roof is flat, crafted from dark gray stone shingles. Lighter bricks are arranged in a delicate flower pattern on the front of the house. *Charming.*

The air is crisp, tinged with the faint scent of fallen leaves. Smoke curls lazily from chimneys, adding to the idyllic atmosphere of Gary's neighborhood. Each of my heartbeats resonates with my footsteps on the paved curb as we approach Gary's house.

Max holds my chin and pulls it up to face him. He skims a light finger down my cheek.

"I love you," he whispers before we ring the doorbell—and the temperature between my thighs plummets.

A dog rushes to the front door at the sound of the bell, its barks hushed by a soft, trembling voice from within. The founder.

The door swings open. Contrasting with the loud barks of a few seconds ago, a chocolate brown dog welcomes us quietly, tail wagging, tongue hanging. My gaze shoots up to the older gentleman standing by the door.

At first glance, Gary looks older than expected. The creases of his face dig deep into his age-stained skin. Dark brown eyes peer out from beneath bushy gray brows. Though tired-looking, they bear true kindness.

He stands a little stooped as if burdened by the weight of his years, but there's a grace in his movements. A quiet strength defines his jaw, softened by the warmth that shines through his gaze. His nose, slightly crooked, adds character to his round face. A halo of thinning silver-gray crowns his head, leaving most of the line above his forehead bare.

After gently petting the top of the dog's head, he gestures to the hallway and invites us in. The furry companion disappears in a side room; his job here is done.

"Hannah, correct?" Gary's joyful tone relaxes my tensed body instantly.

"Yes, sir. And this is Maximilian. It's an honor to meet you," I say as we make our way deeper into Gary's house.

It's a relatively small house, though the large windows all around make it bright and inviting. The smell of roasted garlic and some kind of herbs float in the air.

"Thank you for meeting us, sir."

"I knew it must have been important if Henry dared mention the co-op." Gary waves an index finger in the air as he softly laughs.

Framed photographs line the faded green walls, capturing moments frozen in sepia tones—a young couple on their wedding day, children laughing, and generations of family gathered around holiday tables. Each picture is a window into Gary's life, into his story. My gaze rakes through the photos and paintings and stops on a portrait of a young, *handsome* man.

"Believe it or not, young Hannah, I was quite the ladies' man back in my days," Gary laughs when he notices where my eyes have stopped.

I nudge an elbow at Max and arch my eyebrows—grinning. Gary was *hot*. Max only rolls his eyes and growls at me in silence—baring his teeth, snapping them in the air. He slaps my ass to move me away from the picture. *Possessive warlock.*

We follow Gary's leisurely pace down the narrow hallway that spans the length of the house. As we reach the end, a cozy, office-like room opens up. The walls are lined with sturdy, dark shelves, filled to the brim with books and free paper. More pictures and oil paintings are scattered on the beige walls—where there's room left, that is.

Two couches face each other in a silent battle of time. One is covered with black, weathered leather, torn open in a few places where the stuffing pools out. The other, a bright orange fabric couch—modern and loud in the quiet design of the room. A round white coffee table separates the two, bearing a few rings of forgotten beverages on its top.

The back of the room holds space for a large desk where I assume Gary writes. There's a multitude of hand-written notes, torn pieces of paper, and pens left open.

We all sit down. I'm so anxious I think I'm about to throw up on the antique coffee table.

"We know a thing or two about sisters," I joke, lovingly looking at Max—as he supports my comment with a genuine laugh—when Gary explains that he started the co-op as an homage to his sister.

The conversation naturally flows between us. My anxiety vanishes—my elaborate plans on *what to say and how* with it. Gary's words work as a time machine where all his memories unfold clear as day for Max and me. My body naturally sinks deeper into the orange couch we picked—the more comfortable-looking one.

"It was my sister's dying wish to bring curious readers, writers, scholars... all of them together," Gary explains, his voice filled with love. "She dreamed of an utopian world where beauty would be shared freely. Where the secrets hidden between pages would be carried from one set of eyes to another. She believed that magic lay in writing."

"You have no idea how much this resonates with me," I say, unable to stop my voice from trembling.

My eyes water as I hang on to every word Gary shares about his sister. I know I would have loved this woman. She never managed to bring people together the way she hoped before she passed, so Gary started the co-op.

"I originally wanted to name it after her but decided against it," Gary continues, shaking his head. "She was a simple, humble woman. She wouldn't want anything named after her." He chuckles, his eyes glossy with memories of his late sister.

Gary shares more life stories, and we do the same in return.

The more Gary tells us, the more similarities I see with Max's story —the unconditional love for his sister, the fact that Gary grew up without his parents, becoming the man of the house at a young age and that he grew up in the very house we sit in.

I realize I was brought to Max because he was meant to meet Gary all along. Beyond the grimoire, beyond the magic, beyond the curse. There's silent guidance and wisdom in Gary's words. In his mere presence.

I gaze at my warlock. His features have softened, his eyes a pool of golden, shimmering liquid. The slight smile on his face speaks volumes beyond the feelings we secretly share through our bond. He feels the same. There's more to Gary than the co-op and the grimoire. Max needed to hear his story for reasons I may never fully comprehend. A tender pinch tugs at my heart. My hand reaches for my magical man's lap.

I anticipated having to lead the conversation, thinking Max would remain mainly silent. However, after Gary and Max both realize how much they share, despite the many years that separate them, Max takes the lead. His heart cracks open for us all to see.

He describes the book we're looking for. Not so much what it looks like but what it contains. He tiptoes around the real reason we are seeking it, but Max insists on how important it is to him. To his sister. To me. Gary silently nods, darting around the room as many questions form in his dark eyes.

"If you have said book, you know you do. You can feel it. I don't need to keep describing it to you, Gary." Max's tone is calm and composed. I remain silent, hanging at his lips, anxiously awaiting the final word.

A million emotions materialized on Gary's face as he considers every word. He shifts his weight on the couch, gently slaps his knees, and sighs. His expression is but a foreign language.

Without a word, Gary slowly gets up. His knees and back crack in the process. He leaves the room without so much of a look in our direction. Max and I exchange confused looks, silently wondering if this is our cue to leave.

Damn it.

Before we can decide, Gary materializes in the doorway, trotting toward us. He sits down and places a small, black, leather-bound book on the table. It resembles a simple notebook.

The leather, though noticeably ancient, kept its shiny, ink-black coat. The book is thin, maybe thirty pages. The pristine cover is a black canvas devoid of any embellishments or markings. No obvious sign of any magic. Its smooth surface reflects the light subtly, giving it a quiet elegance.

I turn my gaze to Max. We've faced disappointment so many times. Countless times, I thought we had found the grimoire, only to swallow my despair like a raging fire coating my throat.

But Max is crying.

Shiny pearls silently roll down his smooth skin, jumping off the edge of his jaw, crashing on his blue jeans. His lips are a thin, trembling line. His black pupils are two flames; golden and red and orange and alive.

"This was my sister's," Gary murmurs. "She found it as a little girl and gifted it to me before she passed. Her most precious possession. It's the very book that pushed me to start the co-op." Gary pauses, grazing over the black leather. "Sometimes, I could swear I hear voices whispering right into my ears. Voices from the book. Something telling me to find a way to share the knowledge contained within. Something nudged at my heart. But I never found the right opportunity."

"Did you ever share the manuscript with the co-op?" I ask Gary.

Gary shakes his head. "Only Henry and my sister have seen it."

A silence falls between us. Max's words come back to mind—how the book was created a long time ago and recently, at the same time. How the event traversed time and universes in a way I don't fully grasp.

"We will have to take this home, Gary. Is that okay?" Max's voice is a bare breath, nearly silent.

I shoot my gaze to Gary, who's considering the question very carefully. We both know this book means a lot to him—he has no idea how much it means to us. Gary's eyes travel around the room as if the answer was written somewhere on the walls.

He gives a slight head shake and chuckles as he tells us, "She would want the book to find its true purpose."

CHAPTER FIFTY-EIGHT

The second my feet hit the mansion's grand entrance, I fall to my knees. Howling. I'm howling.

My throat aches, releasing all the anguish, the anger, and the fear my body has been clinging to for the past weeks. Tears fall freely down my cheeks, forming cold puddles on the ground. My heart is about to jump out of my chest as my palms find the cold floor beneath me.

I can't think. I can't talk. I can't breathe.

The warmth of Max's powerful hand embraces my back. I hear his own sobbing. I feel the energy of relief pulsates through his fingers. A steady beat skimming over my skin that slowly brings me back to the room. I find my bearings again.

We fucking did it. We fucking did it.

My screaming alerted everyone in the house. Both Annie and Joffrey come bolting down the stairs. Joffrey kneels down to my height and cups my wet face. I meet his gaze and find a silent question inside it. A million silent questions.

I faintly nod, sobbing some more, drawing a small smile on my lips.

Joffrey jumps up and screams, his arms crossed over his stomach as he bows. More screams. Of joy. Of relief.

Annie walks toward Max and crashes on his chest. He embraces her, laying a soft kiss on her wrinkled forehead.

There's no time to waste. Max needs to break the curse. Immediately.

I'm still on the floor when he grabs my hand and swiftly leads me up the stairs. I've never been behind the massive steel door, never stepped foot inside his magical room, but I know that's where we are headed.

He wiggles his fingers, and the door creaks open, the sound of the shifting steel reverberating across the entire house.

The room not only feels like a vault, it somewhat looks like one. All four walls are made of shiny gray steel, reflecting the image of Max's sculpted body as he moves across the room. The center of the space is almost entirely eaten by a massive wooden table.

The table top is barely visible, covered in dried flowers, pieces of paper, candles—consumed and new—jars and other containers. Small plates contain burnt...something. Things I can't identify.

A collection of antique bottles sits nestled among bundles of dried flowers and twine on a nearby shelf. The bottles, adorned with intricate labels written in an unknown language, contain colorful liquids— potions and elixirs crafted with care, I'm sure.

The space smells like lavender and cinnamon. I can't tell if Max fills the room with his scent or if the scent of the room imprints on him. It doesn't matter. There's no window, no way in or out, besides the massive door that seals shut behind us.

Max waves one hand above the table, and it clears instantly—clear of any remains of ash and other dead things. He hasn't made eye contact with me yet—or even said a word, for that matter. I watch him silently lay the book on the table. Both his hands braced on the wood, framing it.

His eyes lock on the bundle of pages, shining their familiar neon green light. His chest fills, then collapses. Slowly. With slightly trembling hands, he finally grabs the leather cover and splits it open. Invisible energy jumps out of the pages and slams its force against the steel walls. I get it now, why they're made of steel.

Some bottles fall, shattering on the ground. Pieces of paper go flying around the room. The dried flowers are nothing but dust now, filling the air. Max shoots a concerned gaze up at me. In a silent nod, I confirm that I'm okay. The energy rippled along my skin like a wave of heat. But it didn't hurt. Not really.

"This is it," Max whispers.

"Can I look?" I shyly ask.

Just like the magic within The Collector's realm, the magic bound to the grimoire silently pulls me in. A magnetic draw I can't quite control. I need to know every word on the yellowed, crinkled pages. To touch the grain of the paper. Make one with it. Though it's difficult, I've learned to resist my urges when it comes to dark magic.

Max holds out his hand. I eagerly grab it and join him. But I can't make out any familiar words. The sentences on the pages aren't in a language I know. The symbols and shapes seem like they should be words, but they don't make sense.

"I can't..."

"I know," Max interrupts. "It's an ancient language, forgotten by many, even among our kind. My parents taught us. Being ambitious had some...perks, I suppose. They wanted to control a lot of things. With knowledge comes power."

"I want to help," I admit.

Max considers my words for a brief second, scanning my face with his irresistible emeralds, pausing at my lips. My cheeks heat up. He closes his eyes as he holds a flat hand above the spellbook. He chants something I, yet again, don't comprehend. The lines on his forehead grow deeper. The corner of his eyes creases.

I want to devour him. Magic looks good on him.

After a few seconds, Max opens his eyes. A grin spreads across his face when he realizes I haven't stopped looking at him for one second. He's a movie I could watch over and over again. My gaze follows when he jerks his chin toward the book.

My jaw drops. I can read it now. Whatever spell he cast upon the grimoire translated it for me.

"That should do," Max says.

We skim through the pages, one by one, looking for the perfect spell. The Collector's lover was undeniably angry. The woman devised quite the torturous set of spells to get back to her ex-lover. All are carefully hand-written within these pages. From physical and mental pain to ways of temporarily blocking his powers, invading his mind, giving life to his deepest fears, and, there it is... get out of a pact.

Max hovers his hand over the page. Our gazes meet. He silently nods. My heart turns into a drum. My blood hits every corner of my body with such intensity it almost hurts. The hot red liquid is traveling too fast within my veins.

We fucking did it.

CHAPTER FIFTY-NINE

Max grabs both my hands. He pulls me in, a featherlight touch. His hips meet mine. A sharp breath escapes me as I appreciate how hard he is, his pants stretching thin to contain the length of his desire. He lazily runs his fingers down my back, all the way down to my bottom. He tenderly cups my butt cheeks. Though I barely feel the pressure under his careful, calculated touch. The warmth emanating from his hands is doing all the work.

"Do you have any idea what I have in store for you, my love?" Max breathes at the base of my neck.

I shiver. My head naturally falls back, offering my neck. His warm breath runs the column of it. Before I know it, I will embrace the softness of his lips on my skin. I will feel the tip of his tongue claim my neck, his teeth claim my earlobes. His fingers will play the strings of the most sensitive areas of my body, collecting them as his own.

My body ignites with an insatiable hunger, a primal longing that consumes me whole. Desire courses through me like wildfire—the kind of fire not even Max can control.

"You better get to work then," I order.

Max chuckles. "I thought you wanted to help?"

My elbow digs into his ribcage as a response. "What can I do?"

"Let's gather ingredients."

Max flattens the page, and we graze over the ingredients required to perform the spell.

The list is surprisingly short, and, at first glance, the spell seems *fairly* easy to execute—considering the incredible outcome. Excitement is taking over my body. I shift on my feet, tapping my fingers on the wooden table like a child waiting for ice cream. We quickly reach the last ingredient on the list.

I blink.

And blink again.

I shake my head before redirecting my gaze to the last line of the ingredient list.

What the...?

Max's anger travels through our bond.

"No, no, no..." he frantically repeats, running his fingers over the page as if the last words were a mistake, something he could erase. Scratch away. Rewrite.

My stomach lurches, a sickening sensation creeping up my throat until it feels as if it's lodged in my mouth. The walls are closing in, crushing my skull inch by inch.

"No, no, no!" Max is screaming.

Everything within his reach is now scattered on the floor. The sturdy steel comes in handy for containing his anger, too. The noise inside my head is unbearable—roaring chaos. A raging storm takes over. A heavy emptiness settles over me. I want to read the words over, but my vision is blacked out.

A virgin's soul.

The last ingredient hit Max and me like a bag of bricks. The spell requires a virgin's soul. I almost forgot that we were dealing with dark, ancient magic. I can't apply my human logic to this. Seeing how Max is reacting, I suppose even in the magical realms, a virgin's soul is—at the very least—frowned upon.

I'm suffocating inside this damn room. I reach for the heavy door, but it won't budge. I cry out, slamming the unforgiving material with both hands. My fingers crack against the thick metal. Max doesn't look in my direction. My kneeled king waves a hand, and the door obeys.

The air of the mansion digs a tunnel into my lungs. Windows have been left open, granting access to the crisp autumn air.

I find Joffrey sitting on the floor. He's been waiting for us. I watch the hopeful light in his eyes vanish instantly when he takes in my current state. I'm shaking, sobbing, suffocating. Every step I take is clumsy, threatening to fail.

"Hannah..." Joffrey whispers as he rushes to me, lodging his arm under my shoulders to hold me up. "What happened?"

CHAPTER SIXTY

"I will do it if you ask me. I will do it for you and Alice." Max's tone is grave. Flat. There are so many emotions encapsulated inside of it that none come through.

We have yet to talk to Alice. We haven't told her we found the grimoire.

"He's joking, right?" Joffrey says in my direction, scoffing. "What are you going to do, Maximilian? Pick up a girl in the street and ask her if she's a virgin? And then what, we just shoot her in the backyard? Are you out of your damn mind?"

I nervously chuckle at the insanity of it all.

We gathered in the living room, numb and confused and angry. Joffrey has spent so much time with us that he's clearly grown quite comfortable around Max.

Annie's footsteps hit the ground above our heads. She's carefully tending to Brandie and Maggie. I suspect she's avoiding the reality that just hit us all in the face.

Max dismisses Joffrey's comment completely and locks his eyes with mine. He braces his arms on his knees to make sure I truly hear every single one of his words.

"I don't think you understand, Hannah. I would cover every single star, one by one until there is no light left to shine on the world. If it takes me a million lifetimes. If it means loving you freely, I would suffocate the sun with my bare hands."

His words hurtle over my skin, seep through every pore, through my flesh, and down to my bones.

Gods, I love him.

"No one will die because of me, ever again, Maximilian," I say in a bare breath, reminding myself of the lives we lost.

Alice and I have a little over a day left to live.

We don't know what The Collector will do with Brandie and Maggie's souls. I want to believe he will release them once he collects us. *Once he gets his hands on a Forstthorn.* That they were both nothing but a reminder of his wickedness, of his extensive powers.

So many people have suffered greatly in the name of our love. So many have paid for a magical pact they know nothing about. A world they don't know anything about. No part of me can accept the idea of sacrificing another human life to save ours. It's out of the question.

"There must be another way," Joffrey begs. "We have the fucking book. Isn't there another spell in there?" His question floats in the air between us.

I haven't read every spell, but if there was one, Max would know. Some incantations would mess with The Collector, sure. Cause great pain. Surely not enough to free us all, though. We all remain silent a little longer.

Joffrey jumps up. "Fuck this!"

That sums it up pretty well.

Max's fingers lace between his neck, looking down. "I can't live in a world where you don't exist," he whispers tremblingly.

I get up and find the open seat next to my magical king. I release his hands and interlace his fingers with mine. My head falls on his shoulder. I will miss his lavender and cinnamon scent the most. Joffrey is pacing around the room, screaming and swearing. His eyes filled with the blood carried by his tears, or his anger, or both.

"I want her to come back. I want her to be safe with you guys." I sigh my words, each syllable a soft exhale that brushes against the air, looking at Max, then Joffrey.

Joffrey scoffs. My wish for Brandie holds no weight against the will of the beast holding her captive right now. And I can do just that—*wish*.

"I want my memory erased if she doesn't come back," Joffrey says to Max as he collapses on the leather couch opposite us. "I know. I'm a coward. I get it. But I can't do it, man. I can't do it without her."

There's no judgment in Max's gaze when he nods and agrees. No part of him wants to convince Joffrey otherwise. Max knows damn well what it's like to live with the knowledge of your true love gone.

I slap my lap and exhale. "I want everyone to go refresh." There's no room for negotiation in my tone. "We will meet in one hour for one last dinner. There will be no tears. I want everyone to think of one of their favorite memories. We will share them. I want love and laughter. Force yourself if you have to. I don't give a shit. I want our last night together to be memorable." I order the small group.

CHAPTER SIXTY-ONE

As the sun dips below the horizon, casting hues of gold and crimson across the sky, we gather in the dining room—the room I barely ever sit in. I prefer the coziness and the familiarity of the kitchen—but tonight is special. We have under twenty-four hours left together.

For the first time since I met The Collector, I'm not rushing. Not tonight. I have spent the last seven days counting every hour as if someone was sliding a sharp blade between my shoulders, and I braced for every inch. Every second ticking dragged me closer to a terrible end. My eyes constantly locked on the passing time.

But tonight, there's a grim sort of peace washing over me. I have accepted my fate. Tonight, I will not rush; I will not fight the precious hours we have remaining. I will relish every second I get to spend around the people I love the most.

I haven't talked to my parents, haven't said goodbye. Max will cast a spell on them after I'm gone. I refused to know the details. I left it all up to him to come up with the best scenario for them.

Alice portals from the coven. The air inside the mansion turns to ice when she arrives. Her hair is up in a beautiful, intricate bun that looks like someone placed a blooming flower on her head. Her makeup is flawless, embellished with dark red lips—accentuating her already sharp cheekbones and frosty blue eyes.

She opted for a long, black dress. Tight at the bodice, cascading freely down her long legs to the floor. The black fabric is thin enough to reveal her pearl-like skin under her breasts and around her thighs. Lethally beautiful, just like her brother.

Her face is a mask of calm. She may have accepted our outcome, too. Or maybe she locked her emotions away in a small iron cage for the night—or forever.

Jazz is playing in the background—a light, happy melody to support the mood.

The table is set for a feast fit for royalty. In the center, a golden roast glistens, its savory scent wafting through the air and setting our mouths watering. Surrounding it, Annie prepares an array of dishes, each more delectable than the last: platters of roasted vegetables and bowls of creamy mashed potatoes. A basket of warm, crusty bread sits on the edge of the table, its aroma mingling with the sweet scent of freshly baked pastries. Glasses brimmed with fine wine, their ruby-red depths reflecting the soft glow of candlelight flickering across the room.

Joffrey laughs at the amused confusion written on my face. "It's true!" He insists. "That's my favorite memory of Brandie!"

"Meeting *me*?" I lift my hands in the air, laughter bubbling up, and everyone around the table joins in. "That doesn't make any sense, man!"

"It does! Because that's when I *knew* she talked about me," Joffrey breathes in a laugh, his eyes glistening with a joyful light. "You were *so* obvious, Hannah," he smirks, arching an eyebrow.

"Oh, I'll be damned!" No pun intended.

I really thought I was being discreet that day. Of course, I already knew everything about Joffrey's achievements. Of course, Brandie shared details I had never asked for. But I was pretty sure I had it under control. I take another sip of the delicious wine to calm the uncontrollable laughter.

Max has claimed the seat next to mine. He occasionally slides a warm hand under the table to meet my knee. His feather touch skims the skin of my lower thigh, up and down, tracing lazy circles on my lap.

The emotion is overwhelming his fiery pupils. Our last night together. And yet, we'll never be *truly* together. We'll never *truly* hold each other.

"I think my favorite memory of you, Hannah," Alice breaks the comfortable silence after taking another sip of her whiskey—she's so much like her brother, "Is that one night you let loose at game night. You're cute when you have too much to drink." She tilts her head and winks at me.

Both she and Max share an amused smile. My throat bobs as I faintly shrug my shoulders. It's a night that happened before Max erased my memories. A cherished moment I will never get back. Ever.

I hoped that, with time and proximity, I could get some of my memories back. That, triggered by the intensity of my love for Max, something would come to light. But nothing. It's all gone. For good.

The frustration must be evident on my face—as much as I try to hide it—because Max clears his throat and offers a toast. To us. To love. His voice quavers as he raises his glass, each word a fragile whisper on the verge of breaking—clumsy and trembling. The emotion is palpable, making his every syllable heavy with sadness and heartfelt sincerity. But it's exactly what we all needed.

The night reaches its thickest and darkest as we lounge around the dining table. Dirty dishes and tons of used glasses have piled up—we forbid Annie to clean up.

I lean deeper into my chair as I gaze over *my* family. The family I chose for myself. A sense of deep anger grips my guts as Brandie is missing. All because of me. *She* should be here. I should be the one locked up in a spiritual prison for eternity. But I refuse to let the feeling take over me—it's a raging internal battle. I can't spoil our last night.

I run a lazy hand through Max's hair and rest it on the back of his neck, caressing his skin with the tip of my fingers. He faintly jerks his chin towards the balcony door. I take the hint.

I lean against the cold stone rail of the broad paved terrace, looking up at the stars. Max's body towers over mine, as close as the curse allows. I caress both his cheeks. I embrace the quiet of the terrace. The quiet of the endless garden stretching in the darkness behind us. The light of the partial moon bounces off his curls, gifting him a silver crown. He looks like a true king. *My* true king.

"So, every single one of them, huh?" I joke, pointing at the starry sky above our heads, repeating his own words. *I would cover every single star, one by one.*

Max chuckles, "And some."

His proximity has always lit an undeniable fire inside me; maybe tonight—our last night—we could consume it. The idea has been lingering since I decided on this last dinner as a family. What if we ended this with a bang?

My hands find the valleys of Max's chest, fisting the top of his shirt. I lean in with a grin, pressing my hips against his, grinding against his body, guided by sheer desire.

"Hannah," he breathes into my ear.

"I want this. I want you." I lace my arms behind his neck, closing the hair-thin gap between our bodies.

"We can't..." There's hesitation in Max's voice, as if, for the span of a heartbeat, he considered it too.

"What is there to lose?" I argue. "Please, Max..." I beg, intensifying the dance of my hips against his pants.

What *is* there to lose? I will be gone before I know it. My body a sheer memory of who I used to be. My soul locked away in hell for eternity. Why could I not be with my lover just once before ending it all?

"Babygirl," Max murmurs, his voice a low growl. "I want you, too."

"Take me, Max. Take me, please." I beg, my body shaking from the weight of this all-consuming desire.

Max slowly pushes me away, bringing us back to the safe zone.

"If I do this, he will take you the very second I lay a hand on you," Max says, defeated. "I won't even have the chance to feel you. Let alone taste you. It'll be all over before I can take my next breath. And I want every single second I can get with you, Hannah."

His eyes travel the length of my face as if he's just now really *seeing* me. We fall into a tender silence, rocked by the brisk wind of the night playing in the fallen leaves. It never reaches us as Max casts a warm shield around us.

"Promise me something, Maximilian."

"Oh, we are using full names, are we? Am I in trouble because I said no?" he grins.

I slap his forearms and lay a severe look on him.

"Anything, my love," he says.

I fill my lungs fully. "You need to promise me you will never complete the spell. To get us back."

Max's gaze instantly shoots to the side, avoidant and hurt. His jaw ticks, underlying his pursed, trembling lips. His eyes fill with the colors of hell, burning and raging. All the anger and wrath he's been bottling up tonight shoots up and floods his golden pebbles. All the emotions I forced him and our friends to swallow. To cage up. They're all right here, consuming my magical lover entirely.

His fist strikes the stones behind me with a resounding thud as he works to regulate his breath. The sound resonates through the quiet night, and I notice how the stone yields, molding to the muscles of my back and offering a soft landing for Max's fist. The house is protecting its master from harm.

He *has* thought of it. I knew it. He's considered it. I have, too. I don't need his hands on me to know that both are still clenched into fists against the stone rail, now hard again.

"Promise me," I insist.

A faint, forced nod is all I get in response. It's enough for me. For now.

CHAPTER SIXTY-TWO

I leave the group for a moment and head upstairs to my bedroom. I know we're not catching any sleep tonight, and the tight, red, sleeveless dress I chose for our last dinner together is getting less and less comfortable. I need sweatpants and a T-shirt if I want to make it through the night.

I allow my gaze to travel around my bedroom one more time. Over every single detail of this space I now call mine. Over the books tightly pressed together on the shelves beside the bed.

Max chose this very room just for me—the first night he asked me to stay at the mansion. He thought of it as a safe space, away from the danger of Willowbrook. My fingers trail behind me, tracing the edges of the bed, the dresser, the shelves. In slow motion. A small, sad smile tugs on my lips. I swallow the water ironically burning my eyes.

I wonder what The Collector's realm will be like.

Where will we sleep, if at all? What will we wear? Will it be burning, loud, and smelling of decay? The complete opposite of the grandiose castle where the beast lives?

I pick white sweatpants and Max's black T-shirt—left on the chair where he spent every single night for the last seven days. It smells of lavender and cinnamon; of course it does. I run my hands over the comfortable, warm fabric, taking a deep breath in. The familiar scents fill me up, calming my breathing and heart down. If I must pick an outfit for the afterlife, this is what I want—so I can carry Max's scent with me for eternity.

As I head for the staircase to find my friends again, a faint—almost inaudible—drumming sound catches my attention. It comes from the floor above. Something yanks at my heart, ordering me to follow it. I quietly eat the stairs as if walking on air. I wander the hallway of the last floor, not knowing exactly what I'm looking for. As I walk past Max's bedroom, I stop at the door.

His room belongs in a magazine; trendy, organized, pretty much spotless. Black curtains mirror the ink black of his silk sheets. A blood-red rug sits under a large green Victorian dresser. Massive bedposts support a canopy made of the finest material—I can't help but think that I will never use them in spicy, kinky ways.

Not a sound to be heard but this strange, unclear drumming. I pass the large windows open to the infinite night, one by one, following the corner of the hallway. Past the turning point is Max's working room.

The floor is different here. The hardwood has given way to large, cold stones. The kind you wouldn't expect inside a house. The steel door is still wide open. After the hammer that fell on us earlier, Max must have forgotten to seal it. The buzzing in my ears turns to ringing as I get closer.

I glance into the room, my eyes landing on the table where the damn spellbook lies open. After everything we've endured, the suffering that surrounds us, it's inconceivable that a single line in that damn grimoire could seal Alice and me to our doom.

I walk to the grimoire to lay a cold, resentful gaze over it one more time. Such a small piece of literature, holding such a heavy weight over our lives. I run my hand over the grainy page, grazing over the one spell. *Just one more time.* I thought it'd be all over in a blink. And yet. This damn list of ingredients. I murmur every single one of them to myself, building my own personal hell. One by one.

Until the last fucking one. *A virgin's soul.*

No. Wait. Fuck.

Wait.

I rush down the stairs, eating them two by two. A broken ankle is always better than an eternity in hell.

"Read this," I order Joffrey and Alice.

They both shoot me a confused look, wondering out loud if I've gone crazy. Max jumps off his chair like a cat sprayed with water when he realizes what I just launched across the table.

"Read!" I bark.

Joffrey reads out loud, going over the short list of ingredients, his tone flat, resembling a kid doing his homework. Alice reads silently, but her eyes fly wide open when she reaches the last line.

"Okay," Joffrey says, "A virgin soul. I know that, Hannah."

"Read it again."

He repeats the same words. "A virgin soul. Do we have to rub salt on the wound? I thought this dinner was supposed to stay positive."

I scan Alice's and Max's faces. They heard it. They heard Joffrey's words. Alice's features remain frozen, but I clearly see the light ignite in her icy eyes. I see how her eyebrows fly up and how her jaw hangs open ever so slightly.

CHAPTER SIXTY-THREE

Max shuts his eyes.

"How did we miss it?" He whispers, both hands braced on the table, silent tears streaming down his perfect face.

"I don't know, I don't know," I admit, shaking my head as I throw my hands in the air.

I'm pacing around the room, giggling and scoffing. The beating in my heart is out of control at this point. My legs are shaking. The floor has turned to clouds, or marshmallows, or some kind of mushy texture beneath my feet. The house is holding its breath. I can sense it.

"What are you guys talking about?" Joffrey grows impatient. "A virgin soul. We knew that much," he throws his hands in the air.

"A virgin soul, Joffrey." Alice finally motions her lips, her words a bare breath. "Not a virgin's soul," she corrects him.

"What difference does it make?" he challenges her, frustrated.

Everything I've learned at the conference a few months earlier flashes in front of my eyes. The speaker session on paganism I attended. I don't know how Max and I missed this *literal* life-saving detail.

"A virgin soul is not necessarily a virgin's soul," Alice explains. "A virgin soul means a *pure* soul. Like a child's, for instance. A virgin's, of course, but also certain animals. Like a dove's soul. A soul that's not spoiled by greed, lust, or evil."

All colors drain from Joffrey's face when the realization dawns on him—I'm pretty sure he's about to be sick.

There will be no shooting someone in the garden. Max hasn't moved. His eyes locked on the table before him. His chest painfully rises and falls as his breathing intensifies. His tears are now a continuous, glowing stream.

"Where do we find one?" Joffrey screams. He jumps around the dining table, darting around the room. His cheeks are flushed. There's no time to waste. "Can you summon a dove?" his eyes run the distance between Alice and Max, questioning them.

"Not easily," Alice confesses. "But the coven's property is full of them. They are protectors of the magical realm."

Alice trots toward me, grabs my hands, and brings them to her mouth. She presses a strong, thankful kiss on my fingers. "You are my hero, Hannah."

I can barely see her pupils behind the tsunami inside her ocean eyes.

My mouth runs dry—a strange mix of excitement, relief and worry. I could see the bright light waiting for us at the end of the tunnel but couldn't spot the traps still possibly hidden in front of us.

Alice portals back within minutes, holding an oddly relaxed and calm bird. Its feathers are the white of pearls. Beautiful black diamonds for eyes. Max gently grabs the animal and orders me to follow him upstairs. There's no time to spare. My lover turns around to face me when we reach the steel door.

"I can't have you in here with me." Worry stretches the corners of his mouth.

"I'll be waiting for you. Right here." I gesture to my feet.

He chuckles. A faint nod. Max's eyes rake over each of my features, spending precious minutes scanning every inch of my body.

"I love you," he finally says in a breath. "I can't wait to kiss you."

"Don't make me wait too long, warlock." A feline grin on my face as I grab the space between his thighs. A handful of it. Grazing the barrier of his thick pants for the last fucking time.

"You're evil, Hannah Scotch."

I merely incline my head as I say, "You have no idea."

Before the door seals behind him, I tell Max, "Make sure it won't suffer, will you?" Jerking my chin towards the delicate bird still nested in his hands as I swallow my guilt as best I can.

"Promise. It will fall asleep peacefully." Max's gaze is truthful as he gently pets the small white head between his fingers. I didn't expect anything else from him.

The heavy metallic door slams shut in its usual shout. A deep sigh escapes me, tears spilling like shattered glass, scattering fragments of emotion across my face. My frame quivers. I collapse onto the stone floor, bracing for impact as my back meets the sturdiness of the wall.

And I wait.

Long minutes go by before I notice anything. The eerie silence creeps inside my heart. I didn't expect the vault door to betray what was happening on the other side—no sound is escaping this room, that much I know. But I was hoping for a sign. Something to reassure me, to show that things are going as expected. That Max is safe.

Instead, I watch in horror as the stone floor cracks open.

Emerging from under the door, large fissures—like roots sprawling underground—spread across the room, breaking the stones from wall to wall. I shriek, pressing harder against the wall. The entire house is shaking, the ceiling giving up small pieces of white concrete.

Dust is filling the space quickly. From inside the cracks, angry fire erupts. Glowing red and orange flames burn high from below the stones, menacing.

I grab my knees and hold them tight to my chest. More tears overflow like a river breaking its banks. The door yields a sound, after all. A guttural, otherworldly voice emanates from the room where Max is locked. It sounds angry. The sound comes from nowhere and from every corner, every wall, every stone, all at the same time. It sends a shivering down my spine, like needles piercing my bones.

Sinister shadows slither forth from hidden crevices, their tendrils snaking across the walls around me like serpents. They emerge with a ghastly hunger, their forms shifting and morphing with an evil fluidity. The shadows seem to take on a life of their own, twisting into grotesque shapes that mock the laws of nature. I squeeze my eyes shut and force myself to count to ten, just like Dad taught me as a child.

I barely reach five when a piercing screech flies through the air, coming from inside the room. I don't recognize Max's voice or anyone I might know. I attempt to take a grounding breath. I *must* trust him. It takes everything in me to fight my instincts and not run to that damn door.

Time crawls, each minute a drawn-out eternity. I don't know the time or how long Max has been trapped performing the spell. The heat within the mansion is sourced by hell. My face is covered with a blend of tears and sweat and remains of dust.

The air smells like charcoal and ash. I can barely breathe or see—the air is thick from the fallen ceiling and pieces of walls.

I cover my ears and close my eyes. I feel crushed. Oppressed by the scene around me. The flames, the shadows, the shaking walls, the voices and eerie giggles. It's too much. It's taking over me. It's winning.

And then, *nothing*.

CHAPTER SIXTY-FOUR

The silence is deafening. It's as though the whole house had blinked after waking from a nightmare. Though the wide cracks in the stone-paved floor still glow this hellish red, the dancing shadows on the walls have vanished. The trembling has stopped —but it doesn't make what's left of the room any less eerie.

I run both palms over my eyelashes, chasing away the dust. My body aches from sitting so tightly. I release my numb limbs and push myself up. The surrounding scene is that of a battlefield. The mansion is hurt. I can tell by the strange, heavy breathing of the walls. The missing pieces of concrete. The broken stones.

The steel door finally slams open with a loud *bang*, and the outline of Max's powerful body appears, standing in the frame.

He's nothing but a shadow contrasted by the bright light of the room behind him. He's breathing heavily, slightly bent over. His eyes turned into two dark wells of black abyss, like he harnessed the deepest rings of hell and held them there. I slowly walk toward him, yielding only a step or two in his direction.

My eyes scan him for a movement, a word. He leans against the frame of the door. I barely recognize his features. I must look somewhat terrified at the sight because he doesn't wait much longer to blurt out, "We've done, *babygirl*. We've done it."

His words float between us for a moment, emphasized by his feline grin. They strike me when they land, shattering me. My body starts shaking uncontrollably. The accumulation of stress, anxiety, and fear of the past weeks leaves me all at once. Only when I start sobbing can I catch a full breath, filling my lungs up fully. I hold my head in my hands, covering my eyes.

"We have?" I mumble behind my fingers, stumbling on every syllable.

Have we? Have we really beat the curse? Have we tricked the Collector of Souls for good? Is Alice safe? Am I?

We've been clawing our way out of this curse for weeks on end. Leaving us bloody and exhausted and desperate. We've walked to hell and back, hoping to set everyone and ourselves free.

We just wanted love. Freedom.

It's been weeks of turmoil and despair. A string of infinite hours sitting in silence, wondering if we will ever see a way out of this mess. It's been never-ending days wondering what a life without each other would be like—and if we even would want to live it at all.

As my hands release my swollen eyes, I look up at Max. I *truly* see him.

He's shirtless. His jeans are ripped in multiple places. His torso and face are covered in bleeding scratches, signs of a terrible fight with whatever forces he had to overcome in there.

There's ash smeared over most of his bare skin. Sweat pearls on his forehead and on his chest. I don't think I could ever grasp the terrors he had to face *alone* to end this nightmare. I would take the pain and carry it all by myself if I could. I would do anything to relieve him from the memories of what he fought behind that door. Memories that will most likely haunt him forever.

Limping, my king makes his way towards me, ignoring the cracks and destruction around us. He kneels at my feet and grabs my hands. Though his eyes are still endless pits of darkness, I see a gentle warmth in them—it will morph back to fire in no time.

For the first time, he kisses my hand. *Fully*. No more brushing my skin with the wind of his breath. The softness of his full lips claims me. Eats me whole. I close my eyes. He lays a kiss on every finger. He takes his time. After every kiss, he licks the tip of each of my fingers, looking up at me with hunger.

We've done it.

Max stands and picks me up in a swift motion that I barely have time to notice. His muscles like stone against my small body. He presses my back against the wall behind me, and his hands find my bottom to hold me up.

I take the hint and lock my legs around his waist. The distance between us grows smaller by the second. I welcome the searing heat of his touch, losing myself in the burn of his skin against mine, oblivious to the blood, the sweat, the ash. With one hand, Max brushes away the hair partially covering my face.

"I see you, my love," he says, diving into my eyes.

It's not just joy that creeps up my spine. It's not quite excitement either. It's something else entirely—and new. Our heartbeats sync up. When his chest rises, mine falls. We are one.

I hold my breath when I notice Max's face move closer to mine. When I think I will finally taste my lover for the very first time, I hear the familiar whooshing of a portal behind me. With a playful grin, he forces me through. I shriek.

CHAPTER SIXTY-FIVE

Though I have never laid here, I recognize Max's sheets instantly. The silk brushes the bare skin of my arms. Comfort and warmth embrace me with both arms. *I'm home.* Max is holding himself above me, just a whisker's breadth apart.

His gaze sails from my eyes to my mouth and back. A smile stretches his face, seemingly permanently carved onto his mouth. He licks his bottom lip slowly. He's getting ready to feast.

Before I can make a sassy comment, the tip of his tongue meets the corner of my lips. He traces their edges with a warm, claiming lick, leaving a trail of sheer desire behind. A low, guttural growl escapes through his teeth. Time stops as the sting between my legs grows stronger.

He grabs my hip with one hand, pressing his fingers deeper into my side. He finds my cheek and lays a soft caress there. His curls mingle with my long hair—so close his eyelashes graze my face.

Max finally crashes his lips against mine with a loud sigh of relief. We can touch. We can kiss. We can feast off of each other. A soft kiss, at first. I swear fireworks are going off around us. It's like a bolt of lightning, electrifying and exhilarating as if every atom in my being was alight with the intensity of our connection.

My nails dig into the warmth of his back in response, pulling him closer. A deep growl rumbles up his throat.

His tongue finds mine, grazing my teeth, the inside of my mouth, in a sensual dance. The thin layer of fabric covering the bundle of nerves between my legs is flooded. Max's kiss is claiming, possessive, animal. His tongue strikes mine, clicks, again and again, to the rhythm of his moans. His hips press into mine every time his tongue licks my own.

Maximilian tastes like pleasure itself.

He smooths his body over mine, covering my skin with every fragment of his. In his gold and green pools dance both feral desire and genuine love. It's an exquisite mix, a perfect combination. I let the sensation wash over me as I trail my fingers, drawing the valleys of his back muscles. He lets his head down again, and I offer the curvature of my neck as a gift. He obliges, moaning.

"You are delicious, Hannah."

His warm, damp tongue trails the length of my neck, from my ear to my collarbone, occasionally grazing my skin with his teeth.

We belong together.

He bites into my neck. I've been craving him for so long that I'm about to explode. I'm so consumed by him that I didn't notice how he tore off my clothes in one quick movement, leaving nothing but the intricate lace of my underwear between our bodies. There's no safe barrier now, is there?

My breasts harden as a plea for more when they meet the skin of his chest. He's powerful and unbending against me. His hips push to make one with my lower region as he groans in my ear, "I want to *own* you, Hannah."

The words send a shot of bliss down my spine, and I arch my back to get even closer. I need to be his. Max's tongue works its magic as I'm incapable of moving, laying defenseless on my predator's bed. He follows the shape of my collarbone. From the edge, he draws a line down to my nipple.

His tongue rests there for a moment, clicking, swaying, and claiming. As incredible as the fire felt on my body before we could touch, nothing could compare to the warm touch of his hands and the possessive strikes of his tongue. I howl out of pleasure when the sting of his teeth owning my nipple traverses through my body.

"Fuck," I breathe out.

"Patience, my love," Max teases in answer.

He pushes himself up and off the bed. Using the familiar move, Max rearranges my body with a wiggle of his fingers. I find myself seated at the edge of the bed, braced on both hands. Max finds my mouth again. His lips a delicious treat I fully embrace.

One of my arms snakes behind his neck to keep him close. I would devour his face if I could. His lips. His tongue. He keeps kissing me—claiming me as his own.

A sharp breath races out of my lungs when his thumb presses on the delicate and sensitive spot between my thighs, enjoying the wet warmth waiting for him there. He growls as he draws lazy circles.

His breath intensifies as more fingers meet between my thighs. He plays with my lower lips, up and down slowly. Finally, he plunges three fingers inside of me. My nails dig into his back. I moan, pushing my hips upwards to take it all in. His finger-play intensifies, speeds up.

He plays inside me as if he knows the space like the back of his hand. Every move is more delightful than the last. I hear his chuckles as my breath sharpens, my soul slowly leaving my body.

Just before he sends me over the edge, Max abruptly stops. He pulls his fingers out and brings them to his mouth. He licks every single one of them, painfully stretching time, looking at me with playful mischief.

Max cups my face with both hands, plunging his gaze into my eyes. He kisses my cheeks softly. My forehead. My nose. Back to my lips.

"I love you," he whispers.

I loop my arms around him and intensely, sensually kiss him back. I graze a hand over his chest, stopping where he's been cut. The blood has started to clot. I clearly see bruises now, too. I run a light finger over his wounds, wincing. Tears crowd my eyes at the thought of what he's been through. The ashy-looking smears have mixed with his blood and sweat, darkening his golden skin.

I brace myself up to kiss his neck, his chest, and every scratch and cut I can reach. His fingers strike my hair.

"I'm fine," Max whispers in my ear. "I'm okay."

With the thumb that was playing the chords of pleasure just a minute ago, he wipes a fallen tear on my cheek. I close my eyes as both his hands frame my face again.

The pressure between my thighs grows. A strong nudge at my entrance. I didn't realize that Max took his pants off. Sneaky warlock. Our bare skins make one, his hips carefully lodged between mine. He's hard, warm, and thick, pushing gently at my entrance, begging for permission.

I lock my legs around his waist. Using my calves, I press against his lower back. My wetness happens to be the perfect ally. Though he thought he was in control, Maximilian penetrates me. Hard and deep.

He growls, stunned by my unexpected move, then chuckles. I moan louder than I ever have. I add to the pattern of scratches already covering his skin as I feel him, giving myself entirely.

Max leaves a string of kisses from my neck to my breasts, thrusting his hips with intensity. Every move steals a loud moan out of me. Our hearts beat the same rhythm. Max fills me, repeatedly. I scream his name. He grins.

"Burn for me, Hannah Scotch." He playfully orders, using his own words from a past situation.

Nothing compares to the antithesis of his hard length and soft skin. He fits perfectly. We were always meant to be. His eyes turn to sheer fire as his thrusts intensify. I beg him for more. The closer I get to losing myself, the tighter my grip on the back of his neck gets. His hands are framing my head, holding on to my hair.

He moves faster and faster until I make one with the desirable pump inside of me. Maximilian moans my name—I scream his—as we both climax together, holding each other tightly.

The room disappears. All my senses are on high alert as I let ecstasy take control over my body. I'm shaking, incapable of managing such intense emotions.

The sweat of his chest drips onto my breasts. Max collapses onto me. His breath comes in ragged gasps, like waves crashing against the shore after a storm, each inhalation a desperate attempt to capture the lingering ecstasy of release. We lay here in silence as one. His arms are lodged under my back. My legs are still locked around his waist.

When the room around us materializes again, we both laugh. A genuine, uncontrollable laughter. Of relief, of love, of lust. All the emotions we intended to suppress for weeks bubble forth like a brook cascading over smooth stones.

Max repeated the process two more times.

By the time we decided to get cleaned up and let reality settle, my body was numb—every inch pleasured and pleased and satisfied.

I was gifted with an extra orgasm as we took a long-drawn bath together, the rising sun filtering through the floor-to-ceiling windows of Max's bathroom. The colors of the morning were starting to spill over the black canvas of the night.

By now, I should have been dead. *Collected.*

CHAPTER SIXTY-SIX

"I was going to give you two five more minutes before I came knocking." Her voice is a crystalline melody, creating ripples in my blood.

Max had hinted at the fact that everyone was safe as an excuse to keep working on my body before we left his room.

My stomach jumps up and down at the sight of her. I bolt toward Brandie, crashing into her like a hurricane reaching the shore. Her arms embrace me. We both crumble on the floor, sobbing and screaming. My trembling mirrors hers.

When she finally softens her grip, I grab her cheeks and scan her face —mainly looking for any sign of injury. She's as beautiful as ever, her ocean eyes filled with star-like light. She doesn't even seem tired. She smells of roses and other exotic scents.

We stay on the floor for a moment longer, a small hill of flesh and cries and hugs. Relief washes over me like a cool breeze on a scorching day, melting away the icy grip of fear that had clenched at my soul. The weight of our separation lifts from my shoulders, along with the guilt, replaced by an overwhelming sense of gratitude.

She's safe. She's alive. She's back.

"Will you stay with us for a few days, please?" I beg Joffrey and

Brandie as I find Max's side again. His fingers lace with mine as he presses a kiss on the side of my head.

"We'll be back soon, but I am taking this one away in the afternoon," Joffrey answers, pulling Brandie in.

Joffrey's eyes meet mine with a silent agreement. I faintly nod. Next time I see my best friend, she will have a ring on her finger.

Questions burn my throat and threaten to jump off my lips, but I rear them in. I want to know how it was—on the other side. I want to know what the beast did to her, how terrible my vengeance needs to be. But I don't say a word. Some things are better left unsaid—for now.

I spot the silver mane made of silk crowning Alice's head, peeking from behind Joffrey. The icy blue of her eyes blurred from the tears. She takes a deep breath before she runs to me. She squeezes both my forearms and silently stares, a smile crinkling the corner of her eyes.

"Did I mention you were my hero?" She attempts to say in between sobs.

Her tiny body embraces mine. Contrasting with her frozen touch, Max's heat covers us both from behind my back.

My family.

CHAPTER SIXTY-SEVEN

The ringing of my phone pulls me out of my slumber. I stretch like a cat after a nap in the sun—exactly what I was doing. The mansion's paved terrace faces south. I took advantage of the off days I granted myself—deciding that The Book Nook could stay closed for a couple more days.

I giggle and wave a dismissive hand, not bothering to look over my shoulder. I know Max is staring at my half-naked body from one of the windows, most likely fantasizing about what he will do to me once I come back inside. He's been amazingly creative since he broke the curse, leveraging his perfect body along with his fire magic. Making me melt every time.

Annie's breaking voice shoots out from the kitchen, reaching for the sky above. Her pitch is *too* high, her tone trembling. I jump off the lounging chair and cover myself before rushing towards the glass doors.

Annie's been cooking all morning. I wouldn't be surprised if she injured herself.

When I enter the kitchen, Max is already standing on the other side —he too alerted by the urgency of Annie's voice. His features hardened, his eyes host a raging, unnatural fire. His jaw ticks.

Distracted by the apparent panic and anger covering my warlock's face, I didn't notice the two hooded figures standing by Annie's side in the corner. Two females, tall and skinny, wearing sage green hooded robes that flow down to the floors in one elegant wave.

One of them pulls her hood down, revealing striking beauty. Her thick hair is the black of the winter night, falling on each side of her neck down to her stomach. Her skin reflects the sun filtering through like a jewel on display. She's quite literally sparkling. Her eyes meet mine for a brief moment before they bounce back to Max. Her lips are full, betraying the weight of unsaid words.

I know instantly—they are witches.

I throw a confused look at Max, who has not met my gaze yet. He's staring at the floor, his fists clenched by his sides.

"He's taken her," Annie sobs. She pulls on Max's arm, threatening to collapse.

"We let our guard down, Maximilian. It was supposed to be all over." The black-haired witch attempts to explain, her voice the frequency of the wind. "He struck in the middle of the night."

"Alice," I whisper as the realization dawns on me.

The Collector of Souls has taken Alice.

"He took her soul?" I ask in a breath.

"No," the witch addresses me directly. "He took her. He took her body. She's in his realm now."

I open and close my mouth. Alice is now the Collector's captive. He didn't simply take her soul. He took *her*.

"But why?" I whisper, my voice trembling.

Everyone in the room exchanges a look I recognize too well—they know something I don't.

That's when it hits me. The truth I think I knew in my heart from the beginning. The missing puzzle piece that has been feeding my gut feelings this whole damn time. Somehow, I knew. I could sense it. I read it in the silent gazes and fainted nods. I read it in the tears Alice shed. I read it in her trembling fingers when the beast's name was mentioned. Maybe I should have known instantly when Alice mentioned she had been invited to his realm before.

I was blinded, but it was all around me this entire time. I simply refused to see it.

"It's her," I start, collapsing on one of the chairs. "Alice is The Collector's lover. She's the one he betrayed. She's the woman who wrote the spellbook and erased her own memory." I take a slow breath.

"This whole time..." My eyes narrow on Max.

Remorse flashes in his eyes, already begging for forgiveness. Max walks towards me, but I redirect my gaze to the witches. Only the one who has spoken meets my gaze.

This entire time, the Forstthorns lied to me. Annie, too. All of them. They expected me to crack the code and never thought I was worthy of the whole truth. Anger simmers within, fueled by the realization that I've been kept in the dark, manipulated by those I held closest. A pervasive feeling of being used overcomes me, like a pawn in a game I never knew I was playing.

Max whispers my name, but I ignore it. The witches remain silent, immovable glimmering figures in the kitchen.

I manage to swallow the anger burning my lungs as I say to no one in particular, "So what now?"

Max's golden skin starts to glow. His eyes are now neon green, filled with sheer rage, fixated on the void that seems to have been born before his eyes. His usually full lips are a thin, hard line.

"Now, we go to war," he says in a low, rumbling voice.

"The Realms will not follow you into battle, Maximilian," declares a voice I know all too well, dripping with unwarranted confidence and familiarity. It's a voice that, in reality, has no business being here right now.

Brandie.

She appears in the doorway, an aura of intensity and a sense of belonging exuding from her. My jaw drops as I take in the sight of her— my best friend's face, body, and smile, once so familiar, now seem like uncharted territory.

I pause at the slightly pointed ears peeking out from either side of her head, struggling to emerge through her thick blond mane. She's the same, and yet she's different. Confusion bubbles up inside me, threatening to flood the mansion. Before I can utter a word, before Brandie can explain why she's here, how she knows, and what she means, Max cuts me off.

"They will if they know the truth," my magical lover says, unfazed by Brandie's presence, statement—or ears.

ACKNOWLEDGMENTS

First and foremost, to the incredible creatives who stood by me through every twist of this journey, elevating this story with your passion and talent: Nadia, Marisa, Bri, Brandi (with no e), and Dahlia. Your kindness, insight, and artistic vision have been a gift. I cannot express enough gratitude for the beauty of your hearts and the brilliance of your help.

To my husband, for his unwavering patience and boundless support as I navigated this wild adventure. You may or may not have inspired Max—but you certainly inspire me.

To my daughter, who doesn't know it yet, but inspired me every step of the way and silently pushed me to reach my dream of becoming an author. I love you more than any creative word could describe.